THE HALLS OF MONTEZUMA

(THE EMPIRE'S CORPS—BOOK XVIII)

CHRISTOPHER G. NUTTALL

The characters and events portrayed in this book are fictitious. Any similarity to real persons, living or dead, is coincidental and not intended by the author.

Text copyright © 2020 Christopher G. Nuttall

All rights reserved.

Printed in the United States of America.

ISBN: 9798696470733

No part of this book may be reproduced, or stored in a retrieval system, or transmitted in any form or by any means, electronic, mechanical, photocopying, recording, or other-wise, without express written permission of the publisher.

Cover By Tan Ho Sim
https://www.artstation.com/alientan

Book One: *The Empire's Corps*
Book Two: *No Worse Enemy*
Book Three: *When The Bough Breaks*
Book Four: *Semper Fi*
Book Five: *The Outcast*
Book Six: *To The Shores*
Book Seven: *Reality Check*
Book Eight: *Retreat Hell*
Book Nine: *The Thin Blue Line*
Book Ten: *Never Surrender*
Book Eleven: *First To Fight*
Book Twelve: *They Shall Not Pass*
Book Thirteen: *Culture Shock*
Book Fourteen: *Wolf's Bane*
Book Fifteen: *Cry Wolf*
Book Sixteen: *Favour The Bold*
Book Seventeen: *Knife Edge*
Book Eighteen: *The Halls of Montezuma*

http://www.chrishanger.net
http://chrishanger.wordpress.com/
http://www.facebook.com/ChristopherGNuttall
All Comments Welcome!

CONTENTS

PROLOGUE I vii
PROLOGUE II x

Chapter One 1
Chapter Two 10
Chapter Three 19
Chapter Four 28
Chapter Five 37
Chapter Six 46
Chapter Seven 55
Chapter Eight 64
Chapter Nine 73
Chapter Ten 83
Chapter Eleven 92
Chapter Twelve 101
Chapter Thirteen 110
Chapter Fourteen 119
Chapter Fifteen 128
Chapter Sixteen 137
Chapter Seventeen 146
Chapter Eighteen 155
Chapter Nineteen 164
Chapter Twenty 173
Chapter Twenty-One 182
Chapter Twenty-Two 191
Chapter Twenty-Three 200
Chapter Twenty-Four 209
Chapter Twenty-Five 218

Chapter Twenty-Six 227
Chapter Twenty-Seven 236
Chapter Twenty-Eight 245
Chapter Twenty-Nine 254
Chapter Thirty 263
Chapter Thirty-One 272
Chapter Thirty-Two 281
Chapter Thirty-Three 290
Chapter Thirty-Four 299
Chapter Thirty-Five 308
Chapter Thirty-Six 317
Chapter Thirty-Seven 326
Chapter Thirty-Eight 335
Chapter Thirty-Nine 344
Chapter Forty 353

AFTERWORD 358
HELL'S HORIZON PREVIEW:
   Prologue 366
   Chapter 1 369
   Chapter 2 385

PROLOGUE I

FROM: *The Dying Days: The Death of the Old Order and the Birth of the New.* Professor Leo Caesius. Avalon. 206PE.

IN HINDSIGHT, we should have expected more organised competition.

As we saw in previous volumes, the Terran Marine Corps saw Earthfall coming and took steps to preserve themselves and—hopefully—rebuild the Empire they'd sworn to serve. Small groups of marines were assigned to isolated worlds at the edge of explored space—including Avalon, a story explored in my earlier volumes—with a mandate to protect and preserve what remnants of civilisation they could. Others were withdrawn from more populated—and inevitably doomed—worlds to await the final end. And, when Earthfall finally came—somehow catching us all by surprise despite years of planning and preparations—the corps started liberating and recruiting the trained and experienced workers who would assist the marines to preserve civilisation.

All of this did not take place in a vacuum. Earthfall led to utter chaos, to wave after wave of destruction sweeping across the Core Worlds. Planetary governors seized power, only to be consumed by the chaos as uncounted billions were swept out of work and unemployment benefits came to a sudden end. Imperial Navy officers declared themselves warlords and started building empires of their own, most falling prey to ambitious subordinates or supply shortages within a very short space of time. Old grudges burst into flame, unleashing a cycle of attacks and revenge responses that ended with entire planetary systems burning to ashes. We do not know how many people died in the first few months. It remains beyond calculation.

It was during a recruitment mission, as detailed in the prior volume, that the marines discovered they had a major rival. The Onge Corporation, previously ruled by Grand Senator Stephen Onge (who died during Earthfall), had established a major base on an isolated world, Hameau. This alone would be concerning, but further investigation revealed that Hameau was a corporate paradise, a seemingly-ordered world held in stasis by a combination of extreme surveillance and a cold-blooded willingness to remove and terminate troublemakers before they became a serious threat. It was clear, to the marines, that Hameau represented the future…as seen by the Onge Family. The upper classes would have considerable freedom, while the lower classes would be trapped within a social system that would keep them from either rising or rebelling. If this wasn't bad enough, the sociologists believed the long-term result would be utterly disastrous. Hameau would either stagnate to the point it entered a steep decline—not unknown, amongst worlds that refused to permit a degree of social mobility—or eventually be destroyed by a brutal and uncontrollable)uprising.

The marines therefore decided to intervene. Landing troops on the surface—the planetary defences were strong enough to keep the starships from securing the high orbitals and demanding surrender—the marines carried out a brilliant campaign that ended with the capture of the capital city, the effective destruction of the planetary government and them being firmly in control. Everything seemed to have gone their way until the enemy reinforcements arrived, too late to save the world…but quickly enough, perhaps, to destroy the marines.

There was no hope of negotiation. The new arrivals rapidly landed troops themselves, trying to destroy the marines on the ground while skirmishing with starships throughout the local system. The marines, unable to retreat and unwilling to surrender, continued the fight, aided by elements of the local population that didn't want a return to the days of corporate control (or had compromised themselves to the point they couldn't hope for mercy from their former allies). The fighting continued for weeks, with severe effects on the local population and infrastructure, until the marines lured the enemy forces into a trap and smashed them in a single, decisive blow.

However, it was not the end of the war. How could it be? The Onge were now aware of the Marine Corps, just as the Corps was aware of the Onge. With—still—little hope of a peaceful settlement, the two factions girded themselves to continue the war...

...All too aware that whoever won would determine the fate of the galaxy.

PROLOGUE II

ONGE (INCONNU), SHORTLY AFTER THE INVASION OF HAMEAU

"INVASION FLEETS DO NOT COME OUT OF NOWHERE," Director Thaddeus Onge said. He clasped his hands behind his back as he stared out the window overlooking the gardens of paradise itself. "Where did *this* one come from?"

He turned, keeping his face carefully blank. The original reports had been unbelievable. Hameau had been safe. *Should* have been safe. The only force that could have challenged the planet's defences was the Imperial Navy; and the Navy was a fracturing ruin, torn apart by admirals and generals who'd declared themselves warlords and set out to snatch as much military power as they could. Thaddeus had been confident, as the reports continued to flow in from what remained of the Core Worlds, that it was just a matter of time before the last embers of empire faded and died. There'd be room for a whole new order when the dust settled, he'd been assured. This time, the *right* people would be in charge.

His eyes drifted across the table. The *right* people hadn't been in charge for generations. The Grand Senate had been dominated by a hereditary aristocracy that had lost track of what was important centuries ago. They'd been too stupid and inbred to know the truth, that he who paid the piper called the tune. They'd lashed out at giant corporations, all the while sucking up to them for donations. Bribes, in truth, except they lacked the fundamental trait of the honest politician. They didn't stay bought. Thaddeus's family had worked its way into the elite for decades, only to discover the empire was already a rotting corpse. They hadn't needed long to start planning for the future.

Thaddeus looked at Vice Director Hayden James McManus, Director of Corporate Security. "I ask again," he said. "Where did this invasion fleet *come* from?"

"The preliminary reports indicate the fleet belongs to the Marine Corps," McManus said. He sounded as if he didn't believe his own words. "The naval records we obtained suggest the fleet does not exist."

"Officially, this planet does not exist," Thaddeus said, waving a hand towards the window and the gardens beyond. "Not as a corporate headquarters and haven for a new order, certainly. The marines probably have as much experience as we do in keeping things off the books."

He sighed, inwardly. The corporation had spent *decades* building the planet into a citadel, all the while doing everything in their power to ensure the Grand Senate and the Imperial Navy never had the faintest idea it existed. The looters would start levying taxes the moment they worked out something was up, he'd been warned. They couldn't let the bastards know what was happening until it was too late to object. They'd *known* Earthfall was coming…

…Yet, it had taken them by surprise.

"And they invaded the planet," Thaddeus said. "*Why?*"

"We don't know," McManus said. "But they must have had a sniff of our activities."

"More than just a sniff, if they're launching a full-scale planetary invasion," Vice Director Maryanne Mayan said, sardonically. "The cost alone must be immense."

"Yes," McManus agreed. He looked at Thaddeus. "If we predicted

Earthfall, sir, they must have predicted it too. They must have had their own plan to take advantage of the crisis."

"It isn't a crisis," Thaddeus corrected, mildly. "It's the new reality."

He let out a breath. The corporation had laid its plans carefully, yet they'd been overtaken by the sheer *violence* of events. Grand Senator Onge, Thaddeus's father and mentor, had never made it off Earth. Rumour insisted he'd tried to seize power, only to be killed by...by *someone*, depending who was telling the story. The Solar System was a burned-out ruin, hundreds of worlds had fallen into civil war or outright anarchy...the scale of the disaster was beyond human imagination. Thaddeus knew the plan. He'd grown up knowing the plan. He knew he had to collect useful people, bring them to his small cluster of worlds and *wait*. He had a nasty feeling the plan had gone spectacularly wrong.

The Corps was always loyal to the Emperor before the Grand Senate, he thought. The corporation had subverted thousands of army and navy officers, but not a single active-duty marine. *What the hell are they doing?*

"Our plan was always to shape the new reality," Maryanne pointed out. "Doubtless, the marines have the same idea."

Thaddeus couldn't disagree. There was no hope of putting the empire back together. The networks of interstellar trade that had once bound thousands of stars into a single entity were smashed beyond repair. The supply chain was a joke, money was worthless...outside a handful of worlds that had managed to maintain a certain independence from the empire itself. The marines weren't fools. They wouldn't have attacked and invaded an entire planet for *nothing*. No, they had to have their own plans for the post-empire universe. Thaddeus wondered, grimly, what those plans might be. He couldn't imagine them being compatible with his own.

"There's no point in disputing the facts," he said. His father had delighted in pointing out that the *Grand Senate* had often disputed the facts, right up until the moment they could dispute them no longer. "We have to take action. Fast. General?"

"I'm already putting together a response," General Jim Gilbert said.

He was corporate royalty, but he'd served in a dozen engagements in the army before returning to the corporation and, eventually, taking control of its military. "Many of our ships are on recruitment, but we have a small task force that *should* be able to drive the marines away from the planet and land troops. If we get there in time, we should be able to reinforce the defences and crush the invaders. If not, we can boot the invaders off the planet the hard way."

"Doing immense damage to the planet's industry and population," Vice Director Vincent Adamson said. The Director of Human Resources didn't look pleased. "They're not going to thank us for turning the entire planet into a battleground."

"With all due respect, sir, the entire planet is *already* a battleground," Gilbert countered, bluntly. He'd always been plain-spoken, something that had kept him out of the very highest levels. "We have a choice between retaking the planet, whatever the cost, or abandoning it to the enemy. And it won't take them long to realise they've merely stumbled on the tip of the iceberg."

Thaddeus nodded. Hameau was a major investment, and one they'd worked hard to conceal, but it was hardly the only one. The marines would find references to Onge in the planetary datafiles…if, of course, they hadn't already deduced its existence. And then…Thaddeus shook his head. He couldn't allow the marines, of all people, to determine the future of the human race. Their idealism would lead, inevitably, to the *wrong* people taking power once again, dooming the post-empire universe to yet another series of crashes and disasters. No, they had to be stopped. They were committed. They'd been committed from the moment the marines had first landed on Hameau.

And they don't know what sort of hornet's nest they've stumbled into, he told himself, firmly. It was impossible to believe the marines knew the truth, if only because they would have invaded Onge rather than Hameau. *We have a chance to smash them before they recover from the shock.*

He looked at Gilbert. "Are we safe here?"

"It's impossible to be sure, sir," Gilbert said. "But our defences are formidable. We've been bringing newer and better weapons online since Earthfall, when we no longer needed to hide anything from prying eyes. We've also sent out courier boats, recalling the remaining starships from their missions. And, with your permission, I'll call out the militia as well."

"Which will be expensive," Adamson said.

"And the militia may not be entirely trustworthy," Maryanne added.

Thaddeus nodded, sourly. One couldn't give the common man any power, at least not until he proved himself...and all political power, at base, came out of the barrel of a gun. Too many planets had been ruined by politicians who pandered to the masses, or cowered in front of mobs, for him to be sanguine about calling out the militia. Even if they were trustworthy, even if they could be kept under control, it would be taking experienced men away from their jobs. The economy would tumble.

"We have no choice," he said. Hameau had been intended as a military incubator. That plan, like so many others, had crashed and burnt in the wake of the invasion. "We have to move, now, to regain control of events."

"And quickly," Gilbert said. "The Corps trains its people to maintain a high operational tempo at all times."

Adamson scowled. "And in plain English...?"

"They move fast, trying to keep the enemy off balance long enough for them to come out ahead." Gilbert smiled, humourlessly. "We're the enemy, in case you were wondering."

"They picked this fight," Thaddeus said, before an argument could start. "And we're going to end it."

"Yes, sir," Gilbert said. "The task force should be ready to depart within the week."

Thaddeus nodded. If they were lucky, it was not already too late...

CHAPTER ONE

What went so terribly wrong, when it came to interstellar capitalism and the eventual—inevitable—slide into anarchy?
—**Professor Leo Caesius**
The Rise and Fall of Interstellar Capitalism

"AREN'T WE DONE WITH THIS FUCKING PLANET?"

Captain Haydn Steel hid his amusement at the subvocalised comment as he inched his way through the industrial complex, making sure to keep himself out of sight. The district had been battered by repeated bouts of fighting, from the thunder runs that had put the marines in charge of Haverford to the corprat invasion that had driven the marines back out again and the local insurgency that had torn the city apart until the fighting finally came to an end. The latest government had, thankfully, managed to evacuate the refugees to a makeshift camp outside the city, in hopes of bringing the district back to life. Haydn had to give them points for trying, if nothing else. They were showing more initiative than the average planetary government.

"I thought we were really done," Rifleman Jeff Culver said. "What are we doing here?"

"Sniper hunting," Command Sergeant Mark Mayberry growled. "Or weren't you paying attention at the briefing?"

Haydn ignored the byplay as he scanned the surrounding streets and buildings. An enemy sniper, perhaps more than one, had opened fire on a pair of surveyors an hour ago, killing one and wounding the other. The marines had been ordered to find the snipers and catch them—or kill them—before the area could be reopened. Haydn feared, as the marines moved from shadow to shadow, that they'd have to kill the men. The vast majority of the enemy soldiers had surrendered, when they'd been promised amnesty. Those who remained active were either loyalists or war criminals. Or simply convinced they wouldn't be allowed to surrender. It wasn't uncommon for snipers to be killed out of hand.

Sweat prickled on his forehead as he peered towards the nearest skyscraper. It looked dangerously unsafe. A missile or shell or *something* had crashed through the building without detonating, smashing a chunk of the concrete and probably damaging the frame. The windows were shattered, pieces of glass littering the ground beneath his feet. It would be the perfect place for a sniper to hide. Haydn had seen snipers hit targets over five kilometres away. The skyscraper would let the bastard shoot right across the river and into the heart of the city. Haydn feared what would happen if the sniper started taking pot shots at random civilians...

Most of the poor bastards don't want to come out of their houses, he thought. *And who can possibly blame them?*

He keyed his throatmike, muttering an update to the distant controllers. There weren't *many* marines on the ground, not now. The former insurgents were trying to maintain order—the new government needed to *try* to stamp its authority on the planet—but they were neither armed nor trained for crowd control. It would be a long time, with the best will in the world, before the planet calmed down to the point everyone could relax. Haydn wished he could call on the rest of the company, if not the entire regiment. A few thousand marines would be more than enough to flood the entire area and flush out the sniper.

And our snipers are keeping a watch for him, he thought, as he held out his hand to count down the seconds. *They'll shoot if they catch a glimpse of him.*

He cursed under his breath as he slipped out of the shadows and ran across the road. The marine snipers were good, terrifyingly good—they bragged they could castrate a man with a single shot—but they couldn't fire unless they had positive identification of the target. Merely carrying a gun wasn't enough. They had to wait until the sniper took aim before they put a bullet in his head. Haydn understood the political requirements—the local government couldn't afford to look weak, as if it was allowing the marines to shoot civilians at random—but he wished that whoever had come up with the policy was the one on the front lines. It was a great deal easier to issue blanket Rules Of Engagement when one wasn't at risk of being shot.

Glass crunched under his boots as he reached the edge of the lobby and crashed inside, rifle swinging from side to side as he searched for targets. Nothing moved, not even a mouse. The signs of looting were all around him. Paintings had been yanked from walls, drawers pulled out of the receptionist's desk and dumped on the floor…their contents stolen and probably sold for scraps. There were no papers…Haydn guessed the office had been completely paperless. Or the papers had been used for fires. The locals had had a nice city once. Two successive invasions and an ongoing insurgency had ruined it.

Probably taught them a few bad habits too, he thought, as the rest of the squad joined him. *How long will it be before they start settling disputes with violence?*

He put the thought out of his mind as they finished sweeping the ground floor, then sealed the lifts and headed upstairs. There was no power, not any longer. There'd been few, if any, independent power generators on the planet, rendering the entire district largely powerless. A faint smell hung in the air as they reached the first floor and peered inside. The office looked looted, stripped of everything that wasn't nailed to the floor. Haydn felt a flicker of sympathy for the workers as he swept the chamber, noticing how they didn't have so much as the *illusion* of privacy. Or any real control over their lives. They couldn't even adjust their desks and chairs. It struck him as cruel and unusual punishment. He was in the military and even *he* knew that complete uniformity was a bad idea. He'd hate to have to wear BDUs designed for someone smaller than himself.

I suppose it bred good little corprats, he told himself. The office kitchenette was as bland and boring as the rest of the office. The powerless freezer stank of rotting food. He was amused to notice the looters had taken the cleaning supplies, although he knew it wasn't funny. Someone could make a pretty good IED, with a little ingenuity. *And it sure as hell would have kept them in their place.*

He tensed as he heard something above him. A footstep? A bird? He hadn't seen many birds in the city, but urban wildlife might well have started making a comeback now large swathes of the city had been effectively abandoned. Haydn exchanged signals with Mayberry, then inched towards the stairs. By his assessment, they were going to be moving up to the damaged part of the building. The skyscraper didn't *feel* as though it was going to collapse at any moment, but the shattered walls and damaged interior would make a good sniper nest. If nothing else, it would be very hard to pick their way upwards without making some noise.

Haydn considered his options as they studied the stairwell, then started to inch up to the next floor. The air blew colder, carrying with it the unmistakable scent of unwashed human and human waste. It didn't smell like a dead body...Haydn grimaced. They hadn't seen many dead bodies since they'd begun their sweep, although he wasn't sure why. Perhaps the corprats had collected the corpses and buried them in a mass grave. It was the sort of thing they would have done, if they'd realised it *had* to be done. His lips quirked. Of *course* they'd do it. They'd wanted to bring the city back to life as quickly as possible too.

The sound came again as they reached the top of the stairs. Rubble lay everywhere, providing all the cover a sniper could possibly want. Haydn could imagine a skilled sniper setting up a bunch of nests, perhaps even an optical sensor to allow him to track his targets without a spotter... or revealing himself to prying eyes. There might even be an automated gun...the corps didn't use them, unless they were in a clear war zone, but the corprats might have different ideas. Who knew? The sniper probably already considered himself doomed.

He unhooked a stun grenade from his belt, held it up so his team could see what he had in mind, then hurled it through the door and into the exposed zone. Blue-white light flared. The grenades weren't as effective as the media made them look—Haydn wanted a few moments alone with the producers who made those wretched flicks—but anyone caught in the blast would have a few moments of stunned disorientation, at the very least. He leapt forward, rifle in hand. The section was deserted. There was no sign of a sniper or...

Something moved, above him. Haydn barely had a moment to notice before another grenade fell from the upper floor. Haydn shouted a warning and dived for cover, an instant before the grenade exploded. The floor shook violently. Haydn breathed a sigh of relief they weren't in a confined space, then scrambled forward and up the next flight of stairs. The sniper had to be stopped before he got away. He heard someone snap off a shot behind him, the bullet cracking through the ceiling. He couldn't tell who'd fired, or if they'd hit anything. Another explosion shook the building a second later. Haydn felt a flicker of fear. It was hard to escape the sense the entire building might come tumbling down within seconds.

He crashed into a dark shape. The sniper bit out a curse as they tumbled to the floor, fists pounding against Haydn's armour. Haydn headbutted him, feeling his nose break under the force of the impact. The sniper had clearly been enhanced, probably illegally. He almost snorted as the sniper kept hitting him, trying to beat him to death. The corprats had broken hundreds of laws, just by setting up a colony that was technically off the books. Why on Earth would they stop breaking laws *now*?

His fingers found the knife at his belt, drew it and stabbed upwards. The sniper was wearing body armour too, but it wasn't designed to cope with knives. Haydn guessed the sniper's masters had seen the advantages—the armour was very good at coping with bullets—and chosen to overlook the disadvantages. The sniper let out a breath as the knife was thrust further into his chest, flailing uselessly as he gasped for breath. Haydn pushed him over and stared down at him. The sniper looked...no different from any of the other soldiers he'd fought and killed in the last few months.

"Lie still," Haydn said, quietly. If he could take the sniper alive...the spooks would have a field day. The poor bugger was clearly enhanced to the max. "We can do something..."

The sniper gurgled, then lay still. Haydn cursed under his breath as he checked the man's pulse, just in case he was faking it. Enhanced or not, a knife to the gut had proven fatal...it looked as though Haydn had punctured the man's heart. A team of medics with modern equipment might have been able to save him, but the closest medics were on the other side of the river. Haydn pulled out the knife, wiped it with a cloth and returned it to his belt, then started to search the body. The sniper hadn't been carrying much. It looked as though he'd abandoned everything that might have identified him, something *else* that was technically against the law. Haydn was mildly surprised the corprats had broken *that* law. Terrorists and insurgents did it all the time, but the corprat soldiers were supposed to be better. They, at least, had superiors who could hold them accountable... and be held accountable, in turn, for their subordinates.

A shot cracked past. Haydn darted to one side, seeing another sniper—no, a spotter—standing by the far door. He cursed and unhooked another grenade from his belt, hurling it towards the enemy soldier. The soldier dived back, retreating further into the skyscraper. Haydn called in the contact as he picked himself up and chased the man. He wanted—he needed—to take this one alive.

"Give up," he shouted, as he crashed through an open door. The wooden shape hung off its hinges. "Give up and we'll take you alive!"

He jumped into the next room, just in time to see the enemy soldier diving down a garbage chute. Haydn was tempted to follow him, but it would be a good way to get stuck. The rest of the corps would *never* let him forget it. Instead, he yanked a third stun grenade from his belt and dropped it down the chute. The sniper might be armoured, but in such close confines it probably didn't matter. He heard a curse, followed by a thump. It dawned on him, a moment too late, that the sniper had probably lost his grip and plunged down. Hopefully, he'd had enough sense to make sure there was something soft underneath.

"Sergeant, check the rest of the building," he ordered, as he ran back to the stairs. The one advantage of a city designed by soulless corprats was that the city was practically uniform. Learn to navigate around one skyscraper and you'd know how to navigate around all of them. "I'm going to snatch the prisoner."

He ran down the stairs and into the basement. It stunk, a grim reminder that no one had been collecting trash for months. He could hear someone kicking in the semi-darkness. The garbage chute opened into a giant metal drum on wheels…Haydn had a sudden horrified vision of someone getting stuck inside, then being driven to the furnace and incinerated with no one being any the wiser. He had no idea how the sniper intended to get out. Perhaps he could tip it over from the inside, with a little effort, or scramble up the outside of the chute.

"Marine Corps," he shouted. If the sniper wanted to take a final shot at him, now was the chance. "Surrender and we'll get you medical attention. Resist and you'll go to the grave."

He listened, but heard nothing beyond a faint whimpering. He sneaked up on the drum, grabbed hold and yanked it over. A torrent of rubbish—and a twitching sniper—fell out and landed on the concrete floor. The sniper had clearly taken the brunt of the blast and fallen hard, breaking at least one of his legs. Haydn secured his hands with a plastic tie, then searched him roughly. Getting the sniper to the medics was going to be a pain, but it could be done. He had no doubt of it.

"Sir, the building is clear," Mayberry reported. "There's no trace of anyone else."

Haydn nodded, unsurprised. If there were more enemy holdouts, they'd have scattered over the city. They wouldn't run the risk of being trapped, not as a group. Haydn wouldn't hesitate to call down fire from the orbiting starships to smash the enemy, rather than risk the lives of his men trying to root them out and take them alive. The corprats would certainly assume the worst, if they were smart. There was no way the city could be brought back to life before the corprats were exterminated.

"I'll meet you in the lobby," he said. "Tell the medics I have a patient for them."

He searched the enemy sniper quickly, finding nothing. Again. The enemy had dumped everything, even his weapons. Haydn guessed there was a cache of supplies somewhere not too far away. The corprats hadn't had much time to prepare for an insurgency—another insurgency—but a skilled junior officer with enough guts to take the lead might just lay the groundwork before it was too late. And his superiors would probably take a dim view of it. Corprats disliked people showing even a *hint* of independent thought...

And maybe I'm completely wrong, he thought, as he carefully picked up the twitching body and carried it up to the lobby. Moving a wounded man was dangerous, but the medics wouldn't come any further into the building. The corpsmen were just too valuable to be put at risk. *These two might have set off on their own.*

"Raptor inbound, sir," Mayberry reported. "The medics will be here in a moment."

"And then we can sweep the rest of the area," Haydn said. He cursed under his breath. They needed the entire regiment, not a single under-strength company. He knew the score as well as anyone—they were short of trained marines—but it was worrying. They were running the risk of being caught out by superior forces and taking a pounding. "Any word through the grapevine on reinforcements?"

"Nothing, sir," Mayberry said. "There's a vague report we might be heading back up there."

"You'd think they could make up their minds," Culver said, as he joined them. "Where are we going tomorrow?"

"There's never a dull day in the corps," Haydn said. He grinned. "The only easy day was yesterday. Who dares, wins. And a bunch of other clichés."

Culver made a face. "And no hope of shore leave?"

Haydn shrugged. "I dare say they'll try and organise something," he said. He hadn't heard anything, but marine officers understood their men needed leave every so often. *Everyone* needed time to decompress, preferably in an environment where no one was trying to kill them. "But I have no idea when or where."

"There has to be something to do here," Culver said. "Hunting. Fishing. Shooting…"

"Yeah," Haydn said. He understood the younger man's feelings. He just knew they had other problems. "But our duty comes first."

CHAPTER TWO

It's a hard question to answer. Certainly, a number of theories have been advanced that have their roots in ideology rather than the real world.
—**Professor Leo Caesius**
The Rise and Fall of Interstellar Capitalism

"I THINK WE NEED TO MAKE SOME HARD DECISIONS," Major-General Miguel Foxtrot said. "To whit, what are we going to do about Onge?"

Major-General Gerald Anderson nodded, curtly, as he sat at the conference table on HMS *Havoc* and studied the display. The debriefing notes were all too clear. They'd severely underestimated the enemy and now... they were caught in a trap of their own making. It had been costly enough landing an invasion force on Hameau, an invasion force that had nearly been destroyed by the arrival of enemy reinforcements. They'd won a series of bloody battles, only to discover they were facing a multi-star corporate polity. And now they could neither abandon the campaign nor push it to a speedy conclusion.

He kept his face under tight control. Major-General Miguel Foxtrot was a friend, but...he hadn't been there. Not when it counted. Foxtrot and his division had arrived too late, after the enemy force had been shattered, the remnants forced to surrender or head for the hills in hopes of hiding out long enough for a second relief force to arrive. He hadn't had to grapple with the prospect of being the first marine officer to *lose* a campaign, a defeat that could have easily led to the end of everything. Gerald had no illusions. There were only a handful of new marines in the pipeline and, until they established a new training base, there wouldn't be any more. The battle could have shattered the remnants of the corps beyond repair.

"There are three options," Captain Kerri Stumbaugh said, bluntly. Her position was a little awkward. On one hand, she was in command of the ship and the flotilla; on the other, she was an auxiliary and therefore not wholly part of the corps. "We sit on our asses and do nothing, at least until we have orders from Safehouse. We send out messengers to Onge and seek a mutual understanding. Or we find a way to take the war to them before they realise what's happened and launch another invasion."

"I know," Gerald said. "Do they know what's happened?"

Kerri frowned. "We defeated their fleet and retook the high orbitals a week ago," she said, slowly. "Assuming they had someone watching the fun from a safe distance, someone who returned home as soon as they realised we'd won, they'll know what's happened in a week or so."

"Assuming nothing happens to that ship in transit," Foxtrot pointed out.

"It would be unwise to *count* on it," Gerald said. "So…they'll know in a week. What will they do?"

"It depends." Kerri looked at her hands. "We just don't know enough to make any real guesses. They may have enough ships to risk launching a second invasion, as you said, or they may pull in their horns and concentrate on home defence…all the while trying to locate our base. Right now, our only real advantage is that they don't know about Safehouse. That will change."

"So, we've got them off balance," Foxtrot asserted.

"They know we attacked this world," Kerri said. She waved a hand at the bulkhead and the planet beyond. "They'll have to assume we might attack their world next."

Gerald nodded, feeling the weight of the universe resting on his shoulders. "And where are they?"

Kerri smiled. "They did manage to destroy a lot of their records before we secured their ships," she said, "but they didn't manage to destroy everything. Sloppy work, if you ask me, even if it *would* be expensive to put the ships back into working order once their datacores had been destroyed. We know where they're located…or, at least, where the enemy ships *were* before they came here."

She tapped a console, bringing up the holographic starchart. "Inconnu," she said. "Officially, at least. The planet was discovered a few hundred years ago, apparently; settlement rights passed through a network of shell companies and suchlike before the incorporation of the Inconnu Development Corporation. We cross-checked with records on the surface, such as they are; the IDC is a subsidiary of the Onge Corporation. The spooks think the Onge took the planet and developed it as a refuge, just like Safehouse."

Foxtrot shook his head in amused disbelief. "And none of the beancounters even *noticed*?"

"There's a bunch of tax breaks and suchlike to development corporations," Kerri said. "Or there were, at least. As long as no trouble came out of Inconnu, there shouldn't have been any reason for the beancounters to take an interest. I suspect the Onge were secretly pulling strings behind the scenes all along, just to make sure no one *did* take an interest. The Imperial Revenue Service was underfunded for decades before Earthfall. I imagine they had plenty of easier and more worthwhile targets to go after."

Gerald nodded. He'd been in the corps long enough to know the score. Development corporations with big budgets had no shortages of friends on Earth. Getting in on the ground floor of planetary development could be a very solid investment, if one didn't mind waiting a few decades for it to mature. It didn't matter, he reflected sourly, that the colonists themselves were often dirt-poor, even when they weren't being exploited by their masters. As long as the developers had the money, they could do whatever they liked. And the marines often had to clean up the mess.

"So, it's basically just like Hameau, except on a larger scale," Gerald said. "It might be too big a target for us to handle."

"Quite possibly," Kerri said. "The Onge have—had—practically limitless resources. They owned industrial nodes and shipyards, including a bunch of facilities that built weapons and supplies for the Imperial Navy. If the defences *here* were pretty tough, I dread to imagine what they'll have emplaced to defend their homeworld. There's no hope of them feeling the urge to hide now."

"Yes," Gerald agreed. "They can defend themselves openly now."

He felt his heart sink. Hameau had been defended beyond the bounds of sanity for any *normal* colony world. The Empire had never cared for colonies having the means to defend themselves. He was still astonished the developers had gotten away with it. Surely, someone would have noticed. But it probably wouldn't have mattered. The whistleblower would have been bribed or threatened into compliance, if he didn't wake up one morning to discover he'd been declared a criminal and sentenced to immediate transportation. The IRS had been so badly riddled with corruption that it was practically a criminal organisation in its own right. Gerald wouldn't have been surprised to discover its managers had been subverted long ago…

And they're all dead now, he thought, with a flicker of vindictiveness. The IRS had been blamed for everything, even when it hadn't been at fault. The taxmen had always proven convenient scapegoats. They were blamed for doing their jobs and *not* doing their jobs. *They all died on Earth.*

"We need hard data," Kerri said. "And most of the prisoners are unwilling to talk."

"We could encourage them to talk," Foxtrot pointed out.

"They surrendered," Gerald said, sharply. He had no qualms about forcibly extracting information from terrorists, insurgents and enemy forces that refused to adhere to the laws of war, but the Onge had fought a remarkably clean war. "We cannot force them to talk."

"Even when the information in their heads might make the difference between victory and defeat?" Foxtrot leaned forward, playing devil's advocate. "They might know something *we* need to know."

"I'd be surprised if they did," Kerri said, before Gerald could formulate a reply. "The vast majority of captured crewmen and soldiers knew very little, at least as far as we could tell. Their superiors didn't invite them to the briefings."

"And even if they did, what they know lacks any context," Gerald said. The prisoners might talk freely and truthfully, yet unintentionally mislead the interrogators. "If they talked about Landing City, who knows *which* Landing City they mean?"

Foxtrot grimaced. "I'm sure they can fill us in on a few basic details," he said. "If nothing else, they can tell us how their society works."

"We already *know* how their society works," Kerri said, sharply. "No privacy. No freedom. A giant nest of worker and soldier and police ants, with strict enforcement and little hope of promotion. And that's what they intend to export to the rest of the galaxy."

"It has to be stopped," Gerald agreed. He couldn't believe the corprats would succeed—the larger the system, the greater the chance of its inconsistencies tearing it apart—but they'd leave a ruined galaxy in its wake. "And that means we have to act fast."

"We take the war to them," Foxtrot said. "And quickly."

Gerald studied the display for a long moment. "How quickly can we get there?"

"It'll take a few more days to finish reloading the transports," Kerri said. "The majority of the newcomers"—she nodded to Foxtrot—"are already on their ships, along with their equipment. There'll be a lot of grumbling about the lack of shore leave, but…too bad. The squadron itself is ready to go. However, we will be running the risk of leaving Hameau uncovered."

"And the Onge have already shown they can land an army relatively quickly," Gerald agreed, sourly. The dumpster trick had been brilliant, if one didn't mind running the risk of being unable to withdraw in a hurry. He supposed it said something about the corprat mindset. They'd treated their soldiers as expendable. "Can they retake the high orbitals?"

"It depends on what they bring to the party," Kerri said. "There are gaps in the defences, thanks to us. We're tightening up the holes, again, but it won't be enough if they send an entire fleet. They were certainly rich and powerful enough to operate an entire squadron of battleships."

Foxtrot raised an eyebrow. "Would they? I always thought the Imperial Navy's admirals were overcompensating for something."

Kerri smiled, but it didn't touch her eyes. "Back in the old days, the battleships were of purely limited value. Maybe not quite white elephants, but certainly *grey*. There wasn't a peer power…there hadn't *been* a peer power for centuries. The battleships were good for intimidation, but anything else they did…well, smaller ships could have accomplished their tasks just as well. Cheaper, too. Those battleships were money sinks. But now…I don't know. Their plans must assume that, sooner or later, they'd encounter peer powers."

"And it doesn't take a battleship to fry an entire planet," Foxtrot pointed out. "A handful of c-fractional strikes would be quite enough to do that."

"If they wanted to kill everyone on Hameau," Gerald said. War or no war, the planetary population was one of the best-trained in the galaxy. They'd already started finding ways to expand beyond the corprat limits. Given time, Hameau might become a jewel of the new universal order. "They wouldn't commit genocide."

"Desperate men do desperate things," Foxtrot said. "Time may not be on our side."

Gerald considered it for a long cold moment. The path to hell was paved with good intentions. Hell, he'd always preferred dealing with power-hungry warlords because they could be relied upon to do what was in their best interests. An insurgency could find itself going down the path to madness, to mass slaughter and even genocide, before it realised what it was doing. Desperate times bred desperate measures…and, with each successive decision, it became easier to do the next. And the next.

The Onge aren't fanatics, he thought. *They're corprats, with one eye permanently fixed on the bottom line. They won't cross the line into genocide.*

He shivered. He hoped he was right. Corprats often made the mistake of regarding people as interchangeable and disposable tools—*Human Resources* had much colder implications than *Personnel Department*—and they might just decide that, if they couldn't have the trained personnel, no one else could have them either. Hell, Gerald himself had blown up ammunition dumps and equipment sheds to keep them from falling into enemy hands. He'd never sentenced millions of people to death, but human history was a liturgy of atrocities that had been considered unthinkable... at least until someone had not only thought of them, but carried them out.

"We need intelligence," he said. "We'll continue the interrogations, of course, but it is unlikely we'll get much of anything from the POWs. We also need to at least *try* to talk to them..."

"They may stall long enough to prepare their haymaker," Foxtrot warned. "It's happened before."

"Yes." Gerald took a breath. He was a veteran of politically-charged negotiations that no one had expected to go anywhere, except the distant politicians who'd been trying to look good in front of their fellows. The enemy had often used them as a chance to rearm their troops and plot their next move, while the marines had had their hands tied by their political masters. That, at least, was no longer a concern. "We agreed we'd send back the POWs if they refused to join us. They can take a message back to their superiors for us."

"And we'll follow in its wake," Foxtrot said.

"Quite." Gerald allowed himself a tight smile. "We'll let them keep one of the freighters. Kerri, you'll escort her home. That'll give you a chance to carry out a tactical survey of the system, before sneaking out and linking up with us outside detection range. If they refuse to discuss terms, we'll find a way to take out their orbital defences and land troops."

"We can take the remainder of the enemy fleet with us," Kerri said. "They can launch missiles, if nothing else."

"Yes," Gerald said. "I also want to insert a Pathfinder or two. We're going to need more intelligence, particularly things we can't learn from orbital observations. Who's in charge, what are they doing…that sort of thing. The higher-ranking prisoners have been able to tell us some details, but not enough. We may be able to win the war overnight if we can get our hands on the people who can order a surrender."

"As long as their subordinates don't have standing orders to ignore orders from captives," Foxtrot pointed out. "We do."

Kerri laughed. "Have you ever known a corprat who'd agree to issue such orders?"

Gerald had to smile. Corprats *loved* being in control. The idea of diluting their authority, let alone conceding that there might be a time when their authority no longer mattered, was anathema to them. And while *his* subordinates had standing orders to ignore anything he might say if the enemy held him at gunpoint, he doubted his opposite number had anything of the sort. Who knew? Gerald trusted his subordinates. He doubted the corprats felt the same way.

"No," he said. "But there's a first time for everything."

He leaned forward. "We have orders to finish the war—and quickly," he said. "And that means taking the offensive. At the same time, we may discover that we've bitten off more than we can chew. We will certainly *try* to talk to them, all the while preparing the first and hopefully final blow."

"We cannot afford to get bogged down," Foxtrot agreed. "We'll have to take some risks."

"And learn from our mistakes," Gerald said. In hindsight, they'd grown *far* too used to being the best. They'd made a whole string of mistakes during the operation, from unspoken assumptions of technical superiority to their training making up for the shortage of numbers. Gerald hated to admit it, but they'd been luckier than they deserved. "The post-campaign assessment is going to be a pain in the ass."

"Let us admit it freely, as a civilised people should," Foxtrot quoted. "We have had no end of a lesson, which will do us no end of good."

"Quite," Gerald agreed. "Kerri, prepare your ship and the transport freighter for departure as soon as possible. Once we finish the interrogations, we'll transfer the prisoners who want to go home to the freighter and send them off. There should be enough starship crew to handle the ship. If not…"

"We can arrange for our crew to fly her home, then jump ship before the enemy realises we're there," Kerri said. "I'll arrange it."

"I have to write an updated report to the Commandant," Gerald added. "And then we'll be getting back to work."

"No rest for the wicked," Foxtrot agreed. "I'll start drawing up invasion plans immediately."

"Just remember to credit your staff," Gerald said, dryly. "They're the ones who'll do all the work."

He smiled. Foxtrot would supervise the work, perhaps even sketch out a vague idea, but it was his staff who'd turn the concept into an operational plan. Not, he supposed, that it would be a very detailed plan. They simply didn't know enough about the enemy homeworld. The files were untrustworthy. He was all too aware that everything in the databanks, beyond basic planetary details, might have been made up out of whole cloth.

"Yes, sir," Foxtrot said. He stood, then paused. "Can I nominate myself for ground commander?"

Gerald laughed. "Is it a reward or a punishment?"

Foxtrot pretended to consider it. "It depends," he said, finally. "Which one will get me on the ground?"

"Wait and see what we find," Kerri advised. "For all we know, there'll be no defences and the entire operation will be a walkover."

"It might," Gerald agreed. The corprats could have spent *trillions*, literally, on securing their homeworld. They'd had a budget the Imperial Household would envy. "But I wouldn't bet money on it."

CHAPTER THREE

The capitalist, some say, is little better than a robber baron, little better than a feudal lord. He takes from those who don't have enough already and hoards it to himself, leaving the poor to starve.
—**Professor Leo Caesius**
The Rise and Fall of Interstellar Capitalism

IT WAS, ALL THINGS CONSIDERED, the worst place Julia Ganister-Onge had ever been.

She scowled as she sat in the hard metal chair and looked around the chamber. It was very clearly a prison, even if it was a little more comfortable than she might have expected. The bed was uncomfortable, the clothes were itchy and the toilet very crude. She'd asked the guards for her cosmetic supplies, or even for a basic eReader, but they'd said no. She was a prisoner, and prisoners had no rights.

She'd heard all the horror stories, when she'd first started to work for the family. Her mother had wanted Julia to put her ambition aside and marry someone from the corporate ranks, someone who would be boring and utterly useless…someone she'd rapidly grow to loathe. Her mother hadn't hesitated to point out the dangers, if Julia fell into enemy hands. The corporate world had been poisonous well before Earthfall. Julia might be killed, or enslaved, or raped, or even brainwashed. It was funny, Julia reflected sourly, that her mother had never talked about the threat of *boredom*. She would almost sooner have been put in front of a bulkhead and shot.

Her stomach churned with the bitter bile of failure. Recruiting Admiral Nelson Agate had been her mission, and she'd been willing to do whatever she had to do to get him onboard, but staying with him had been her choice. Her gamble. Admiral Agate had been on the way up and, with her clearing his way and handling the politics, he would continue rising until he was right at the very top. Or as close to it as an outsider could come. Julia had had no concerns about developing a relationship with him, about—eventually—becoming his wife and bearing his children. It was her duty, both to the family and herself. But now the dream was ashes in her mouth. She hadn't seen Admiral Agate since he'd surrendered. She had no idea what had happened to him.

And it won't matter, she thought, savagely. *We failed.*

She stared down at her hands. She'd gambled and lost and…there was no way in hell they'd ever allow her another shot at the golden ring. The corporation was *good* at isolating incompetents, at putting them in places they could do no harm. She was family, so she was fairly sure she'd wouldn't be thrown out the nearest airlock, but she wouldn't have a chance to reach the heights again. There was no room for failure at the very highest levels. The entire corporation relied upon its leadership being the best it could possibly be.

The blank walls seemed to mock her. She *knew* she was being watched, even though she was alone. She understood, too late, how the starship crewmen must have felt. She'd been their political commissioner. She'd controlled the monitors that watched them, every hour of every day. She'd never abused her power—she hadn't watched them undressing or making use of the privacy tubes—but…she doubted they'd feel the same way. Her skin prickled every time she used the toilet. She couldn't even turn out the light.

She stood and paced the compartment. How long had it been? She had no idea. Days? Weeks? Months? Her hair didn't seem to have grown any longer, but...she honestly wasn't sure. The marines had interrogated her once, asking questions she had no intention of answering, then abandoned her. She wondered, morbidly, if she'd been forgotten, if they'd put her in a cell and forgotten all about her. One day, perhaps they'd open the hatch and get a terrible shock. Or...

It can't have been more than a few weeks, a month at most, she thought. *My hair would have grown all the way down to my ass.*

She glared at the lights. They never changed, even when she went to sleep. No one made her keep a schedule, no one insisted she got in or out of bed...she was honestly unsure if it had been more than a day or two. Her head hurt every time she thought about it. Perhaps she was being drugged. The automated food dispenser only offered gruel and cold water. The former tasted like cardboard. Perhaps it *was* cardboard. God knew there'd been all sorts of bids to recycle crap, when she'd been a little girl. She doubted any of it had been particularly worthwhile in the long run.

Her eyes swept the bulkheads, looking for the monitors even though she knew it was futile. The monitors she'd used were so small they couldn't be seen with the naked eye. The crew would have needed security gear to find them, let alone remove them, gear they—of course—weren't allowed to have. She couldn't find the monitors either, even though she could guess where they were. She knew where *she* would have placed them. Three or four in all the right places would have ensured there was nowhere to hide, nowhere she could do something to escape...she snorted at the thought. There were videos and flicks featuring super-strong men and women smashing through hullmetal bulkheads as though they were made of paper. The real world was rarely that obliging. And it didn't come with a laugh track, either.

The hatch hissed. Julia turned and straightened, trying to pretend she was in her office as the hatch opened completely. She considered trying to jump the interrogator, but what was the point? There was nowhere to go. And besides, she had no real combat training. She leaned back as the marine walked into the cell, her eyes narrowing as she took in the sight. The marine was a mousy woman, with long hair and a uniform so shapeless she looked as though she was trying to hide herself. Julia felt a flicker of contempt, then concern. The marine was almost certainly trying to look harmless. And that meant...what?

"Good morning," she said. Her voice felt rusty...how long had it been, really, since she'd spoken a single word? A week? A month? A year? "Welcome to my humble abode."

The marine smiled, rather wanly, then turned and walked towards the table. Julia's eyes followed her, silently noting that her arms were rather more muscular than one might expect from such a mousy woman. It was an act, no different to the act *she'd* been taught to put on when she was a teenager. Fake it until you make it was pretty good advice...she wondered, sourly, why a marine would *need* the act. Perhaps she wanted to be underestimated. Julia doubted it was working. She was acting like a servant in a great house, not a prison interrogator. Surely, she'd know it was hard to feel superior when one was in a goldfish bowl...

Just like everyone else, Julia thought, bitterly.

"Please, sit," the marine said. Her hair spilled over her face, nearly hiding her eyes. "We have much to discuss."

Julia sat, crossing her arms under her breasts. "Do I have a choice?"

"You can stay here, if you like," the marine said. "Or there are other places you can go."

"I suppose." Julia frowned at her interrogator. "Do you have a name?"

"Rachel," the interrogator said. "And you're..."

"Julia," Julia said. She was too tired to keep the sneer out of her voice. "As I'm *pretty* sure you already know, given that I gave my name to the *last* interrogator."

"Quite." Rachel looked forward. "Tell me about Inconnu."

We call it Onge, Julia thought. She tried to jolt her sluggish brain into high gear. If the marines had name-checked Inconnu...it meant they knew where the corporation was based. Or did they? They would hardly have needed to ask *her* if they already knew everything. *How much do they actually know?*

Her mind raced. She could lie to them, except...she had no idea how they'd react if they caught her in a lie. All the horror stories suddenly seemed very real. In hindsight, she should have gone for one of those courses on resisting interrogation. Should she tell the truth? Should she lie? Should she say as little as possible and hope they didn't have ways of making her talk? She was supposed to be immune to truth drugs, but it had never actually been tested. And she knew she had little tolerance for pain.

"It's a resort world for the corporate elite," she said, finally. It was true, if one left out practically everything. "I grew up there."

Rachel seemed unsurprised. Julia wondered, not for the first time, if Admiral Agate or one of his subordinates had started talking. She didn't have much to look forward to, if—when—she got back home, but they had even less. She'd have turned her lover—her former lover—into the scapegoat, if she hadn't known she was too far beyond salvation. She couldn't hope to escape the consequences of her failure.

"You must have had an interesting life," Rachel said. "What was your childhood like?"

"Boring," Julia said. She knew, intellectually, she'd been lucky...but she had a hard time believing it. She was minor corporate royalty and yet she'd grown up in a world of staggering luxury. The idea of growing up in a ghetto, scavenging and perhaps even selling herself for food, was utterly alien to her. "It was safe and warm and boring."

"I see." Rachel's eyes crinkled, just slightly. "Tell me about your world."

Julia considered refusing, but she couldn't see how the information would help the marines. She talked about her childhood, about her teenage years, about her decision to make her bid for the golden ring...Rachel listened quietly, sometimes asking questions to bring out more detail. Julia wondered, suddenly, if she was saying more than she should. She'd told the marines a great deal about how Onge actually worked.

But it won't help them, she thought. *All I've done is told them who's in charge.*

"That's very interesting," Rachel said, when she'd finished. "We have a question for you."

She leaned forward. "We promised you that we'd repatriate all POWs as soon as possible, if they wanted to return home. Do *you* want to return?"

Julia frowned. She'd never really expected the promise to be kept. "And if I say yes, what'll happen?"

"You'll be transferred to a freighter and shipped home," Rachel told her. "Whatever happens after that is in the hands of your government."

"And only a few hundred of us want to go home?" Julia wasn't sure she believed *that*, but if the marines were only letting one freighter go… the total couldn't be much more than five hundred. "Can I talk to them?"

"No." Rachel shrugged. "Not now, anyway."

Traitors, Julia thought. *There were hundreds of thousands of spacers and soldiers attached to the fleet…*

Her blood ran cold. God! How many had died in the last few weeks? The marines had practically drowned an entire army! Thousands…tens of thousands…she didn't want to think about it. Her stomach clenched at the thought. There might only be a few thousand survivors, if that. Some of the people who wanted to go home might not have come with the fleet, but instead…they might be surviving members of the planetary government. She wondered what sort of reception *they* feared, or deserved. No one had expected an invasion. But they hadn't done a good job of fighting it off, either.

She put the thought to one side and leaned forward. "Does Nelson want to go home?"

"Nelson?" Rachel paused for a moment, as if she was considering her next words very carefully. "Admiral Agate? I believe he wants to stay."

Julia gritted her teeth as the stab of betrayal ran through her. It was hard to blame the admiral, not when he'd be busted all the way down to… whatever was below midshipman, even if they had to make up a new rank just for him. And yet, she had spent enough time with him to like and respect him as more than just a meal ticket. She was tempted to ask if he wanted her to stay with him, but she didn't have the guts. In truth, she was scared of the answer.

She looked down at the metal table, her thoughts whirling through her mind. Her duty was to the family, to the corporation they'd created and the new galactic order they intended to build. And yet, what fate awaited her when she got home? Death? Exile? Permanent inconsequence? Or what?

And if I stay, she asked herself, *what can I expect?*

She had no idea. Again, she didn't want to ask. It was possible the planetary government—the *new* government—would insist she be put on trial, even though they'd surrendered on terms. It was also possible it wouldn't do anything for her. She might be assigned to a settlement and told to work or starve. Or…she didn't know. She just knew she didn't want to face it. She…

Someone has to warn the family of what's coming, she thought. She thought they'd listen to her. She'd been at Admiral Agate's side, watching as he and General Rask had directed their forces against the enemy. They should have won. They…someone had to explain what had happened, rather than leaving the head honchos in the dark. Who knew? Perhaps it would buy her something more than permanent irrelevance. *If they listen to me…*

"I want to go home," she said. She wanted to keep her voice calm, but she knew she'd revealed too much of her desperation. She wanted out of the cell. She wanted to go home. She wanted the universe to start making sense again. "When do we leave?"

Rachel smiled. "Two days," she said. "You'll be transferred tomorrow and held within the freighter until she departs. I hope that's satisfactory?"

Julia shivered. She hadn't expected things to move so quickly. The marines were *efficient*. All of a sudden, Admiral Agate's tales seemed very reasonable. She swallowed, hard, and cleared her throat.

"What choice do I have?"

"You can stay, if you like," Rachel said. "The planet below needs settlers. They'll be quite happy to have you, if you're prepared to work. There's a whole bunch of starship crewmen with skills the planet desperately needs. They're looking at high salaries and the chance to build a whole new life.

Even the ones without skills have a chance to better themselves. Their children will have a chance at a good life."

"Really." Julia felt another surge of bitterness. The universe had had a place for her, before the fleet had been defeated. Now...she couldn't hope for much. "And do you think *I* have skills that are desperately needed?"

"You might be surprised," Rachel said. Her face was so expressionless Julia *knew* it was an act. The woman was laughing at her behind her mask. "You clearly have *some* skills."

Seduction and manipulation, Julia thought. She doubted either skill would be useful on the planetary surface. She'd gotten away with a lot, in the past, because of the family name. Here...she supposed the best she could hope for wasn't very good at all. *I'm no good with my hands.*

"Not enough," she said. What could she be? A whore? A high-class courtesan? She wondered, suddenly, if there was any difference between what she'd done for the family and outright prostitution? Perhaps there was...it had been for a cause, not for something as tawdry as money. "I'd like to go home."

"As you wish," Rachel said. "I do have a few more questions..."

Julia groaned, inwardly, as Rachel started firing more questions at her. She'd made the mistake of talking and now...she couldn't *stop* talking. The unspoken threat of not being allowed to go home after all haunted her mind, keeping her under firm control. Thankfully, there were a lot of things she simply *didn't* know. She knew very little about the planetary defences, or about the remainder of the navy. She grimaced, inwardly, as she realised Admiral Agate probably knew a great deal more. There was no point in trying to lie. She wasn't even sure she could mislead them...

She rubbed her forehead, feeling a headache starting to throb beneath her temples. Perhaps they'd dosed her with something, or perhaps...it didn't matter. All that mattered was that she'd told them too much and yet, not enough. She didn't *know* enough.

"I need a rest," she mumbled. She didn't expect to get anywhere, but she wanted to ask anyway. Her brain felt as if it was going to explode. She wanted to bury herself below the thin blankets in hopes of getting as little light as possible. "Can I get a nap before I get shipped home?"

Rachel stood, brushing down her baggy uniform. "If you wish," she said. She held out a hand. Julia shook it automatically. "And if you want to change your mind, you can do so at any moment before transfer. After that…good luck."

She walked to the hatch. Julia watched her go, fighting the temptation to ask if there was something she *could* do on the planet. Something…she shook her head. She *had* to go home. She *had* to report, even if it meant condemning her career to the dustbin of history. She had to tell the family what was coming…

And Nelson is staying here, she thought. *He'll tell them everything he knows.*

CHAPTER FOUR

The flaw in this argument is that it assumes that 'wealth' is a fixed amount. A pie, in effect. One can take all the pie and leave everyone else with none. But this isn't true of capitalism.
—**Professor Leo Caesius**
The Rise and Fall of Interstellar Capitalism

"I MUST SAY, THAT BAGGY OUTFIT and terrible wig makes you look ravishing," Specialist Steven Phelps said. "Will you keep the trousers on for me?"

Specialist Rachel Green gave him the finger as she straightened up, brushing down her oversized uniform. She'd dressed down for the interrogation, in hopes of weakening Julia Ganister-Onge's mental defences, but it was hard to tell if it had had any real effect. The poor woman hadn't been remotely trained for captivity, let alone forced to run through the dreaded Conduct After Capture course. Julia was pretty close to breaking, if indeed she hadn't broken over the last week. The cell was designed to disorient anyone unlucky enough to find themselves inside it.

"I think you need your eyes checked," she said. "You're going blind."

"I'll have you know I bribed a doctor to give me a clean bill of health," Phelps teased her. "And all it cost me was turning up in perfect health."

"Then you're in to a very weird scene," Rachel said. "I always knew you were a terrible pervert."

"You wound me," Phelps said. "There's nothing wrong with being into girls in baggy outfits…"

Rachel rolled her eyes as she removed the wig and placed it in a locker, then headed into the washroom to change into her regular uniform. Pathfinders didn't *have* to wear formal uniforms, as long as they weren't on parade, but she didn't see any need to wear civilian clothes while she was onboard ship. Besides, there were just too many *real* civilians onboard. The last thing she wanted was to be mistaken for one of them. Her teammates would never let her forget it.

She stripped down and inspected herself in the mirror, then pulled her BDUs on and walked back out. The scars from the previous engagement had healed nicely, although the medics had warned her to take it easy for a few days. Rachel was fairly sure they were joking. She wasn't really *capable* of taking things easy. Besides, there was always something for the Pathfinders to do. Rumour had it they were going to be redeployed any day now, although no two rumours agreed on when and where. Rachel had a private bet with herself that they were going to be inserted on another corprat world. The spooks had insisted on asking questions to get the lay of the land—the *lie* of the land, they'd joked—and that could only mean one thing,

"I'm ready," she said. "And if you say anything about my uniform…"

Phelps held his hands up in surrender, then fell into step beside her as they left the interrogation cube and made their way through the giant ship. The Marine Expeditionary Unit was buzzing with life, from marines running rings around the main corridors to auxiliaries and crewmen stowing gear as they prepared the starship for departure. She felt a handful of eyes watching them as they walked onwards, admiring eyes. Pathfinders were the best of the best, the most capable Special Forces unit in history. Everyone wanted to join them.

She smiled. She'd heard all sorts of rumours about other units, about SF groups so black that no one below the commandant himself knew they existed. The Green Lights, the Marine Corpse...she had no idea if they were jokes, or distractions, or *real*. It was quite possible she'd *never* know. The elites would invite her to join, if they wanted her, but otherwise...she shrugged. Secrets were secrets for a reason. She was trained and enhanced to keep her from being interrogated, yet...who knew? Anyone could be broken if the interrogator tried hard enough. What she didn't know, she couldn't tell.

The remainder of the team, Specialist Michael Bonkowski and Specialist Tony Perkins met them outside Officer Country. Rachel wasn't sure she liked *that* designation, not on a starship built for the corps and crewed by marines. The idea of a whole separate section for officers felt like blasphemy, when the officers were supposed to share the perils of the men they commanded in battle. Rachel had met quite enough army officers who *didn't* to know how important it truly was. And yet...Officer Country was more than just Major-General Anderson's office. It was the home of the planners and beancounters who made the deployment work.

It helps they're on detached duty, she thought, as they stepped through the hatch. *They know what's important. They simply haven't had time to lose track of it yet.*

The office hatch was open. They were expected. Rachel smiled as they filed in, feeling like she'd been summoned before the headmaster to explain herself. Again. She wondered, idly, how the junior marines thought when they saw the elite go directly into the Major-General's office. Envy? Or pity? The junior marines had captains and lieutenants and even sergeants between themselves and their ultimate superior. It would be years before the riflemen qualified to join the elite themselves.

If they ever do, she thought, grimly. *The Slaughterhouse is gone.*

She straightened to attention as Bonkowski took the lead. "Pathfinders reporting for duty, sir."

"Good." Major-General Anderson looked harassed, for someone who'd just won one of the most shattering victories in modern history. The marine corps had met its first real test in decades and won. "We have another mission for you."

Rachel nodded, shortly. She assumed the team hadn't been summoned to discuss the weather. There might be some grumbling about shore leave, or lack thereof, but they knew their duty. She'd rest when she was dead. Besides, unless they were wanted back on the planet, there'd be some time to rest before they reached their next destination. She didn't bother to speculate. She'd get the details shortly.

"We're going to be sending the prisoners back in two days, as you know," Anderson said, adjusting the holographic display. "What you don't know is that you're going to be going back with them."

"Cool," Phelps said.

"Quite," Anderson said, as Bonkowski shot Phelps a sharp look. "Your orders are to insert yourself into their society and be ready to assist, if—when—the invasion fleet arrives. I can't give you any more precise instructions, because I don't know what you'll find when you get there, but ideally you'd avoid anything that might reveal your presence before it's too late."

"Yes, sir," Bonkowski said.

Rachel had a different thought. "Do you expect to insert us with the POWs?"

"If you believe that's the best way to do it, then yes," Anderson said. "However, I would be very surprised if they didn't take the POWs into custody the moment they returned home."

"And getting to the planet without getting detected might be impossible," Bonkowski said, thoughtfully. "Even if they don't know what they did here, they're bound to have newer and better sensor nets covering their homeworld."

Rachel nodded. She'd handled some of the interrogations herself and monitored the others. The POWs hadn't known *much*, but the ones who'd been born on Onge—as they called their world—had been a wealth of information. They'd told Rachel how their society worked, how everyone was listed in a database…a database most of them considered to be holy writ. The weak point was obvious. If they could get onto the database, they could move around freely. Anyone who questioned them would be told they had authorisation...

So all we have to do is get on the database, she thought. It wouldn't be the first time she'd sneaked into an enemy-controlled system, either by forging the right documents or simply taking someone's place. *It shouldn't be too hard.*

"We'll hitch a ride on the freighter," Bonkowski said, firmly. "And jump ship before it gets boarded and searched."

"You have complete freedom," Anderson said. "Just make sure you're in position to be useful when the time comes."

"Yes, sir," Bonkowski said. "We won't let you down."

Rachel smiled as they saluted, then left the compartment and headed to their private section to hash the operation out properly. The chance to devise their own operational plan, to call on whatever stores and personnel they needed to make it work...heaven. Assuming, of course, they survived. She was too experienced to believe that everything would go perfectly. Midway through the operation, they might find themselves having to improvise... her imagination provided too many possibilities. She'd faced religious nuts who'd believed that anyone held prisoner had been defiled and could no longer be trusted. They'd gunned down their own people rather than take them back.

The corprats won't do that, she thought. *If nothing else, they'll need to know what happened to their fleet.*

She frowned. It was one hell of a gamble, although—from what she'd heard—standard naval doctrine insisted that a fleet should be accompanied by a picket ship just to keep an eye on things from a safe distance. There was a good chance the bad guys already knew what had happened. They had to know there was no point in killing the former POWs. And... if nothing else, the returned POWs should be one hell of a distraction. It would keep them looking in the wrong direction.

"So, we have our orders," Bonkowski said. He was, technically, the team lead. They were all experienced enough to have few qualms about putting the plan together as a group, then following orders when they went into the fire. They'd all proved themselves long ago. "Get to the planet, blend in and wait."

"Sounds very simplistic," Phelps offered. "Should we try to seduce the head honcho while we're at it?"

"You're not allowed to watch those dumb spy comedies anymore," Bonkowski said, curtly. "Go get a sex life instead."

"They're not comedies," Phelps insisted. "They're what some overpaid hack thinks a spy genuinely *does* for a living."

"And, according to those hacks, we're all ultra-violent drooling morons who chant like football fans when we're on the battlefield," Rachel pointed out. "I don't think their opinions can be taken seriously."

"And they're probably dead," Perkins offered. "There's room for some *real* stories now."

Phelps snorted. "They did a story about an army garrison on some shithole world once," he said. "It was very realistic. The grunts spent most of their time standing guard and sitting about doing nothing, while cramming ration bars into their mouths. It was so boring it never got so much as a second episode."

"You can write something better, when you're older," Bonkowski said. He keyed the holographic projector. "The official files say the planet has nothing more than a handful of outdated Orbital Weapons Platforms. Anyone want to bet that's true?"

"Not a hope in hell," Rachel said. She was used to gambling, but she disliked the idea of being on the wrong side of a sucker bet. "I thought we'd taken the enemy admiral prisoner."

"We did," Bonkowski confirmed. "And he's been spilling his guts. Problem is, he doesn't know very much about the planetary defences. Lots of shit was compartmentalised, apparently."

"Wise of them," Phelps commented, sardonically.

Bonkowski nodded. "Frankly, they're either trying to mislead us deliberately or they know so little they're misleading us by accident. There's a pair of orbital elevators and suchlike, and a whole bunch of stations in orbit, but none of the POWs can say what they are. Not with any great certainty, at least. The chances are good some of them are industrial nodes and others are weapons platforms, but they don't know which is which. We might not know until the weapons platforms start shooting."

"There'll probably be less debris in orbit too," Rachel commented. "An orbital drop is unlikely to work."

"We'll be dead before we know we're under attack," Perkins agreed. "But we can probably get onto the orbital stations, with a little effort."

"Yes." Bonkowski tapped the display, bringing up an image of the captured freighter. "We can't insert ourselves into the prisoner compartments. The ship itself will be flown by the POWs, which means that joining the crew isn't a possibility either. We'll be riding on the outside until the ship reaches its destination, then jumping off and making our way to the enemy stations. At that point, we'll have to wing it."

Rachel nodded. Getting into the station wouldn't be difficult. The Empire had standardised everything centuries ago, including airlocks. They could open an airlock from the outside and get into the station, although—unless they were very careful—there was a good chance they'd set off the alarms. The corprats probably wouldn't seal their airlocks. They wouldn't want to take the risk of trapping someone outside when they were running short of air.

Accidents happen, particularly when someone makes them happen, she thought. She had plenty of experience in arranging them herself. *And the station is probably large enough for us to sneak around without being detected.*

She frowned. "Do we have copies of the enemy personnel files?"

"Not enough," Bonkowski said. "We have copies of the files for this world, but not for Onge itself. And we'd better get used to *calling* it Onge too."

Rachel nodded. "Best case, we replace a bunch of people long enough to make their lives miserable," she said. "Worst case, we hide in the ducts until the time comes and *then* make their lives miserable."

"Worst case, we get caught and shot," Phelps pointed out. "Anyone got any famous last words?"

Perkins smiled. "I told you I was ill!"

"Back to work," Bonkowski said. "We have an operation to plan."

"Sir," Phelps said.

• • •

It had been years, Captain Kerri Stumbaugh thought sourly, since she'd set foot on an Imperial Navy battlecruiser. The design had always annoyed her, speaking more to the Imperial Navy's desire for big and spectacular starships rather than workhorses that could actually do the work. They didn't even have the firepower of the battleships, although—she acknowledged—this ship had battered her squadron badly before she'd been forced to surrender. Cruisers could do everything battlecruisers could do and cheaper, much cheaper. One could buy and operate ten cruisers for the cost of one battlecruiser. The corps certainly had.

Although the navy's finances were a mess before the end finally came, she reminded herself, dryly. *Between corrupt officers and a shitty procurement system, they probably spent more on screwdrivers than they did on this ship.*

She walked onto the bridge and looked around with interest. The Onge Navy didn't seem to have made many improvements, although what they had done had been disconcertingly good. The battlecruiser's sensors were better than she'd thought, the missiles top-of-the-range...it was lucky, she supposed, that she'd had an ace up her sleeve. Their first real engagement between capital ships could easily have gone the other way. The Onge had trained their crews very well. She made a mental note to *learn* from the battle. It could have ended very badly indeed.

"Captain." Chief Engineer George Daniels stood from behind a battered console. He looked as if he'd been working constantly for the past few days, without so much as a shower or bed. "Or is it *Commodore* here? I can never tell."

"Either." Kerri shrugged. She'd met Imperial Navy officers who'd throw a fit if they weren't addressed by their proper rank, but she'd never been that concerned. She was in the corps, not the navy. Besides, she wasn't on *her* ship. "Can we get her to move?"

"Barely." Daniels shrugged as he wiped his hands on his uniform trousers. "There's not *that* much damage to her hull, Captain, but they damaged the datacores beyond easy repair. I'd say take her to a shipyard, if we had the time. We've done a lot of jury-rigged crap to get her moving again, but she won't have anything like the flexibility she *should* have. The rest of the squadron is not that much better off."

"I see." Kerri frowned. The battlecruiser was little more than a sitting duck if her systems couldn't interact. Her hull was tough, but not that tough. "How much can you do with automation?"

"Very little," Daniels said. He removed a datapad from his belt and held it out to her. "The datanet is shot to hell. There's a bunch of systems that survived more or less intact, but can't talk to each other. My crews can rig up a wireless system to make it work, but a couple of solid hits will knock it down again. Like I said, she needs a shipyard."

"Which isn't likely to happen, not any longer," Kerri said. The corps had small shipyards and mobile repair ships, but they weren't big enough to handle a battlecruiser. The giant shipyards that had supplied the Imperial Navy had been dying for years, before the crunch finally came. "Can she make a voyage through phase space?"

"Yes, as long as you're careful," Daniels said. "But I wouldn't try anything risky with her unless I wanted to die."

"Got it." Kerri smiled. She'd had an idea. It was crazy, the sort of idea that would get someone marched in front of a court martial in the old days, but it might just work. "Get as much done as possible, then ask for volunteers from your crew to sail her."

"Aye, Captain," Daniels said. He sounded as if he didn't believe his ears. "If you take her into harm's way...I don't think she'll come back."

"I know," Kerri said. She reached out and touched the battered command chair. "As long as she does what we want, she'll be fine."

CHAPTER FIVE

Imagine three people: a lumberjack, a carpenter and a builder. They may see themselves as independent, as separate people, but in truth they are part of a chain that leads from relative poverty to wealth.
—**Professor Leo Caesius**
The Rise and Fall of Interstellar Capitalism

JULIA AWOKE, SHARPLY, as the hatch hissed open.

She'd been asleep…she wasn't sure how long she'd been asleep. Her eyes felt leaden, as if she'd stayed awake for days—helped by mil-grade coffee and stimulants—and only just fallen asleep when the hatch opened. She wondered, as she blinked tiredness from her eyes, if she'd been drugged. It would be almost laughably easy. They controlled her entire environment. Doping the water or ration bars—or even piping gas into the compartment—would be simple. She forced herself to sit up and look at the hatch. A lone man was standing there.

Julia scowled. He wore a suit of featureless armour, covering him from head to toe. It was impossible to see a face behind the helm, impossible to know who was intruding on her privacy. Julia felt her expression harden, knowing—even though she didn't know *how* she knew—that she was being scrutinised. The armour was intimidating and the grim certainty she could never point out the man in a crowd was worse…Corporate Security used the same trick, she'd been told. It was impossible to punish a man if you didn't know who he was.

"On your feet," the marine ordered. The voice was completely atonal. "Come with me."

Julia stood on wobbly legs. "Shouldn't I be cuffed and shackled for this?"

The marine showed no visible reaction. "Do you want to be?"

"No," Julia said, after a moment. They didn't need to bother. She was helpless, lost and completely alone. "There's no point."

The marine beckoned her to follow as he turned and walked through the hatch. Julia sighed and did as she was told, passing from one metal compartment to another. The air smelled of too many people in too close a proximity, but there was no one in view save for her and her captor. The skin on the back of her neck prickled as they walked on. They were being watched by unseen eyes. Julia gritted her teeth, feeling the sensation grow stronger. She felt as if she was walking to her execution.

They said I could go home, she thought, as they passed through another pair of airlocks. *They said…*

The gravity field shifted, slightly. She stumbled, nearly falling to the deck. The marine put out a hand to steady her, Julia leaned on his arm gratefully. The armour felt cold and hard. Admiral Agate had said something about it, once…she couldn't remember. Not, she supposed, that it mattered. She wasn't a trained marine, let alone a superhero from an action flick. There was no hope of kneeing her captor in the groin and fleeing. She literally had nowhere to go.

Another airlock opened. A gust of air washed across her nostrils. She grimaced. The air smelled of oil and sweat, a stench that nagged at her mind. The marine didn't slow as they walked down a long tube and through yet another airlock. The deck started to thrum beneath her feet. It dawned on her, too late, that they'd moved from starship to starship. The marines had docked another ship to theirs and marched her over…

A young man, wearing a simple shipsuit, waited for them. "Commissioner Onge?"

"Ganister-Onge," Julia corrected, waspishly. She wasn't about to allow her family name to be mangled. The intermingling of bloodlines was vitally important to ensure the family remained healthy, escaping the curse of inbreeding and hereditary illness. "What can I do for you?"

"I'll take her from here," the young man said. "Thank you."

The marine nodded, turned and withdrew. Julia glanced back in time to see him pass through an airlock and, presumably, back onto the mothership. The hatch closed...she wondered, idly, if the marine had looked back at her before it was too late. Not that it mattered, she supposed. They'd never see each other again.

"We have prepared a cabin for you," the young man said. "If you'll come with me...?"

Julia gave him a sharp look. "Who's *we*?"

"Those of us who want to go home," the young man said. "If you'll come with me..."

Julia hesitated, then allowed him to escort her through a warren of metal corridors. The ship—one of the troop transports, she guessed—was heaving with people. They passed a dozen compartments crammed to bursting with former naval and army personnel, men and women trying desperately to find somewhere comfortable to sit and wait for departure. The transport hadn't even left orbit and there was already friction, she noted; she shuddered at the thought of what conditions would be like in the next few days. Even if they flew at their best possible speed, it would be at least a week before they reached Onge. The decks might turn into warzones. It was not going to be a pleasant flight.

They could at least have offered us security, she thought, numbly. *It would've made the trip so much more bearable.*

A hatch opened. She peered into a tiny compartment, barely large enough for a single adult...she couldn't help thinking it had been intended for a child. The bunk was tiny, the washroom barely large enough to accommodate her...she wasn't even sure she could shut the door. She silently prayed she didn't have to share with anyone. There simply wasn't enough room.

"There's a datapad in the compartment under the bunk," her escort informed her. "I'm afraid it's currently disconnected from the starship's datanet, but you can play games on it if you wish."

Or start writing my report, Julia thought. She'd tried not to think about it while she'd been held in the cell, but now…now she had to work out what she wanted to say. It wasn't easy to imagine something that wouldn't get her disowned, if not sent into permanent exile. *What the hell am I going to say?*

She shook her head. "What time are we leaving?"

"Five hours, they say," the young man said. "But we just don't know."

Julia nodded as she sat on the bunk, her head brushing against the upper compartment. She looked up, puzzled. Was the section meant for two people after all? Or…she dismissed the thought with a wave of her hand as her escort bowed and retreated, the hatch closing softly behind him. She had a nasty feeling she wouldn't be welcome, if she left the tiny cabin and headed for the bridge. A chill ran through her as she remembered the former POWs she'd seen below decks. What would happen if they rioted? Could they take the ship? She wondered, for the first time, if she'd made a mistake. Should she have stayed behind and accepted asylum?

You have a duty to your family, she told herself, severely. *And you damn well have to live up to it.*

• • •

"I haven't done this since training," Perkins said. "Are you sure this is safe?"

Bonkowski snorted, rudely. "I thought we were Marine Pathfinders, not Junior Cowards."

"They do a hull scan, they'll know we're here," Perkins said. "It isn't as if we're riding on the hull in suits."

Phelps glared at the pair of them. "We're safe enough, as long as they don't overhear you two arguing," he said. "We'll just have to put up with each other's company for a week."

Rachel snorted as she settled back within the compartment. The giant troop transport had been a warren even before she'd been battered and forced to surrender by the spacers. The engineers had patched up the worst of the damage, allowing them to hide the Pathfinders in what was supposed to be a vented and isolated compartment right next to a gash in the hull. They'd done a good job of both isolating the section and linking it into what remained of the ship's datanet, ensuring the Pathfinders would have plenty of warning if someone decided to search the depressurised sections. Rachel silently prayed they wouldn't even *think* of trying to make repairs while the ship was in phase space. The Pathfinders would have to abort the mission if they were discovered.

She looked around, concealing her displeasure. She'd been in tight spaces before, but not for very long. There'd always been a sense she could get out for a walk, even when it ran the risk of attracting enemy fire. Here… there was too great a chance someone would realise they didn't belong and raise the alarm. The spacers had done a good job of mingling enemy personnel from a dozen different units, in hopes of giving the Pathfinders some cover, but it was too risky. She sighed, inwardly, as she reached for her datapad. They'd downloaded copies of all the interrogation reports, including the more pointed questions aimed at enemy personnel who'd requested asylum. They probably guessed the marines intended to infiltrate Onge. Why else would they ask for details that made little military sense?

Someone might not realise something is wrong if they don't recognise us, she mused, *but they'll sound the alarm if they realise we're not wearing the right uniforms.*

"It feels like being in prison," Bonkowski said. "Which one of us is the snitch?"

"In prison, you meet a better class of person," Perkins said. "I have to share a room with you?"

"I'm being punished for something," Phelps mused. "I'm a ruddy kindergarten teacher."

Bonkowski snickered. "Are we there yet? Are we there yet?"

"Don't make me come back there," Phelps said. "Tony, I want you keeping an eye on the sensors. The moment anyone comes near the compartment,

I want to know about it. Rachel, keep monitoring the enemy personnel. We don't want them starting a mutiny in the middle of the flight."

"No," Bonkowski agreed. "For once, it wouldn't work in our favour."

Rachel nodded as she picked up a datapad and started to flick through the live feed from the sensor nodes. The entire ship was wired to a degree that bothered her, even though she'd given up on privacy since she'd joined the marines. A person couldn't so much as pass wind without alerting the sensors and triggering an automated investigation. She had the feeling the system could be simply overloaded, with a little effort, but that would probably set off *more* alerts. The corprats claimed it was for the good of the workers...she rather doubted anyone believed it. The system was designed to head off rebellion before it ever got off the ground.

She felt her eyes narrow as she peered into the POW compartment. The former prisoners had only just arrived—the transport hadn't so much as left orbit—but it was clear that trouble was already brewing. Men were bickering, despite the best efforts of the handful of repatriated officers. Rachel wasn't surprised. They'd lost a *lot* of their authority, when the fleet had been bested in space and the infantry smashed on the ground. Perhaps it would have been better to leave the officers with their firearms...she shook her head. The transport was too close to the planet for anyone's peace of mind. They couldn't risk a well-timed mutiny leading to utter disaster.

"The hatches are solid," she said, more to herself than to her comrades. "They can't get out."

"Not without the right tools," Phelps agreed. "You got the feeling this ship was designed to do double duty as a prisoner transport?"

"I guess so," Bonkowski said, seriously for once. "The entire ship is a honeycomb of sealed compartments. I don't think they intended to give their troops the freedom of the vessel."

Rachel shivered. She'd spent her entire career in the corps. She'd been treated as a responsible adult from the moment she'd passed through Boot Camp and entered the Slaughterhouse. She was expected to follow orders, even if she didn't understand them; she was expected not to go wandering when she was onboard a transport or MEU. The enemy soldiers, however, were treated like overgrown children. Or prisoners. She was fairly sure such treatment would breed resentment. There'd be a chance to take advantage of it.

"I'll tell you what else they didn't bring," Bonkowski said. "Porn! The WebHeads didn't find so much as a single naked photo in their datafiles."

Phelps snorted, rudely. "Do you ever think about anything else?"

"Sir?" Bonkowski struck an innocent pose. "Is there *anything* else?"

Rachel laughed, then returned to work.

...

"Captain," Lieutenant Tomas said. "We have established solid communications links with the Pathfinders on *Botany Bay*."

Kerri nodded. "Keep forwarding the results of the interrogations to them," she ordered, calmly. "And do your level best to keep us off their sensors."

She leaned back in the command chair, feeling a pang of guilt. Any spacer knew the danger of fiddling with the sensors while underway, let alone deliberately weakening them to create a blindspot. *Havoc* could hide within the blindspot and shadow the transport all the way to Onge, hopefully without the enemy crewmen knowing they were being followed. In theory, they could emerge along the phase limit behind the transport and remain undetected…if, of course, anyone was watching. There was no solid data on what communications or sensor capabilities the enemy possessed. The analysts had assumed the worst. Onge might be as heavily defended as Sol itself, before Earthfall.

And if we've buggered their sensors too far, they might just run into something they should have been able to see, she thought. Weakening the sensors was one thing, but actually corrupting the datanet codes…she shook her head, sharply. She understood the reasoning behind the act. She just didn't like it. *At worst, we'll have to break cover and warn them if they're about to crash.*

"Captain," Ensign Susan Perkins said. "Major-General Anderson has cleared us for departure. The transport is powering up, ready to leave orbit."

"Helm, prepare to leave orbit as planned," Kerri said. She felt a thrill of excitement banishing the guilt. She was mistress of her ship, but—as long as she flew in company with two Major-Generals—not in sole command of her destiny. As long as the mission lasted, she—and she alone—would be in command. "Tactical, establish the sensor mask once we're clear of the high orbitals."

"Aye, Captain."

Kerri smiled as she studied the display. The troop transport was a lumbering brute of a ship. She hadn't even had a *name* until some marine with a sense of humour had dubbed her *Botany Bay*. *Havoc* could run rings around her with ease, although the transport wasn't *entirely* harmless. A ship that size could do a hell of a lot of damage if someone rammed her into a planet. The marines had taken the precaution of rigging a nuke to blow the ship to atoms, if the crew tried. Kerri doubted any of them were suicidal, but…they'd agreed to go home to a government that was unlikely to welcome them with open arms. Perhaps they *were* suicidal.

You'd go back to the corps, even if you were staring down the barrels of a court-martial, she told herself. It wasn't a pleasant thought, but it was true. If she failed so badly…she'd owe it to the corps to help them learn from her failure. She wondered, idly, if the enemy personnel felt the same way. *Why would they not?*

A low thrumming echoed through the ship. "Captain," Commander Joaquin said, formally. "We are ready to depart."

"Take us out of orbit," Kerri ordered.

The thrumming grew stronger as *Havoc* glided out of orbit and fell into position behind *Botany Bay*. Kerri couldn't help feeling they were so close to the other ship that the enemy crew could see them with the naked eye, although she knew it was impossible. *Havoc* was a big ship, but she was tiny compared to the sheer immensity of deep space. A chill went through her as the ships picked up speed, her vessel quivering as if she wanted to rush past the transport and burst into FTL the moment she crossed the phase limit. Kerri resisted the urge to do just that. They had to remain in the blindspot if they wanted to be sure of not being detected.

Shadowing a ship through phase space isn't easy at the best of times, she thought. She'd spent a chunk of her pre-Earthfall career chasing pirates, but—even with the best crew and sensors in the known galaxy—she'd rarely been able to track a pirate ship back to its homeport. Even a comparatively primitive ship could escape, just by random course changes and dropping sensor decoys in the right places. *We've rigged everything in our favour and we still might lose the bastards.*

She put the thought out of her head and forced herself to wait. It was unlikely, the analysts agreed, that the enemy would assume their system hadn't been probed. There were probably enough ships coming and going, even in the post-Earthfall days, for an intruder to sneak into the system. Hell, a sufficiently determined intruder could drop out of phase space well short of the limit and make his way into the system, in the certain knowledge he could not possibly be detected. It would take weeks, if not months, but it could be done.

We have to assume their sensor net is good, she reminded herself, sharply. *And that they're just as paranoid as we would be, if we were in their shoes.*

Shaking her head, she settled down to wait.

CHAPTER SIX

The lumberjack goes to the forest, cuts down a tree and lays claim to the trunk. We will say, following the classic rectal extraction method, that the trunk is worth roughly ten credits. Does the lumberjack have, therefore, ten credits?
—**Professor Leo Caesius**
The Rise and Fall of Interstellar Capitalism

HAVERFORD HAD PROBABLY LOOKED BETTER, Captain Haydn Steel thought as the company marched towards the edge of the city, before two successive invasions and an insurgency had torn the city to bits. A number of districts had been reduced to rubble, their inhabitants either killed in the fighting or forced to flee. The all-seeing planetary datanet had been a shadow of its former self before the new government had ordered it dismantled, the massive files of surveillance data on every last member of the population unceremoniously deleted before someone could try to argue for their retention. Haydn was fairly sure it was just a matter of time before someone would've done just that. It was easy to make a claim that spying on everyone was good for public safety.

But it might be a while here, he thought. The snoops had been lynched, when it became clear the datanet was a thing of the past. People who'd enjoyed spying on their neighbours had discovered, too late, just how much they were loathed. *It'll be at least a generation before they start forgetting the downsides of limitless surveillance.*

He put the thought out of his head as they reached the edge of the city and marched onto what had once been a bowling green. Haydn wouldn't have known, if it hadn't been flagged up on the final mission briefing. The green looked as if someone had driven an entire brigade of tanks over the grass, turning it into mud before crashing into the buildings and smashing them into the ground. It was hard to believe it had ever been anything other than a sea of mud. He shook his head as he slowed, the marines forming into a ceremonial march. His opposite number from the planetary militia was waiting for him.

"I relieve you," the planetary officer said. "And I thank you for your service."

"I stand relieved," Haydn said, wondering who'd introduced the militia to military formality. "And I wish you good luck."

They exchanged salutes. Haydn held his a moment longer than necessary, then led his men off the field. The planet had welcomed the marines—mostly—but he was fairly sure there were a *lot* of locals who resented them. The people who'd been on top a few months ago, of course...the people who'd lost friends and family in the fighting. The two invasions had killed hundreds of thousands of people, directly or indirectly. It wasn't fair to expect the people who'd lost loved ones to be *thankful*. Haydn just hoped they wouldn't seek revenge or turn into bitter-enders. Either way, it would end badly.

He frowned as they marched onto the road, passing a company of drilling militiamen. The locals were enthusiastic, and a bunch of them had military training and experience, but they still struck him as being woefully unprepared for modern war. There was a shortage of experienced officers who could be trusted. The planetary government had offered amnesty to anyone from the enemy force willing to sign up and share their experience, yet...could they be trusted? Haydn had his doubts. Betrayal tended to be habit-forming.

"I'm sure there was a spaceport here," someone muttered behind him. "Once upon a time…"

Haydn nodded. The spaceport had served briefly—far too briefly—as a Forward Operating Base. He and his men had left the planet when the enemy reinforcements had arrived, taking the last flights out of the spaceport before incoming missiles and shells had turned it into a pile of rubble. Good thinking on their part, he acknowledged sourly, although a little too late. Major-General Anderson and his staff had already decamped when the missiles came roaring in.

I guess we weren't the only ones learning as we went along, he thought. *They could have killed our CO and decapitated us if they'd moved a little quicker.*

He put the thought out of his mind as they walked towards the shuttles. The enemy POWs had cleared what remained of the landing pads and runways, allowing the shuttles to come and go without hindrance. A command vehicle had been parked on the edge of the spaceport, surrounded by a pair of mobile defence units and a sensor truck. It would be enough to handle traffic, at least until the local government started to rebuild the spaceport into something usable. Haydn figured that day was a long time off. The locals simply had too many other problems right now.

Colonel Foster met them as they reached the edge of the spaceport. "Captain," he said, once they'd exchanged salutes. "Your shuttles will be arriving shortly."

Haydn nodded. Saluting was as clear as sign as any that the command staff believed there was no longer any serious danger, not on the surface. They weren't allowed to salute in combat zones. He relaxed, slightly, and watched as more marines flowed towards the shuttles, their officers and sergeants organising them for departure. They'd be back on the MEUs by nightfall, then…they could take a break. It wouldn't be much—the MEUs were hardly pleasure boats—but it would be something. The men could unwind and relax, while Haydn and the other officers planned their next move. Haydn had heard the rumours. There was practically *no* chance they were going straight back to Safehouse.

He waited, feeling sweat trickling down his back as the day grew hotter. The military was fond of 'hurry up and wait,' and the marines were no different. He ignored some grumbling from the ranks, as long as it stayed low. They could have stayed on patrol, partnering with the militia as they learnt the ropes, or found somewhere to relax on the surface. Haydn suspected the brass feared an incident, although they would have been hard-pressed to put their feelings into words. It wouldn't be the first time a peaceful exit deal was ruined by an idiot acting like an idiot.

A flight of shuttles roared overhead and landed. Hatches snapped open, allowing their occupants to march out. Engineers, military and civilian. Haydn had helped rescue some of them personally, before the marines had been ordered to Hameau. He hoped they'd find it easy to blend into their new homeworld, or—if they didn't—that they'd have no trouble leaving and going somewhere else. Trained personnel were worth their weight in gold, these days, but they couldn't be forced to work. Resentful people in sensitive places could do a hell of a lot of damage before they were stopped.

"Good luck, Captain," Foster said. He waved at the shuttles. "They're all yours."

Haydn nodded and led his men through the hatch and into the shuttle. It was designed to carry an entire company of marines, although—normally—the unit was spread out over two or three shuttles to ensure that one hit didn't take out the entire company. Another sign, he supposed, that the brass felt relatively safe. There were no snipers with HVMs lurking close to the spaceport, or what remained of it; there was, he assumed, very little enemy presence at all. He gritted his teeth as the shuttle rocked, the hatch banging closed and the pilot starting his wretched prattle. In his experience, it was very hard to exterminate an entire enemy force. The snipers he'd chased down earlier might be nothing more than the tip of the iceberg.

And we don't know how many enemy soldiers got drowned when we blew the mountain and unleashed the flood, he reminded himself. Thousands of bodies had been swept downwards to the sea. The locals had picked up a number of dead soldiers and taken their bodies to mass graves, but thousands had never been found and buried. It was quite possible that some of them had survived and gone rogue, living off the land in a demented bid to continue the war until they died. *The locals are never going to be sure they're all gone.*

He shook his head as the shuttle powered up its drives, then leapt for the sky. The normal evasive manoeuvres were also gone. A good sign, but also something that bothered him. Better to take precautions and look paranoid than *not* take precautions and wind up dead. He tried to put the thought out of his mind as he keyed the datapad and linked into the shuttle's communications systems. *Havoc* had departed orbit, two days ago. He felt a flicker of discontent, which he ruthlessly suppressed. He'd had no reason to think his brief affair with Captain Stumbaugh would last. There'd certainly been no guarantee his unit would be assigned to *Havoc* again. And there was no way he could ask.

Major-General Anderson would not be pleased if I tried, he thought. *He wouldn't want personal feelings interfering with our duties.*

The shuttle's gravity field twisted as it docked with the MEU. Haydn felt the stomach-twisting sensation, feeling—once again—as though the world was slightly out of kilter. He'd never quite gotten used to it, although he'd learnt to keep the reaction under control. There were poor bastards who honestly couldn't handle it. They tended to stay planetside and never leave their homeworlds.

Poor bastards, he thought.

Command Sergeant Mayberry raised his voice as the hatches opened. "Report to your berths, then relax," he barked. "And don't leave your compartments without permission."

Hayden smiled at the handful of good-natured groans. The MEU was *designed* for the Marine Corps. There was no such thing as Marine Country on a ship that was owned and operated by the Marine Corps. But they had to stay in their berths, at least until the ship was underway and they could move about without getting in the way…he smiled. No one was going to be shooting at them. For real, at least. He made a mental note to arrange more training time in a day or two. It would keep them busy.

He watched the men hurrying through the hatch, then nodded to Mayberry. The Command Sergeant would keep an eye on them. He returned his datapad to his belt and headed through the hatch himself, making his way down to the briefing room. As always, it was a scene of organised chaos. Holographic images glided around like ghosts, brushing shoulders with flesh and blood officers from the MEU. He was mildly surprised they weren't meeting in person, although he supposed he shouldn't have been. The only thing all the rumours agreed upon was that the two divisions would be moving out within the week.

"Captain," a voice said. "Major-General Anderson requests the pleasure of your company."

Hayden turned to see Lieutenant Gold, looking as tired and harassed as the rest of the officers. The corps was designed for hasty movement from planet to planet, but loading up the marines and their equipment—and ordering replacements for everything lost during the campaign—was never easy. It didn't help, he supposed, that so much of the original chain of command had been shot to pieces during the war. There would be so many gaps in the manifests that the pre-Earthfall Inspectorate General would have a field day.

"I'm coming," Haydn said. A request from a senior officer was an order. There was no point in trying to deny it. "He's in his office?"

Gold nodded, then hurried off to do something else. Haydn felt a flicker of sympathy as he made his way around the compartment, passing a bunch of logistics officers who were waving datapads at each other as if they were weapons. The marines had expended more ammunition during the fighting than anyone had expected, if the reports were accurate. It would take time, time they didn't have, for the factory ships to start replenishing their stockpiles. They were lucky, he reflected sourly, that the second division had arrived. They'd have enough supplies to handle a major engagement.

Major-General Anderson's hatch was closed. Haydn pressed his hand against the scanner and waited. Anderson would have left the hatch open if he wanted people to just walk in and out of the office...Haydn snorted at the thought. Senior officers thought they were owed a little privacy. They probably were—if nothing else, they had to handle matters junior officers weren't supposed to know about—but it still irked him. He rather suspected he'd change his mind when—if—he reached such rarefied heights himself.

The hatch hissed open. Haydn stepped into the office and looked around with interest. It appeared no more permanent than a FOB in the middle of a warzone, complete with collapsible furniture, portable datapads, and holographic projectors. A lone drinks dispenser was parked against the far bulkhead. Haydn suspected it was designed to send a very clear message to visitors as well as its owner, a reminder that no one—not even the Major-General himself—would remain permanently on the giant starship. They'd be going in harm's way soon enough.

And the starship is one hell of a target, if any enemy warships start prowling around, Haydn thought. He came to attention and saluted, smartly. *The entire division might get blown away if she is caught and trapped before she can retreat.*

"At ease," Anderson ordered. His voice was gruff, suggesting he wished he was somewhere—anywhere—else. The senior officers had to do a *lot* of paperwork, even though the corps cut it down to the bare minimum. There'd been Imperial Army officers who did nothing but paperwork. It probably wasn't a coincidence that their units tended to be the least capable on the field. "Welcome back, Captain. Help yourself to coffee."

"Thank you, sir," Haydn said.

He relaxed, slightly. If he was being offered coffee, he probably wasn't in trouble. He poured himself a mug of coffee from the dispenser, added a hint of sugar and turned to face his ultimate commanding officer. It wasn't the first time they'd met. Major-General Anderson was *good* at talking to his subordinates, making sure he had a clear picture of what was actually going on. Haydn admired that in him. It was all too easy for a senior officer to look down from his lofty perch and completely miss the little details.

"You did good work down there," Anderson said. "Do you think the city is relatively stable?"

"Relatively, sir," Haydn said. "The local economy has been shot to hell. They're eating ration bars and drinking recycled water…"

"A known cause of civil unrest," Anderson said. His lips twitched in a faint smile. "And the enemy snipers?"

"We captured or killed every enemy soldier we encountered, sir," Haydn said. "However, I cannot guarantee we got them *all*."

"No, of course not," Anderson agreed. "Some of them will throw away their weapons and try to blend into the crowd. Others will bury their weapons and wait for a chance to strike again."

"The locals will handle them," Haydn said. "They might not be entirely fond of us, sir, but they're even *less* fond of their former overlords."

"We can, but hope." Anderson looked him in the eye. "Are your men ready for deployment?"

Haydn hesitated. "We lost seven men during the battle in space," he said. He felt each and every one of those losses. He'd have to spend time writing to their families, if their families were still around. Earthfall had shattered everything. The families could have fled the chaos or…or died, caught up in one of the civil wars that had started tearing the remnants of the empire apart. "Three more were wounded, but should return to active duty within the next two months. The remainder are…tired, sir; tired but ready to resume their duties if necessary."

"It may become necessary," Anderson said. "We'll be leaving the system within the next two days and heading for the RV point. Depending on what *Havoc* finds, we may be going straight into action. We just don't know."

He keyed a terminal and brought up an image. Haydn leaned forward. A cone…a small emergency landing pod? No, the scale was too big. A dumpster, designed to land enough supplies to set up a small colony in a single drop. He frowned. The basic *idea* of using them to land troops had been around for centuries, but the Onge had been the first people to actually *risk* it. Their troops had had no line of retreat. They could have been caught on the ground, if the defenders had had enough warning, and annihilated. No wonder they'd expended so much firepower on flattening anything that so much as *looked* like a threat. They didn't dare risk letting their forces be pocketed and destroyed before they had a chance to deploy.

"We may need to get a lot of troops to the ground in a hurry," Major-General Anderson said. It was easy to tell he wasn't remotely happy about it. "This may be our only option."

"All or nothing," Haydn said. He felt a thrill of excitement, mingled with fear. It would be daring…the sort of daring idea that was best suppressed unless they were truly desperate. Were they? "Sir?"

"Yes," Anderson said. His face was grim. "Prepare your men. We may have no choice, but to risk everything on a single throw of the dice."

"Yes, sir," Haydn said. "We could land an entire regiment with a dumpster."

"Yes," Anderson agreed. He lowered his voice, echoing Haydn's thoughts. "And there'll be no way to get them off in a hurry if the operation goes badly wrong."

CHAPTER SEVEN

No, of course not. He has, at best, the potential for ten credits. The value of the trunk depends on the beholder. One person may value it highly, another may see it as just...useless wood. The trunk is only worth ten credits to the right person. And, of course, unless the lumberjack sells the trunk it will be effectively worthless.
—**Professor Leo Caesius**
The Rise and Fall of Interstellar Capitalism

THE HATCH BLEEPED, ONCE.

Julia looked up. The voyage hadn't been as bad as she'd feared, once they'd dropped into FTL and left Hameau behind. The crew had served ration bars and water and otherwise insisted she stay in her cabin, but... she told herself she should enjoy the flight. Admiral Agate had once told her about officers who'd told their men to enjoy the war, as the peace was going to be terrible. Julia understood how they felt. She was going to be in deep trouble the moment she stepped off the transport, if not before. Someone had probably already reported home, just to destroy Julia's career. It was what she would have done.

"Come," she said.

The hatch hissed open. The young man—Ensign Taros—stuck his head into the compartment and saluted. Julia hid her irritation with an effort. Taros didn't seem to be able to decide if he should be treating her as a lowly civilian, on the ground she was a guest on the transport, or kissing her ass because she was corporate royalty. Julia was tempted to point out that kissing her ass was likely to end badly, if only because her career was about to fall so far and so fast she'd probably wind up on the other side of the planet. Anyone who stood too close to her would be struck by the disaster. Anyone she recommended for promotion would probably be demoted instead.

"Commissioner." Taros saluted, again. "The Captain wants you on the bridge."

Julia stood, brushing down her ill-fitting tunic and tucking the datapad under one arm as she followed him out of the hatch. She had grown to loathe the cabin in the last few days, even though she *knew* it was vastly superior to sleeping in the onboard barracks or cargo holds. The air smelled faintly unpleasant, as if the life support was reaching the limits of its capacity. Julia knew little about starship mechanics, but she knew enough to be concerned. If the atmosphere went bad, they were doomed. The thought wasn't reassuring.

She breathed a sigh of relief as she followed Taros onto the bridge. It was small and cramped, compared to the battlecruiser's command deck; it looked as if someone had thrown a dozen consoles together at random and wired them into a holographic command network. A middle-aged man sat in the centre of the compartment, looking as if he were worried and trying to hide it. Julia didn't recognise him. He probably hadn't been assigned to *Hammerblow*. He'd have some other commissioner keeping an eye on his behaviour.

"Commissioner," the captain said. "I'm Captain Arbroath. Thank you for coming."

You could have invited me at any moment, Julia thought as she shook his hand. She knew she was being unfair and she didn't really care. *It wasn't as if I was doing anything more important than trying to find a way to blame everything on someone else.*

"Thank you," she said. "What's happening now?"

"We're about to drop out of phase space," Captain Arbroath informed her. "I thought you would like to contact your superiors."

Julia gave him a sharp look. She was no expert, but she wasn't a complete ignorant either. "I thought it took at least ten hours to get a message from the phase limit to the planet."

"It does," Captain Arbroath confirmed. "However, we're running on empty here. Our life support is on the verge of breaking down. We need to offload at least a third of our passengers within the next twenty-four hours or we'll be in deep shit."

"I see," Julia said. "Why didn't they give us more life support?"

"They did," Captain Arbroath said. "But the datanet is too badly battered to handle it. If they hadn't hardwired the course into the navigational system, I wouldn't be entirely confident we're heading to the right place. We rely so much on our computers that we're lost without them."

Julia nodded, curtly. "I'll transmit as soon as we arrive," she said. "And hopefully...they'll listen."

She took a seat and waited, watching the displays as they counted down to zero. The reports were largely incomprehensible, but she understood some things. On impulse, she tested the datanet. It was so slow and crude it felt like something out of a museum. She shook her head, then swallowed—hard—as the transport ground her way back to realspace. Julia's stomach heaved. She had to force herself not to be sick. Judging from the noise behind her, not everyone had been so lucky.

"The communications console is ready," Captain Arbroath said. The display lit up, showing a handful of planets orbiting a star. If there was anything close enough to be a threat, it wasn't showing up. "Commissioner?"

Julia took a breath, trying to decide what to say. The week in transit suddenly felt very short...too short. She suddenly didn't want the voyage to end. She told herself, sharply, not to be stupid. The life support was already failing. Soon, they'd suffocate in their own wastes. She wanted to live. She wanted to...she wasn't sure what she wanted. All her hopes and dreams had died when *Hammerblow* had surrendered.

"This is Julia Ganister-Onge, Political Commissioner attached to OSS *Hammerblow*," she said. "We require assistance. I say again, we require assistance. This ship's life support is failing. We require immediate assistance."

She sat back, allowing Captain Arbroath to take over and explain what was actually going on. It was unlikely anyone would refuse, now the transport had declared an emergency, but it was impossible to be sure. She tried to tell herself they wouldn't let *her* die, yet…she had to admit she was an embarrassment. Her family might be happier if she died a long way from home, rather than returning in failure. And yet, they needed to know what had happened. Didn't they? If someone had been watching the battle from a distance and slipped back to report…they wouldn't know everything. She hoped…

"That's the message sent," Captain Arbroath said. "We'll be heading in-system now."

Julia looked at him. "Shouldn't we wait for permission?"

"We don't have time," Captain Arbroath said. "It'll take ten hours, more or less, for the message to reach Onge. Even if they reply at once, which they won't, it'll still take another ten hours for the message to get here. We have to head to the planet, to the orbital station, and hope to hell they let us dock without delay. If they don't…"

He waved a hand at a display. Julia couldn't understand what she was seeing, but she was sure that a line of red lights was nothing good. She shook her head as a dull rumble echoed through the giant ship, a grim reminder that her realspace drives had been badly damaged during the fighting. Tenos had even told her that there were entire sections that were still depressurized, effectively unreachable. Given the limits on the life support, Julia thought that wasn't a bad thing. They simply didn't have the capacity to spare.

"Just get us there as quickly as possible," Julia said. Her eyes lingered on the display. A lot of icons that should have been present *weren't*. The cloudscoops, the asteroid miners, the in-system transports…all gone. She told herself the sensors had been badly damaged during the engagement.

"And hope they take us in without an argument."

"Hopefully," Captain Arbroath agreed.

• • •

"They've just transmitted a rather worrying message," Rachel said. "Their life support is on the verge of conking out."

Phelps nodded, his expression grim as he paced the tiny compartment. Rachel understood. They'd timed it well, in hopes of convincing the enemy defences to let *Botany Bay* enter orbit without searching the transport from top to bottom, but she knew it was quite possible the locals wouldn't believe the message. There was no way to verify the ship's distress without actually being there and *that* would take time the ship and her passengers didn't have. She felt a little guilty. It wasn't the worst thing she'd ever done to carry out her duties—she had a long list of things she regretted, for one reason or another—but that might change if the air turned poisonous before the ship could be unloaded. She'd never sentenced thousands of people to death...

She turned her attention back to the live feed from the ship's sensors. The system was rather more densely populated than the files suggested, although *that* wasn't a surprise. The files had been hopelessly out of date before Earthfall had destroyed them. Onge had at least five cloudscoops—and probably more, given that one gas giant was on the other side of the primary star—and hundreds, perhaps thousands of asteroid mining colonies. She guessed the corprats had stepped up their recruiting missions, snatching up trained personnel from every star system within range. Why not? It was what they'd been doing when the marines first discovered their existence.

"You do realise they may not be very welcoming?" Perkins looked up from his blanket. "They might just put a missile in our hull from a safe distance."

"They'll want to know what the passengers know," Phelps pointed out. "And blowing up an entire ship of ex-POWs will be shitty for morale."

"Assuming anyone finds out about it," Bonkowski countered. "This ship could easily be branded an enemy vessel, just another raider full of pirates that got blown away before they could start shooting holes in a handful of asteroid colonies. You take a PR specialist and he'll turn the worst atrocity in human history into a just and necessary act."

"Wankers," Perkins commented. "For all they know, this ship is carrying a bunch of conditioned assholes with orders to assassinate their bosses."

"They can handle the risk," Phelps said. "And, like I said, they'll want to know what the passengers know."

Rachel turned her attention back to the latest datapacket from *Havoc*. There probably wouldn't be any more, at least as long as the situation remained stable. The POWs had offered hundreds of insights into enemy culture and civilisation, although there was no way to know what was missing until it was too late. Rachel was used to winging it, but she preferred to have at least a *rough* idea of what they were getting into. She'd be happier making a blind drop to the surface. There, at least, they could sneak around and spy on the locals, building up a picture of their society before they tried to get inside. It would be simpler...

Not that we'd have any more chance to get out, if things go wrong, she thought, as she leaned back against the bulkhead. *If we get caught, we're toast.*

Perkins sat up and checked his datapad. "If the crew manages to keep the speed up, they'll enter orbit in twenty hours or so."

"Then we'll be ready to jump ship," Phelps said. "Get some rest. I want to be well away from the ship before they start searching her."

"And hope we can find somewhere to hide," Rachel said. The suits were designed to be hard to detect, but they weren't *cloaked*. Crossing a sensor net would reveal their presence as surely as sending up a sensor flare. Hell, they could be spotted with the naked eye, if someone got lucky. "We'll have to hack their datanet if we want to get in."

"True," Phelps said. There was an edge in his voice that hadn't been there before. The voyage had been wearing, even though they'd done very little. "But one problem at a time, all right?"

"Yes, sir," Rachel said.

THE HALLS OF MONTEZUMA

...

The giant mansion had been designed, Director Thaddeus Onge had been told, in a style that dated all the way back to the family's roots on Old Earth. Thaddeus himself hadn't been so sure. It looked as if a dozen different styles had been merged together to produce a building that would have been elegant, if it hadn't been so...*jarring*. Personally, he suspected the building designer had taken his ancestors for a ride. The ancestral mansion was long gone, assuming it had ever existed in the first place; it was difficult, judging by what few records had survived centuries of unrest on Earth, to be sure the mansions in photographs had genuinely belonged to them. Anyone who claimed photographs couldn't be faked was either ignorant or a liar.

Not that it matters, he thought as he let the dogs race around the garden. *The future is ours, and to hell with the past.*

He smiled, and tried to relax. Someone—he'd forgotten who—had once joked that anyone who wanted a friend on Earth needed to buy a dog. He was becoming depressingly aware that that was true on Onge, too. Everyone wanted something from him, from simple investment to...to anything. Thaddeus had an entire staff charged with handling requests for money, meetings and everything else along those lines, but some things couldn't be left to them. Thaddeus *had* to keep on top of his work or the project his ancestors had started would be as doomed as Old Earth herself.

His eyes narrowed as he peered into the distance, towards the growing megacity and the orbital elevator beyond. The city had never been intended to get so large. In hindsight, it might have been easier to spread it out a little...even though it risked losing the advantages of concentrating so much talent and resources in a relatively small space. It had been turning into a major headache even before Earthfall, when they'd started recruiting trained personnel and their families and rushing them to safety. Thaddeus knew Onge was safe—the PDC on the distant mountaintop was a grim reminder of the family's investment in security—but the influx of so many refugees was causing its own problems. The planetary society was never intended to take so many newcomers so quickly. In hindsight, they should have invested more in farms and farming and little hamlets...

"Your Lordship!"

Thaddeus turned. Daisy, his aide, was hurrying towards him, carrying a portable communicator in one hand and a datapad in the other. Thaddeus scowled, then concealed his irritation as best as he could. Daisy had been with him long enough to understand the importance of dog-time. She wouldn't interrupt him unless it was truly urgent. It could cost her a position that made her one of the most influential people on the planet.

"Yes?"

"General Gilbert called for you," Daisy said. "He insisted it was urgent."

"It probably is," Thaddeus said. General Jim Gilbert didn't like his political superiors interfering in purely military decisions. He wouldn't have contacted his ultimate superior if it hadn't been necessary. "Let me talk to him."

He took the communicator and held it to his mouth. "Jim. What's happening?"

"Sir," Gilbert said. "A troop transport, one of the ships from Admiral Agate's fleet, has returned. She's insisting she's overcrowded with former POWs and requesting urgent permission to dock."

Thaddeus blinked. "Former POWs?"

"Yes, sir," Gilbert said. "We don't have a solid briefing yet, but from what we've heard Admiral Agate appears to have lost. "

"...I see." Thaddeus controlled himself with an effort. He didn't know enough. Not yet. "When will this transport arrive?"

"Roughly nine hours from now," Gilbert said. "If their messages are accurate, their life support is failing and they desperately need to offload some passengers before it's too late."

Thaddeus forced himself to think. What had happened? Admiral Agate had had enough firepower to smash his way to Hameau, punch his way through what remained of the defences, clobber the marines from orbit and land troops to mop up what remained of the invaders. He shouldn't have been *defeated*. What the fuck had happened? It was impossible to believe the marines were deploying battlecruisers, let alone battleships. The manpower requirements alone should have made it difficult, if not impossible.

"Sir." Gilbert audibly gulped for air. "We need to let them dock at one of the immigration stations. It's designed to handle thousands of sudden arrivals."

"They could be lying," Thaddeus pointed out. "Do we have any real proof?"

"I've already got shuttles *en route* to check out the story," Gilbert said. "However, sir, we have to proceed on the assumption they're telling the truth."

"Yes." Thaddeus let out a breath, then started to rattle out orders. "Clear the immigration station. Get everyone already there off before you let the freighter dock. Then…hold the newcomers until we have a chance to assess their story. Total news blackout. No messages off the station without prior permission. Make sure they haven't been conditioned or anything."

"Yes, sir," Gilbert said.

"And call an emergency meeting, to be held one hour from now," Thaddeus continued. "We need a plan. Quickly."

"Yes, sir," Gilbert echoed.

Thaddeus passed the communicator back to Daisy, then looked at the dogs. They were still gambolling happily, unaware that their human had bigger problems. Thaddeus envied them their innocence. They didn't understand what had been lost. They didn't understand what might *still* be lost. The timing was horrible. His day had been ruined.

"Order one of the boys to come and take over," he told Daisy. There was no point in trying to retrieve the day. "And then have coffee brought to my study."

Daisy curtseyed. "Yes, sir."

CHAPTER EIGHT

A smart student might argue, at this point, that the lumberjack could burn the trunk for firewood. This is obviously true. But... the value of the trunk would remain stable right up until the trunk was burnt to ashes, whereupon it would be definitely worthless. The lumberjack's potential wealth would drop, sharply.
—**Professor Leo Caesius**
The Rise and Fall of Interstellar Capitalism

"COMMISSIONER," CAPTAIN ARBROATH SAID. "They're dispatching a shuttle to investigate."

Julia nodded. Her entire body felt as if it was creaking helplessly. She'd declined suggestions she should go back to her cabin, then drifted off to sleep on the bridge. The chair hadn't been comfortable, but…she forced herself to stand, wishing—again—for a long bath and a massage. She'd settle for a shower and a change of clothes. She was ruefully aware she stank. She wasn't alone. The entire crew smelt terrible.

"Have them dock as soon as possible," she said. The air tasted stale. She tried to tell herself she was imagining it. It didn't work. She could almost hear laboured sounds coming from the air processors. "Have you told them I'm onboard?"

"We forwarded a datapacket, yes," Captain Arbroath said. "I assume they've had a chance to look at it."

Julia forced herself to sit and wait as the shuttle flew closer. The sensors were battered almost to the point of uselessness. If the shuttle hadn't been broadcasting an IFF signal, they wouldn't have been able to track it at all. She shivered, wondering if they were on the verge of crashing into an asteroid or even an entire planet. The odds of accidentally ramming an asteroid were very low—dense asteroid fields only existed in bad flicks—but it was hard to escape the impression that she didn't have the slightest idea what was going on. The planetary defences were probably already locked on the hull. If they came too close, without permission, they'd be blown to atoms.

"The shuttle is requesting permission to dock," an officer said. He looked up from his console. "Captain?"

"Open the forward hatch," Captain Arbroath ordered. "And let them enter alone."

Julia shot him a sharp look. Naval protocol insisted visitors had to be greeted by the ship's officers, if not the commanding officer personally. She supposed they weren't exactly dealing with a normal boarding party. Captain Arbroath keyed his console, bringing up the live feed from the handful of remaining interior sensors as the shuttle docked. Julia watched, silently, as the hatch opened and four armoured men entered the ship. They were so heavily armoured she couldn't help wondering what they thought they were walking into. An ambush? A trap? Or...or what?

She tensed as the armoured figures made their way towards the bridge. This was it. This was...she swallowed, hard, as it dawned on her she was committed. Hell, she'd been committed from the moment she'd refused the offer of asylum. Her reports had been included in the datapacket...she shuddered, her mouth suddenly dry. Her superiors had had nearly thirteen hours to read the report, then decide what to do with her. She wondered if the boarding party had orders to open the airlocks, depressurise the entire ship and direct the hulk into the primary star. It was paranoia, but...she shook her head. Her superiors wouldn't condemn everyone on the ship to death for *her* failures. Unless...

The bridge hatch opened. Julia felt a flash of *déjà vu*. The newcomers weren't carrying their weapons at the ready, but otherwise they reminded her of the marines boarding the battlecruiser a few short weeks ago. She knew she should stand to greet them, but her legs refused to cooperate. The featureless helms were terrifying. She couldn't see so much as a rank badge, let alone a nametag. There was no hope of complaining, again, if she didn't know who she should be complaining about.

"Welcome," Captain Arbroath said. "As you can see, this ship is in poor condition."

The boarding party walked to the consoles and plugged their suits into the local nodes. Julia watched, all too aware they were scanning every last inch of the ship. If anything looked wrong...she gritted her teeth, cursing as she remembered just how many of the internal datanet nodes were beyond repair. The boarding party would have to search the ship physically, if they wanted to make sure the ship was completely harmless. That would take hours. The passengers didn't have time.

"The ship will be guided to an immigration station," an armoured figure said. Julia guessed he was the commander. "You will be held there until your future has been determined. Any resistance will result in the destruction of your vessel."

Julia saw Captain Arbroath's lips tighten at the words. He wasn't a pirate, flying on a pirate ship. He was a decorated officer in the Onge Navy...he didn't deserve to be treated like a criminal. None of them deserved to be treated like a criminal...her heart sank as she realised it was just a matter of time before she was marched before her superiors and ordered to explain. She wished, not for the first time, that Admiral Agate had accompanied her. She could've hidden behind him when their superiors started allocating the blame.

One of the boarding party remained at the helm. The others started calling in more shuttles. Julia guessed they were going to start uplifting passengers and shipping them directly to the immigration station, rather than risk leaving them on the ship. The transport's condition was obvious. Julia had no doubt the ship's life support was on its last legs. The shuttles couldn't hope to make up the difference.

She sat back and watched the display as the planet came closer. The giant immigration station was emptying rapidly, if the hundreds of shuttles flying around the structure were any indication. They wouldn't want to risk contaminating the immigrants, the willing and the unwilling alike, with bad news from a distant world. She wondered, idly, if anyone outside the navy and government knew the ship had arrived. She'd heard rumours of hidden datanet channels used by hackers, allowing underground groups to share information, but they'd never been anything more than rumours. The official line was that they didn't exist and never would. Julia had been in corporate service long enough to know that might well be untrue.

"Commissioner Ganister-Onge?"

Julia looked up. One of the faceless men was looking at her. "Yes?"

"You will accompany us," the faceless man said. "You have an appointment."

In Samarra, Julia thought, darkly. She wondered if she had time to go back to her cabin and splash water on her face. Probably not. The newcomers had discouraged crewmen from leaving the bridge, even as they'd landed more and more armoured troopers on the hull. She suspected they were readying themselves to deal with a riot. *I suppose I should be glad they're offloading me before the ship docks.*

She stood. "I'm coming."

• • •

Rachel watched, coldly, as more and more armoured troopers flooded onto the transport and started to search the corridors. It was clear, from the flurry of activity, that whoever was in charge was making it up as he went along, but she had to admit he was doing a good job. The boarding party had confirmed the transport's life support was about to fail, then taken control and steered her towards the giant immigration station. Rachel doubted the corps could have done much better. There really hadn't been many other options if the corprats wanted to keep the passengers alive.

She frowned as she studied the live feeds from the sensors and compared them to the files. The latter were almost laughably out of date. The transport's sensors were picking up hundreds of orbital structures, from a pair of giant anchors for the space elevators to orbital weapons platforms, industrial nodes and asteroid habitats. It looked as though they'd prefabricated the platforms, then hastily assembled them shortly after Earthfall. Rachel was morbidly impressed as she continued her scans. The corprats had practically thrown the whole thing together in zero time.

It's astonishing what one can do if one has an unlimited budget and a complete lack of scruples, she mused. There was a great deal of radio traffic, seemingly uncensored. She was pretty sure it was monitored closely for signs of wrongthink. *If they'd had more time, they might have risen to dominate the entire sector.*

She shifted uncomfortably inside the Pathfinder suit. The suit was designed for long-term occupancy, she'd been assured, but there was nothing the designers could do to make it more comfortable. She would have preferred to remain in the blister, outside the suit, but the risk of detection was too great. A sudden burst of vented air would draw attention, if the enemy was feeling paranoid. The last thing they needed was the transport 's hull being swarmed by *more* enemy soldiers. They'd sell their lives dearly, but they'd end up dead.

More icons appeared on the display. There were surprisingly few warships—she reminded herself that meant nothing, as the sensors were far from mil-grade—but there were thousands of shuttles, worker bees and interplanetary ships in clear view. The latter might well be dangerous, even if they didn't have FTL drives. There was no problem in arming them... hell, the corprats might have just bolted a handful of missile launchers to their hulls in hopes of providing more firepower at the crucial moment. She checked the laser communicator was sending messages back to *Havoc*, relaying everything they'd picked up to the cruiser. She'd be making her own survey of the system, but she couldn't get too close. The risk of detection was dangerously high.

"They're moving the commissioner to the shuttle," Phelps said, pressing his helmet against hers. "I think we should ride along."

Rachel nodded. The high orbitals were *glowing* with everything from active sensors to radio and radar beacons. The corprats were clearly very aware of the danger of cloaked ships. She thought they could remain undetected, if they jumped ship and headed for the nearest asteroid habitat, but it wasn't a sure thing. Riding on the shuttle would be easier and safer, particularly if it headed straight for the anchor. Rachel was fairly sure it would. The sensors suggested, very strongly, that there were no shuttles heading to the planet itself.

Odd, she mused. *But not important at the moment.*

She felt a thrill of excitement as they performed one final check of the suits and what remained of the blister, then opened the hatch and stepped out onto the hull. There was nothing left to alert the enemy to their presence, if—when—the scarchers opened up the depressurised section and investigated. What little evidence they'd left over the last week had already been disintegrated or hurled into space. By the time it was found, if it ever was, it would be too late.

They communicated using hand gestures as they made their way across the hull to the enemy shuttlecraft. They'd picked the transport with malice aforethought—the hull wasn't remotely smooth, making it harder for motion detectors to pick up on their presence—but she knew better than to take it for granted. The shuttles were standard designs, copied from the Imperial Navy. She hoped the corprats hadn't made any improvements. The analysts had suggested the corprat designers had reserved the really advanced technology for themselves, for the day they'd declare independence, but Rachel doubted they were that clever. It was far more likely the Grand Senate and the Imperial Navy had refused to pay for pure research that might or might not lead to usable technology. They'd been at the top of the heap. They wouldn't want something that might upset the order of things.

And Earthfall did it anyway, she thought, as they reached the shuttle. Her sensors warned her the craft was already powering up its drives. The corprats wanted their answers yesterday. She felt a flicker of sympathy for the poor commissioner, even though she was...well, a commissioner. The woman was at the mercy of superiors who wouldn't want to hear the truth. *They wanted to hold everything in stasis...*

The Pathfinders attached themselves to the hull, concealed themselves out of direct eyesight and waited. The shuttle disengaged and spun away into interplanetary space. Rachel waited, her mouth suddenly dry. They might have to jump off in a hurry if the shuttle headed towards a shuttle-bay, rather than a docking port. There was no way to know. Rachel would have preferred the docking port herself, if she was transporting dangerous prisoners, but...it wasn't as if the prisoners were physically dangerous. It was what they *knew* that made them so dangerous. She assessed the radio chatter as best as she could, trying to determine what—if anything—had leaked out. It was impossible. The chatter came in fits and starts. It was difficult to tell what was important and what wasn't.

She tensed as the shuttle approached the giant anchor. Space elevators were normally attached to asteroids, but the corprats had thrown together a giant space station and attached the elevator cable to that instead. She puzzled over it for a long moment, wondering why they hadn't used an asteroid. Was there some advantage to the design? Or hadn't they wanted to take the risk of bringing another asteroid into orbit? It wasn't as if they hadn't already brought a number into orbit...maybe they'd had some idea that hadn't quite panned out. Or maybe she was overthinking it. The corprats might have simply wanted to put an elevator anchor together as quickly as possible.

Phelps caught her attention as the shuttle reduced speed. It looked as though they were heading towards a docking port. Rachel breathed a sigh of relief. Jumping ship so close to the giant station risked detection...they might be taken for space junk and fired upon without the enemy ever knowing what they'd done. She kept her eyes open as the station grew larger and larger until it dominated the horizon, noting how many different structures had been woven together into one. There would be plenty of room to hide on the hull, she told herself. They'd just have to be very careful when they tried to find a way in.

The shuttle slowed, then docked. Rachel felt a shudder running through the craft as its gravity field merged with the station's. She stood, disengaging her maglocks and jumping through space to land on the station's hull. The horizon seemed to shift, a twist in perspective that had never failed to make her head hurt. She gritted her teeth as she crawled over the hull, feeling naked and exposed. The rest of the unit followed her, looking for a place to hide. They'd have to hang out on the hull until they got inside and blended into the local population. Thankfully, there were so many people on the station that no one could hope to know them all.

As long as we can fool the security monitors, she thought as they found an exposed sensor node and started to work, *we can fool everyone.*

Her lips curved up. People tended to believe in technology, even though they shouldn't. It was easy, with the right training and equipment, to insert *anything* into the files and have it believed. The corprats had devised one hell of a surveillance system—she still shuddered when she thought how easily it had been misused—but they rested far too much faith in it. She had no doubt it could be turned against them. If nothing else, they could hack themselves new identities within the system and be taken for Onge personnel...

Concentrate, she told herself sharply. *If this goes wrong, we're doomed.*

Data flowed into her HUD as she linked into the enemy system. The sensor node wasn't tied to the main datanet trunk, but it didn't matter. Someone had melded the two systems together, probably out of a desire for convenience. Her lips curled into a cold smile. One could install the most advanced security system in the known universe and some yahoo would *still* do something to weaken it, even if it was something as minor as setting the password to 'password.' Whoever had rigged the system had created a back door into the main datanet and probably didn't even *know* it. She guessed he was no WebHead. Most people didn't even *begin* to understand what went on inside their datapads, let alone how easily they could be hacked and turned into enemy spies. The corprats probably saw that as a feature, not a bug. They'd see a great many advantages in spying on their people.

Her smile got bigger as more and more data opened up in front of her. The high-security files were still sealed—and there would be datanodes that were physically isolated from the datanet, unless she missed her guess—but she already had enough access to start building false IDs for them. It helped, she supposed, that the corprats were already scrambling to deal with a major crisis. People were being moved around so rapidly that none of them really knew what was going on.

Good, she thought. *We can use that.*

Phelps brushed his helmet against hers. "Can we get in?"

"Yes," Rachel assured him. She'd done it before under far more challenging circumstances. She might not be able to create completely new cover identities, but she could hijack a handful and put them to work. "Just give me a few hours to put together the fake ID codes."

"Hurry," Phelps advised. "We can't hang out here forever."

CHAPTER NINE

Instead, our lumberjack sells his trunk to the carpenter.
The carpenter pays ten credits for the trunk, therefore turning
the lumberjack's potential wealth into actual wealth, thus
allowing the lumberjack to buy whatever he wants to buy.
—**Professor Leo Caesius**
The Rise and Fall of Interstellar Capitalism

JULIA FELT...AWFUL.

Her minders—she tried not to think of them as guards or prison wardens—had allowed her to shower, then subjected her to a long series of security procedures that were designed to ensure she posed no threat, humiliate her or both. They'd gone over everything in cynical detail, pressing sensors against her skull to monitor her brainwaves and then inserting smaller probes into each and every of her orifices. She'd expected to be asked questions, not poked and prodded like…a piece of meat. She felt sick and violated by the time the ordeal was finished, with the minders throwing a shipsuit at her and ordering her to dress before she faced the next challenge. Julia was tempted to plead for food and a nap, even for a simple nutrient drink, but she had enough dignity to keep her mouth shut. If they couldn't tell she was hungry, their medical probes needed work.

They escorted her into a dark room and pushed her into the exact centre, then ordered her to wait. Julia knew what was coming, but it was still a shock when beams of bright light flared around her. The chamber was designed to intimidate, to leave her feeling naked, alone and facing a handful of shadowy questioners. She knew the procedure, but she'd never faced it before. Not like this. She wondered, not for the first time, if she'd made a terrible mistake in returning home. Someone had to be the scapegoat. Someone...that someone was probably her.

"Julia Ganister-Onge," a voice said. It was completely atonal. It could have come from any of the figures or none of them. Hell, some of the figures might be nothing more than holographic illusions. She knew better than to touch them. "Your report is neither complete nor conclusive."

Julia said nothing. They were trying to unsettle her. She knew the drill as well as they did. They'd fire charges at her, in hopes of getting her to say something they could use against her. Clearly, her status within the family was in doubt. They wouldn't have treated her so badly if they'd considered her a full member, with full voting rights. And yet, they'd addressed her by her full name.

"You were sent to restore order on Hameau," the voice said. "What happened?"

"We lost," Julia said, bluntly. They'd had *hours* to read her report, along with whatever Captain Arbroath had submitted. They *knew* what had happened. "We were defeated by the marines."

There was a long chilling pause before the voice spoke again. "Why?"

Julia took a breath, then started to go through the whole story. The arrival at Hameau. The first engagement with the enemy fleet. The landings. The ground engagements, against both the marines themselves and the local insurgents. The final desperate push against the marine positions, broken by a tidal wave of water; the engagement with the enemy fleet, ended by boarding parties storming the battlecruiser and her escorts. And the surrender...*her* surrender. She felt her heart sink as she finished outlining the story. She should never have headed home. Someone else could have reported to the family. She should have stayed on Hameau and hoped for the best.

"And you decided to come home," the voice said. "Why?"

"Because someone had to report," Julia said. She put as much lipstick on a pig as she could. "I had to make sure you knew what had happened."

The voice said nothing. Julia couldn't keep herself from peering into the darkness, even though she *knew* she wouldn't see anything. The holograms wouldn't offer any more detail than a vague report from a subordinate hoping desperately his boss wouldn't look too closely and see the problems… she winced, inwardly. She was too close to that mindset for her peace of mind. Not that it mattered. She was in deep shit. The odds of her being allowed to retire gracefully were terrifyingly low.

She kept her voice under tight control as the voice threw question after question at her, often forcing her to repeat herself. She tried to hide her growing tiredness—and fear and frustration—as they went over the same points time and time again, perhaps in hopes of catching her in a lie. They wouldn't *want* to believe, she knew. They'd sooner believe Admiral Agate had turned traitor and set off to carve out an empire of his own than accept they'd lost to an outside power. A few weeks ago, the shadowy men facing her had *known* they were the heirs of empire. Now…

"The invaders claimed to be the Terran Marine Corps," the voice said. "Do you believe they were telling the truth?"

"Admiral Agate believed so," Julia said, carefully. She wouldn't know a marine from a civil or corporate guardsman. "I have no reason to doubt him."

"And yet he could be wrong," the voice said. "Or lying."

"I have no reason to doubt him," Julia repeated. She felt her voice start to crack. "And, whoever they are, they won."

"Yes." There was another pause. "Did they give you any hint of their future plans?"

"No," Julia said. "They did hint they might be open to discussions, but…nothing too concrete."

"Understood," the voice said. "We will have more questions for you later. Until then, you can get some rest. We'll bring you down to the planet shortly."

"Yes, sir," Julia said, relieved. She wondered, again, who was hiding behind the holographic masks. Her father? Her uncle? A relative she'd never met? It was possible. "I...I thank you."

The holographic images vanished. The lights came on. Julia heard the hatch opening behind her and turned as the minders entered. This time, she was almost pleased to see them.

...

Director Thaddeus Onge watched through a small array of sensors as Julia Ganister-Onge was escorted out of the interrogation chamber and down the corridor to a luxury suite that doubled as a holding cell. Julia had no way to know it, but her body had been under constant monitoring from the moment she'd been transferred to the anchor station. The slightest hint she'd told a lie would have set off alarms right across the system, providing more than enough excuse to subject her to an even more thorough interrogation. She hadn't shown any hint she was lying, although it had been clear she wasn't sure of a few things. Thaddeus didn't blame her. Indeed, it was a good thing. If she'd been trying to construct a false narrative, one based on a misinterpretation of the truth, there would have been fewer holes in her story.

"It is impossible," Vice Director Hayden James McManus said. "The marines are a small military force. They couldn't invade and occupy an entire planet!"

"They have." General Gilbert spoke quietly, but firmly. "There's no way to avoid the simple fact that that's exactly what they've done."

Thaddeus looked at Gilbert's holoimage. "I take it there's been no time to interrogate the others yet?"

"No, sir," Gilbert said. "We're still unloading the transport and providing urgent medical care. However, we have had time to scan their reports and compare them. There's a lot of ass-covering in places, I think, but the general gist is pretty much identical. The marines came, saw and conquered. And then they defeated Admiral Agate and captured most of his fleet."

"Through a deep-space boarding action," Thaddeus said. "Why didn't Admiral Agate see it coming?"

"Unknown, sir," Gilbert said. "The later interrogations might shed some light on the question, but right now…sir, we have to assume the worst."

"They hinted they might be interested in peaceful discussions," Vice Director Vincent Adamson said. "The galaxy is big enough for both of us."

"Diplomacy is another word for playing nice and making honeyed promises while you assemble a big stick," General Gilbert said. "We don't know how much war materiel the marines have hidden away, but can it match us?"

Thaddeus made a face. He knew *just* how many trillions of credits had been invested in settling a cluster of star systems and secretly developing them into first-rank worlds without setting alarm bells ringing right across the empire. He knew just how many ships he'd dispatched to collect trained personnel, willing or not, and bring them to the cluster, trading safety for service. The marines had a small fleet—as far as the official records were concerned—and they clearly had more ships that had never been officially registered, but…how many? He couldn't imagine it was *that* many. The Terran Marine Corps had always been short of manpower.

But they might have kept half their manpower off the books too, he thought. His lips curved into a faint smile. *Someone should lodge an official complaint.*

He put the thought aside and leaned forward. "General, what do you think they'll do?"

"I think they'll come here, as soon as they feel they can win," Gilbert said. "They may not know it, but they have a window of opportunity right now."

Thaddeus grimaced. Two-thirds of the navy was on collection duty. Half of the remainder had been dispatched with Admiral Agate and was now either destroyed or in enemy hands. It wasn't clear if the captured ships were still usable—the reports had been vague on that point—but Gilbert was right. They had to assume the worst. Onge was armed to the teeth, with powerful orbital and ground-based defences, but there was no way they could take the offensive again until the remainder of the navy returned. He cursed the irony under his breath. The steps they'd taken to safeguard their worlds, the seed of a new empire, might have weakened them instead.

"Do they know?" McManus seemed unimpressed. "They can hardly count on us exposing ourselves."

"They will have interrogated the prisoners," Adamson said, quietly. "Admiral Agate would certainly have had something to offer."

"Traitor," McManus growled.

"He might not have been given a choice," Gilbert pointed out. "There are plenty of ways to extract information from an unwilling donor."

"He was supposed to be immune to them," McManus said. "Or was I misinformed?"

Thaddeus held up a hand. "Right now, we have to assume the worst," he said, nodding to Gilbert. "In the short term, the marines can do a great deal of damage to us. In the long term, we should have the edge."

"If we can find their base," Gilbert said. "It could be anywhere."

McManus glared. "Surely it can be found..."

"There are *billions* of stars within the galaxy," Gilbert said, dryly. "There's a very good chance the marines established a major base outside the Core Worlds themselves. We'd have, at best, millions of possible star systems to search. We could reduce the number of possible targets by making assumptions about what sort of world they'd choose, but if one of those assumptions turned out to be wrong..."

Thaddeus considered it while Gilbert and McManus exchanged sharp remarks. The empire was immense. Had been immense, he corrected himself. There'd been hundreds of known and unknown colonies beyond the rim, beyond the edge of formally explored, claimed and settled space. And yet, he doubted the marines would want to go *that* far from the Core Worlds. They'd have to invest in infrastructure, if nothing else. The costs would skyrocket to the point no black budget could hope to hide them. And yet...

was that actually true? Costs were high because the bigger corporations hadn't had any interest in finding ways to lower them. Thaddeus had seen the reports. Given time, and a small degree of investment, isolated worlds could catch up at speed...

They'll want to be close to the political centre of empire, he reminded himself. *And that means their base has to be somewhere near the core.*

"Right now, we concentrate our fleet and stall for time," he said. "How long until they can take the offensive?"

"Unknown," Gilbert said. "However, I doubt they can take the offensive very quickly. They would need to maintain a garrison on Hameau, replace whatever men and materiel they lost during the fighting...they may even be unsure where to go."

"They sent their prisoners back here," McManus snapped.

"Yes," Gilbert agreed. "But is this world, which is listed as a relatively minor colony world, the core of our operations? Or is it just another Hameau?"

"Admiral Agate could answer that question," Thaddeus pointed out. "We concentrate the fleet. We prepare our defences. We send out diplomatic missions and say *nice doggy* a lot, while we gather our forces and scout out their positions. If nothing else, we can raise the spectre of launching another invasion of Hameau...or even scorching the entire planet."

"There are steps we can take to strengthen our defences here," Gilbert said. "We need to start bringing more and more of the newcomers into the planetary defence network."

"They're not indoctrinated," McManus objected. "They might be more loyal to the empire..."

Thaddeus raised his eyebrows. "*What* empire?"

McManus scowled. "Sir, with all due respect, we would be better relying on men who've served us for decades."

"Most of whom are on the fleet," Gilbert said, quietly. "We don't know if we can trust the ones who returned home."

"No." Thaddeus rubbed his forehead. "Do you think they've been conditioned?"

"We tested Julia Ganister-Onge thoroughly," Gilbert said. "There should have been *some* sign if she'd been conditioned. It would have had to have been a rush job, one that would have left scars on her mentality... scars we could detect when we monitored the activity within her brain. She *could* have agreed to serve them willingly, which wouldn't have left any telltales for us to see, but I don't think so. We certainly didn't catch her in a lie."

"No," Thaddeus agreed. "Let her rest, then have her shipped down to my estate. She can offer her insights, if she wishes to regain her former post."

"If you think she can be trusted," McManus growled. "Is she good for anything?"

"I do need a new aide," Gilbert offered.

Thaddeus laughed. "Find your own," he said. "I need her on the surface."

"Yes, sir," Gilbert said.

"This is a challenge," Thaddeus said, addressing the entire group. "We knew there would come a time when we'd face a peer power, a force that would challenge us. We didn't expect it to happen so soon, but it did. We need to handle it quickly and decisively and I have faith we can and we will. Any final issues?"

"Just one," Adamson said. "What do we tell the people?"

"Nothing, not yet," Thaddeus said. "And make it clear to your staff that anyone who leaks anything, even the slightest hint, is going to be unceremoniously fired."

Out an airlock, his thoughts added, silently. *Or perhaps straight into the sun.*

"Yes, sir," Adamson said.

• • •

Rachel felt her heart starting to pound as she opened the airlock, her implants telling the local processors a string of comforting lies. The locals actually *implanted* their people with trackers, as if they were condemned criminals...she shuddered, feeling sick even as *her* implants started to put out the same signal. Earth had tried a similar system, but it had never gotten off the ground. The logistics of implanting everyone from birth had been completely unmanageable. Here...the corprats seemed to have managed. She put her disgust out of her mind as she inched into the airlock, knowing she was on the verge of complete success or utter defeat. If she'd missed something, the airlock would seal itself until a security team arrived to investigate.

She breathed a sigh of relief as the outer hatch closed behind her, the inner hatch opening a moment later. The corridor in front of her was empty. The anchor station's sensors had sworn blind the entire section was deserted, but Rachel hadn't been too impressed. If she could hack the system from the outside, someone on the inside could presumably do a much better job. She'd been through enough transit stations to *know* they were infested with smugglers, criminals and even terrorist supporters. It was astonishing how few people realised they'd be first against the wall when the revolution came until it was too late and they found themselves against the wall.

The airlock cycled again. Phelps stepped out, his armoured suit looking faintly out of place. Rachel waited for the others, then led them down the corridor and into a deserted living suite. There'd be time to get undressed, wipe themselves down and blend into the station's population while she put together more complete IDs. They shouldn't attract any attention, as long as they didn't do anything suspicious. The automated systems would think they were authorised to be onboard and do nothing.

"I stink," Bonkowski said, as he removed his armour. "Next time, can we try to sneak onto a resort world?"

"You'd be bored within a day," Phelps said, removing his helm. His face looked pale and sweaty. "Rachel?"

"I'm just poking holes in the system," Rachel said. Like all large networks, the enemy system seemed to assume that anyone who got through the airlocks was authorised to be there. As long as it didn't kick a query up to a living human, it should be fine. "Give me a couple of moments."

"And then we get to work," Perkins said. He struck a dramatic pose.

"Do I look ready?"

"You look like a complete asshole," Bonkowski said. "Perfect!"

"It's the uniform," Perkins said. "Why do they make their people dress like this?"

"Because anyone who doesn't stands out," Rachel said. She could see the logic. She could also see the glaring hole in the enemy defences. "Shall we get to work?"

Phelps grinned. "Yep."

CHAPTER TEN

The carpenter then puts his skills to work on the trunk, cutting away the branches and bark and sawing whatever is left of the wood into long planks. This does not reduce the value of the wood. Instead, it increases it. The planks themselves may be worth around one hundred credits, even though they're smaller than the original trunk. The debris, too, may be worth something as firewood.
—**Professor Leo Caesius**
The Rise and Fall of Interstellar Capitalism

IN SPACE, KERRI REMINDED HERSELF, *no one can hear you scream.* It was a cliché so old, it predated spaceflight by decades, a cliché so old that few people knew where it had originally come from. *She* wouldn't have known, if she hadn't gone through a training simulation based on one of the remakes of the ancient flick. It was plain common sense—sound didn't travel in space—and yet hardly anyone believed it. She could have held a keg party on the bridge and none of the enemy sensors would have heard a thing, yet her crew would have been horrified if she tried. They spoke in hushed voices, when they spoke at all. The slightest sound made them jump.

Kerri smiled, although there was little real humour in the thought. A jumpy crewman might bring the active sensors online if he got a fright, revealing their presence to every sensor within the system. Or...her imagination provided too many possibilities, each one more worrying than the last. The system steadily unfolding in front of her, revealing its secrets one by one, was an order of magnitude more industrialised—and defended—than Hameau. Onge itself was far too close to first-rank status for her peace of mind.

She leaned forward as more and more data flowed into the display. The planet was heavily defended, with everything from orbital battlestations to hundreds of automated defence and sensor platforms. The giant anchor stations were probably armed too, along with the asteroid habitats. There were surprisingly few starships within sensor range—she'd expected an entire fleet to back up the fixed defences—but the locals clearly thought they didn't need mobile fleets. They might be right, she acknowledged sourly; it was hard to get a solid look at the planet from so far away, but her optical sensors had already picked out a handful of planetary defence centres as well as towering megacities. The locals might well assume they didn't need the fleet to see off anything smaller than the Imperial Navy.

Which no longer exists, she mused. *They may not even realise we're coming at them.*

She shook her head. The enemy commanders knew what had happened to Hameau. They'd start interrogating the returned POWs immediately, then decide to do...what? She didn't know. It defied belief that the ships she could see—and the ones that had been lost at Hameau—represented the entire enemy fleet. A corporation with a dozen major shipyards under its control could easily put together a much larger force, even if they'd had to keep it off the books. And yet...she remembered just how many shipyards had been destroyed, or seized by warlords, in the months since Earthfall. It was quite possible the corprats couldn't rely on anything outside their small cluster of colony worlds.

Her eyes narrowed as her stealthed probes fanned out across the system. There were a surprising number of asteroid mining stations, some apparently independent...although not *that* independent. The corprats would have enough monopolies on everything from fresh food to interstellar shipping that they'd be able to keep the rest of the system in a vise, if one that wasn't very obvious as long as they didn't put pressure on it. Kerri doubted the asteroid miners had any illusions about how dependent they really were. Spacers couldn't afford to let themselves believe in illusions. Everything had to be solid, or the weak links would get people killed. She'd dated a RockRat once. She knew how they thought.

"Captain," Lieutenant Kiang said. Her voice nearly made Kerri jump. "I've prepared some projections on industrial output."

"Good," Kerri said. "Let me see them."

She keyed her console, bringing up the projections. The planet seemed to have a surprising amount of industry on the ground, something odd for a world settled by a corporation. They could easily have set up an entire *halo* of orbital industrials, if they'd had time. Perhaps they'd planned a more gradual shift to space-based units or…there were some advantages, she supposed, in remaining on the surface. They already had a pair of space elevators. It was unlikely they'd build an entire orbital tower, let alone four, but they didn't *need* one. They could send everything they needed to orbit via the elevator.

We could do something with that, she thought, before she caught herself. She'd seen the videos of Earth's orbital towers falling one by one, each one crashing with the force of a dozen asteroid strikes. *Or perhaps we should be careful* not *to take them out*.

"Interesting," she mused. "What are they doing on the surface?"

"They may be trying to avoid a declaration of independence," Kiang said. She was young, but strikingly cynical. "The asteroid colonies might let their personnel have a degree of freedom—too much freedom. On the surface, social control would be a great deal easier."

"True," Kerri agreed. The RockRats had been born from independence-minded asteroid settlers who'd realised, thousands of years ago, that they didn't *have* to put up with orders from distant beancounters who manifestly didn't have the slightest idea what was actually happening. The immensity of space had ensured the RockRats simply outlasted the fools who'd thought they could be forced to work. "Is it worth a little inefficiency to keep control?"

"I believe so," Kiang said. "The vast majority of their output could be churned out on a planetary surface. There'd be no need to cross-train the workers or give them any hint they could rise higher. I guess the really rebellious ones would be steered towards the army or simply given a one-way ticket towards the nearest penal colony. It certainly matches what we were told by the POWs."

Kerri shook her head in disbelief. Haydn had insisted they were facing an alternate civilisation, rather than a mere corporate monstrosity, but she hadn't really believed it…not until now. The corprats were condemning everyone, including themselves, to a living death and eventual bloody collapse. By the time the end finally came, there would be no one with the experience to make a post-collapse society work. Did the corprats think they had a solution? Or were they foolishly convinced their plan was going to work?

She glanced at the communications console. "Have we picked up anything from the Pathfinders?"

"No, Captain," Ensign Susan Perkins said. "We pinged the platform four hours ago. There was no update."

Kerri nodded, tartly. There was a possibility—she'd known it from the moment she'd received her marching orders—that she might lose contact with the Pathfinders completely. They might not be *able* to send a message to the platform…hell, they might try to send a message, completely unaware it wasn't reaching its destination. They knew there wouldn't be any acknowledgement. If the enemy picked it up…

She felt the hours slowly crawl by, one by one. Their orders were to spend four days surveying the system, unless they had to leave early. She wondered, grimly, if her subordinates had managed to get enough of *Hammerblow's* systems back online to allow her to fly to the RV point, accompanied by the remainder of the captured ships. It was a shame they couldn't use her as a Trojan Horse to get into weapons range. The enemy knew she'd been captured.

And if they didn't, she mused, *they sure as hell know now.*

Kerri stood. "Commander, continue our survey," she ordered. "I'll be in my ready room."

• • •

If there was one advantage to the enemy state of alert, Rachel decided, it was that they were rushing officers and crew all over the system without any pause for thought or reconsideration. The losses they'd suffered at Hameau *had* to have hurt worse than she'd thought. They'd clearly not *expected* to have to deploy a mid-sized army across the interstellar void at a couple of weeks' notice…she admitted, rather sourly, that they'd done a remarkable job. The marines could hardly have done better and their divisions were *designed* for hasty deployment. Now, the cracks in the enemy personnel departments were starting to show.

"You have your records," she said. They'd spent the last few hours in a temporary suite, posing as crewmen waiting for their next assignment. "Are there any questions?"

She smiled, grimly, as she recalled the facts and figures she'd forced herself to memorise. Lieutenant Hannah Gresham would have been astonished to discover she hadn't been assigned to the lost fleet after all…Rachel had gone through the files very carefully, making sure there were few—if any—people who might have known Lieutenant Hannah Gresham before her departure and death. She'd been on one of the enemy ships that had been destroyed in the final engagement, her presumed friends killed with her…there was always the possibility of running into someone who knew her, but the risk was as low as possible.

"I think so," Perkins said. "Why did you take the prime job for yourself?"

"I'm a bitch." Rachel stuck out her tongue. "And there weren't *that* many places we could go."

She smiled. Lieutenant Hannah Gresham looked—*had* looked—a little like Rachel. Not enough, perhaps, for Rachel to fool someone who'd known her well, but as long as she was spared that encounter, she would be safe enough. The others hadn't been so easy. She hadn't wanted to assign them to military units where they'd be the FNG and therefore carefully watched, or risk having them sent right across the system. Their covers were slightly looser than hers.

"We can't expect perfection," Phelps said, shortly. "Don't fuck up."

Rachel watched him and the others go, then breathed a silent prayer. There were so many people coming and going that it was hard to believe they'd be noticed, but she wasn't *completely* confident that she'd jiggered the records properly. There were too many gaps in her knowledge of the enemy datanet for her peace of mind. The defence systems were completely isolated from the rest of the network, unsurprisingly. Hackers had caused so much damage, back on Old Earth, that only a fool would allow his weapons to be hooked up to an all-encompassing datanet. She'd heard stories about hackers who'd triggered missiles in their launch tubes, but her instructors had insisted they were nothing more than stories. It was hard to believe anyone would rig a system that would allow a hacker to do *that*.

Although there have been terrorists who blew themselves up while making bombs, she reminded herself. *And simple human laziness opens gaps for evildoers to do evil.*

She glanced at herself in the mirror and let out a faint sigh. Lieutenant Hannah Gresham looked pretty, in a butch sort of way. The ill-fitting uniform looked faintly absurd. Rachel would almost have preferred a uniform intended to show off her curves, such as they were. In her experience, people preferred to stare at breasts rather than faces. It irritated her to use such a simple trick, but if it worked...

The timer bleeped. She headed for the hatch, hoping and praying the lockers they'd stolen would remain undisturbed. They'd fiddled with the records to make sure they were assigned to transient workers, and should therefore be left alone, but there was no way to be entirely certain. Onge was a planet of sneaks, spies and government snoops. She kept her face under tight control as she passed through a series of airlocks, her implants pinging the datanodes as she went along. The shuttles were already arriving, their complements of personnel being directed towards the assembly point. There'd be so many new faces mingled together that no one should notice one more.

She smiled as she joined the throng of junior officers and crewmen. Some of them were clearly young, probably born on Onge and recruited directly into the Onge Navy. Others, older and more experienced, were clearly ex-Imperial Navy. Rachel studied them from behind her bland expression, wondering if there were ways to disrupt the smooth functioning of the enemy military. In her experience, inter-service rivalry was a pain in the ass even when everyone had the same boss. Now, after Earthfall, who knew where the chips would fall? It was quite possible the locals would resent the newcomers and vice versa.

They followed a handful of senior officers into a giant auditorium, where tired-looking uniformed bureaucrats held out assignments. Rachel braced herself, knowing that she was approaching the moment of truth. If she'd made a mistake, if the beancounters hadn't added Lieutenant Hannah Gresham to their list, she might have to try to fight her way out. She didn't dare let them take a good look at her. The implants were designed to be difficult to detect, but difficult was not the same as *impossible...*

"Lieutenant Hannah Gresham," the officer said. He held out a datachip. "Report to Section-31G. Immediately."

"Yes, sir," Rachel said.

She allowed herself a moment of relief. The hacking had worked. The man hadn't noticed anything wrong. She felt a thrill of excitement as she turned and headed up the shaft towards the command core. Someone had taken a look at her credentials and assigned her right where she wanted to be! She'd done everything in her power to ensure she'd be assigned to the right place, but there'd been no guarantees. The handful of officers she passed paid no attention to her. She was too junior to be worthy of their interest.

The soldiers on guard outside the command core checked her ID twice before allowing her to proceed to her duty station. Rachel found it irritating, although she was careful not to show it. Alert guards meant trouble, even if there was nothing wrong with the legend she'd crafted around the dead lieutenant. They might intervene if she started a gunfight in the middle of the command core…if, of course, she had a gun. She'd had to leave her weapons behind, in the locker. The only people allowed weapons on the anchor station were senior officers and security guards. She'd have to take one of their guns if she wanted to use it.

A middle-aged man blocked her way. "You're late," he growled. "What happened?"

Rachel pasted a cringing expression on her face. "I had to find my way up here," she stammered, trying to look like a mouse hiding from a hawk. "I…I've never been on a station like this before."

She tried not to roll her eyes at his expression. The deception irked her—she could kill him with a single blow—but it served a useful purpose. He would never speak so rudely to Phelps, who looked big enough to snap the asshole in two effortlessly, yet he would never see him as harmless either. It was enough to make her want to snort. Very few people were completely harmless, even the ones who were so weak they couldn't lift a hand to defend themselves. She'd had to deal with the consequences of too many weak men who'd been pushed too far, or so they insisted, to have any sympathy for them.

"We'll discuss it later," the man said. He spoke to her as if she were a young and particularly stupid child. "I'm Commander Archer, your section CO. You *are* checked out basic tactical duties, are you not?"

"Yes, sir," Rachel said. She judged she could let a little irritation slip into her voice. The tactical systems were standardised, as far as she could tell. The corprats hadn't been interested in devising something new, not when half their recruits came from the Imperial Navy. There would be no surprises, not here. She might have problems on a pirate ship, where a dozen different systems would be spliced together, but not here. "I have certifications in…"

THE HALLS OF MONTEZUMA

"I don't care," Commander Archer said. He jabbed a finger at a console underneath a chair on a dais. "That's your station. Familiarise yourself with the system before you go on duty. You'll be under my supervision until I say otherwise. Understand?"

"Yes, sir," Rachel said. The thought of his supervision made her skin want to crawl. She had no trouble recognising the petty resentments of a man who'd been promoted past the limits of his competence, a man who knew he'd never be anything worth mentioning and intended to take it out on as many people as he could before he was finally discharged. "I understand."

He pushed her towards her seat, then stamped off to make someone else's life miserable. Rachel sat, activating the console while carefully glancing around the command core. It was larger than she'd realised, an interlocking network of consoles, stations and chairs intended to remind everyone at the bottom that that was precisely where they were. She thought she saw an officer she vaguely recognised at the top, from her younger days. An Imperial Navy officer who'd taken the corprat shilling...

Dumb bastard, she thought. She turned her attention to the console and started to work. She'd been ordered to familiarise herself with the system and that was precisely what she intended to do. Her supervisor could hardly make a fuss if he caught her following orders. There would be time to cause trouble later. *Anyone who places their faith in corprats is heading for a nasty fall.*

CHAPTER ELEVEN

Our carpenter, therefore, has successfully turned a ten-credit trunk into a hundred-credit pile of planks (plus whatever the firewood is worth). But, again, this is potential wealth. It needs to be turned into actual wealth.
—**Professor Leo Caesius**
The Rise and Fall of Interstellar Capitalism

"**THANK YOU FOR COMING**," Director Thaddeus Onge said. "I understand it wasn't easy for you."

I didn't think I had a choice, Julia said, as she shook his hand. *You certainly didn't try to offer me one.*

She winced, inwardly. The summons hadn't allowed any room for *creative* interpretation. She was to be escorted down the elevator to the megacity, then flown to the Director's estate. It would have pleased her more if she'd known what to expect when she finally reached the end of the line. The last two days had not been pleasant. The interrogators had drawn information out of her she hadn't known she knew, then told her to wait. She hadn't needed them to tell her that her fate was being decided at the very highest levels.

"Please, take a seat," Director Onge said, indicating an armchair. "Tea? Coffee? Or something stronger?"

"Tea, please," Julia said. All the *best* people drank tea. And it was probably her last chance to drink an expensive brew. "Thank you for inviting me."

She sat, looking around the office with interest. It was large, although size alone didn't matter when the corporation ruled an entire cluster of star systems. The decor, on the other hand, showcased both wealth and taste. The combination of paintings, artworks and other refinements suggested a mind in perfect tune with itself. She thought some of the artworks were surprisingly cheap, and hardly exclusive, but they blended neatly with the overall scheme. Perhaps there was a message there, for those with eyes to see. Or perhaps she was simply reading too much into the scene. Director Onge didn't *need* to play petty power games.

A secretary, wearing a low-cut dress, appeared with a tray of tea and biscuits. She put them on the small table, then withdrew as silently as she'd come. She looked like a menial servant, but Julia was fairly sure she was a great deal smarter—and more influential—than she looked. The director didn't need to spice up his office with arm candy either. There were entire divisions dedicated to providing escorts—sexual partners—to meet all tastes. The director could order whatever he liked from them, if he wished.

"You've been through a hard time," Director Onge said. "I'm sorry we had to be so...rigorous upon your return."

Julia nodded, curtly. Director Onge sounded sincere, although she knew it was probably manipulation. He looked so much like a calm parental figure, right down to the greying hair, that she *knew* he used cosmetic surgery and bodyshaping. He could have turned himself into a Greek God if he wished, something that would have suggested a lack of basic confidence in himself. Julia reminded herself not to underestimate the director. He was, to all intents and purposes, the unquestioned ruler of his world. The board wouldn't unite against him unless he *really* screwed up.

"I quite understand," she said, as graciously as she could. There was no point in making a fuss and it might win her some points. "You had to be sure I was still me."

"Quite." Director Onge took a sip of his tea. "How do *you* think we should proceed?"

Julia blinked, surprised. She was very low in the corporate hierarchy... she'd been very low even before her career had fallen straight into the crapper. The idea of the *director* himself asking her opinion was completely alien to her. Her opinions were supposed to pass through at least five levels of corporate bureaucracy before they managed to get anywhere *near* the director. She knew from grim experience her superiors would take full credit, at least for the ideas *their* superiors liked. The corporate world was still very much a dog-eat-dog universe.

She forced herself to think. She'd expected, at best, to be told to go back to her family's mansion, get married and forget about working her way to the top. Instead...was she being tested? Given an opportunity to redeem herself? Or...she smiled, suddenly, as it dawned on her she didn't have much to lose. Her life was no longer her own. She couldn't hope to steer her course any longer. There was a kind of freedom in that, she supposed. She didn't have to worry about the worst because the worst had already happened.

"I think we need to prepare for the worst," she said. "The marines already took one planet from us. It's just a matter of time until they come for the others."

"And they'll be coming out of the darkness," Director Onge observed. He quirked one eyebrow. "Unless you *know* where they're based?"

Julia shook her head. Admiral Agate—she felt a pang at the thought—had explained the problem of locating the enemy base in great and tedious detail. The base was very small, a cosmic grain of sand set against a beach so large as to defy imagination. He'd reasoned that it couldn't be *that* far from Earth, if only because the marines would need to keep in touch with their political masters, but that still left hundreds of possible locations. Hell, the base might be so carefully concealed that a survey ship might pass through the system, detect nothing and assume the system was deserted.

"And that's the problem," Director Onge said. "Can we share a galaxy with them?"

"I don't know, sir," Julia said. "I don't know what sort of universe they have in mind."

She considered it for a moment. The marines were...the marines. They'd been the empire's shock troops. They killed people and broke things. They weren't charged with rebuilding planets devastated by war, nor any of the other functions that were generally left to NGOs, government bureaucracies and corporations. She'd never figured the marines might set out to create a state of their own. What did they have in mind? Military dictatorship? She knew enough history to know that would be a very bad idea.

"That's something we need to know," Director Onge said. "We also need to know what *else* they've been doing."

He took another sip of his tea. "The marines were ordered to abandon Earth, shortly before Earthfall. The orders came from the Grand Senate itself, but...I wonder if the marines planned it that way. They certainly didn't try to argue when they pulled units off the surface and headed into deep space."

"And so they survived Earthfall," Julia said. "They knew it was coming."

Director Onge snorted. "Anyone with *eyes* knew it was coming."

He shook his head. "They returned you and the other POWs. Keeping you captive would hardly have posed a problem. There's plenty of unsettled territory on Hameau they could have turned into a makeshift POW camp. Dropping you on an island would be sufficient, I think. They could have given you enough food to feed yourselves and then put you out of their minds. But instead they sent you back. Why?"

"I don't know, sir," Julia said. "They did hint they'd be open to talks."

"Indeed," Director Onge said. "Sending you back is a message in itself. They don't care about what you and your fellows can tell us. Worse, they know where we are. They can find us. They can *reach* us."

Julia felt her blood run cold. "What did the other POWs tell you?"

"Nothing of great use," Director Onge said, sardonically. "I think they might have kept back any POWs who might have told us anything of tactical importance. They certainly wiped the freighter's datacores and damaged the datanet before they sent her back, although"—he frowned—"there was something screwy about the sensors. The hardware itself was in good shape, but the software controlling them had been badly corrupted."

"Odd," Julia agreed. She didn't know what it meant and didn't really care. "Perhaps they didn't want to take the time to do it properly."

"Perhaps," Director Onge said. He finished his tea and put the cup back on the saucer. "Do you think we can come to terms with them?"

"No, sir." Julia threw caution to the winds. She'd either rise again or… stay in the corporate doghouse. "They attacked one of our worlds, without the slightest hint of provocation. They came out of the dark and opened fire. Whatever they have in mind—military dictatorship or the rise of the old regime—bodes ill for us."

"You may be right." Director Onge stood, indicating the meeting was over. "You'll be staying here for the moment, as one of my advisors. Daisy will show you to your suite. You may record messages for your family, if you wish, but they might not be delivered for a while. There is still a complete news blackout."

Julia frowned. "Are there no rumours?"

"There are always rumours," Director Onge said, as his secretary stepped into the room. "But most people don't have the slightest idea what's happened."

"Yes, sir," Julia said. She had her doubts. People would notice that *Hammerblow* and the rest of the squadron had left, never to return. The rumours would grow as they spread from place to place, as more and more people noticed the army units hadn't returned either. She winced, inwardly, as she considered the problem. Too many units had been sent to their doom. "When are you going to tell them?"

"We'll see," Director Onge said. "I'll speak to you later."

Julia curtseyed, then followed Daisy out of the room.

• • •

Rachel prided herself, at times, on showing as little reaction as possible to overbearing commanding officers, particularly ones who didn't know what she was or simply didn't care. She'd met her fair share of uniformed idiots when they'd been working with the army, men and women who'd been promoted because of family connections or because someone was trying to fill a quota...but Commander Archer was pretty much the worst. She honestly had no idea how *he'd* been promoted. His file didn't so much as *hint* at corporate connections.

She sighed, inwardly, as the shift came to an end. Commander Archer had a foul temper, wandering hands and a complete lack of common sense. It was clear the entire department hated him, men and women alike. There was no unity, no sense of shared purpose...Rachel couldn't help wondering if the corprat commanders were bothering to keep an eye on their subordinates. Commander Archer's behaviour was just *asking* for someone to stick a knife in his back, perhaps not metaphorically. It only took one resentful person in the wrong place—or, rather, the right place—to do one hell of a lot of damage. And someone with enough cunning could do it and make sure Commander Archer took the blame.

Her relief arrived. She passed the console to him, assured him that nothing had happened that required immediate attention, then stood and filed through the hatch. Commander Archer was busy harassing another girl and paid no attention to her. Rachel silently promised him a painful death when she had a chance, even though cold logic told her his stupidity worked in her favour. The only thing that united his department was shared hatred of the pointy-haired boss. The crew might not sound the alarm if she did something that looked like it would embarrass him.

I can't count on it, she reminded herself, as she made her way to the cabin. There were so many officers and crew coming and going that she had to share a compartment with ten other people. The grumbling amused her, if only because she'd slept in worse places. *It only takes one person to set off the alarms.*

She put the thought out of her mind, then concentrated on accessing the local security monitors. Convincing them to pay no attention to her was easy. Convincing them that she was still in the sleeping compartment, even when she was somewhere else, was a great deal harder. She hoped Commander Archer didn't intend to come and seek her out...the bastard probably peeked on his subordinates through the security monitors, as well as everything else. No wonder the division was a seething mass of resentment. The corprats were too stupid to let people vent. She honestly didn't understand it. Did they really think people were nothing more than tools, tools that could be easily replaced?

Probably, she thought, as she slipped through the hatch and headed down. The station was gradually filling with people, making it harder to find a place that could be isolated from the security network. *They certainly don't seem interested in developing their personnel.*

She snorted at the thought. The training modules she'd endured, with Commander Archer breathing down her neck, had been laughably easy. She'd faced harder problems when she'd been a child, playing with computer games. She had no idea how the vast majority of the anchor station's personnel would cope, when faced with a *real* emergency. They should be running emergency drills time and time again, just to ensure their people knew what to do. Her lips quirked, humourlessly. Perhaps Commander Archer had argued against emergency drills. It would certainly showcase his department's failings.

Phelps met her as she stepped into the compartment. "The others can't make it," he said, shortly. "They've been assigned to a different section to make up a numbers shortfall."

"Ouch." Rachel cursed under her breath. They could have found a privacy tube and pretended to be lovers, although even *they* weren't safe. Or maybe not...someone might have asked questions if they couldn't watch the act. Damn it. "How did you get out of it?"

"Luck of the draw," Phelps said. "That...and my supervisor seems to like me."

"Lucky you." Rachel shook her head. "I've collected a ton of information. I couldn't get at anything classified above a certain level, but there's enough to help plan the operation."

Phelps nodded. "Does your supervisor suspect anything?"

"I don't think so," Rachel said. "He's an asshole who seems to have dedicated his life to making his staff miserable. I don't think he's paying anything like enough attention to his duties."

"How terrible," Phelps said, with heavy sarcasm. He took the datachip she passed him and slipped it into his pocket. "When are you expected back?"

"Technically, I'm off duty for eight hours," Rachel said. "Practically, I should probably get back before someone asks what happened to me."

"Or spots that you appear to be in two places at once," Phelps agreed. "I'll send the datapacket in an hour, then…we'll be alone."

"Again." Rachel had to smile. They'd been alone from the moment they'd boarded *Botany Bay*. "At least we could probably steal a starship and make a run for it here."

"Yeah," Phelps agreed. "It could be a lot worse. We could be at the bottom of the gravity well."

Rachel shrugged. "Check in with the others when you get a chance," she said. "I'll try and be here tomorrow at the same time."

"Two days from now," Phelps said. He waved a hand at the bulkhead, his mouth twisting as if he'd bitten into a lemon. "Better not to let them see us close together."

"Understood." Rachel made a face. "Good luck, sir."

"And to you," Phelps said.

Rachel nodded, then turned and walked back to the command core. Phelps was right. If someone noticed her and the other three together… who knew *what* sort of conclusion they'd draw? The corprat system was as caste-ridden as some of the less developed worlds she'd visited, back before Earthfall. They seemed to believe command staff, even very junior officers, shouldn't have relationships with yarddogs and stevedores. Better to have her groped by Commander Archer than allow her to have a perfectly consensual relationship with someone below her…

It makes sense, she told herself. She could see the logic. She just didn't like it. *They don't want people from different departments talking.*

She felt her heart sink as she reached her bunk and carefully linked herself back into the security monitors. *Havoc* would be leaving the system shortly, once she received the final datapacket from the Pathfinders. And then...she'd go to the RV point, carrying with her the information Rachel had painstakingly collected. She knew it would be useful. She just hoped it would be enough. There were so many things she didn't know, so many blanks she'd had to fill in through educated guesswork...she'd made that clear, in the report she'd put together when she'd been pretending to sleep, but she knew too many of her superiors had Optimists Selective Hearing Syndrome. They wanted to believe...

Her mind raced. She'd deduced a lot, from the location of some of the planetary defence centres to the capabilities of the orbital defence network. It certainly *looked* as though the corprats had blundered when they'd sent most of their available ships to Hameau. The fleet lists were intimidating long, but most of the listed ships were nowhere to be seen. Were they on deployment? Hiding under cloak? Did they even *exist*? Her superiors would want to believe they were far away, that they would be unable to intervene before the matter was settled one way or the other. She understood the impulse, she admitted silently. She wanted to believe, too.

Anderson knows better, she thought, as she closed her eyes. She'd served with Major-General Anderson before. The man knew not to believe *everything* he read in the reports. *And he'll make sure the others know it, also.*

But it was a long time before she finally managed to fall asleep.

CHAPTER TWELVE

Now, the carpenter increased his potential wealth by chopping up the trunk. That's obvious. But there's a second factor involved. Planks and firewood are simply more useful than trunks. There are more potential buyers for planks than there are for uncut trunks. The carpenter has not only prepared the wood for sale. He's increased the number of potential buyers.
—**Professor Leo Caesius**
The Rise and Fall of Interstellar Capitalism

THERE WAS SOMETHING FUNDAMENTALLY WRONG, Kerri had often thought, about interstellar space. It was an illusion—there was no way to tell, with the naked eye, if she was in interstellar or interplanetary space—and yet it was painfully hard to shake. The fleet was completely alone, over five light years from the nearest settled world. There would be no hope of assistance if they ran into trouble; there would be no hope of signalling for help if the phase drives failed, leaving them stranded in interstellar space. Even if they powered up the sublight drives and pushed them to the limit, it would be over a decade before they reached safe harbour. If, of course, they reached it at all.

The fleet floated in the darkness, illuminated only by running lights and signal beacons. She smiled, despite the chill, as her eyes picked out the giant MEUs, the handful of escort ships and the small cluster of captured starships. They weren't practicing signals discipline, something that both amused and irked her. There was little chance of detection, so far from the enemy homeworld, but it was a bad habit. She supposed it made a certain kind of sense. They were so far from safe harbour they *needed* the beacons. It was easy to believe someone could get lost in the darkness and never find their way home.

She shivered, then put the thought aside. "Communications, transmit the datapacket and the analyst reports to the MEUs," she ordered. "And get me a laser link to Commander Halibut."

"Aye, Captain," Ensign Susan Perkins said.

Kerri stood. "I'll be in my ready room," she said. "Put the link through when it's established."

She felt her heart beginning to race as she stepped into the ready room, leaving her XO in command. They were about to launch an invasion...their *second* invasion. She poured herself a mug of coffee and sat at her desk, her eyes moving automatically to the near-space display. Haydn was on one of those MEUs, preparing his unit for deployment...she felt a flicker of amusement, mingled with irritation. The urge to have sex before she went back into harm's way was overpowering, but it had to be ignored. She was an experienced officer, not a teenage girl.

The terminal bleeped, displaying the latest reports from the analyst deck. They'd gone through everything the Pathfinders had sent, putting together a surprisingly detailed assessment of the enemy system. Kerri couldn't help thinking it wasn't anything like comprehensive enough. They knew a lot about how the system worked, by connecting the data from the Pathfinders to the reports from the prisoner interrogations, but they didn't know how the system was *defended*. Kerri's survey reports had noted hundreds of defences—and orbital stations she assumed were armed—but there was no overall picture. There was just too much they didn't know.

And what we don't know can hurt us, Kerri thought. She took a sip of her coffee, morbidly contemplating the possibilities for outright disaster.

If we're wrong about how many ships they have in the system, we could lose.

The terminal bleeped, again. "Captain," Ensign Perkins said. "Major-General Anderson is requesting a conference."

Kerri nodded. "Put him through."

She sat upright as the Major-General's image appeared in front of her. "Sir."

"Captain," Anderson said. He nodded to her. "Congratulations on the success of your mission."

"It was relatively easy for me, sir," Kerri said. She had no intention of claiming credit she didn't deserve. "It was the Pathfinders who did the *real* work."

"Regardless, you've told us a great deal about their defences," Anderson said. "We're currently refining one of our operational plans for invasion. When the planners have finished putting everything together, I'd like your opinion. You'll be in command of the first part of the operation."

Kerri nodded. "We'll be going with one of the Romeo concepts?"

"A variant on Romeo-4," Anderson agreed. They'd drawn up the rough concepts before *Havoc* had shadowed *Botany Bay* to Onge, but they hadn't been able to finalise the plan until they knew what they were facing. "The goal will be to put a major force on the surface as quickly as possible, while launching a major propaganda offensive."

"And doing enough damage to convince the locals to rise up in support," Kerri said. She had her doubts. The Pathfinders had made it clear that Onge was a seething cauldron of bitter resentments, but there was a sizable gap between mute resentment and outright rebellion. As long as the locals feared their government would retain power, they would be reluctant to put their lives on the line. "We'll have to move fast, sir. Those missing ships will return, sooner or later."

She made a face. The POWs had been very talkative, but there was a great deal they simply didn't know. Where had the enemy sent their ships? When would they return? They clearly hadn't been *expecting* to find themselves fighting a full-scale war and yet intelligence had been heavily compartmentalised…she frowned as she considered the possibilities. There were just too many ways things could go spectacularly wrong and yet…the projections were clear. The Onge had to be stopped now, while it was still possible. Given a year or two, their position might become impregnable. The corps couldn't hope to match their production, even if it maintained a qualitative edge.

"I am aware of the risks," Anderson said. "And I have advised Safehouse of my decision."

"Yes, sir," Kerri said. "I understand the logic."

Anderson gave her a look that suggested he knew what she was thinking. In the old days, a commanding officer might time the notification to ensure his superiors couldn't put the brakes on before it was too late to keep the operation from going ahead. In the old days…she swallowed, hard. In the old days, even a complete failure wouldn't prove fatal to the corps or the empire itself. Now…losing an entire division—*two* entire divisions—would be a disaster beyond imagination. The corps might never recover from the loss of so many trained men and their equipment.

"Prepare your ships," Anderson ordered, curtly. "Once the plan is finalised, I want you ready to deploy at a moment's notice. We'll move in two days."

Kerri nodded. That was fast, but they'd already laid most of the groundwork. The MEUs were loaded, the enemy ships rigged with slave circuits… she made a mental note to ask for volunteers to crew the captured ships. They'd draw immense fire, once the enemy realised what they were doing. The battlecruiser was tough, but she wasn't designed to soak up so much fire on her own. And there was nothing she could do about it either.

"Yes, sir," she said. "Will we be alerting the Pathfinders?"

"No." Anderson grimaced, suggesting he wasn't pleased by his decision. "They know what to do."

"Yes, sir," Kerri said, again. "With your permission, I'll get straight to work."

Major-General Gerald Anderson leaned back in his chair the moment the image vanished, trying to clear his mind. Senior officers could not afford to let themselves get bogged down in details...that way led micromanagement and a tendency to miss the forest for the trees. His staff could handle the logistics, taking the plan they'd devised and adapting it to fit the intelligence they'd obtained from Onge. *Havoc* and the Pathfinders had done well. They'd learnt a great deal about how the enemy society actually worked.

It has two weak points, not one, Gerald observed. *And we only need to take advantage of one of them to win.*

He closed his eyes for a long moment. It was obvious Captain Stumbaugh had doubts. She wasn't the only one. They'd grown up in a universe where they could lose battles—they did lose battles, no matter what the spin doctors and PR specialists claimed—but never lose the war. There'd always been a hard limit on just how much they could lose...until now. He wasn't blind to the risks. The stakes were incredibly high. He was gambling with an entire division, with hundreds of thousands of full-fledged marines. Losing even *half* the force would be a disaster that would make Han look like a child's temper tantrum.

And yet, he didn't see any choice. The corprats had evolved a government...an extremely repressive government that would not, that *could* not, allow any other form of government to exist. Corporations had their place—capitalism was so much better than anything else that it was hard to put it into words—but they couldn't be allowed to dominate the galaxy. They'd crush competition and doom themselves—and their people—to stagnation and death. He'd read reports suggesting the corprats had killed breakthroughs in everything from FTL drives to fabrication nodes, just to ensure they stayed on top. He believed them. The reports from the first planet they'd invaded were all too clear. The locals had been trapped in a living death.

Which means we gamble everything on one throw of the dice, he thought. *And if we lose...I take full responsibility.*

He snorted, rudely. No one outside the corps, at least in the Core Worlds, had ever taken full responsibility for anything. The Blame Game was a demented version of musical chairs, with chairs added or taken away at random while the music threatened to die time and time again before it actually did. Who could blame them, when the rewards for success were so low and the consequences of failure—or at least being saddled with the blame—were so high? And yet...he shook his head. It didn't matter *who* accepted the blame. The corps would be staring down the barrels of a disaster fully as great as the nuclear screw-up on Parris, without the ability to regenerate itself. Hell, this time there would have been plenty of warnings about potential disaster. The red team had taken a sadistic delight in drawing up hundreds of disastrous scenarios.

His intercom bleeped. "Sir, Major-General Foxtrot is on the line."

"Put him through," Gerald ordered.

"Gerald," Foxtrot said. "You should have let me put my name on the plan."

"You can share the credit if it works," Gerald said. It was something of a pointless exercise—a disaster wouldn't be redeemed by putting the CO against the nearest bulkhead and shooting him—but he'd do his best to spare his counterpart the shit sandwich that would be coming his way if the operation failed. "If it fails, you can swear blind you never knew me."

"And that I was in the bath, singing noisily, while my division went into action," Foxtrot said, dryly. "Somehow, Gerald, I don't think the Commandant would buy it."

Gerald laughed. "Maybe you could claim you were having an orgy," he said. "It would be a *little* more believable."

"Don't knock it 'til you've tried it," Foxtrot countered. "Seriously, though, I have signed off on the plan. I'm not going to let you take *all* the blame. Just two-thirds of it."

"I love you, too," Gerald said, dryly. "How about you take half the blame?"

He shook his head. "Miguel, if this goes wrong there will be quite enough blame to go around."

"Yes." Foxtrot studied him for a long moment. "Gerald, like I said, I have signed off on the plan. If I had doubts, if I thought the plan needed to be modified or cancelled before it even got off the ground, I would have said so. I would have demanded we check with Safehouse before going ahead. But I didn't, because I believe the plan will work. And I will not let you share the blame alone."

"Then we can share the same firing squad," Gerald said. "Or the same pod as we get dumped on a penal colony."

Foxtrot laughed. "Yes, sir," he said. He made a show of consulting a datapad. "The first wave of landing forces have been transferred to the dumpsters. Your units have been reinforced by elements of mine…I'll make you pay for that later."

"I'm sure you will," Gerald said. He would have preferred to spend more time integrating the two divisions, but they simply didn't have time. "Thankfully, there's been no FNG nonsense."

"There aren't any FNGs here," Foxtrot reminded him. "Every bootneck is an experienced man."

"And we're about to drop them into hell," Gerald said. He looked at the terminal. The plan looked bloodless. He knew it would be anything but. The loss projections were just numbers, yet each and every one of them represented a living, breathing marine. And the casualty calculations for the local population weren't much better. He knew they were partly based on guesswork, but…"This could go horribly wrong."

"You always get pessimistic before the drop," Foxtrot said. "Perhaps you should go back to having the shakes instead."

"I got over them," Gerald said. They shared a mute look of commiseration. "It was a hell of a lot easier when I wasn't responsible for anyone but myself."

• • •

Haydn kept his thoughts under tight control as he walked into the briefing room and took his place amongst the other officers. The company had spent the last two weeks practicing with the dumpsters, all too aware they couldn't test the concept itself until they were actually dropped into the planetary atmosphere. Haydn had interrogated the handful of enemy survivors, the poor bastards who'd ridden the last set of dumpsters down to the surface, but they hadn't been able to tell him very much. The dumpsters were safe until they weren't.

And one of them broke up during flight, Haydn reminded himself. It was impossible to be *sure*, but the sensor records certainly suggested the dumpster hadn't been struck by a missile or a shell. *The people inside burned to a crisp well before their remains hit the surface.*

Ice washed down his spine. He'd made dozens of drops, orbital and suborbital, in his career. They held no terrors for him. And yet, the dumpster concept bothered him more than he wanted to admit to anyone. They would be strapped inside, unable to move until they reached the ground…unable, even, to take some time to recuperate before they had to get out and fight. Jumping from a shuttle in full armour would be a cakewalk, compared to dropping from orbit in a dumpster. He felt a flicker of unwilling respect for the corprats. They'd done pretty well, damn them. It helped that their grunts probably hadn't been offered much of a choice.

Major-General Anderson took the podium. Silence fell.

"*Havoc* has returned from Onge," Anderson said. "The intelligence she has collected has been uploaded to your datacores, allowing us to finalise our plans. We'll be proceeding with a variant on Romeo-4."

Kerri is back, Haydn thought. The thought brought a thrill, one he hastily suppressed. *I won't get to see her before all this is over.*

A holographic image of a planet, zooming in on a giant city, appeared behind Anderson. "We have two objectives. First, we will be dropping the dumpsters right on top of the enemy aristocracy. Their leadership is based here, in a cluster of large mansions a relatively short distance from the megacity and the space elevator. If everything goes according to plan, we will be able to decapitate or capture the enemy leadership. If not, we will seize the megacity and the factories beyond while pushing the local population to revolt. Either the planet surrenders, or we ensure its masters can do no further damage."

Haydn smiled. The plan was audacious, to say the least. It offered a reasonable chance for outright victory—if the enemy leadership could be *convinced* to order a surrender—while making life difficult for anyone who wanted to mount a counterattack. It wouldn't be easy to get troops into the area without tearing up the landscape and risking the lives of their aristocracy, assuming—of course—there were troops on hand. He'd seen projections that suggested the enemy had sent most of their available forces to Hameau.

Nah, he thought, wryly. *We couldn't possibly get that lucky.*

"Study the intelligence carefully," Anderson said, "but remember there are gaps in our knowledge. There are things we don't know. If you have doubts, raise them."

An officer lifted a hand. "Can we punch a hole through the orbital defences?"

"We think so," Anderson said. "It won't be as big a hole as we might like, but there should be enough room to land troops on the surface. They'll probably try to shift their orbital platforms to fire on us, but the fleet will be running interference."

And if the area is crawling with aristos, they'll hesitate to drop nukes on us, Haydn told himself. Even a clean tactical nuke would do a hell of a lot of damage. *If nothing else, they won't see this coming.*

He frowned. That wasn't true. The *enemy* had been the first to use dumpsters to land an entire division of troops. Sure, the concept had been discussed for centuries, but they'd been the first ones to actually try it. And if the fleet failed, if the defenders were not held hostage by human shields...

We can do it, he told himself, firmly. He studied the data as it scrolled up in front of him, noting all the questions left unanswered. *And once we capture the space elevator, we can take control of the entire planet.*

CHAPTER THIRTEEN

Indeed, the law of supply and demand is one of the most fundamental rules of basic economics. If supply goes up in line with demand, prices remain even; if supply goes up and demand remains stable, prices fall; if supply falls and demand remains stable, prices rise. This is so basic, so elementary, that it is rarely taught or discussed in schools, which perhaps explains why the empire ran into so much trouble in its final years. But we're getting ahead of ourselves.
—**Professor Leo Caesius**
The Rise and Fall of Interstellar Capitalism

"**She's as near to ready** as she'll ever be," Commander Halibut said.

Kerri stood on *Hammerblow's* bridge and eyed her consoles thoughtfully. The engineers had done well, replacing enough of the ship's datanet to allow them to control her from a specially-rigged shuttlecraft attached to her rear docking port. The jury-rigged network wouldn't survive, once enemy missiles started burning holes in the battlecruiser's hull, but it should last long enough to give her a chance to do real damage. It was just a shame she couldn't get into point-blank range before opening fire. There were so many sensor stations orbiting Onge that she *knew* a cloaked ship would be detected and blown away before it had a chance to react.

And they wouldn't be fooled by any fake IFF codes, she mused. The enemy CO had managed to wipe *those* from the datanet. Even if they'd been captured, the enemy defenders knew the battlecruiser had been captured. They wouldn't let her into firing range without asking some very tough questions. *We'll just have to take the hard way through the defences.*

She glanced at her subordinate. "Did you pack the missiles into the hull?"

"Yes, Captain," Commander Halibut said, patiently. "She'll be firing double salvoes until she shoots herself dry or gets blown to atoms. It's a shame to lose all those missiles, but I don't see any choice."

"No," Kerri agreed. She'd met enough beancounters who'd refused to supply weapons and ammunition on the grounds it would screw up their bureaucratic accounting. The corps was a great deal smarter about it. There was no point in holding back the missiles if they might make the difference between victory or defeat. "Did you fix the targeting sensors?"

"We did our best," Commander Halibut said. "If we lose the network, Captain, she'll fire on anything that looks remotely threatening. The dumpsters should be safe…"

"I hope you're right," Kerri said. Accidents happened, even if everyone took the right precautions. She knew that all too well. "The remainder of the fleet will keep a safe distance from the assault force."

She frowned. The Imperial Navy would never have agreed to the plan. But then, the Imperial Navy had been a deeply conservative organisation led by admirals who'd been in their second or third centuries. Kerri understood the value of institutional knowledge, but there were limits. She'd heard reports that many of those admirals had been murdered by their subordinates after Earthfall. She understood *precisely* how those subordinates felt.

"The engineers will be leaving shortly," Commander Halibut informed her. "The remainder of the crew will head down to the shuttle and get set up. We'll be ready to jump ship when they start throwing brickbats at us."

"Don't try to be a hero," Kerri said. She was tempted to take command herself, even though she had a responsibility to the squadron. "Just jump ship and go ballistic. We'll pick you up afterwards."

"Understood." Commander Halibut smiled, thinly. "Can I call myself *Captain* while I'm in command?"

"Sure." Kerri smiled back. "Just remember you don't *have* to go down with the ship."

She turned away, unwilling to allow her doubts to show on her face. The battlecruiser offended her sensibilities—*Hammerblow* cost too much and offered too little in return—but sending the ship to her death still bothered her. Kerri doubted the corps would have bothered to repair the ship and put her back into service, but still…she shook her head. If they won, it would be worth the cost; if they lost, it wouldn't matter. They would have too many other problems.

Commander Halibut remained on the bridge, installing the final software and testing it before the battlecruiser was thrown back into the fire. Kerri headed to the shuttle hatch, looking around at the damaged and stripped corridors. The spooks had searched the ship from top to bottom, looking for anything that could offer insight into enemy thinking, while the engineers had removed everything of value. She smiled, humourlessly, as she recalled the report. The sweep had found a cache of porn, but little else. *Hammerblow's* interior had been too closely monitored to allow the crew to develop any rebellious tendencies.

They weren't even allowed to keep diaries, Kerri thought. The corps had always encouraged its people to keep a record of what they'd been thinking at the time, although she'd rarely recorded her innermost thoughts. The Onge didn't seem to allow its people to keep even harmless logs. *They didn't give their people any freedom at all.*

She shuddered as she peered into a deserted cabin—it had belonged to the commissioner, who'd apparently had the power to override the admiral and the captain on their own ship—and then clambered into the shuttle. The pilot closed the hatch behind her, disengaging from the doomed battlecruiser and heading back to *Havoc*. Kerri felt a guilty pang as she looked at the transports, worker bees buzzing around them as they made the final preparations. Haydn was over there, readying himself for the drop into enemy territory. She was tempted to go see him…she shook her head. She'd be put in front of a court-martial and probably dishonourably discharged if she tried. Their relationship wasn't quite illicit—she wasn't a full-fledged marine—but it would certainly be an abuse of her position. It wasn't as if *everyone* could do it.

After this, everyone needs some shore leave, she thought. *And we'd better get it before we go back to war again.*

• • •

"Captain," Rifleman Frederick Palin called. "I have a sudden urge to take sick leave."

Haydn snorted. No one was very happy about the dumpsters, although the younger marines saw them as a chance to do something new and to hell with the risk. The older ones were smart enough to calculate the odds and have second thoughts. He didn't blame them for grumbling. He wanted to grumble, too.

"The medics will give you two painkillers and send you straight back here," he said. "You'd be better off staying where you are."

"They'll give him the anal probe instead," Rifleman Gillian Moulder said. "I think he's got something stuck up his ass."

"I'm sure it'll come shooting out when we hit atmosphere," Palin said. "I think…"

"That's enough," Haydn said, firmly. Marines had always joked when they were on the verge of going into battle, but…there were limits. "You can apply for your sick leave later."

He felt a chill as he walked through the immense dumpster. It was nothing like a shuttle. The interior was crammed with scaffolding, cradling the tanks and other vehicles until the time came to open the hatches and drive onto enemy soil. The tank crews were positioned next to their vehicles, checking and rechecking the straps time and time again. Haydn understood. If a tank came loose and started flying around inside the dumpster, a lot of marines were going to be injured or killed. Beyond them, electronic warfare crews were powering up their gadgets, testing them and powering them down again. They couldn't afford a failure on the surface.

The chill grew stronger as he walked past a platoon of marines writing or recording their final messages to their friends and families. They knew, as well as he did, that there was a very good chance those messages would never be delivered. The corps had scooped up as many relatives as it could, in the desperate bid to abandon the known boot camps and barracks before it was too late, but thousands of people had simply vanished without trace. They'd died on Earth or one of the innermost Core Worlds, worlds that had gone straight down into violent civil war. Or...

He looked at the metal bulkhead, wondering if the Onge Corporation had scooped some of them up. It was quite possible. Marines came from every background, including engineering. Some of them had been quietly recruited for Safehouse and other concealed bases, others...others had been left alone until Earthfall. Had they been snatched by the Onge? It was definitely possible. They might have more friends than they thought on the planet ahead

But no way to be sure, he thought, as he turned and headed back to the command platoon. *We certainly can't count on it.*

"Captain," Command Sergeant Mayberry said. "The company is present and accounted for."

Haydn nodded. He'd have preferred more time to train, particularly with the newcomers from the 3rd Marine Division, but they'd make do with what they had. They didn't have a choice. He clambered into the webbing and secured himself, then unhooked his datapad and brought up the files on the LZ. It was no surprise the official files were worse than useless. They insisted the LZ was nothing but forest. *Havoc's* long-range scans revealed otherwise.

And we have to be very careful how we storm the mansions, he told himself. *We simply cannot afford to kill the only people who can surrender.*

He winced, inwardly. They weren't fighting fanatics. The corprats were trained and well-equipped, but they didn't have the fanatical urge to keep fighting after the war was clearly lost. They would surrender, he thought, when they realised that further resistance was pointless. He suspected the brass had sent back the former POWs to make it clear there was a life after surrender. Fanatics often told their followers that they'd be killed—or tortured, raped and *then* killed—when they were captured. The bastards did it to keep the poor buggers fighting while they ran for the hills.

Bastards, he thought. *And if they keep fighting, we'll tear their world to pieces.*

Command Sergeant Mayberry webbed himself up beside Haydn. "This should be interesting."

"May you live in interesting times," Haydn agreed. He'd *always* lived in interesting times. Some historian was going to turn the mission into a holographic educational program...probably cleaned up, with all the swearing replaced by bleeps or nonsensical words. He wondered if the man would bother to read the actual reports before he started to put together his sanitised version. "Remember, we aim to take prisoners first."

He leaned back against the webbing. The top brass had put together a picture of the enemy command structure, but there were too many gaps for his peace of mind. The spooks hadn't known anything like enough before Earthfall messed up what little they *did* know. They insisted that Grand Senator Onge was dead, but refused to say *how* they knew. Haydn groaned, inwardly. He'd feel better when they were on the surface. Until then...

"Get some sleep, sir," Mayberry advised. He closed his eyes. "We'll be there shortly."

"I know," Haydn said. He checked his timer. Ten hours. Probably. Experience had taught him it was only an estimate and probably not a very good one at that. "You get some sleep, too."

• • •

"The squadron is ready to depart," Lieutenant Holmes said. "They're just awaiting your order."

Major-General Anderson stood in the MEU's CIC, feeling an unsettling guilt gnawing at his thoughts. It was *traditional* for marine commanders to lead their men from the front or as close to it as possible. He'd landed on Hameau as soon as possible, then commanded the campaign from a command vehicle as close to the trenches as his bodyguards would allow. He knew he'd be landing on Onge, eventually, but…he wished he was accompanying the first wave. Foxtrot could handle his duties and, if worse came to worst, take command of the retreat.

His eyes lingered on the display. Fifty-seven starships, lined up in a formation that looked shockingly unprofessional. Anderson didn't care, as long as it did its job. The lead squadron held position at the front of the fleet, spearheaded by the battlecruiser and a handful of other captured ships. And, behind them, the transports…he felt another pang of guilt. He should be there, riding the dumpsters down to the planet. He owed it to his men to face the same risks.

"Good," he said, finally. "Are the drones ready to go?"

"Yes, sir," Holmes said. She indicated the display. "They'll be deployed as soon as we reach the system."

Anderson nodded. It was a shame there was no hope of making a stealthy arrival, as they'd done at Hameau, but the planet was surrounded by extensive sensor arrays. They'd have to drop out of phase space a *long* way from the limit to be sure of remaining undetected, something that would add weeks to their transit time. He could see some advantages, but the risks were just too high. The enemy would have a chance to reconcentrate their fleet and start looking for Safehouse.

They've probably deduced a few things about Safehouse's location, Anderson thought. He'd done it himself, as a mental exercise. It was cheating, in a sense, because he'd already known the answer…and yet, he was grimly aware an enemy analyst might draw the same general conclusions. Searching the entire galaxy was impossible, but isolating a few hundred possible targets and keeping them under covert observation was doable. Barely. *We can't afford to give them time to recover.*

His heart quailed at what he was about to do. It would be easy to wait for orders. It would be easy to pass the question up to his ultimate superior, the Commandant himself. He understood, now, why so many beancounters couldn't make decisions to save their lives, even when they had so little at stake. They could lose everything if they made the wrong call. It was easier and safer to pass the buck to their superiors, who would—of course—feel the same way. And they didn't have to worry about the future of the entire galaxy.

Bastards, he thought.

The universe seemed to hang on a knife edge. It would be so easy just to let someone else make the final decision. He'd spent half his career trying to deflect political and military micromanagement from people who manifestly did *not* know what they were doing, but now...he almost wanted it. He almost wanted someone to tell him what to do. He almost laughed at the irony. He'd wanted freedom and responsibility; now he had it, and he didn't really want it at all.

He laughed. *Be careful what you wish for*, he thought. *You might just get it.*

Holmes cleared her throat, nervously. "Sir?"

Gerald turned to her. "Send the signal," he ordered. He was tempted to come up with something dramatic, but the propaganda experts could do that after he was safely dead. He was sure they'd come up with something good. He'd always had a feeling that half the sayings attributed to Major-General Carmichael, the effective founder of the corps, had been made up after he'd retired. "Begin."

"Yes, sir."

• • •

"Captain," Ensign Perkins said. She sounded calm, but there was a hint of nerves in her voice. "We are cleared to begin."

Kerri nodded. The plan was as good as possible, with a hundred possible variants explored in the simulations...she scowled, reminding herself that the simulations were only as good as the information fed into them. A single ship that hadn't been noted, logged and accounted for would be more than enough to disrupt her plans. She thought she'd worked out enough ways to retreat, but...there would come a time when they'd be committed. There'd be no way to retreat.

"Signal the squadron," she ordered. The doubts nagged at her mind. She did her best to ignore them. It wasn't the time. "We'll depart in two minutes."

"Aye, Captain."

"And if there are any problems," Kerri added, "I want to know about them now."

She leaned back in her chair as the squadron powered up its drives, readying itself for the jump into phase space. The enemy star glowed in the display, waiting for them. Kerri knew they'd be detected the moment they dropped out of phase space, but it didn't matter. They'd planned for that. She'd be more worried if they ran into an enemy fleet the moment they crossed the phase limit.

And that's about as likely to happen as me being promoted to Supreme Empress of the Known and Unknown Universe, she thought. She couldn't even begin to calculate the odds of that happening, but she was sure they were very low indeed. They'd even taken care to randomise the exit coordinate to make life hard for any would-be interceptors out there. *That's not going to happen.*

A dull whine echoed through the ship as her drives reached a crescendo. Kerri studied the power curves, an unpleasant feeling lingering in her belly. Something might go wrong—something might go wrong at the worst possible time—she gritted her teeth. She'd planned for everything she could imagine, up to and including a total drive failure. The squadron could continue the mission without her...

Which isn't the worst possible outcome, she mused. It would be embarrassing, but survivable. She'd been through worse. *The worst would be losing the entire fleet.*

She looked at the helmsman. "On my command, take us into FTL," she ordered. She felt a flicker of the old excitement. It was time to put her doubts aside and make war. "Now!"

CHAPTER FOURTEEN

We will assume the carpenter sells his planks to the builder. He has made more money than the lumberjack, which doesn't seem fair, but he also has more demands on his resources. He has to pay for his supplies and tools out of his earnings. Whatever's left is profit.
—**Professor Leo Caesius**
The Rise and Fall of Interstellar Capitalism

COMMANDER ARCHER WAS ON THE PROWL.

Rachel bit down her annoyance as the man marched past, as if he was a demented marionette on strings. It hadn't taken her too long to check the files and determine that yes, Commander Archer had been passed over for promotion multiple times. She was mildly surprised he hadn't been reassigned to an asteroid settlement or a monitoring station in the middle of nowhere, although she supposed that he might cause even more damage when he didn't have someone looking over his shoulder. Or suffer a fatal accident that was nothing of the sort. She rather suspected Commander Archer's superiors found him useful. If nothing else, they could be sure he was no threat.

She kept her eyes on the console, watching the live feed from the vast array of sensor platforms deployed around the system. The original design had been hugely expensive, to the point that only Earth and a handful of Core Worlds had invested in them; the corprats had improved the design to the point they—and hundreds of other worlds—could monitor their system without needing to invest in colossal arrays. The design would have been admirable, she thought, if the corprats hadn't been the enemy. She made a mental note to ensure the designs were stolen and copied, at the end of the war. Their advancements could benefit thousands of worlds if they came without strings attached.

And the sensor arrays aren't so easy to duplicate, she mused. *They could have made billions if they'd sold them before the collapse came.*

Her lips quirked. The corprats had also devised vastly more efficient cloudscoops, but there was nothing special about them. The big corporations had pushed through laws mandating safety measures that made standard cloudscoops vastly more expensive, ensuring they had a monopoly on production and distribution. There was no reason anyone with a space-based industry couldn't duplicate their work or come up with a similar design of their own…

"What are you smiling at?" Commander Archer was right behind her. "What's so funny?"

"I was merely remembering last night's entertainment," Rachel lied, smoothly. It wasn't easy to look nervous, but she managed. "It was very funny."

"Keep your eyes on your console," Commander Archer snapped. "We don't want anyone slipping past us!"

He stamped off. Rachel hid her amusement as she looked back at her console. She was mildly surprised he hadn't bawled her out for thinking about last night's flick, but who knew? Perhaps it would have been taken as a sign of disloyalty. It hadn't taken her long to realise that *no one* had any faith in the Corporate Security Division. They certainly didn't think it could be *reasonable*. It was about as sensible as the average theocratic police force, preferring to jail and execute a dozen innocent men rather than let one heretic go free. She doubted the system would last forever, but it hardly mattered. It would do one hell of a lot of damage before it fell.

She forced herself to keep her eyes on the display. The system was preparing for trouble, although it was clear no one knew what form that trouble might take. Worker crews were rushing from place to place, moving so rapidly they often outran the security personnel who were supposed to be monitoring them. She'd listened in on an argument between a work supervisor and a security officer, an argument that had had to be resolved by higher authority…an argument that, under normal circumstances, shouldn't have happened at all. And everyone was so intent on covering their rears against charges of everything from incompetence to subversion that they were making mistakes…

A bunch of cunning smugglers could probably establish an entire supply chain, if they were careful enough to ensure they didn't set off any alarms, she thought. She was certain there *was* an underground, if only because secret police states tended to breed them like dogs bred fleas. *Everyone would be too scared of making waves to rat them out.*

She frowned. The last two days had been…edgy. She'd been kept too busy to have more than a brief meeting with the others, leaving her feeling dangerously exposed. The random security sweeps were growing more frequent, each one increasing the risk of discovery at the worst possible time. She'd done her best to plot out ways to escape, if she was uncovered, but she was all too aware there weren't many options. The anchor station was huge, and she knew how to subvert the automated monitoring systems, yet the security officers could seal the hatches before searching the structure from top to bottom. Rachel knew she'd sell her life dearly, if there was no other choice. She also knew her death would probably be meaningless in the greater scheme of things.

It's not like I could set the fusion cores to blow without a lot of preparation, she mused, as she kept her eyes on the live feed. Commander Archer was harassing a young crewwoman who looked too young to be on the deck, but it was just a matter of time before he returned his attention to her. She didn't like killing people, yet…oh, she was going to enjoy killing him when the time came. *There's a limit to how much damage I can do.*

Her console bleeped. She tensed, feeling a sudden rush of excitement as the long-range sensors detected an exit splash on the very edge of the phase limit. A *large* exit splash, ten light-hours away. Her heart started to race. It looked as if a small squadron of ships had arrived...the invasion force? It was certainly possible. She hadn't expected any advance warning. There was no way to signal the Pathfinders without alerting the enemy to their presence.

Commander Archer looked like a bear with a toothache as he stomped over to her. "Report!"

"Multiple starships exiting phase space," Rachel said, calmly. There was no *proof* it was the invasion force. Not yet. They'd be waiting some time for sublight reports from the more distant monitoring stations. "At least seven ships, maybe more."

"And where are they now?" Commander Archer glared at the screen. "Where are they?"

"We won't have realtime data until they come a lot closer," Rachel said. Any competent officer worthy of the rank would know *that*! She guessed Commander Archer expected to be fielding demands from his superiors fairly soon. "If they come on a least-time course..."

"I didn't ask for your opinion!" Commander Archer tapped the console, then straightened up. "Keep an eye on them!"

"Yes, sir," Rachel said. She was tempted to ask, precisely, what she should be keeping an eye on. The unknown starships were well beyond active sensor range. It would be hours, at the very least, before the planetary defences got a lock on them. "Should we forward the alert up the chain?"

"I'll take care of that, you stupid bitch," Commander Archer snapped. "Keep an eye on them!"

He stamped off. Rachel noticed a pair of operators shooting her sympathetic looks. She felt a pang of guilt. Those poor bastards were risking their careers, if anyone caught their movements on the security monitors. And they were doing it for an enemy infiltrator...never mind they didn't *know*. They'd be for the high jump if their superiors realised what they'd done. Bastards.

She concealed her amusement as she looked back at her console. Commander Archer would probably contact his superiors, passing the alert up the chain to whoever was in ultimate command. She guessed he'd try to claim credit for the early detection, as if he'd been watching the console personally until the enemy ships made their appearance. She wondered, idly, what would happen. The orbital commander should technically declare an emergency, but...if he did, a lot of time and effort would be wasted as defences went online and personnel scrambled for shelters. The cost would be staggering. If it was a false alarm, the orbital commander would be in deep shit.

Which is why it is never a good idea to punish people for being careful, she thought. She kept a wary eye on the monitors as she planned her next move. If the invasion was about to begin, she knew what she had to do. *They start covering their asses instead of covering yours.*

...

Thaddeus rather liked breakfast, for all that he rarely had time to sit back and enjoy it. The first meal of the day was the most important one, with scrambled eggs, toast and bacon—washed down with coffee and tea—preparing him for the rigours he'd face the moment he walked into his office. He'd always preferred to eat breakfast alone, but he'd invited Julia Ganister-Onge to join him. She was his guest, after all. The least he could do was share his breakfast with her.

He studied her with interest as she sipped her coffee, presumably studying him too. She was pretty enough, although too young to be interesting. His lips quirked at the thought. Most people weren't interesting to a man in his second century, particularly a man who could have all the sex he wanted—with whoever he wanted—just for the asking. Julia would have to be older, smarter and much more experienced to capture and keep his interest. Right now, she would have to work hard to overcome her disgrace.

Thaddeus wasn't sure she could climb out of the hole without a *lot* of luck and careful planning.

Daisy entered, carrying a datapad. Thaddeus sighed as he took it and scanned the list of actionable items. The system was gearing up for war and everyone, even the people who were supposed to know better, wanted his input before any final decisions were made. It was a flaw in the corporate government, he acknowledged sourly; there was no way the leadership could empower their subordinates without risking trouble, yet...powerless subordinates *had* to forward all decisions to their masters. There was no way to open upper management without risking all sorts of problems. If nothing else, the corporate royalty would object—strongly—to newcomers being offered plum jobs.

Good enough to marry into the family, but not good enough to be trusted with real opportunities, he thought. *And their children might lack the kind of intelligence that attracted us to their parents in the first place.*

"There's a dispute between two contractors on a deep-space station," he said, more for the sake of making conversation than anything else. "How would you handle the situation?"

Julia looked up, slowly. "I would find out what had happened first," she said. "And then I would make whatever decision seemed appropriate."

A very corporate answer, Thaddeus thought. The poor girl had lost a little of her determination to fight, to carve out a place for herself. She thought—she had to think—that her career was deader than Earth herself. *But then, it wasn't a very fair question.*

The door opened. Daisy hurried into the room. Thaddeus looked up, alarmed. His secretary was supposed to be having her own breakfast, after bringing him the morning reports. She wasn't supposed to interrupt him unless it was truly urgent. He tensed, wondering just what had happened. If it was another dispute that had gotten out of hand, he'd have everyone involved shot. What was the point of being on top if one couldn't rely on one's subordinates to show a little common sense from time to time?

"Sir," Daisy said. "Orbital Defence has picked up a handful of unknown starships entering the system. They are requesting permission to declare an emergency and put the defences on alert."

Thaddeus took a moment to think. "Where are the ships now?"

"Unknown," Daisy said. "Orbital Defence states that they could be here within six hours, perhaps less."

"Really?" Julia sounded a little more animated. "If they were detected on the phase limit, they're at least twenty hours away."

"But we don't know when the contact was actually made," Thaddeus said. He ground his teeth in frustration. Orbital Defence knew what to do if enemy starships appeared from nowhere, firing missiles in all directions, but what should they do if the enemy was some distance away? Whatever decision they made, someone would insist it was the *wrong* decision and demand satisfaction. "They could be a great deal closer."

He thought, rapidly. If he gave the command...it might unite the board against him, but it was unlikely. Too many of them owed him favours. They'd need a far greater cause to put those favours aside and stick a knife in his back. And then...

"Inform Orbital Defence that they have permission to declare a system-wide emergency," Thaddeus said. If he was any judge, the deep space facilities would have sounded the alert anyway. They were out on the edges, hopelessly isolated if the enemy decided to take a crack at them. It was part of the reason the system's industrial infrastructure was concentrated around the planet itself. "And that they are to keep me informed."

Daisy curtsied and withdrew. Thaddeus looked at Julia. She had returned her attention to her plate, as if the issue of an enemy fleet was of no importance whatsoever. Thaddeus couldn't help feeling a flicker of amusement. Her input would certainly be interesting.

"What do you think?"

"I think we need to prepare for the worst," Julia said. She sounded disinterested. It was almost certainly an act. "They're coming."

Thaddeus nodded, although he had his doubts. Onge was heavily protected. There were layer upon layer of orbital and ground-based defences waiting for the enemy. It was a shame no one had ever managed to produce a working planetary force field—the techs claimed it was possible, but usable hardware was sorely lacking—but it hardly mattered. Anyone who tried to land on the planet without permission would be shot to pieces before they made it through the upper atmosphere. It was possible the marines were simply making a demonstration. It was possible. The marines presumably understood the virtues of intimidation as well as he did.

And they can keep us guessing simply by flying around the edge of the system, he thought, sourly. He was no fool. The wear and tear on expensive equipment—and people—would be all too noticeable. *They'd wear our people down before making their move.*

...

Rachel made a show of rubbing her eyes as she sat at her console and monitored the incoming fleet. If she hadn't had her implants, and years of training, she would probably have slipped off her chair and fallen to the deck. As it was, a quarter of the crew had had to be relieved at short notice. She was surprised Commander Archer hadn't chosen to take a nap himself. But then, General Gilbert had taken command. Commander Archer probably didn't want to look bad in front of his ultimate CO.

Particularly when he can't blame everything on us, Rachel thought. She couldn't imagine a way anyone, even someone as versed in interdepartmental conflict as Commander Archer, could pass the blame to his subordinates. *It won't be long before he starts seeing things.*

She frowned as she studied the sensor readings. The incoming fleet appeared to be goose-stepping around the system, feinting at asteroid settlements and cloudscoops before withdrawing back into the inky darkness of interstellar space. Her console was steadily filling with distress calls, each one pleading for starships that simply didn't exist. The planetary defence squadron was under strict orders not to leave orbit, let alone plunge into interplanetary space. Reading between the lines, Rachel was sure General Gilbert had already written most of the deep-space facilities off.

She doubted *that* would do wonders for interplanetary relationships.

And yet…her eyes narrowed. The fleet should have closed with the planet by now. It knew it had been detected. Hell, it had made no attempt to *avoid* detection. Rachel had worked closely with marine and naval personnel. They were very far from incompetent. They had to know they'd been detected…a thrill shot through her as realisation dawned. They wanted to be detected! They wanted the enemy keeping their eyes on them. They wanted…

She smiled, despite herself. The diversion didn't *have* to be smaller than the main attack. It just had to be noticeable. And it *was* noticeable. Everyone, right across the system, was keeping a wary eye on the enemy fleet. They simply didn't have time for anything else.

"What are they doing?" Commander Archer demanded. His voice sounded as though he was on the verge of breaking. "Why are they just… staring at us?"

General Gilbert shot him a sharp look. The general looked as if he was on the edge of exhaustion. A handful of his staff had already taken stims, despite the risks. Rachel was surprised they hadn't gone to bed. As far as they knew, the threat was still several hours away. They could snatch a few hours of sleep before returning, revitalised, to face the incoming hordes. Instead, they were almost mesmerised by the enemy fleet. She accessed the orbital sensors and studied them carefully, half-expecting to see a cloaked fleet sneaking up on the planet. If the ships on the display were a division, they had to be running cover for something…

Red icons materialised on the display. Alarms howled. But it was already too late.

CHAPTER FIFTEEN

The builder takes the planks and works them into a house. The total value of the house is now one thousand credits...yes, a gross understatement, but easy enough to follow. Our ten-credit tree trunk has become a hundred-credit pile of planks and now a thousand-credit house. With each stage in the process, the total value of the wood has increased until it offers the promise of a vast potential profit.
—**Professor Leo Caesius**
The Rise and Fall of Interstellar Capitalism

COMMANDER NORMAN HALIBUT KNEW, without false modesty, that he'd probably never have another chance to command a starship in combat. He was a trained engineer, a profession that ensured he would never be out of work…but also one that guaranteed he wouldn't be allowed to venture into danger very often. It was easy enough to remove a malfunctioning node and slap a replacement into position—anyone could do it—yet it was a great deal harder to repair a damaged node on the fly, rewire the datanet on short notice and jury-rig a life-support system to keep a crew alive long enough to be rescued. Norman had come to realise, long ago, that his career had been the victim of his own success. He was simply too valuable to be risked.

He tried to suppress a thrill of excitement as *Hammerblow* glided closer to the planet. He and his crew were sitting in a shuttlecraft, effectively commanding the giant battlecruiser through remote control, but it was the closest he'd ever been to starship command. The jury-rigged command and control network was working better than he'd feared, allowing him to steer the ship towards her target. It would start to fail the moment the enemy defences returned fire, despite the multiple redundancies he'd worked into the system, but it didn't matter. The battlecruiser wasn't expected to survive the coming engagement. Norman would have resented that, under other circumstances. The battlecruiser could have been repaired and returned to service, given time. But they just didn't have the time.

Sweat ran down his back as the range steadily closed. How long did they have before they were detected? Their emissions were dialled down as low as possible—the cloaking device should have muffled what little they hadn't been able to reduce to nothing—but the enemy sensor arrays were very good. Norman had even made a small bet with himself that they wouldn't get anywhere near the high orbitals before they were detected. He touched his console, making a tiny adjustment in the starship's course. She was heading directly towards a giant orbital battlestation. Sooner or later, she *would* be detected...

His finger rested on top of the firing key. The passive sensors were picking up all sorts of targets, ranging from the remote sensor units to orbital defence platforms. The anchor station and the asteroid habitats were off-limits—no one *wanted* to knock one of the asteroids out of orbit and cause a full-scale disaster—but everything else was a legitimate target. There were so many that his engineer's soul was almost offended by the targeting data, as if they couldn't concentrate on a single target. It didn't matter, he reminded himself. The idea was to disrupt and degrade the enemy network, not smash it to a pulp.

The display flashed red. Norman didn't hesitate. He pushed the firing key, unleashing a full-scale salvo towards the enemy positions. The missile pods they'd bolted to the hull spat fire and fury a second later, unleashing everything they had in a single burst. The design was hugely inefficient, but it wasn't a problem. They needed to put as many missiles into space as possible before the enemy recovered from their shock and opened fire. Norman had calculated it wouldn't take more than a few seconds before the enemy started shooting. A salvo of missiles *would* concentrate a few minds.

"Drones deployed," Ensign Harper said. He'd volunteered for the mission, which made him a brave man, a fool, or some combination of the two. "ECM going online now."

"Understood." Norman ramped up the drive, throwing the battlecruiser towards the giant battlestation. The drives couldn't take the acceleration for long—the designers had skimped a bit, for reasons he didn't understand—but they wouldn't have to. "Anders, prepare to disengage."

He smiled as the display sparkled with more and more red lights. The enemy defences were finally returning fire. Their targeting was a little skewed, automated systems thrown off by the drones and ECM, but they were rapidly closing on the battlecruiser. Her point defence went live, adding to the mix by firing plasma and laser pulses at the incoming missiles… they could have made a longer stand, he acknowledged, if the point defence wasn't forced to engage the enemy sensor platforms as well as everything else. As it was…

A dull rumble ran through the shuttle as four missiles ploughed into the battlecruiser. The hullmetal took the brunt of the impact, but there hadn't been time to patch all the holes from the *last* engagement. The alerts flashing up in front of him suggested that half the wounds had just sprung open again. Laser beams stabbed deep into the battlecruiser's hull. He silently thanked all the gods that he'd removed as much as possible, then depressurised the starship's interior. It wouldn't slow the destruction down for long, but every second counted.

His lips quirked as another volley of bomb-pumped lasers stabbed into the hullmetal. The enemy hadn't realised how well their *first* volley had worked. He guessed the ECM was doing its job. Half the incoming missiles were wasting themselves on sensor ghosts and decoys that were effectively worthless. They certainly posed no real threat to the enemy defences. Hell, normally the sensors would have no trouble isolating the decoys from the *real* ships. Now...the system had taken such a battering, the command and control network so badly weakened, that it couldn't even focus on the ships that were actually launching missiles. There was no better way to separate the real ships from the ghosts.

Be grateful, he told himself, sharply. *If they knew where to fire, they would have blown you away by now.*

Another shudder ran through the ship. He switched the systems to automatic. They wouldn't hold for long, but...he glanced at Anders as the automatics took over. "Disengage from the hull," he ordered. "And then go ballistic."

"Aye, sir," Anders said. "Disengaging...now."

The shuttle rocked. The gravity field seemed to twist around them, an unpleasant sensation Norman had always likened to his breath catching in his throat, as they spun away from the giant battlecruiser. He prayed, silently, that between the sensor distortions and the exploding warheads, no one was paying attention to a tiny shuttle heading *away* from the planet. The odds were in their favour—no one would care about a shuttle when there was a full-scale invasion going on—but he knew, better than most, the role chance played in interstellar warfare. There was a very good chance that someone would mistake them for a stealthed weapon and blow them away...or that they'd simply be swatted in passing by one of the bigger ships, with no one on either side ever quite aware of what was happening to them.

He gritted his teeth and turned his attention back to *Hammerblow*. The proud battlecruiser was gliding steadily towards her target, her weapons still firing in all directions. Damage was mounting rapidly—she was venting live plasma from a drive node, suggesting the containment tubes had been breached—but she was still moving. The battlestation was bringing its heavy weapons to bear on her, yet her forward armour was holding. Barely. Norman smiled. It looked as if the days they'd spent cannibalising armour from two of the other captured ships and welding it to the battlecruiser's prow had not been wasted after all.

"My God," Anders said. "She's going to make it."

"Yeah." Norman felt his smile grow wider as the battlecruiser smashed into the battlestation and wiped it from existence in a blaze of radioactive plasma. He didn't think—then—of the hundreds of lives that had been blotted out in a single catastrophic moment. He didn't care about the waves of debris spinning out in all directions, including chunks of hullmetal that were likely to make it through the planet's atmosphere and hit the surface. "She did it."

He felt a prickle at the corner of his eyes. *Hammerblow* had been his ship, if only for a few short days. He mourned her loss, even though he knew he would never have been allowed to keep her. And...

"She lived up to her name," he said. "And now, we're out of the fight."

He settled back in his chair. They'd keep moving until they were well clear of the engagement, then head for the RV point. If they were lucky... they'd be picked up by friendly forces. If not...he shook his head. The engagement might still go badly, but...right now, the enemy had worse problems. They didn't have time to worry about a shuttlecraft fleeing the battle. Norman and his crew should be safe.

His lips curved into a humourless smile. *Of course, if they catch us and figure out what we did, we'll be very far from safe.*

• • •

Kerri watched, torn between awe and a very primal fear, as the enemy battlestation disintegrated. The designers had made the battlestation tougher than a battleship—they didn't have to cram military-grade drives into the hull—but they couldn't have prepared her for a giant battlecruiser ramming herself into the battlestation. There was no armour in existence that could stand up to *that*. The sheer insanity of the tactic made it hard to predict. No one, not even the Imperial Navy, would throw away a multi-billion credit starship on a whim.

A shame we couldn't cram her hull with explosives, she thought. The battlecruiser had expended most of her missiles before meeting her fiery doom. *The blast might have been even bigger.*

She put the thought aside as the remaining automated ships advanced towards the planet. They were tearing a hole in the enemy defences, shooting missiles and projectiles towards the orbital platforms and the PDCs below. The latter were only just starting to shoot, even though they had enough plasma weapons to make one hell of a difference. Kerri suspected they were reluctant to risk blowing holes in the orbital industries. They *needed* to keep those facilities intact.

"Continue firing," she ordered. They'd cleared a gap in the enemy defences. "And deploy the second wave of drones."

"Aye, Captain."

Kerri settled back into her chair and watched. The automated ships were soaking up one hell of a lot of fire. Good. Their crews were already on their shuttles, heading away as fast as they could. The ships were doomed, but it didn't matter. She'd never intended for any of them to survive the battle. The more fire they drew, the less that would be aimed at the *real* threat. The ships inching into high orbit had to be protected as long as possible.

And as long as they're confused about what we're trying to protect, she told herself, *the harder it will be for them to tackle the real threat.*

She smiled, coldly. "Contact Captain Summand," she ordered. "Inform him he may begin Phase Two when ready."

"Aye, Captain."

• • •

Rachel was all too aware that the Terran Marine Corps based its doctrine on speed, surprise and hitting the enemy where it hurt. The corps had always been outnumbered on the battlefield, forcing it to rely on maintaining a high operation tempo to keep the enemy from recovering its balance and striking back. But now...Major-General Anderson and his staff had outdone themselves. The battlecruiser had wiped an entire battlestation out of existence and that, combined with the damaged or destroyed orbital sensor platforms, had thrown everything into confusion.

"Link the command and control networks through the anchor station," General Gilbert snapped. There was no hint of panic in his voice. Rachel was morbidly impressed. "We'll take control of the defences."

Good thinking, Rachel thought, as Commander Archer echoed the command. She tapped her console, doing her level best to look like she was handling the job while moving as slowly as possible. The anchor station was designed to serve as an emergency command and control centre, but the system had never been tested. *You might have saved the day if I'd allowed you the chance.*

She watched as the operators struggled to bring their systems back online. The orbital network was continuing to fragment. It looked as if a bunch of sensor nodes had gone down, then come back up again and started targeting friendly units. Rachel guessed that one of her comrades had engaged in a little sabotage before the shit hit the fan. It had probably been Bonkowski. He'd always had an evil sense of humour.

And their system isn't making it easy for us to replace the dead controllers, she thought, with a flicker of amusement. *We don't have the permissions we need to take control.*

"Unlock the system," General Gilbert ordered. His thoughts had clearly been moving in the same direction. "Hurry!"

"But..." Commander Archer started. "Sir..."

"Do it!" General Gilbert rounded on him. "We don't have time to argue!"

Rachel kept her face carefully impassive as more and more options appeared in front of her. The staff were working hard, their minds concentrated by incoming fire and the grim certainty they could no longer be blamed for anything. The system might be designed to log each and every keystroke, and assign them to an operator, but not once it had been unlocked. Rachel knew it would work for them. The fear of being blamed for making an entirely understandable mistake was gone. Thankfully, it also let her get on with a little sabotage.

She worked hard, assigning platforms to target ships that looked like drones and fiddling with their systems to ensure the odds of actually hitting anything were very low. General Gilbert was handling things well, she conceded; he'd even managed to silence Commander Archer and a handful of other timeservers. She caught herself glancing at his back, wondering if she could kill him and get the hell out before they riddled her body with bullets. Only the grim certainty she couldn't hope to escape kept her in her seat. If they saw her kill him, they'd wonder what *else* she'd been doing.

Alarms howled through the command core. "Incoming shuttles! I say again, incoming shuttles!"

"Target them," General Gilbert ordered. "Quickly!"

Rachel smiled. Between her fiddling and the badly-degraded sensor network, it wasn't likely they'd be able to hit more than one or two shuttles before they clamped onto the hull and boarded the anchor station. The internal security systems were designed to deal with dissidents, not marines in powered combat armour. She wondered what they'd do once the station fell into enemy hands. Fire on the anchor and risk disaster? Or simply disconnect and hope the marines wheeled up the cable before it was too late?

General Gilbert's voice rose. "Command staff, switch command to the ground-based systems and then head for the elevator cable. Now."

Rachel stared. He wanted them to ride the cable to the ground now? It was insane! Nuclear warheads were detonating outside the station, each sending out more and more waves of electromagnetic disruption. And yet... she could see his logic. The cable hadn't drawn fire. It wouldn't. It might give him a chance to get the knowledgeable command staff off the station before it was captured. She thought, fast, as the rest of the staff scrambled to their feet and headed to the emergency tubes. She could still do a lot of damage if she remained on the station, but the chance to follow the commanding officers was not to be missed.

She hoped the others were safe as she joined the exodus. The three other Pathfinders had found menial positions. It was unlikely they were on any evacuation lists. Hell, she wasn't entirely sure *she* was on any lists. She'd inserted herself into the records, and tightened up the references over the last few days, but the longer she remained in place the greater the chance of something going wrong. The slightest slip-up could result in disaster.

But the entire system is already a ruin, she thought. *They'll be lucky if they don't lose track of everyone after this.*

Commander Archer pushed past her as they made their way down to the elevator pod. Rachel felt a hot flash of contempt, mingled with irritation that her safety depended on an imbecile with wandering hands. Commander Archer deserved to have an accident, perhaps several accidents...she shook her head as they reached the pod. She'd have a chance to do even more damage, if she kept her head down and paid attention to her surroundings. Who knew? They might be so desperate for trained and experienced personnel they wouldn't pay any attention to glaring red flags.

She kept her implants connected to the datanet as they boarded the pod and strapped themselves in. The fleet—the incoming fleet—was lost in a haze of sensor distortion. She guessed, from the damage to the system, that all of the Pathfinders had performed individual acts of sabotage. She prayed, silently, that they'd make it out of the fire. Phelps and the others owed her drinks. She probably owed them drinks too.

The pod lurched, then fell towards the planet. Rachel closed her eyes and tried to get some rest. There was nothing else to do. Whatever happened in the future, she knew that—for the moment—she was out of the fight.

CHAPTER SIXTEEN

It's easy to argue that this isn't fair. The poor lumberjack on the bottom has only realised a tiny percentage of the value. He has a mere ten percent of the carpenter's earnings and an even smaller one percent of the builder's earnings. A simplistic mind, looking at this, would declare it unconscionable.
—**Professor Leo Caesius**
The Rise and Fall of Interstellar Capitalism

GENERAL DEVOID GANISTER was not having a good day.

In fact, he reflected sourly as he sat in the command pit, he'd not been having a good month. It hadn't been *easy* to get his young relative Julia into a position of some considerable power and trust, an exercise that had cost the family subset a great deal of trouble at the time and even more when she returned in defeat. The Ganister branch of the family had seriously considered disowning her and swearing blind she'd never been one of them...a tactic they would have used without hesitation if they'd thought it would have worked. Instead...he put the thought out of his head as the battle unfolded on the big display. The enemy, the marines or whoever they were, had done a hell of a lot of damage in the first few seconds of war.

His eyes tracked hundreds of pieces of debris falling towards the surface. Most of them would burn up in the atmosphere, but a number were large enough to hit the ground and do real damage. The PDCs were already engaging them, even though it limited the amount of firepower they could deploy to assist the orbital defences. The enemy fleet itself was within range, but just far enough from the planet to be hard to hit. And it was a multitude…he was entirely sure that the vast majority of enemy contacts were nothing more than sensor decoys, if only because the enemy wouldn't have had to pussyfoot around if they had thousands of starships under their control, but it wasn't easy to separate the real contacts from the fakes. It was impossible …

Alarms howled. "General!"

Devoid spun to face Commander Ringo. "What?"

"They're targeting us, sir," Ringo said. "They're launching *missiles* at us."

For a moment, Devoid honestly didn't believe what he'd been told. Missiles? Shipkiller missiles? Deploying them against a planetary surface was a violation of every law in the book. There was a better than even chance of causing an atrocity that would give the Bombardment of Kali a run for its money. And yet…he blanched as he saw the trails lancing towards the PDC. The enemies were mad! They were insane! They were going to kill a sizable percentage of the planet's population…

"Priority orders," he snapped. "Retarget all systems. Take those missiles out!"

"Aye, sir," Ringo said.

Devoid forced himself to think through his shock. The enemies were utterly insane. They could have drenched the PDC in KEWs and been fairly sure of doing real damage, without putting the rest of the planet at risk. An object striking the surface at a reasonable percentage of the speed of light…it would take out the PDC, he supposed, as well as most of the surrounding area. The Imperial Navy had experimented with all sorts of anti-PDC weapons. Thankfully, most of them had been field-tested on uninhabited worlds.

He reached for his console to send an alert, then stopped himself. There was no point. There were no precautions that could be taken, in a handful of minutes, that could make a difference. The disaster was going to shake the entire world. The people lucky enough to have bunkers might discover they'd become death traps. And the people outside the bunkers might discover the living would envy the dead...

Two missiles vanished from the display, picked off by the planetary defences. Two more kept coming, followed by a wave of KEWs. Devoid snorted. The invaders had moved well beyond mere *overkill*. The PDC was buried within a mountain, the fusion cores and living quarters well below the surface, but the impact would be enough to tear the complex open and kill everyone inside. There was no time to order an evacuation. Even trying to get his people out would expose them to enemy fire. And yet...he frowned. Something didn't quite make sense.

The display blanked. "What?"

"The enemy warhead detonated, sir," Commander Thistle reported. "They did considerable damage to the sensor arrays..."

Devoid stared at her as she continued her report. It made no sense. Why fire a shipkiller at the planet and detonate it a moment before it hit its target? They'd blasted the mountain with nuclear fire, roasting anyone unlucky enough to be in the open, but they could have cracked the PDC open like an eggshell. Why...they'd damaged the sensors and melted the point defence, but it could be fixed. The main communications trunk was safely below the ground. The PDC had been damaged, yet...

The ground shook. He recalled, too late, the KEWs. Understanding dawned. The invaders had used the shipkillers as a distraction—they'd threatened the entire planet as a distraction—without ever intending to let them hit the ground. The KEWs...the entire complex shook, time and time again, as the projectiles smashed into the armour. Devoid cursed as he looked at the damage reports. The upper levels had been devastated. The heavy weapons and sensors had been smashed beyond repair. They'd even cracked the plasma containment chambers. Fires were raging over the scorched mountaintop. There was no hope of opening the airlocks and escaping before the fires died.

He shook his head as more and more reports flashed in front of him. The PDC was still technically intact, but it didn't matter. They could no longer engage the enemy. They were, for better or worse, out of the fight.

And that means they have a clear path to the surface, he thought. He had no doubt what was coming next. *They're going to invade.*

• • •

"Captain," Lieutenant Tomas said. "I can confirm that two of the enemy PDCs have been disabled. A third is still operating, but appears damaged. Its rate of fire has been significantly reduced."

Kerri allowed herself a moment of relief. Using shipkillers to engage a planetary target had been risky. They'd worked as many safety precautions into the programming as possible, to the point they'd taken the risk of *not* inflicting enough damage on the PDCs to blind them. And yet...she smiled. The risk wasn't one she wanted to take again, but it had worked.

"Signal the dumpsters," she ordered. The skies were as clear as they were going to be. The enemy were clearly trying to redirect their remaining defence stations into position to close the gap, but they didn't have the time. "Tell them to drop."

"Aye, Captain," Ensign Perkins said.

"The marines have boarded the anchor station," Lieutenant Tomas added. "They've secured the command and control system. Captain...they report that the station has been locked out of the main network and the datanodes have been partly destroyed."

"Unsurprising," Kerri said. She'd hoped they'd capture the enemy command network intact, allowing them to shut it down completely, but she hadn't counted on it. No defence planner worthy of the name would leave such a glaring weakness in place, even on a world as interconnected as Onge. "Order them to secure the cable, then wait."

She turned her attention to the display. The transports were moving into position, deploying the dumpsters one by one. The technique was centuries old, but it was rare for humans to ride the dumpsters down to the surface. An impact that would damage a piece of solid equipment would kill a human…she shook her head. The enemy had done it and made it work. Anything they could do, the marines could do better.

And Haydn is in the first wave. She'd checked. *If he doesn't make it down…*

"Captain," Lieutenant Tomas said. "The dumpsters are dropping now."

"Begin transmitting," Kerri ordered. The enemy would try to lock the signals out of their datanet, but it wouldn't be easy. Their system had been shot to hell in the last ten minutes. "And order the boarding parties to try to insert more signals into the network."

"Aye, Captain."

...

"This is worse than making a HALO drop through a storm," someone muttered.

Haydn was tempted to agree. Parachuting through a storm was dangerous as hell. The rain alone could be painful, if not lethal; the wind could pick a parachutist up and toss him too high to survive or tangle the chute or slam him into the ground or…there were just too many possibilities, each one worse than the last. And yet…the dumpster was shaking violently as it plunged through the atmosphere. He felt completely helpless. It felt as if he were riding a rock as it fell to its doom.

It isn't that bad, he told himself. He thought he could hear the metal creak behind him. He'd ridden emergency escape pods, but they'd been far smaller and safer. Something crashed in the distance…he prayed, silently, that it wasn't one of the vehicles. It could start crushing marines or smashing through cables or even destabilising the whole dumpster and sending it wildly off course. *We could be on a starship falling towards the nearest star.*

"There was an old book about an alien race that invaded a planet," Mayberry said. "They shot themselves out of giant cannons and practically rammed their target. They survived."

Haydn scowled. He couldn't tell if Mayberry was trying to distract the men or distract himself. The whole concept sounded absurd, except…they were doing it. The Onge had already done it. Maybe the landing part was practical...maybe. Shooting a dumpster out of a cannon, without crushing the crew to bloody paste? He mulled it over as the dumpster shook, again and again. It might be possible, if one had the right sort of technology. But if one did, why not build a proper starship? The whole concept sounded like something drawn up by a scientific illiterate.

He probably didn't know what was possible, Haydn thought. He'd read a handful of scientific romances from the pre-space days. The corps had preserved them for reasons that had never really been explained. Half had just been laughable. The other half had remained universally true, even centuries after the people and places they referenced had been forgotten. *Perhaps they didn't have starships in those days.*

"There's no such thing as aliens, Sarge," Rifleman Scully said. "They just don't exist."

"Hey, someone found some pretty odd ruins on a world beyond the rim," Rifleman Muldoon put in. "Strange ziggurats, weird houses build for weirder creatures. They weren't human."

"Faked," Scully said. "You look in any market along the rim and you'll see a handful of fake alien relics. You might even see a pair of skulls belonging to a single person...one for when he was an adult and one for when he was a child."

Muldoon laughed. "People actually believe that crap?"

"My recruiting sergeant told me that women go mad for men in military uniforms," Scully said. "And you know what? He was lying through his ass."

"You have to look good in the uniform." Muldoon snickered. "It isn't my fault you look like a beached whale with a BO problem..."

The dumpster lurched again. "I probably shouldn't have tried to pick up girls on Atlanta," Scully said, mournfully. "Oh, what a fool I was. They see the military as a pool for losers."

"They'll have probably changed their minds by now," Muldoon said. There was a hint of cold satisfaction in his voice. "Atlanta is right on the edge of disputed space."

Haydn couldn't disagree. The university world had been peaceful and pacifistic to a fault. The greatest threat the academics had faced had been polite arguments over grants from the imperial authorities. They'd even banned the military from recruiting there, on the grounds it would sully their peaceful paradise with violence. He doubted it was anything like as peaceful now. The academics would probably make things worse by appealing to an authority that no longer existed, an authority the neighbouring warlords knew very well no longer existed. And they couldn't hope to defend themselves…

The buzzer rang. The marines fell silent and braced themselves, an instant before the retrorockets fired. Haydn had made hundreds of drops into hostile territory, but this…he thought, just for a second, as though someone had kicked him in the butt. The techs had assured him the dumpster's lower plating could survive anything short of a bomb-pumped laser, but he hadn't felt particularly reassured. The impact didn't have to blow them to atoms to throw them off-kilter and send them crashing to the planet below.

The gravity field seemed to invert itself, just for a second. There was a final thunderous impact, then total silence. Haydn shook his head, wondering if he'd gone deaf. Marines always laughed and joked, making light of the death that awaited them…now, he couldn't hear a thing. Fear gripped him, just long enough to send ice through his heart. Was he the sole survivor? It didn't seem possible. And yet…

"Any landing you can walk away from is a good landing," Mayberry said. "Sir?"

Haydn disengaged himself from his webbing and scrambled to his feet. His legs felt wobbly, as if he'd fallen back to the days when, as a young recruit, he'd made his first parachute drop. He hadn't been anything like scared enough, he recalled. Now…he wondered, as he checked his weapons and led the command platoon towards the opened hatches, if the corps would be making more dumpster drops. When it worked, it worked.

And one tiny mishap would be enough to wipe out a regiment, he thought. *We wouldn't have tried it here if we weren't desperate.*

His HUD flashed up warnings as he peered out of the hatch. The dumpster had crashed down in the middle of a forest...no, it was too well-tended to be a forest. A large garden...he recalled some of the video games he'd played as a child, the ones that had invited him to pretend he had limitless resources, and shuddered. The garden in front of him was easily large enough to take an entire regiment of marines. He could see a mansion in the distance, nearly a mile from the landing zone. It looked like a building out of a historical flick.

The remainder of the platoon hurried past him, scrambling up the side of the crater and spreading out. It didn't *look* as though they were under attack, as if the enemy was hurling shells or missiles towards them in a desperate bid to smash the dumpster before it started unloading its contents, but that could change at any moment. He keyed his throatmike as he jumped down and walked up the side of the crater himself, ordering the logistics staff to get the air defence units out as quickly as possible. The planners had sworn blind the first wave would get down on the ground before the enemy had a chance to react, and he supposed they'd been right, but it was just a matter of time before that changed. The enemy would be scrambling to react to the invasion. It wasn't as if they'd landed on the very edge of settled territory. They were far too close to the megacity for the enemy's piece of mind.

He reached the top of the crater and looked back, just in time to see the first ADV emerge from the dumpster and drive up beside him. Its sensors were already sweeping the air, looking for targets. The logistics crew were laying down struts, making it easier for the follow-up vehicles to get out of the crater. Haydn ground his teeth in annoyance. The crater...they should have expected the crater. None of the reports had suggested the impact would create one, but—in hindsight—it was bloody obvious. They hadn't been planning to land in the middle of a spaceport!

I suppose we're lucky we didn't set the forest on fire, he thought, grimly. He could see plumes of smoke rising from the distant mountains. There was a PDC there, if he recalled correctly. The plan had called for it to be taken out with maximum force. He guessed the plan had worked. An active PDC would have blown the dumpsters to atoms well before they reached the surface. *It could have been worse.*

He joined the rest of the platoon as the marine continued to file out of the dumpster and form up. The remainder of their equipment was being unloaded slowly, but they didn't need it. Not yet. He smiled as a pair of tiny drones were launched into the air, even though they were easy targets for modern antiaircraft systems. If nothing else, their deaths would tell the marines something useful. They'd know where the enemy wanted to defend and was willing to risk revealing their position to do so...

Mayberry saluted. "Captain," he said. "The company is ready to advance."

"Good," Haydn said. "Follow me."

He pointed towards the distant mansion, then started to walk. Time wasn't on their side. The enemy had used dumpsters themselves. It stood to reason they had a plan for dealing with the sudden arrival of a large body of troops. Hopefully, they'd hesitate to use WMD on lands owned and occupied by corporate royalty. A single nuke would shatter the timetable beyond repair.

In the distance, he heard the sound of guns.

CHAPTER SEVENTEEN

And yet, is this true. Each successive party in the process brings his skills and experience to the task of creating wealth. The lumberjack's sole job is to cut down a tree, a relatively simple task. The carpenter's role requires a certain degree of training and experience as well as tools. The builder's role requires still more training and experience.
—**Professor Leo Caesius**
The Rise and Fall of Interstellar Capitalism

JULIA FELT...ALONE.

She *was* alone, to all intents and purposes. The director didn't seem interested in inviting her into his innermost sanctuary, the office from where he ruled the world. She wandered the corridors of his mansion, marvelling at how many luxurious rooms were completely empty. Director Onge practically lived alone. He had no wife; his children were grown and working their way up the corporate ladder...he didn't even have a live-in mistress. His servants and dogs didn't count. They gave Julia a wide berth as she walked from room to room, wondering what was going to happen. If the marines had finally arrived...

Her thoughts ran in circles, threatening to plunge her into depression. There was nothing for her, not any longer. She was surprised she hadn't been sent into exile—or back to the subset of her family in disgrace—even though the director seemed to value her input. She supposed it must be a new experience for him. He could talk to her about anything without having to fear her plotting. She didn't have a hope of unseating him and taking his place.

She frowned as she walked past a line of long windows, staring over the garden. Nothing moved below her, save for a handful of birds flying through the air. The garden looked perfect, too perfect. It was a rock garden in the truest possible sense, everything placed so perfectly as to rob the scene of any randomness. The landscapers had created something wonderful, yet sterile. Her eyes lingered on a treehouse on the edge of the forest, as neatly sculptured as the rest of the garden. She wondered, idly, what it would have been like to play in the forest as a kid. She'd grown up in a smaller mansion, one crowded with children from a dozen different family subsets. She had never been truly alone.

Not until now, she thought. *Not until...*

The windows shattered. She hit the floor instinctively, hands moving to cover her head as pieces of stone and glass crashed down around her. The windows were designed to be *tough*. If they'd been broken...her thoughts spun madly. The marines were still hours from the planet, weren't they? She forced herself to stand and peer through the shattered window, looking towards the city. Smoke was rising from the far side of the forest. She could see a conical shape that hadn't been there before. It was...she froze as she realised *precisely* what it was, a heartbeat before a second fell from the skies and crash-landed nearby. A dumpster. Two dumpsters. She was looking at an invasion beachhead...

Someone screamed. Julia turned to see a maid, staring at the mess. The woman—girl, really—looked shocked out of her mind, mumbling about cleaning up the halls. Julia started to slap her, then stopped herself. Admiral Agate had told her, time and time again, that the marines were trained to move fast. They didn't have long, perhaps no more than a few minutes, before the dumpsters started to open and disgorge their contents. An entire *army* had just landed on the director's front lawn.

She cursed her decision to wear a simple dress as she turned and ran down the corridor. The mansion felt unsteady, as if the impact had damaged the foundations. If she'd worn a pair of trousers instead...she stopped and ripped the lower half of her dress away, even though it cost more than the average corporate worker would make in a year. The ground shook, again. A third dumpster? She tried to calculate how many marines had just landed, then gave it up as a bad job. There was little hope of resistance. The mansion didn't have more than a handful of guards, none of whom were—presumably—trained to cope with a full-scale invasion. Julia knew *she* wasn't trained to cope with it either. They had to get out before the noose tightened around them.

The door to the innermost chambers looked solid. Julia hesitated, wondering if she should try to run herself or find somewhere to hide... somewhere she could surrender, once the marines had finished securing the mansion. They wouldn't kill her...probably. They hadn't said anything about terms and conditions, when they'd let her go. And yet...if she could get the director out, she could write her own ticket. He wouldn't fail to reward her. The Onge Family hadn't risen to the very heights of power by ignoring those who saved their lives.

She pushed the door open. The director was sitting in a chair, staring at a set of holographic images. Julia knew enough to tell the orbital defences had taken one hell of a beating. The anchor station was flashing red. One of the massive battlestations was missing. Admiral Agate had told her the defence stations were *designed* to soak up fire...what the hell had happened to the missing station? A new superweapon? Or sabotage? There was no way to know.

"Director!" Julia raised his voice, throwing caution to the winds. "They're landing outside!"

The director looked up at her, a multitude of emotions crossing his face. He hadn't realised...she didn't know how he hadn't realised something was terribly wrong. The mansion had been hit by a series of earthquakes...she yanked at his arm, pulling him out of his chair. It crossed her mind, not for the first time, that he was *old*. He was in his second century. It occurred to her to wonder, as she half-dragged him towards the door, just how long her generation would have to wait before they tasted true power for themselves. The director's kids were old enough to be her *grandparents*. And yet, they were still dependent on their father.

"Julia," the director managed. He snapped back to normal as they hurried down the corridor. "What are you doing?"

Julia bit down a sarcastic reply. "The marines have landed outside, sir," she said. Another shudder ran through the mansion. She thought she could hear gunfire, although she had no idea who was shooting. As far as she knew, there were no friendly troops near the mansion, no one who might come to their rescue. "We have to get out of here."

She forced herself to think. The marines would be advancing on the mansion. They'd probably surround the building before they crashed through the doors and searched it from top to bottom. And that meant… if there were any emergency escape tunnels, she didn't know about them. The director seemed to be veering in and out of shock. He was in no state to tell her anything. Worse…if there were tunnels, there was a very good chance they'd been collapsed by the dumpsters. She'd heard all sorts of horror stories from the last war.

"This way," she said. The director's aircar was probably their best bet. There were horses in the stables, but she had no idea if they could get to them in time. And the poor beasts probably couldn't outrun a man in powered combat armour. "Quickly!"

The building shook again. She could *feel* the marines closing in, even though they appeared to be alone. The servants had made themselves scarce, probably cowering under tables as they waited for the marines to round them up. Julia didn't blame them. They weren't trained to handle a full-scale invasion. Normally, the director would have been moved to a secure location…she snorted in irritation. They should have done it at once, even though they'd thought the marines were on the other side of the system. It would be better than being caught with their pants around their ankles.

Or in a completely inappropriate dress, she thought as they rushed into the garage. *If I'd known this was going to happen...*

She found herself smiling as she shoved the director into the passenger seat, then powered up the aircar and drove it straight at the garage door. The hatch opened automatically, allowing her to fly into the open air. It had been a long time since she'd flown personally, rather than allowing the automatics to handle it, but she hadn't forgotten. She breathed a silent prayer of thanks that her parents had permitted her to learn when she'd been a teenager. *And* that the director's aircar was exempt from the normal rules. The civilian population had probably already discovered their aircars were grounded for the duration. *They* weren't allowed to take the helm themselves.

Her mind raced. There was a simple road leading from the mansion to the megacity and the nearby installations, but the marines would probably have sealed it already. She took the aircar off the road, flying over the forest as low as she dared. Sensor units weren't totally reliable at low-level, she recalled someone saying. The marines had surprised her people by flying so low they'd practically touched the ground. Sweat trickled down her back as she glanced over her shoulder. There were armoured figures on the lawn. She ducked, although she knew it was useless. If they launched an HVM at the aircar, the passengers would be dead before they knew they were under attack.

"Head to the megacity," the director said. "I have to take command."

Julia hesitated, then did as she was told. The sound of shooting died away behind her as they flew onwards. She looked up, wincing as she saw pieces of debris burning through the upper atmosphere. The planet's defences were impregnable, she'd been told. It looked as though the marines had proved the defenders wrong. Again.

"We'll have to stay low until we get there," she said. She had no idea what they'd find, when they reached the city. Knowing her luck, the defenders would mistake the aircar for an incoming missile and shoot it down. "And then..."

She grinned as the aircar picked up speed. They were clear. She had no doubt the marines would regroup and advance towards the megacity as fast as possible, but—for the moment—they were clear. She felt a flicker of the old excitement, even though they were very far from safe. She'd faced a challenge and handed it well. The marines had been left eating her dust.

And if I can't parley this into some kind of position, she thought as she glanced at the director, *I'm not the woman I thought I was.*

• • •

"This place is weird," someone muttered.

Haydn was inclined to agree as the platoon advanced on the mansion. It was a towering monstrosity, looking like something out of a history flick than anything practical. The building itself looked intact, but the windows had been shattered…he wondered, suddenly, why they'd used *real* glass when there were far more practical alternatives. He muttered commands into his throatmike as they inched up to the shattered doorway—it looked as if they'd designed doors that were also windows—and stepped inside. The garden room might have been fancy, once upon a time. Now, the shockwaves had knocked paintings from the walls and scattered glass everywhere.

He gritted his teeth as his boots crunched across the floor. The mansion was huge, easily large enough to make him feel small. He'd been on *starships* and slept in *barracks* that were smaller. The Government Houses he'd seen on a dozen worlds had been bigger, he supposed, but they were designed to serve as offices rather than homes for the excessively wealthy. A shiver ran down his spine as he peered into the next room. The mansion should have been absolutely *bursting* with people. Instead, it was apparently deserted.

The sense of unreality grew stronger as they moved from room to room. He directed other units to secure the gardens, making sure that no one could escape and flee into the forest. It felt as if he hadn't brought anything like enough men to search the mansion properly. There were so many corridors and rooms that someone who knew the building well could probably stay ahead of them indefinitely, at least until they started isolating the chambers and deploying sensor drones. If he was any judge, there were probably bunkers and tunnels deep below the surface. The owners had probably decamped the moment the marines had hit the ground.

A figure appeared ahead of them, hands in the air. "Don't shoot! Don't shoot!"

Haydn swore under his breath. He'd come within a heartbeat of putting a bullet through the man's head. The newcomer was a cook, he thought; the man was dressed like a cook from a flick set in ancient times, right down to the silly white hat. He was overweight, something that made Haydn smile. His mother had always told him never to trust a thin cook. He wondered, sometimes, what she would have made of the marine chefs. They were thin, too.

Most cooks don't have to pick up rifles and start shooting, he thought, as the marines searched and bound the cook. *They don't have to work in the middle of a battle.*

"Please don't hurt us," the cook said. He looked terrified, as if he expected to be marched outside and shot. "Please…"

"Us?" Haydn frowned. "How many others are there?"

"The staff are inside," the cook babbled, waving a hand at the door. "Please don't hurt them."

"No one will be hurt," Haydn said, as reassuringly as he could. He raised his voice. "Come out with your hands up!"

He breathed another curse as the servants started to emerge from the giant kitchen. They were a strange bunch, dressed like people from another era. The manservants looked absurd, the maids looked sexy and yet…he shook his head in disbelief. The entire scene was surreal. The marines searched the prisoners, then marched them outside to wait. They'd be unhurt, Haydn told himself as the platoon resumed the search. There was nothing to be gained from hurting or killing them. They'd probably simply be held until the end of the war.

And hope their superiors don't punish them for being taken prisoner, Haydn thought. He'd fought terrorists and fanatics who'd shot their own people for daring to be taken captive. *Who knows what's happened to the poor bastards who wanted to go home?*

He heard a pair of explosions in the distance as they searched the rest of the mansion. The living quarters were huge, much larger than the palatial quarters offered to admirals and senators. There were a handful of rooms that were clearly designed for children, yet it was easy to tell they hadn't been so much as touched for decades. They looked like something out of a horror movie…Haydn shivered as he eyed a doll that was probably worth more than his annual salary. There was definitely something creepy about the place. It felt as if someone was putting on a show, rather than designing rooms for real life.

"Captain, we located a command centre," Mayberry reported. "The spooks want permission to go inside."

"Granted," Haydn said. He was fairly sure the remainder of the mansion was empty. The forward teams had rounded up more prisoners, and they'd captured a maid who'd literally hidden under a bed, but it felt as if the mansion had been seriously undermanned. "Ask the prisoners how many servants normally live in the building."

"Aye, sir," Mayberry said. There was a pause. "They say seventy, sir. We've captured fifty-two."

"If they feel talkative, see what else they'll tell us," Haydn said. He'd once dated a girl who'd worked for an aristocrat on a disputed world. She'd known more of what was going on than her mistress, let alone the spooks. "And inform me if any of it is tactically important."

He walked back downstairs. A forward team was already setting up a command post in what *looked* like a giant dance hall. Tables were being dragged into place and covered with terminals, communications equipment and everything else that might be needed to coordinate an offensive. Outside, he could hear rumbling as tanks and support vehicles moved into place. He paused in front of the display and studied the live feed from the drones. The space between the mansions and the megacity looked empty. He was morbidly sure that would change very quickly.

We didn't dare risk a full-scale bombardment, he thought. *We'd have killed too many civilians for too little return.*

"This mansion apparently belonged to the director himself, sir." Mayberry's voice echoed over the network. "The servants insist he should be here, but there's no sign of him. We know *someone* made it out."

Haydn frowned. "The aircar?"

He wasn't so sure. The director—the planet's ruler, to all intents and purposes—shouldn't have been *alone*. Effectively alone. Any halfway competent close-protection team wouldn't risk packing their principle into an aircar and flying through a storm of missiles and point defence, not if there was any other option. He was surprised they hadn't encountered any actual resistance. The only resistance the first wave had found had been a man with a deer rifle, who'd fired two shots and then surrendered. The locals clearly hadn't expected an actual invasion.

Certainly not here, he thought, grimly. As far as the locals had known, the marines had been light-hours away. *And yet, the director clearly got out before it was too late.*

He grimaced. *There will be no quick end to the war.*

CHAPTER EIGHTEEN

Indeed, the lumberjack has the lowest obligations as well as the lowest profits. The carpenter must invest in tools and materials to carve; the builder must invest in everything from glass for windows to pipes and suchlike to carry water into the house and waste to the sewers. He may even have to invest in sewers! Does it still seem unfair?
—**Professor Leo Caesius**
The Rise and Fall of Interstellar Capitalism

"WAKE UP!"

Rachel opened her eyes. A young man was peering down at her, wearing a uniform she didn't recognise. And she was bound…she nearly triggered her implants, she nearly broke his neck with a punch, before she realised she was merely strapped into a seat. She'd been asleep…she'd been on the space elevator pod. Where was she now?

She made a show of yawning as she looked around. The pod was being evacuated, command staff being hurried out the hatches and into the megacity. Rachel allowed the young man to unstrap her, then push her towards the nearest hatch. The pod was vibrating slightly, suggesting…suggesting what? Was someone trying to pull it back to orbit? Or was the anchor station coming apart at the seams? She had no idea.

"Over here," Commander Archer barked. "Quickly!"

Rachel hid her irritation as she stumbled over to him. The command staff were being marched through a set of corridors, passing through entry stations that looked to have been abandoned at very short notice. Her implants reported a number of pings from the sensors, interrogating the locator implants…she breathed a sigh of relief when alarms didn't start to go off immediately. Her cover remained intact, for the moment. The entire system was probably taking one hell of a beating. She made a mental note to do what she could to complete the fall. Wiping the security database would make it a great deal harder to monitor the population.

The scene outside the elevator base was chaotic. Soldiers and spacers ran everywhere, shouting loudly to make themselves heard over the din. Rachel saw a handful of trolleys crammed with supplies being pushed down the corridor, although it looked as though the orderlies didn't have the slightest idea where they were going. Senior officers were trying to restore order, but they didn't seem to be having much luck. Her lips quirked as they were marched through a pair of secure airlocks and dumped into a barracks. The corprats had probably carried out hundreds of emergency drills, but drills—no matter how detailed—always left out the *emergency*. She guessed the chain of command was pretty badly fragmented.

A mid-ranking officer stood on a chair. "Everyone who was in the command core, step through the blue airlock," he ordered. "Everyone else, stay here."

Rachel nodded to herself as she followed Commander Archer and the others through the airlock into another, smaller, chamber. A large holographic display dominated the room, a section darkened to indicate the absence of any live data. Rachel hoped that meant the invasion force had captured, blinded or destroyed the sensor platforms. Someone might be trying to be clever, but there was a time and a place and it *wasn't* when the entire plan was under attack. Her eyes narrowed as she studied the display. It looked as though groundside facilities had *also* been attacked.

General Gilbert stepped into view. He looked to have aged a decade overnight, his face so haggard that Rachel almost felt sorry for him. His superiors would *not* be pleased, if they survived long enough to demand answers. The corprats seemed to feel that *someone* should get the blame for everything, even if they'd done everything right and still lost. She felt the general's eyes lingering on her and tensed. Commander Archer had a roving eye and wandering hands, but General Gilbert had seemed a far better person. If he was taking an interest in her...

"What happened?" General Gilbert looked straight at Archer. "How did they hit us?"

Rachel concealed her amusement as Commander Archer stumbled through an explanation that was long on technobabble and short on anything useful. The wretched man was *completely* off his game. General Gilbert was no civilian who could be blinded by a barrage of military acronyms and corporate double-speak. He'd see right through the nonsense and be singularly unimpressed. Commander Archer's voice trailed off as his superior started to glare. He'd realised his mistake, too late.

General Gilbert looked at her. "And what do *you* think?"

"They tricked us," Rachel said. It was obvious, in hindsight. She wasn't saying anything the enemy post-battle assessment teams wouldn't say. "They used drones to keep us looking in the wrong direction, while sneaking up from a completely different direction. And they thought outside the box and converted a battlecruiser into a kamikaze ship."

"Madness," Commander Archer said. "They'd have to be insane!"

Rachel leaned forward. If she impressed the general...there was nothing the commander could do to her. His command staff had to have been fragmented, his subordinates scattered across the planet or trapped on the anchor station...he might need someone new.

"Sir, they practically *threw* the battlecruiser at the battlestation," she said. "It was no accident. They made no attempt to change course or even reduce speed. Instead, they closed the range to zero as fast as they could and rammed the battlecruiser into its target. The ship was probably under remote control."

General Gilbert raised his eyebrows. "You do realise that would be difficult?"

Rachel chose her next words carefully. "Sir, all they had to do was get the ship moving in the right direction and firing on every target that presented itself," she said. "They never planned to fight a conventional battle."

"True." General Gilbert looked at Archer. "This young lady is assigned to my staff. So are you. Bring two other orbit-qualified officers too. We're going to the command centre."

Rachel kept her face blank as Commander Archer favoured her with a nasty look. He wasn't pleased. Rachel had embarrassed him in front of his ultimate superior. She'd have to watch her back. If she was any judge, Commander Archer was too petty a man to let that pass unanswered. He'd start looking for a way to get back at her soon enough.

Commander Archer snapped commands at two other operators, both young and pretty, then strode down the corridor. Rachel followed, eyeing his back for the knife. She could probably arrange some kind of accident, perhaps rig evidence to suggest he'd screwed the pooch deliberately…she turned a handful of possibilities over and over in her mind as they walked into a giant command centre. It was larger than the command core on the anchor station, but considerably more chaotic. The holographic display showed hazy red icons on the surface. It was hard to be sure, but they looked alarmingly close.

They managed to land, then, she thought. She'd known there would be landings, but she hadn't been given any real details. What she didn't know she couldn't tell. *And they'll be advancing on the city soon enough.*

General Gilbert was a blur of activity, snapping out commands to operators as he paced the room. Commander Archer stood by the airlock, looking like a sulky little boy. Rachel wondered, idly, if he had any idea how he looked. No one would be impressed, if they saw him. But then, he didn't have anything to do. He had no duties, no nothing. It was just a matter of time until he was ordered to report to the personnel pool.

And that would be great for us, she thought. *He'll run for his life the moment the invaders start shooting.*

She put the thought out of her head as she studied the reports blinking up on the main display. The enemy had been caught by surprise, but they were rallying. She guessed anyone who didn't have duties elsewhere was being redirected to the personnel pool. If there was one advantage to the all-encompassing surveillance state, it was that they knew who was still alive and free. She'd have to do something about that, she decided as she was steered towards a console. The command and control systems were still unlocked. She nodded to herself as she took control of the system and studied the live feed from orbit. Given time, she could cause some real chaos. Given time…

...

Thaddeus had never been in a war. He'd never even been *close* to a war. His father had made it clear, when he was a young man, that there was no hope of anything resembling an exciting career. Thaddeus was doomed to enter the corporate ranks and climb to the top. He knew he'd issued orders that had killed people and stolen their lands—or worse—but he didn't much care. It was hard to comprehend, at times, that the numbers entered in the ledgers represented *real* people. They were just…*numbers*.

He felt numb as the aircar flew towards the megacity. His mansion, his home, had been violated. The marines had smashed their way into the mansion's hallowed halls and torn it to pieces, stamping their boots across his childhood home. He wanted to scream at the universe for allowing such an indignity to happen, but he knew it was completely pointless. There was nothing he could do about it. Or anything. He glanced at Julia, her expression grim as she steered the aircar onwards. She'd saved his life. Probably. There was a bunker under the mansion, but it lacked a direct connection to the megacity. The marines might not have caught him, yet they would have trapped him as surely as a lobster in a pot.

The aircar dropped to the ground. Thaddeus gritted his teeth, resisting the urge to groan even though it felt as though his stomach had been left behind. The vehicle slowed and landed neatly, far too close to a group of armed soldiers for comfort. It dawned on Thaddeus, suddenly, that law and order might have completely broken down. There was no shortage of people on the planet who detested him, just for being who and what he was. If he fell into their hands...

Julia stepped out of the aircar. "Take us to the command centre," she ordered. "At once."

The soldiers checked their ID implants, then hastily passed them to a senior officer who helped them into a groundcar and drove them into the megacity. The streets were churning with people, from civilians staring at the skies to refugees who hadn't been assigned to apartments and workplaces before the marines arrived. Thaddeus hoped they'd have the sense to stay out of the fighting. The marines had given his people a black eye—he conceded the point without much rancour—but they hadn't won. Not yet. Thaddeus promised himself, as they reached the command centre, that the corporation would retaliate. They couldn't have lost everything in a single, catastrophic battle.

He composed himself as they were shown into the command centre. General Gilbert looked about as bad as Thaddeus felt, but at least he was alive. Thaddeus was gloomily aware the Board of Directors was probably already looking for scapegoats—they'd put the search ahead of everything else, including planetary defence—yet right now they *needed* the general. He simply didn't have time to go looking for a new commander. And besides, it wasn't clear—yet—who was to blame. None of the tactical projections had included an invasion force landing within moments of its arrival...

"Director." General Gilbert looked tired, too. "If you'll come with me..."

Thaddeus followed him into a side room, Julia trotting at his heels. Something would have to be done to reward her, when he had the time. He briefly contemplated a selection of possible rewards, then dismissed the thought. Right now, they had more important problems. General Gilbert closed the door, darkened the lights and activated the holoprojector. The image of the megacity and the surrounding countryside was covered with red flecks of light.

"Fifty-two minutes ago, an enemy force crept up on our orbital defences and opened fire," General Gilbert said. "Through unprecedented tactics, they managed to take out Battlestation Alpha One, PDC Three and nearly everything else capable of hitting their ships; through copying *our* tactics, they landed a sizable body of troops on the surface."

"I know," Thaddeus said, harshly. He'd seen the smoke behind them as they fled. The mansion was burning. The bastards had probably done it deliberately. "They chased us here."

"Yes, sir," General Gilbert said. His finger traced a line on the map. "Right now, we think it's just a matter of time before they advance on the megacity. We can't stop them."

Thaddeus glared. "Are you telling me you don't have enough troops to keep them out?"

"Right now, the command network has been seriously degraded," General Gilbert said. "We never expected invasion, not like this. I'm in touch with a number of units, and they're readying themselves for deployment, but they're either out of place or simply unready for action. What forces I *do* have in the megacity are simply insufficient to the task."

Julia cleared her throat. "Why don't you ask the civilians to assist?"

"The average civilian is completely unarmed," General Gilbert reminded her. "There is no time to distribute weapons, even if we had them on hand *and* we trusted them to handle the weapons responsibly. There's certainly no time to make preparations for an insurgency."

Particularly one that could wind up aimed at us as easily as them, Thaddeus mused. He knew how to read a map. The marines were already on their way. *And we can't trust our own people to behave themselves.*

He looked at the general. "How do you intend to proceed?"

"I've deployed forces in hopes of slowing the marines long enough to rush most of our core personnel out of the city," General Gilbert said. "Everyone with some degree of military training, everyone who isn't already needed on the front lines, has orders to join the flood and head west. They'll be taken in by the army as it assembles to push the marines back out of the megacity. We can hold them, sir. We can hold them long enough for the remainder of the fleet to return."

"And then we crush them," Julia said. There was a hint of heavy satisfaction in her tone. "It sounds like a plan."

"I need your permission to destroy as much of the city's infrastructure as possible," General Gilbert added. "If we shut off water and power supplies, the marines are going to find it hard to govern the city…"

Thaddeus considered it for a long moment. He could see the logic. But he could also see hordes of starving people spreading across the land. There was no way they could get more than a tiny fraction of the population out before the marines sealed off the city and moved in for the kill. He'd heard all kinds of stories about cities that had been turned into death traps, bleeding the invaders white, but…they'd relied on the defenders having enough ammunition and time. He shook his head. The war was quite bad enough already.

"No," he said. "Destroy anything the marines can turn against us, if possible, but don't kill the civilians. We don't want to slaughter our own people."

"Yes, sir," General Gilbert said. He glanced at Julia, then back at Thaddeus. "You and your…assistant will be on the first transports out."

Thaddeus nodded. His assistant. Julia might like that. He'd discuss it with her when they had a moment. Right now, it wasn't important. "What about the rest of the board?"

"A handful have reported in," General Gilbert said. "I've advised them to refrain from making contact over the airwaves. The enemy has shown a terrifying willingness to target our leadership. They've also been inserting propaganda into the datanet. If you believe them, they represent the empire and they're here to liberate the planet."

"The empire is gone," Julia said, sharply.

"Yes," General Gilbert agreed. "But people can insert whatever damnfool nonsense they like into propaganda broadcasts. They're gleefully telling our entire population what happened at Hameau."

"I see." Thaddeus made a face. They'd been rumours, of course. A *lot* of rumours. And they'd all been suppressed, suggesting to anyone with an insightful mind that there was some truth in them. Now...the marines were telling a mixture of truth and lies and people would believe them because the corporate news was *all* lies. "Can't you push them out of the datanet?"

"I have teams working on it," General Gilbert said. "Unfortunately, we've had to unlock parts of the datanet to keep our systems online. It's not easy to boot them back out without booting ourselves out as well. Given time, we can isolate our command networks and then shut down all the other systems, but...it will have unfortunate effects on everything from communications to production."

"Either we hold out long enough to mount a counteroffensive or we try to come to terms with them," Thaddeus growled. He had no qualms about opening negotiations and stalling long enough to muster the fleet, but they weren't in a good position to do it. The marines didn't *have* to let them draw talks out as long as possible and they knew it. "We have no choice."

"No, sir," General Gilbert agreed.

His wristcom bleeped. He keyed it and frowned as he read the message, then looked up. "Sir, the enemy are moving towards the city limits. You have to go now."

Thaddeus nodded. "Make them pay," he said. He felt the anger bubble up within him. "General, whatever you do, make them pay."

CHAPTER NINETEEN

It does, again, to those who have never dealt with the problem at first hand. They see the wealth, the profits, and do not see the effort and expenditure that goes into creating that wealth. Indeed, it is capitalism that creates and maintains wealth. What is the difference between a piece of paper and a bank note? The answer is that society, as a whole, is convinced the bank note represents wealth.
—**Professor Leo Caesius**
The Rise and Fall of Interstellar Capitalism

MAJOR-GENERAL GERALD ANDERSON braced himself as the shuttle fell into the planet's atmosphere, flying through the gap in the enemy's defences. The latest reports suggested the enemy were trying to move more air defence vehicles and MADPAD teams into the cleared zone, but they'd clearly been caught by surprise. Gerald was pretty sure the marines would have done better, if they'd been jumped. If nothing else, they would have had a coherent plan for dealing with a full-scale invasion.

And no battle plan ever survives contact with the enemy, he thought. *The enemy, that dirty dog, has plans of his own.*

He forced himself to relax as the shuttle flew lower, then bottomed out a few seconds before it would have slammed into the ground. The compensator field twisted unpleasantly around him as it straightened out, then faded as the shuttle crashed to the ground. Gerald unstrapped himself and hurried for the hatch, followed by his staff. The reports from the ground suggested the enemy hadn't managed to start shelling the LZ yet, but it was just a matter of time. It was what Gerald himself would have done.

The mansion loomed over him as he double-timed it inside. There was no time to appreciate the building or the many fine artworks littered around the complex. The locals were lucky the marines weren't given to looting, although—if the reports were accurate—there weren't many local communities for thirty miles. He hoped the building would have enough value to the enemy they'd hesitate to fire on it...personally, he would have preferred to command the division from a hole in the ground. But they were short on options.

"Sir." Colonel Taggard nodded as Gerald stepped into the giant hall. "The first scout units are ready to go. Follow-up units are taking up position now."

"Good." Gerald studied the display for a long moment. It looked as though the enemy was trying to evacuate the megacity—it didn't even have a name, something that amused him more than it should—although it was hard to be sure. "How much resistance do you expect?"

"Unknown, sir," Taggard said. His finger isolated points on the map. "The enemy has been establishing defence lines, but they've clearly been thrown together at short notice. It looks like they don't have anything like enough firepower to do more than slow us down. We've captured maps of the city itself and located targets. Once the power stations and suchlike are in our hands, we can hold the rest of the city in an unbreakable grip."

"Deploy additional units to cut off their line of retreat," Gerald ordered. He doubted they'd snare anyone important, but he'd prefer to bottle up the enemy forces and deal with them before they had a chance to regroup and face the marines on even terms. "I take it there's been no response to our demands for surrender."

"No, sir," Taggard said. "It isn't even clear if the locals are *hearing* the demands."

"And they might be unable to surrender safely, either," Gerald agreed. He'd fought his way through enemy defences held by men who'd wanted to give up, but knew they'd be shot in the back by their own people if they tried. The locals wouldn't believe the marines could protect them until the marines actually had people on the streets. "We'll do what we can to give them a chance to surrender."

He took a seat and pasted a calm expression on his face. "Signal the forward units," he ordered. "They are cleared to begin the offensive."

...

It was hard, Rachel decided, not to feel a very definite flicker of admiration for General Gilbert. His staff had been shattered, half the units under his direct command had been unable or unwilling to report for orders, but he'd still managed to put together a workable plan. It looked cowardly—she'd overheard a couple of officers muttering nasty comments when they thought no one could hear—yet it was remarkably practical. And it had survived her best efforts. She'd sent a handful of units in the wrong directions, and quietly deleted a number of messages before they reached their destinations, but the plan was still going ahead.

Perhaps I should take him out and run, she thought. She'd downloaded maps of the city into her implants, and she would have no difficulty avoiding the passive security sensors, but she doubted she'd get out alive. There were just too many soldiers swarming the complex, weapons at the ready. *And if I stay here...*

She felt Commander Archer's eyes burning into the back of her neck and scowled. The asshole didn't know it, but he was being more effective than he'd been in years. She didn't dare make any overt *mistakes* while he was watching. The irony burned as she spied a handful of corprat leaders speaking to General Gilbert. One of them looked as if she'd been in a real fight. She'd torn her dress so badly Rachel could practically see her buttocks...

Ice washed through her as she *recognised* the corprat. Julia Ganister-Onge. She looked more ragged than Rachel remembered, when they'd last met face-to-face, but it was *her*. Rachel tensed, hoping Julia wouldn't see through her disguise. She looked very different, yet…Julia's eyes washed over her without showing the slightest hint of recognition. Rachel breathed a silent sigh of relief as she turned her attention back to her console, just as alarms started to ring. The offensive they'd feared for the past two hours was finally starting to begin.

"Alright, everyone." General Gilbert's voice echoed through the chamber. "You have your orders. Evacuate to the buses and don't look back."

Rachel keyed a switch on her console, then stood and joined the throng. She'd programmed a small virus into the system—really, it was barely large enough to be called a virus—but she hadn't dared use it until they were heading out of the chamber. General Gilbert's crews would be wiping and then smashing datanodes, trying to make sure they didn't leave anything behind that would help the marines. They didn't have time for a proper clean-up, Rachel thought, but they'd do their best before they ran too. Unless they intended to stay behind…

It might not last very long, if they do, she mused. She'd had a chance to take the measure of the population monitoring and control system. It was surprisingly robust, at least for the moment. *Once we take command of the system, we can use it ourselves.*

She kept her face impassive as they marched down the building and into the courtyard. A line of giant hoverbuses waited for them, their engines already humming loudly. She was mildly surprised the corprats hadn't gone for something simpler, like most colony worlds, although she had a feeling it was yet another form of social control. She could fix a simple car from a stage-one colony world with ease, but not a modern system. The corprats didn't want their people having any sense of independence. Bastards.

Commander Archer barked orders as the staff scrambled onto the buses. Rachel took a seat and watched, through the window, as the vehicle hovered into the air and then glided onto the streets. The pavements were lined with vehicles, a handful showing signs of recent damage that suggested their owners had suddenly realised they only *rented* them. The traffic control system had taken over and steered them out of the way, then parked and shut down the vehicles completely.

A voice echoed through the loudspeakers. "Stay off the streets. Stay in your homes."

Rachel frowned. Here and there, she could see people defying the order. Fewer than she'd expected, really, but she supposed it make sense. The locals saw their government as an omnipresent monster, with eyes and ears everywhere. Big Brother, on steroids. She hadn't even known that book existed until she'd joined the corps, let alone been allowed to read it. *1984* hadn't been so much banned as comprehensively forgotten.

Commander Archer sat next to her. "I've got my eye on you," he growled, as the bus picked up speed. "Don't think you're so great just because the general listened to you."

Rachel shrugged and looked out of the window. Right now, she had other problems. The invaders would be surrounding the city, unless someone had decided to risk charging straight into unknown territory to seize the elevator. There was a very real chance they'd be intercepted, bringing her mission to an inglorious end. It would be embarrassing as hell. The others would never let her forget being captured by her fellow marines… she wondered, again, what had happened to them. Were they alive? Or hidden away within enemy ranks?

She felt a hand on her thigh. It was child's play to pretend to shudder, to make him think he was getting to her. She'd seduced people before, for the corps, but…she made a silent promise that she was *really* going to kill him. Or ensure he got the blame for something…she tossed ideas around in her head as the bus moved onto the motorway, heading west. A constant stream of cars was leaving the city. She couldn't help thinking of rats leaving a sinking ship.

They can run, but they can't hide, she told herself. *And they know the corps is after them.*

THE HALLS OF MONTEZUMA

...

"Incoming!"

Haydn ducked as a missile flew over his head and crashed down somewhere to the rear of the platoon. The enemy defence lines were weak, but they seemed to be making good use of what they had. They fired a handful of shots at the approaching marines, then scarpered before the marines could pin them down and destroy them. He would have been more impressed if they hadn't been slowing the advance down. The timetable was more than a little vague—the whole plan of attack had been thrown together on very short notice—but it was still frustrating. His peers would never let him forget it if his unit was the last to finish its mission.

The enemy town might have been a nice place to live, once. Now…it had been converted into a strongpoint. He hoped—prayed—the local civilians had had a chance to escape before their dwellings had been repurposed. He couldn't help feeling bad as he hurled a HE grenade into a small house, the kind of building that would have suited a young couple and their children. The defenders hadn't really had a chance to pile up sandbags, remove the glass and do any of the hundreds of other things they needed to do to turn the house into a real strongpoint. The grenade exploded, blowing the walls away and collapsing the roof. He knew he'd destroyed someone's hopes and dreams…

He pushed the thought aside as they pushed through the town. There was no time to be gentle, no time to wrinkle the defenders out while leaving most of the buildings intact. They crashed through a school, hurling more grenades to take out anyone who might be inside before they could escape. A pair of tanks rumbled past, their main guns firing shells towards the distant megacity. Some bright spark on the other side had placed snipers in the towering buildings. The local population was going to pay the price.

The company reached the edge of the town and pressed on towards the power plant. The station had to be captured intact, before the enemy thought to destroy it…or, worse, triggered a major explosion. It was supposed to be impossible to make a fusion core explode, but Haydn had seen it done. And the power plant was right next to the megacity. He tensed as bullets cracked through the air, one hand dropping automatically to the grenades at his belt before he caught himself. They couldn't start hurling HE grenades around a power plant! They'd destroy the systems they needed to keep the power plant online.

He keyed his throatmike and muttered orders. The plant was huge, but—seemingly—a fairly standard design. The inner core would be completely sealed, unless whoever had put the system together was a complete lunatic. The outer layers were armoured too, but they weren't anything like as solid. If they could take the command centre, they could take over the station and shut down the power to the city. It could be worse. They could be assigned to the water purification plant.

Bracing himself, he threw himself forward and into the enemy line. The defenders had no time to react before he cut them down. His men followed, rushing towards the main entrance. There were no convenient windows, not here. The power plant was designed to be as secure as humanly possible. Anyone who wanted to enter had to go through one of two entrances or give up. He eyed the door as reports flowed in from the other units. The power distribution centre was in their hands. If the power plant crew refused to give up, they'd find themselves isolated anyway.

Mayberry worked on the door, packing explosives into the hinges. Haydn felt uncomfortable, even though he *knew* it wasn't as if they were going to crack open the reactor itself. The door shuddered as the charges detonated, then fell to the ground with an almighty *crash*. Haydn hurled a stun grenade into the chamber and waited for it to detonate, then hurried in. The plant's interior was as standard as the rest of it. They had no trouble finding the control room.

"Get away from those consoles," Haydn barked. The operators looked scared, but did as they were told. "Keep your hands on your heads."

He snapped commands to the engineers, ordering them to take control. It wasn't clear if the reactor control system could be isolated from the rest of the planetary network or not. The locals might just shut the whole system down, rather than let the marines keep the occupied city alive. Haydn dreaded to think about what might happen if they decided to screw around with the power systems. Hundreds of thousands, perhaps millions, of people would be at risk.

"Sir," Lieutenant Packer said. "The system has been isolated."

"Very good." Haydn breathed a sigh of relief. "Are the follow-up crews on the way?"

"Yes, sir," Packer said. "They're having to take the long way around, but they're on their way."

Haydn nodded. The marines were steadily surrounding the city, but they hadn't eliminated all the pockets of resistance between the LZ and the megacity itself. They'd have to be dealt with, if they weren't already retreating. Haydn wouldn't have bet against it. The enemy had been caught by surprise, but they'd reacted well. He suspected it wouldn't be long before they started harassing the LZ itself.

"Once they're here, hand over the prisoners and see what they have to say," he ordered, curtly. It was unlikely the prisoners knew much, but they had to be sure. "And then try and get into their system."

He smiled, coldly. It would be hard for the enemy to deny the evidence of their own eyes, once the marines started moving into the city itself. It was possible the locals would join the marines, or simply rise up against their government. It was also possible they'd stay on the sidelines and do nothing. It was the safest course of action, the best thing they could do until they knew who'd won the war.

"And then we'll be heading onwards," he added. "The city is waiting for us."

...

"Sir," Taggard said. He sounded pleased. "The city has been surrounded. The support systems are under our control."

"Good," Gerald said. He hadn't expected to lose the string of minor engagements, but the enemy could have made him pay a far higher price for their facilities. "I take it there's still been no reply to our demands for surrender?"

"No, sir," Taggard said. "We cut off their line of retreat, but..."

Gerald made a face. It was generally considered wise *not* to keep the enemy from retreating, unless one was sure one had an overwhelming advantage. The enemy would fight to the last if it thought it couldn't surrender or retreat. And yet, he hadn't seen any choice. They had to keep the enemy from rebalancing themselves as long as possible.

"Pass the word," he ordered. "The assault is to go ahead, as planned."

He felt his expression grow darker as he studied the display. The megacity was huge. He couldn't afford to put boots on the ground everywhere, not if he needed to continue the offensive into enemy territory. He'd seize a few key spots, then leave the rest alone. He prayed, silently, that the local population would behave itself. The key to keeping unrest from turning into open resistance was to crack down hard, but he simply didn't have the manpower. It was going to take far too long to bring down the rest of the mobile divisions...

We could always try to make a few more dumpsters, he thought. He was relieved, and surprised, the plan had worked as well as it had. They'd come far too close to losing one of the dumpsters to enemy fire. *But that would be just too risky.*

CHAPTER TWENTY

This makes a degree of sense. A large-scale barter economy simply doesn't work. The cobbler cannot trade his shoes for food if the farmer doesn't want or need shoes. Indeed, he cannot obtain leather from the tanner if he has nothing to offer in exchange. Why would the tanner give the leather for free? He wouldn't.
—**Professor Leo Caesius**
The Rise and Fall of Interstellar Capitalism

"I FEEL ALMOST HUMAN AGAIN," Julia muttered.

The maid looked up. "I beg your pardon, my lady?"

Julia shook her head, silently dismissing the maid. She'd had a nap during the flight to the corporate HQ, then a shower as soon as she'd been assigned a room and an attendant. It would be a long time before she ever felt truly safe again—she'd never thought to see enemy troops tramping across the planet, let alone coming for her with blood in their eyes—but she felt she'd done well. She'd certainly saved the director from being captured and forced to order a surrender. Or being killed out of hand. She had no idea what the marines intended to do with the corporate elite.

She towelled herself down, then dressed. The maid had laid out a selection of dresses, most more suitable for the dance floor than a corporate boardroom, but Julia chose the suit and tie. It was not the time to appear as anything but a level-headed businesswoman. She'd saved the director, yet she knew that would only go so far. Too many corporate leaders wouldn't thank her for saving their superior. They would never say anything out loud, but they'd think they could have stepped into his shoes. She finished dressing, tied back her hair into a tight ponytail, and headed for the door. A pair of armed guards fell into position beside her as she made her way down to the boardroom.

Her heart sank as she passed dozens of soldiers and operators running around the complex like headless chickens. None of them had ever expected to be facing a full-scale invasion either, not when the orbital defences should have delayed an enemy force long enough for the military to prepare itself—mentally as well as physically—for the task ahead. Hell, there'd been good reason never to expect a hostile landing. The corporation practically controlled large swathes of the former empire. What it didn't control, it could bribe. Why would anyone expect the empire to launch an invasion? It would be literally killing the goose that laid the golden eggs.

Not that the empire was ever big on common sense, she reflected. She'd been taught how the empire's elite would snatch control of profitable industries from their founders and drive them into the ground. It wasn't malicious, although the founders probably couldn't have told the difference. It was sheer stupidity. *They might think that a costly invasion somehow made sense.*

She walked past a row of terminals, manned by operators who were gabbling quietly into throatmikes. Holographic images flickered around her, some taken from orbital satellites and others from active sensors in the combat zone. She saw a row of tanks advancing along a road, escorted by armed men who constantly scanned the horizon for threats. Behind them, a flight of shuttles flew overhead and landed somewhere to the east. The marines were steadily landing their troops and spreading out. By now, they probably controlled both the anchor station and the planetary terminus. It was only a matter of time until they started sending their troops down the space elevator to the surface.

They don't have unlimited troops, she reminded herself. *They might find that occupying a whole planet is beyond them.*

She composed herself as she passed a cluster of senior officers, speaking in low voices, and walked into the boardroom. A handful of senior directors glanced at Julia, then ignored her. Julia was almost offended, even though she knew she should have expected it. She'd been the most powerful person on the battlecruiser, outranking even the admiral in command of the fleet, but here...she was somewhere below the maids. The maids were probably regarded as more useful. They, at least, were bringing coffee. She smiled at the thought, then took a seat next to the top chair. The director entered a moment later. Julia almost smiled at how quickly the others snapped to attention. The director was *important*.

"Be seated." Thaddeus Onge walked to the head of the table and sat down. He'd clearly had a shower, a change and something to eat. "General Gilbert. Do you have an updated report?"

"Yes, sir," General Gilbert said. He took control of the holographic projector and displayed a map. A red haze—it looked almost like a bloodstain—blurred the land. "As you can see, the marines have secured control of the corporate district and placed Roxon City in a vise. The last reports have made it clear that they're doing their best to maintain a light footprint, but they've occupied the vast majority of critical targets and—therefore—have the city under effective control."

Julia studied him thoughtfully. General Gilbert looked as if he was already on the verge of giving up. He'd passed the stage of being reluctant to give bad news to his corporate masters. *That* wasn't a good sign. Gilbert wasn't *that* much older than Admiral Agate, but he looked and sounded older. If he was giving up...she knew, all too well, that someone had to take the blame. There was no way anyone could *reasonably* blame Gilbert for not foreseeing the marine invasion, but...what did reason matter when there was blame to be placed?

The director frowned. "Are our people not resisting the invasion?"

"We have a handful of deep-cover agents in place, who are attempting to keep us informed," Gilbert said. "They report a considerable amount of looting, civil unrest and—worse—score-settling, but so far the marines have not faced any real resistance. The vast majority of the population is unarmed, director, and unlikely to encounter a marine even if they were. I think there will be more unrest as the marines come to grips with the problem of feeding a megacity, but that will take some time to materialise."

He grimaced. "The marines will also be able to make use of our population control systems," he added. "They'll be able to quash resistance before it becomes dangerous."

"I thought the systems were meant to be destroyed," a director said. She thought she recognised him, but his name escaped her. "Why were they left intact?"

"The computer cores were earmarked for destruction," Gilbert said. "I believe that somewhere between sixty to eighty percent of the command and control datacores *were* destroyed, although it is hard to be sure. Destroying the physical monitors, on the other hand, was impossible. Given time, the marines can simply plug in their own command and control systems and reactive the physical gear. There's very little we can do about it."

"Incompetence," the director snarled.

Julia hid her irritation. She didn't know the director, and she was fairly sure he was light years above her, but she didn't like him. No one had believed there would come a time when the population monitoring systems would have to be destroyed, if only to keep them from falling into enemy hands. General Gilbert could hardly be blamed for failing to destroy them during the retreat. It simply hadn't been possible.

"Not now." Director Onge held up a hand, then looked at another director. "Maryanne, how are our people handling the news?"

"We've instituted a complete media blackout, but there's no way to hide either the flood of refugees making their way along the motorways or the pieces of debris falling from the skies," Vice Director Maryanne Mayan said, grimly. "Officially, the general population knows nothing. We blacked out enough of the enemy broadcasts to keep them from reaching receptive ears. Practically, they know *something* is happening and rumours are spreading rapidly. People are talking, Director, and there's nothing we can do about it. I think we need to make *some* kind of announcement, if only to quell fears."

Which might not be possible, Julia thought. *How many people will side with the marines when they are offered the choice?*

"There will be panic," Gilbert predicted. "We need to continue the call-up without incident."

"We'll have to tell the population something, and quickly," Maryanne said. "It's only a matter of time until the datanet gets hacked."

"We'll consider it later," the director said. "General, can we stop the marines?"

"Yes, sir," Gilbert said. "I believe we can stop them."

Julia kept her face blank. Admiral Agate had said the same thing, so long ago it felt like another life. And he'd been wrong. The marines had traded space for time until they'd gotten the troops where they wanted them, then dropped the hammer. They'd effectively won the war in a single catastrophic battle.

Gilbert indicated the map. "Right now, we expect the marines to take some time to regroup before they push onwards. They will be bringing down their troops and equipment as fast as possible, but they're going to run up against some very hard limits. We can keep them from using the space elevator, for example, by threatening to fire on the elevator cars if we see them moving. They *have* cleared a corridor to the surface, to give them due credit, but they've shot their bolt. They cannot widen the corridor any further. This puts additional stresses and strains on their logistics. Our worst-case projections indicate it will be at least a week before they can resume the offensive."

Julia leaned forward. "What if they use dumpsters?"

"We think that, if they had more dumpsters, they would have used them by now," Gilbert said. "Dumpsters, by their very nature, are dangerous. They're designed for equipment that can be easily replaced, not people.

Using them is a dangerous gamble. The marines would understand the risk as well as we do."

"That didn't stop the marines from using them," Julia pointed out.

"No," Gilbert agreed. "But there comes a time when the risks outweigh the rewards."

He tapped the map. "They simply don't have the forces to occupy the entire planet, so we're assuming their goal—now they failed to capture our leadership—is to snatch or destroy the planetside industrial centers and PDCs. If they succeed, they will win…either directly or simply by destroying our ability to make war. Accordingly, we are settling up defence lines along the motorways—his hand traced lines on the map—and massing our forces for a counterattack. If they come at us, we'll lure them into a maze of defences intended to bleed them white and eventually destroyed them; if they stay where they are, we'll harass them until the fleet is reunited and then destroy their fleet. At that point"—he smiled, coldly—"their forces on the ground can surrender or die."

"Die," the director said. "We have no use for them."

"Let us wait until we win before deciding their fate," Thaddeus said, dryly. "General, it is *imperative* we drive them off-world as quickly as possible."

"I understand, sir," Gilbert said. "But it takes time to call up everyone with military experience, establish defence lines and ready ourselves for the coming engagement. We will win, I believe, but it will take longer than you might think."

"Unless the fleet gets back sooner," Julia said.

"The fleet will need to be reunited first," Gilbert said. "If the ships return one at a time, the marines will pick them off one by one. They got very lucky with the timing."

He paused. "Director, I would like to declare a full, planet-wide state of emergency. We need to do more than just call up everyone with military experience. We need to put everyone to work digging trenches and evacuating townships that cannot be defended, before we try to turn them into strongpoints. And we need to start handing out weapons to people who might find themselves in occupied territory."

"Out of the question," a director snarled. "Do you have any idea how much trouble that would cause?"

Julia smiled, behind her hand. *Do you have any idea how much trouble a full-scale invasion will cause?*

"It will not be easy to maintain control over the population if you're putting them to work," Maryanne said, slowly. "They do not love us, General."

General Gilbert looked at her, evenly. "Hard choices must be made," he said. "The enemy is at the gates. We must hang together or the marines will hang us separately."

...

Thaddeus was not given to hasty decisions. It was something he'd always considered a strength, although he was starting to realise it could also be a weakness. There was time to consider the best course of action when the enemy was light years away, but little time for contemplation when the enemy was at his throat. He'd never expected to be chased from his mansion, not without plenty of warning. He hadn't even taken *basic* precautions to safeguard himself. If Julia hadn't been there, he would have fallen into enemy hands.

He said nothing for a long moment, allowing the directors to argue amongst themselves. He could see both sides of the argument; he could see that both sides had a point. They risked an uprising if they armed the workers, but—at the same time—they *needed* to arm the workers. He doubted there would be any resistance if the workers *couldn't* resist. The marines would have no trouble putting the workers back to work. His lips twitched sardonically as he remembered working his way up the ranks, back when the universe had made sense. It was astonishing what people would do when they were staring down the barrel of a gun. They'd say anything, do anything, sign anything...

His eyes scanned the table. Julia's opinion didn't matter. General Gilbert was seriously outranked by the rest of the table. And the directors seemed split down the middle. Thaddeus silently assessed the situation, wondering who would be the first to try to jump ship. *Someone* would, in his experience. There was always someone wanting to make sure they wound up on top, even if it meant switching sides and leaving their former allies to fight alone. Who would it be? He didn't know. He'd be surprised if the entire table wasn't at least *considering* how to switch sides.

And they'll know how to circumvent the population control systems, he mused. The directors wouldn't take kindly to suggestions they should be watched at all times. That was for the little people. *There's no way even to move against them unless I had solid proof they were planning to commit treason.*

"I think we don't have a choice," he said. "At the very least, we should start putting teenage boys to work digging trenches."

He sighed, inwardly. The schools were designed to turn out the next generation of corporate worker drones. Students who showed hints of rebellion were often steered into the army, the navy or—at worst—quietly sent into exile. The teenagers who were willing to fight were already in the army or earmarked for military service. He cursed Admiral Agate under his breath, not for the first time. The admiral had lost so many trained men that training up new soldiers wasn't going to be easy.

And if we give them guns without proper training and indoctrination, he thought, *they might turn on us instead.*

"Yes, sir," Gilbert said. "However, we will require far more manpower than we have on hand…"

"Start drawing up plans to conscript more," Thaddeus ordered. He looked at the map. "We cannot let the marines keep tearing through our defences."

"I understand," Gilbert said.

Do you? Thaddeus kept his face impassive. *Sooner or later, something is going to break.*

He looked at Vice Director Vincent Adamson. "Draw up an announcement to the general population," he said. "Make sure you convince them that the situation is serious, but is being handled. We don't want them getting the idea we're going to lose. And start preparing them for enemy propaganda. The marines will get their message into the datanet sooner or later."

"Perhaps we should lock down the datanet completely," Vice Director Hayden James McManus said. "The marines have probably captured datanodes in Roxon. They can figure out how to hack the system if they haven't already."

"The system limited our response to the invasion," Gilbert said, sharply. "We had to unlock sections of the military datanet just to rally the troops. Tightening things up now will only cause further confusion and delay, at the worst possible moment."

"I thought it was possible to put an entirely separate military datanet together," McManus snapped. "I was told..."

"Yes," Gilbert said. "We have contingency plans. But we never anticipated having to put one together under fire..."

"Fucking incompetence," McManus snapped. "If you'd been thinking..."

"Enough." Thaddeus spoke quietly, but with immense force. "We don't have time to bicker. Not now. We have too many other problems."

He stood. "You know what to do," he said. "We'll reconvene tomorrow unless something changes."

The meeting broke up as he headed for the door, Julia falling into place behind him. He ignored her as he contemplated his allies, wondering which one would be the first to make contact with the marines. Some of them owed their positions to him, others had been appointed by the Grand Senator himself...he sighed, inwardly. It didn't matter. The moment the rats decided the ship was sinking, they'd throw caution to the winds and try to get off.

And we have to win quickly, he thought. He couldn't avoid the thought. *Or the marines may destroy our society even if we drive them off our world.*

CHAPTER TWENTY-ONE

Money—in whatever form—takes the local economy to the next level. The cobbler sells his shoes, then uses the profits to pay the tanner for the leather and the farmer for food. It doesn't matter that neither the tanner nor the farmer wants or needs shoes. All that matters is that they have something they can trade themselves.
—**Professor Leo Caesius**
The Rise and Fall of Interstellar Capitalism

"KEEP WORKING," COMMANDER ARCHER ORDERED. "Don't take your eyes off the console."

Rachel hid her amusement as the older man stamped up and down, barking orders as if he thought his subordinates would slack off without a great deal of encouragement. She suspected that half the staffers were already working as slowly as they dared, even though there *was* a war on. People like Commander Archer tended to provoke resentment and hatred even when they *didn't* have wandering hands. His staff might not be able to strike openly, but they'd do whatever they could to make the bastard look bad.

Be grateful, she told herself. *You don't want someone smarter assigned to the role.*

She kept her face under tight control as she worked her way through file after file. General Gilbert was doing his level best to regroup his forces, fill in the gaps in his order of battle and prepare for the coming engagement. She had to admit he was doing a good job, although the problems of regrouping under enemy fire would have made the task hellish even without her sabotage. She'd deleted a handful of orders before they ever reached their destination, she'd added transhipment instructions to send desperately-needed supplies to the other side of the planet and carefully altered a number of files to ensure that experienced people were not called up for war. The enemy was so reliant on their datanet, she mused, that it was nothing more than a giant blindspot. She dreaded to think what would happen to any marine officer who became so dependent on something outside his control.

Shooting would be too good for him, she mused. She'd served a term in logistics herself and she *knew* how easy it was for some dingbat staffer to swear blind his depot was full, even when the shelves had been stripped bare years ago. It was almost pathetically easy for a corrupt man to sell off his supplies, then lie to his superiors. The marines had learnt the hard way never to take anything on faith. *People put garbage into the system and they get garbage out.*

She continued to work her way through the files, carefully redirecting a stock of antiaircraft missiles to launchers on the other side of the defence lines. It was a plausible mistake, particularly as she wasn't supposed to know where the air defence units were going. She doubted it would matter, if they realised what she'd done. They'd arrest her for being an idiot and... she'd have to fight her way out. It wouldn't be easy. They'd been gathering troops around the HQ for nearly a week now. She knew she was good, but was she good enough?

The bell rang. Rachel tapped her console, hiding the evidence of her tinkering, then handed the system over to her relief. It still astonished her how little the corprat staffers knew of what actually happened *inside* the computers. They took them far too much on faith. She was careful to avoid

Commander Archer's eye as she stood and left the chamber, heading down to the barracks assigned to the general's staff. Commander Archer had a briefing in an hour, according to his schedule. She had no doubt he'd take all the credit for the staff work. Her lips twitched into a smile, despite herself, as she reached the barracks. *That* was going to bite him, when his superiors discovered his department had played host to a saboteur. He'd have some problems explaining if he'd taken credit for everything.

A chill ran down her spine as she walked into the barracks itself. She'd slept in smaller places—and filthier places—but the barracks was creepy. She hadn't needed her training to spot the security monitors, positioned neatly to cover every last inch of the compound. There was no way to hide, even when one was on the toilet. No one spoke, for fear they might be overheard and misunderstood. Rachel hid her dismay, even though it worked in her favour. The more she talked to her peers, the greater the chance of saying something that would lead to her exposure.

She undressed quickly, feeling a twinge of sympathy for the locals. They had no privacy, nowhere to hide…she remembered, grimly, just how badly the surveillance system had been abused on Hameau. The monitors had been spying on everyone, including children…she felt sick at the very thought. They'd been abused here too, unless she missed her guess. The idea of a completely clean, completely incorrupt, security service was nothing more than a dream. There was always a tendency towards playing stormtrooper, towards becoming a peeping Tom…towards thinking that one knew what was best for one's people. She made a face as she climbed into her bunk and closed her eyes. The planetary broadcasts had been bland to the point of complete uselessness. No one *really* knew what was happening outside their own little worlds.

Which works in my favour, she told herself as she accessed the datanet through her implants and started to work her way through the files. *No one questions their orders for fear of looking bad.*

She felt her heart sink as she studied the files. The population monitoring system watched *everyone*. It ran an incredibly complex series of algorithms to determine who might pose a threat to the established order, then flag them for human intervention. She doubted the system was anything like as effective as the designers claimed, given the inability to make the jump to a true AI. The majority of suspects were nothing more than grumblers, if that. And yet...she tried not to grimace as she realised just how badly the algorithms could screw up their lives. A person who was regarded as suspect could be denied everything from promotion to travel and banking services, their lives destroyed at the push of a button. And people *trusted* the system. They wouldn't bother to actually *think* before they hit the switch to cancel the suspect.

Rachel shook her head in disbelief, then started to compose two messages. The first one would be mailed out to everyone on the suspect list, from people who were on the verge of being cancelled to people who'd grumbled once and never again. She composed it carefully, adding warnings about the danger of reporting the message to higher authority even if one refused to join the rebellion. The *supposed* rebellion. There was a good chance that at least *some* of the suspects would think the message was a sting, but it was unlikely the message could be traced back to her. She'd been tempted to try to blame everything on Commander Archer... she dismissed the thought before she could put it into practice. Better the message seemed to come out of nowhere. If the enemy locked down the datanet, it would hamper them more than anything else.

She sent the message, wondering how many people would reply—and how many people would report it. There was no way to know. The algorithms were so deeply flawed, and yet so pervasive, that there was a good chance that most of the suspects were nothing more than false positives. Rachel had been in the corps long enough to know that everyone grumbled, everyone. The grumbling didn't always mean there was about to be a mutiny. But a bad reaction to grumbling tended to make it worse.

The die is cast, she thought. *And now...*

She put the second message together a little more carefully. The message would go directly to each and every one of the ex-imperial personnel, reminding them of their former loyalties and offering them the chance to switch sides. She was *entirely* sure the security services would pick up on the message, but doing something about it wouldn't be easy. If they treated the ex-imperial personnel with suspicion, they might trigger off a mutiny; if they removed them from positions of power, they'd hamper their war effort...if they ignored the message, they'd give an ambitious little toad a chance to start plotting. Rachel had few illusions about the ex-imperial personnel. Some of them would have been hired for competence, but others would be hellishly ambitious. Who knew how much trouble they'd cause?

If I can keep them second-guessing themselves, she mused, *it'll make it harder for them to organise resistance.*

She carefully worked her way through the system, trying to ensure the blame fell on an ex-imperial officer of uncertain competence. He'd be primed for interrogation, she was sure; he'd tell his interrogators the complete truth, yet they'd never believe him. Why would they, when he'd been prepared to handle everything from direct brain contact to old-fashioned torture? She'd been tempted to try to pin the blame on General Gilbert, but she'd resisted. He would have been thoroughly vetted before being promoted to his current position. There was too great a chance the security services would realise they were being spoofed.

Not that it matters, she thought, as she disconnected herself and drifted off to sleep. *They'll have to take the threat seriously...*

• • •

Harrison Clines, Assistant Vice Production Director, was not having a good day. He'd come into the office to discover a handful of his most trusted personnel had been called up for military service, creating a series of delays that would look very bad on his annual performance review. He'd been hoping to be promoted up the ladder, but that wasn't going to happen unless he managed to fill the holes and boost production once again. He knew what he needed to do, yet...it was impossible. He'd spent the entire morning trying to find replacements, only to discover there were none to be had.

It looked as though all the trained and experienced personnel had been recruited for the military, leaving the factory manned by button-pressers and floor-cleaners. Things would remain stable, as long as nothing broke down. He had a nasty feeling something *was* going to break.

He scowled as he stamped past his secretary and walked into his office. The Vice Production Director, a cast-iron bitch if ever there was one, had torn a strip off him. It hadn't been *his* fault that all available spare parts had been rerouted to the military. It hadn't been *his* fault that they'd received a series of rush orders from the government at the same time they'd lost the ability to handle them. But the bitch hadn't cared. She was hoping for a seat on the Board of Directors and *that* wouldn't happen if she was blamed for the problems. No…she was passing the blame to him. Harrison had no doubt she was already putting together a paper trail that blamed everything on him, a string of lies that no one would dare question too openly. He sat down, opened his drawer and removed the bottle of wine he'd concealed there weeks ago. If there ever a situation that called for a stiff drink, it was this one…

The terminal bleeped, indicating a priority message had arrived. Harrison gritted his teeth in frustration. He was important, damn it. His secretary should handle all such matters. No one would be sending him priority messages unless it was truly important…unless it was his wife. He had no idea how he was going to face her, when he finally went home. She had her heart set on being a director's wife and…if she knew her husband wouldn't be climbing any higher…who knew what she'd do? Bitch and moan, probably. He silently kicked himself for marrying her. Sure, her family had connections, but not *enough* connections. There were younger men on the management teams who would probably jump past him, thanks to *their* connections. Bastards.

He let out a sigh as the terminal bleeped again. He'd better read the message before it was too late. His wife would know, somehow, if he left it untouched. And if it was an urgent governmental message…they'd know. He stared at the walls, all too aware there were few blind spots in the office.

There was no way to be *sure* he'd missed something, when he'd checked the room for bugs. For all he knew, one of them had been carefully hidden to lull him into a false sense of security. It was what the security bastards would do. They spent all their time trying to catch people saying things they shouldn't...

The message unfolded in front of him. *Greetings. If you are reading this message, you are on a list of possible subversives. You are under suspicion. Be aware that receiving this message will be counted against you, even if you report it to the security services. They will not give you the benefit of the doubt. We will. This message has been wiped from the datanodes as it made its way to you. It will be wiped from your datanode shortly too. If you choose to ignore it, we will respect your choice. If you choose to report it...you will be putting yourself in the hands of the security services. You can consider for yourself the possible consequences.*

Harrison felt his heart skip a beat. What? What was...? His thoughts ran in circles. Who'd sent the message to him? And why? Was it a trap? Was he meant to report it? Or would the mere fact of receiving the message be held against him? He didn't know.

The message continued. *We are the underground. We intend to overthrow the current order and replace it with something better, free of the corprats and their peeping Tom security services. We feel that you, a possible subversive, might be interested in joining us. If you reply to this message, we will take it as an expression of interest. If not, you will still receive messages from time to time. We ask you to consider ways you can assist us in building a better world...*

"Shit." Harrison caught himself a moment later. "I..."

He shook his head as he read the last few lines. Who *were* these people? He'd heard rumours of an underground, of course, but nothing concrete. The security services were damn good at rooting out dissidence...his heart seemed to jump as he realised *he* was on a list. He...what the hell did they think he'd done? He'd spoken sharply to one of his contractors...was that it? Or was it when he'd tried to keep his trained personnel from joining the military and getting themselves killed? Or...or what? Had he talked in his sleep? Paranoia washed through him as he reread the message. Who could be trusted? Maybe his secretary had reported him. She'd seemed a little less enthusiastic, last time he'd bent her over the desk and fucked her... perhaps she hadn't really *wanted* it. He swallowed, hard. What should he do? Reply to the message? Or ignore it and hope the underground, if it was the underground, went away? He just didn't know.

The message glowed on his terminal. He thought the screen was concealed from prying eyes, but what if he was wrong? The underground might want him, yet...what if it wasn't the underground? What if it was a test of loyalty? If he sent the reply, he might be confirming that he was a dissident...his heart pounded in his chest. What was he to do? If he made the wrong call, it would kill him. And yet...

Heart thudding, he made his decision.

• • •

"Did you hear the news?"

Rachel looked up, sourly. It was easy to pretend she hadn't slept well. The barracks were uncomfortable even by military standards. The shower dribbled and the towels were rough and the food...it put her in mind of the joke about men deserting when they were threatened with field rations. It hadn't struck her as funny until she'd seen what the Civil Guardsmen had to eat in the field. She'd practically staggered all the way to the mess hall and crashed into a chair.

Fran smiled at her. Rachel found her a little annoying, if only because Fran was young and bubbly and surprisingly calculating. She'd even responded to Commander Archer's advances. Her friendly nature made her more dangerous than someone who was in it for herself. She kept trying to make friends with her fellow staffers...

"No," Rachel said. "What happened?"

"I heard it from Archer," Fran said. She showed no awareness of the monitors she *knew* had to be embedded in the walls. "Colonel Belmar was arrested for treason!"

"He was?" Rachel showed as little interest as possible. The senior officers were supposed to live in their own little world. Staffers like Fran—and Lieutenant Hannah Gresham—were not meant to gossip about them. "What happened?"

"Archer didn't know all the details," Fran said. "But he was caught and marched off in cuffs."

He probably got one of my messages, Rachel thought. She didn't know the colonel. She had no idea which way he would have jumped, if he'd been given the chance. *He got one of the messages and it destroyed him.*

Fran grinned, brilliantly. "What do you think he was doing?"

"I don't know," Rachel said, sharply. She was tempted to remind the younger woman that walls had ears. Literally. "But does it really matter?"

She stood, trying not to feel a pang of guilt. She'd destroyed a man she'd never met. She couldn't help feeling there was something dishonourable in it. And yet...

There's no other way to win, she told herself. *And if we win quickly, the poor bastard might survive the war.*

But she knew, as she headed for the door, that she was almost certainly wrong.

CHAPTER TWENTY-TWO

This is, as a noted and somewhat wordy pre-space sage put it, the root of money. The money itself is worthless. The thing that matters is what the money represents to the users. Money is created by those who turn raw materials (the trunk) into wealth (the house).
—**Professor Leo Caesius**
The Rise and Fall of Interstellar Capitalism

"THEY'VE GOT THE SPACE ELEVATOR TARGETED, Captain," Lieutenant Yang said. "If we try to send down a pod, they'll blow holes in the cable."

Kerri nodded, tartly. The battle in space had stalemated. It galled her, more than she'd admit to anyone, to have so little room to manoeuvre…but there was no point in trying to hide from reality. They'd cleared a corridor to allow them to land troops and supplies on the surface, yet the enemy ground-based defences were strong enough to keep the marines from capturing the high orbitals and hammering the planet into submission. The anchor station was useless as long as the enemy could fire on the cable itself. They'd have to leave the system alone until the PDCs were captured or destroyed.

And there might not be much left of the planet if the war goes on so long, she mused, as she studied the display. *Or when the enemy fleet returns.*

Her heart sank. They'd captured enough intelligence to be fairly sure that two-thirds of the remaining enemy fleet had been scattered across the empire, rescuing and recovering trained personnel. It was just a matter of time until the fleet returned. When it did…she made a face as she studied the fleet list. Ideally, the ships would return one by one and get blown away by her squadron. If they returned as a group, she might be in some trouble. She had the nasty feeling they'd be outgunned.

The intercom bleeped. "Captain, we've picked up a spacer who wants to see you," Tomas said. "He's a Family Man."

Kerri felt a flicker of excitement, which dimmed as she realised the newcomer wouldn't be—couldn't be—Haydn. "Send him up," she said. She glanced at Yang. "We'll discuss the matter later."

Yang saluted. "Yes, Captain."

The hatch hissed open. Kerri looked up with interest, then nodded as Specialist Phelps stepped into the compartment. Phelps hadn't changed in the months since she'd flown him and his squad to Hameau. He was a tall wiry man, without the muscles on his muscles popular entertainment led her to expect, with an air of confidence that suggested he could handle anything. Kerri felt herself responding to it, even though she'd met enough Pathfinders to know they died like everyone else. It was easy to believe there was nothing the tall man couldn't do.

"Specialist," she said. The rank covered a multitude of sins. "It's good to see you again."

"And you." Phelps took the seat she offered him gratefully. "Have you seen anything of the others?"

"No," Kerri said. Phelps had had three others under his command, hadn't he? "You're the first we've recovered."

Phelps grimaced. "We took up four different roles," he said. "I was expecting at least two to make it home."

He stared at his hands for a long moment. His subordinates had a degree of freedom and independence *most* subordinates could only envy, and the mission briefing had assumed they'd be operating independently, but there were limits. It couldn't be easy to know his people were, at best, somewhere within enemy territory. Or dead...their bodies falling into the atmosphere with the rest of the debris. There might never be closure. Kerri was experienced enough to know that starships could be blown to atoms, their crews reduced to dust and less than dust, but...she understood. It was never easy to deal with missing people, even when one didn't know them personally. The Pathfinders were practically family.

"There are quite a few facilities still in enemy hands," Kerri told him. "They might have remained underground."

"I hope so," Phelps said. He looked up, meeting her eyes with a grim intensity. "I need to go down to the planet. I'm useless up here."

"I wouldn't say useless," Kerri said. "We're contesting a number of orbital and asteroid installations..."

"There's nothing I can do here someone else *can't* do," Phelps said. "I could try to sneak into the nearest asteroid settlement, Captain, but they'll be wise to that trick now. There's certainly no hope of getting them to panic and start moving people around again. Down there"—he jabbed a finger at the deck—"I can be more useful. If I'm the last Pathfinder..."

"There's no reason to assume your comrades are dead," Kerri said, sharply. "Pathfinders have survived worse."

"They should have reported back," Phelps told her. "Rachel was on the anchor station. She could have made herself known to the boarding party, when they stormed the installation. Even if the others were cut off, they could have slipped out a message"—he shook his head—"I have to assume the worst. And there's really nothing for me to do here."

Kerri keyed her terminal, bringing up the shuttle schedule. "I can add you to the MEU unloading plan, if you want," she said. "You might have to clear it with the logistics staff. I don't know how much leeway they'll have for you."

"It'll be a start," Phelps said. "Thank you."

"I don't know if I've done you any favours," Kerri said. She nodded to the in-system display. "There's a chance you'll be trapped on the ground. Again."

"We'll cope," Phelps said. "Up here, I'll be useless. Down there, I might make a difference."

"Good luck," Kerri said. She tapped a command into the terminal. "We'll be sending a shuttle to *Roger Young* this afternoon. You can go on it."

"Thank you," Phelps said, again. "I won't forget it."

Kerri nodded, returning her attention to the display as the Pathfinder took his leave. Space looked peaceful, but she knew it was an illusion. The remaining enemy ships were biding their time, waiting for reinforcements to arrive. Kerri hoped and prayed the forces on the ground were enough to win the war before it was too late. They'd be in some trouble if the squadron wound up pinned against the planet. They *really* didn't have much space to manoeuvre if everything went to hell.

If that happens, we'll have to abandon the high orbitals quickly, she thought. *And that means the guys on the ground will be fucked.*

...

Major-General Gerald Anderson had spent most of his service on the front lines, or in offices close enough to the front lines to avoid inspections by officers with better connections than service records, but he'd spent a few months serving as an advisor to a Grand Senator. He'd honestly never understood how the man could surround himself with so much luxury, to the point it was wasteful beyond words. Here...the mansion had been practically empty, with a single owner and a handful of staff. The paintings on the walls were never seen, the rows of books on the shelves were never read...the guest bedrooms were ready for guests who rarely, if ever, came. There was something about the mansion that bothered him, although he couldn't put it into words. Something oddly...*sad*.

He snorted at himself as he studied the display. *Poor little rich man?* He'd known a couple of aristocrats who'd joined the corps and made something of themselves...hell, they'd been quite a few who hadn't gone anything like that far and yet had turned into quite decent people. The mansion owner, the effective ruler of the entire planet, had shut himself away in a hive of luxury...he could have surrounded himself with friends, or at least sycophants, if he'd wished. And yet, he hadn't even had a dedicated close-protection team. Gerald was sure the enemy CEO had felt safe. He'd probably had good reason.

"Sir," Colonel Patel said. "We have secured corridors through and around the city."

Gerald nodded. Roxon City would be a nightmare, if he tried to occupy it. There were just too many people in too close proximity...the early outbreaks of rioting and looting were likely to get worse if the marines didn't stamp on it, but he simply didn't have the forces to keep the city under control. He hated to admit it, yet there was no choice. They'd hold the vital points within the city and nothing else. Thankfully, the local population was largely unarmed. They didn't have the firepower to do real damage.

"Good," he said. "And the refugees?"

"We're billeting them on the estates for now," Patel said. "They seem a little...astonished."

Gerald snorted in cold amusement. He'd been on planets where the higher-ups had demanded all sorts of things for the poor, all of which had to be paid for by the taxpayers and kept a *very* long way from them. Here... he wondered, idly, what would happen if—when—word started to spread. The aristocrats lived in giant mansions, each one big enough to house a regiment of marines, while the workers lived in apartment blocks and single-room flats...if they were lucky. The spooks were already speaking to the refugees, looking for people who might carry messages to their fellows. Gerald doubted they'd be many volunteers, but it didn't matter. They were already getting close to hacking the enemy communications network and filling it with propaganda.

He frowned as he studied the map. The marines were advancing lightly along a broad front to feel out resistance, a tactic he would have preferred to avoid. Strong forces were held in reserve, ready to stamp on anything the scouts couldn't handle; he knew, all too well, that a capable enemy commander might mousetrap the scouts and use them as bait to ambush their reinforcements. His point defence units were moving forward, backing up the mobile missile launchers and artillery as they supported the offensive. It was a shame the enemy point defence was pretty good—he'd started to deduce their positions from where he'd lost drones—but it was no longer a surprise. His men were used to fighting within the fog of war.

"There are patches of resistance along the motorway," Patel informed him. "But the enemy seems more intent on delaying matters than actually stopping us."

Gerald nodded, coldly. Someone on the other side was actually *thinking*. There was nothing to be gained by sending men to do or die, particularly when they would just die. They were sniping at the marines, then falling back towards the defence lines…defence lines Gerald *knew* had to be taking shape. The marines would have to push forward, at the risk of exposing their supply lines to enemy attack. He ground his teeth in irritation. It would be so much easier if they could land shuttles west of Roxon, but the enemy would have a clear shot at them. And there was no way to get around the problem.

We could start pressing their aircars and hover vehicles into service, he mused. *It might let us speed things up a little…*

"Smart of them." Gerald put the thought aside for later consideration. They didn't have time to come up with a whole new logistics system, not when they were advancing as fast as they could. The enemy commander was known to be tenacious. "Keep funnelling supplies around the city. We don't want to get a logistics unit bogged down on the streets."

He frowned. "And see if you can locate some premade dumpsters," he added. "It might let us drop a lot of supplies into enemy positions."

"Yes, sir," Patel said.

• • •

"Incoming!"

Haydn hit the ground as a volley of shells screamed out of the clear blue sky. Flashes of light darted overhead as the point defence units engaged the shells, trying to swat them before they crashed down on top of the marines. The ground shook, violently, as a handful of shells made it through and slammed down. Haydn breathed a sigh of relief as he realised most of the shells had fallen behind the platoon. The company had advanced forward so quickly they'd effectively outrun the shells before they'd been fired.

He crawled forward as, behind him, he heard the self-propelled guns returning fire. Chatter echoed through his earpiece, reporting that enemy guns had been sited within yet another town. Haydn prayed the locals had fled before the shooting started, that the enemy troops had let them flee. The town was doomed. The shells would take out every building that might serve as a hiding place for troops and guns. And if the inhabitants had remained behind, they were doomed too.

The ground shook, again. Haydn forced himself to his feet and ran forward, risking everything as he led the platoon through the field. The enemy hadn't started putting together IEDs yet, but it was just a matter of time. They had enough material on hand to make life truly miserable for the invaders, if they knew how to use it. The corprats wouldn't *want* to teach their people, if only because the training would be very effective against them, but they didn't have a choice. The marines were advancing at breakneck speed.

A hail of bullets shot through the air, dropping lower as the gunner sighted the marines. Haydn dropped again and crawled forward, flashing backwards to his training as he approached the enemy position. Someone had set up a machine gun in what had been a commanding position, before the shells turned the town into a burning wasteland. The gunner was moving quickly, but not quickly enough. Haydn put a shot through his head, watching emotionlessly as the man's body flopped over and hit the ground. He kept moving, readying a grenade to hurl into any further enemy positions. An interlocking network of machine gun nests could have made life interesting—and gruesome—for the marines. Instead, the gunner seemed to have been alone. No shots poured out of the burning town.

Haydn felt sweat trickle down his back as the marines searched the remains of the town. It was hard to guess what the town had looked like, before the shells, although he was fairly sure it had probably looked just like the other corporate towns. They all looked the same, a handful of prefabricated buildings surrounded by homes, schools and shops laid out in a soulless pattern. He peered into what had probably once been a school and breathed a sigh of relief when he saw no one inside. The town had definitely been evacuated. He doubted anyone with any sense would have stayed put when he saw the refugees on the road. The corprats simply didn't have time for crowd control.

He dismissed the thought as a trio of tanks crashed their way through the cornfields and advanced through the town, weapons sweeping from side to side as they looked for potential threats. A pair of Raptors flew overhead, launching drones into the distance. Haydn hoped the enemy point defence would fire on the drones, revealing their locations to the waiting gunners. The enemy had managed to keep the marines from taking control of the air, but...they didn't have control either. They certainly didn't have enough point defence to save their gunners and shoot down the drones. Either way, the marines won.

A tall figure jumped from the tanks and landed neatly by the side of the road. Haydn tensed, then relaxed slightly as he realised the figure had to be friendly. The newcomer straightened up and nodded, rather than saluting. He wore simple camouflage, rather than proper BDUs. Haydn didn't give much for his chances if the enemy caught him. The corprats had fought a relatively civilised war—it was a nice change from terrorists and insurgents, who unleashed horror for the sheer hell of it—but they'd be completely within their rights to shoot someone they caught out of uniform. Admittedly, the laws of war had been a dead letter well before Earthfall…

"Sir," the newcomer said. "Specialist Phelps, reporting."

Haydn raised an eyebrow. "I doubt you're here to check the plumbing."

Phelps chuckled, although the joke had long since lost its humour. "No," he said. "I have to cross the lines."

"You're right on the edge now," Haydn said. He unhooked his terminal from his belt and held it out. "We're here, on the forward edge. The enemy is somewhere to the east."

"Understood," Phelps said. He didn't complain about the lack of data. He'd probably been briefed before he'd ridden a tank to the town. "Are there any refugees on the roads?"

"Some," Haydn said. A flight of missiles roared overhead. He turned his head just in time to see fireballs rising in the distance. "The enemy has been fairly good about telling people to leave their homes."

"They'll find that harder, as the war advances towards their industrial core," Phelps told him. "But I should be able to blend in."

"Try not to get shot," Haydn told him. "We're hoping to push forward again once reinforcements arrive."

Phelps laughed. "I laugh in the face of danger. I stick ice cubes down the vest of fear. I"—he adopted a quavering voice—"I don't want to go!"

"You're uglier than the guy in the flicks," Haydn said. He had no idea why some idiot producer had turned a war movie into an absurd satire, but he supposed it made sure no one took it seriously. "Just keep your head down and your balls covered and you'll be fine."

"Hah." Phelps grinned. "Just try not to shoot me in the back. That would be embarrassing."

"Quite," Haydn agreed. He felt a flicker of envy. The Pathfinders got all the *really* interesting missions. "You'd be the first marine to get shot in the back while running *towards* the enemy."

CHAPTER TWENTY-THREE

And it is simply impossible to produce wealth without a degree of capitalism. Feudal states (the aristocrats own everything and leave the peasants with pittances) and communist states (the state owns everything and doles out what it thinks the peasants need) routinely go through periods of starvation. Why? Because the producers know they won't be allowed to profit from their hard work, so they do as little as possible and nothing more. And there is no way to make them.
—**Professor Leo Caesius**
The Rise and Fall of Interstellar Capitalism

"DIRECTOR," VICE DIRECTOR MCMANUS SAID. "I think we have a problem."

Thaddeus frowned. He'd spent the morning working his way through the reports and putting together a replacement staff to handle the issues he didn't need to. Julia had been a blessing, for all that her ambition was clear to see. She could handle some issues without ever turning into a major threat herself. But she couldn't deal with the security director. McManus reported directly to Thaddeus himself.

"Joy," he said, crossly. The marines had been advancing for the last two days. It was hard to be sure if they'd been slowed down—they certainly hadn't been stopped—by the defenders. "What happened?"

"We arrested Colonel Belmar two days ago," McManus said. "The colonel received an email from an unknown source, offering him a role in a pro-imperial coup. We had a spy on his staff who reported the email to us, before Colonel Belmar could decide what he wanted to do. We arrested him at once."

Thaddeus sucked in his breath. "He didn't report it?"

"No," McManus said. "The email specifically warned him *not* to report it. We have to assume he wouldn't have reported it. He wasn't one of the long-term recruits."

"I see," Thaddeus said. "Have you traced the email?"

"No, sir," McManus said. "The email's trail was wiped from the datanodes. From what little we've been able to determine, it was wrapped in authorisation codes that specifically ordered the datanodes to forward the email—following a path laid down by the sender—and then erase all traces of its passage, without checking with human authority. There's no way to tell who sent the message, not without checking each and every datacore...frankly, sir, my staff believes that it would take years to even *try*."

"And whoever sent it had the right authorisation codes," Thaddeus mused. "How did they *get* the codes?"

"We don't know," McManus said. "It's possible the codes were stored somewhere in Roxon and the marines captured them, although the secure datanodes were ordered wiped and then physically destroyed. There were quite a few senior corporate managers who kept private datacores, even though it was officially discouraged. We don't know what, if anything, was on those cores, let alone what happened to them. There are simply too many missing people for us to be sure."

He paused. "It's also possible that the message was sent by someone from *our* side."

"Someone planning to take advantage of the chaos," Thaddeus said. "Someone planning to sell us out to the marines."

He felt a flash of cold anger. He could name a dozen high-ranking people who were ambitious enough to try to make a deal with the marines, perhaps offering to surrender in exchange for maintaining their positions, and stupid enough to think they could get away with it. They probably assumed they'd get no more than a slap on the wrist if they were caught. Hell, they wouldn't have their positions if they didn't have supporters who'd defend them even if they were caught and convicted of treason. He ground his teeth in frustration. The planet had been invaded. He didn't have *time* to worry about being stabbed in the back.

"Who?" Thaddeus glared at his hands. "And why?"

"We don't know," McManus said. "We have a list of possible suspects, but no solid proof."

His face darkened. "However, there is a second problem."

"Someone else received the message," Thaddeus guessed.

"We suspect so, sir," McManus said. He looked as if he knew he was on the verge of delivering bad news. "It is quite likely Colonel Belmar wasn't the only person who received that particular message. As an ex-imperial officer who was recruited shortly before Earthfall, he was unlikely to rise any higher and he knew it. That's not the real problem, though. The real problem was that there was a second set of messages. These went out to a bunch of civilians."

Thaddeus understood, suddenly, why so many of his relatives had liked the idea of shooting the messenger. "Who? Why?"

"The message offered them the chance to join the underground," McManus said. He sucked in his breath. "We received ninety-four reports from people who received the message. It is quite likely there were many more who got the message and chose to keep their mouths shut."

"Fuck," Thaddeus swore. He rarely swore, but now...he met the younger man's eyes. "Is the message being *believed*?"

"We don't know, sir," McManus said. "The handful of people who openly questioned the news broadcasts have already been rounded up and taken away. They were the idiots, sir. The vast majority of people who don't believe the reports were probably smart enough to keep their mouths closed. There's simply no way to hide the flashes in the sky or the hordes of refugees being moved into the city."

"So they don't believe us," Thaddeus mused. He took a tight grip on his temper. "What's the *point* of sending such messages?"

"If the messages come from the marines, they may be hoping to either convince our military officers to surrender or convince dissidents to stop working," Thaddeus said. "If the messages come from someone in the government..."

His voice trailed off. Thaddeus had no trouble seeing the implications. There would be someone who thought he could deal with the devil and come out ahead. The marines would make whatever agreements they had to make, then break them as soon as they were no longer necessary. Thaddeus knew he had political enemies, including some of the people on the corporate board. And the entire government had enemies from outside...he made a face. They'd recruited ambitious ex-imperial officers who hadn't been able to climb the ladder any further. Those officers hadn't lost their ambition just because they'd signed up with the corporation...

He looked at McManus. "How do you suggest we proceed?"

"We already have a network of commissioners monitoring the ex-imperial officers, but we cannot be sure they'll catch everything," McManus said. "The commissioners were chosen more for loyalty than expertise. Worse, their charges *know* they're being watched and react accordingly. There's no way to know what's in someone's head until they start something, and by then it'll be too late.

"I think we're going to have to double our security measures, even to the point of tying up humans monitoring the ex-imperials in real time," he added. "And that will cause no end of problems."

"Yes." Thaddeus gritted his teeth. "Do we have a choice?"

"A couple of officers deserting their posts could cause a great deal of damage, if they timed it well," McManus said. "If they just ordered their men to surrender, the moment they see the advancing hordes, well..."

He shrugged. "We're also going to need to make a show of strength on the streets," he continued. "More troops around critical positions, more policemen clearly visible...too many people simply forget the surveillance network is *there*. We'd be better off deterring any hostile moves than swatting them once they come into the light. Once they show themselves...it might be too late. We do *not* want to waste time and effort putting down a rebellion on the streets."

Thaddeus met his eyes. "And you think you can do all that without taking troops off the defence lines?"

"We may not have a choice," McManus said. "Until we figure out what's really going on..."

"And find out who's responsible," Thaddeus finished. Who *was* it? He could name a handful of people who could manipulate the datanet, or have their subordinates do it for them, but he didn't think any of them would be stupid enough to try. The marines were breathing down their necks. "We need to warn people not to pay attention to the messages."

"We cannot have them questioning the datanet," McManus warned. "If they stop believing what they see online...sir, with all due respect, we have enough problems caused by trying to assemble a defence at very short notice. There will be further delays—or worse—if people lose confidence in the datanet."

"I see." Thaddeus hadn't considered *that* possibility. "Anything we do will only make it worse."

"Yes, sir," McManus said. "The datanet is supposed to be perfect."

Thaddeus doubted that anyone *really* believed the datanet was perfect. He was all too aware of just how easily a simple mistake could snowball into a hellish nightmare, simply because a piece of data was taken on faith even though it was obviously untrue. And yet...he gritted his teeth. Whoever had used the datanet to distribute propaganda, whatever their motives, had thrown the entire system into doubt. He felt a hot flash of paranoia. The datanet could send a message to each and every civilian on the planet. Why had so *few* people received the message? No...why had so few people *reported* the message? His blood ran cold as he considered the implications.

There was no reason the unknown senders would limit their reach to a few hundred people. They could have sent the message to everyone.

"How many people received the message," he asked, "and said nothing?"

"We don't know," McManus said. "Everyone who reported the message was on a list of possible dissidents, but none of them were considered serious threats. The algorithms pinpointed them, sir, yet...they weren't guilty of much more than grumbling in the wrong places. However..."

Thaddeus cut him off. "So we arrest everyone on the dissident list?"

"Sir, that would mean arresting millions of people," McManus said. "Even if we limit it to the people with three strikes against them, which is normally when we arrange for a human officer to investigate, we'd still be arresting hundreds of thousands of people. Many of them are in vital positions and cannot be replaced quickly, if at all. The chaos and disruption would be immense. There'd be no way to fix the damage. I...I could not advise it."

"The marines might be hoping we'd do just that," Thaddeus said. "We'd be shooting ourselves in the foot."

"More like stabbing ourselves in the chest," McManus said. "I think there's nothing we can do, but watch and wait."

"And doubling patrols on the streets," Thaddeus said. "Do it."

"Yes, sir." McManus stood. "My staff is looking at ways to tighten up the datanet without damaging it. However, it may be impossible to fix the system before the current crisis is resolved."

"Do what you can," Thaddeus ordered. He dismissed the younger man with a wave of his hand. "Keep me informed."

· · ·

Julia had never liked paperwork—she knew no one who did, certainly not amongst the aristocracy—but she'd learned to appreciate its value. Whoever controlled the bureaucracy controlled everything, from the military to the corporation itself. And if senior officers gave up control, they risked watching helplessly as the bureaucracy mutated into a cancer that choked and eventually killed the organisation it was meant to help. Julia detested reading reports, but it was the only way to keep on top of things. It was also a good way to start rebuilding her personal power base. She was mildly surprised the director had let her get away with it.

"Julia," the director said, when he called her into his office. "I have a job for you."

Julia nodded. She was in no position to refuse. She didn't want to be kicked out of his service, not until she had rebuilt enough of her position to find a decent post elsewhere. If she held out long enough, she was sure people would forget her failures. Corporate royalty had very short memories, particularly when they wanted to forget.

"I need reports from the streets," the director said. "I want you to go walkabout and see what you see."

"Sir?" Julia knew it was unwise to question orders, but…this order made no sense. Did the director want to get rid of her? He didn't need to resort to trickery. He could just order her to go and she'd have no choice, but to obey. "I don't understand."

"You are trained in observing people, are you not?" Director Onge met her eyes. "There have been developments, Julia, and I don't know who to trust."

Julia listened to the brief explanation, dropped a curtsey and hurried out of the office. She was trained to watch military officers, not corporate drones, but…she supposed it was a sign the director had some faith in her. She changed into a simple suit—her regular suit marked her out as a high-ranking personage—and hurried through the security checkpoints. It was hard to remember, while she was inside the office, just how many layers of security were wrapped around the complex. She wasn't looking forward to getting back inside. The security officers would insist on checking her thoroughly even though she *was* corporate royalty.

She put the thought out of her mind as she began to walk. She'd never spent much time on the streets—she'd never rubbed shoulders with the drones—but the air felt…tense. The pavements were lined with grounded aircars, all deactivated by the ATC system until the crisis was over. Soldiers and policemen were everywhere, guarding buildings or putting raw recruits through their paces. It was odd to see that inside a city, instead of a nicely-isolated training base on the other side of the planet. Admiral Agate had once told her that training officers and crew required total isolation, just to keep their minds focused on the job. And yet...she pushed the pang of... *something*...out of her mind. The admiral had surrendered to the enemy. He might as well be dead.

Her eyes narrowed as she spotted the wall-mounted viewscreens. Public Relations had been churning out endless news reports that bore very little relationship to reality, although it was hard to tell if anyone realised it. The defenders were pushing the marines back...sooner or later, the cynic in her noted, someone was going to realise the marines had been pushed right around the planet. She glanced at the workers in their drab clothes, their faces carefully blank. It didn't *look* as though they were enthusiastic about the news reports.

Julia kept walking until she was passing through the apartment district. The children were still going to school, their mothers watching them worriedly. There were no older teenagers in view...Julia frowned, then remembered most of them had been conscripted into the labour battalions. She'd read a report insisting the kids had taken to military discipline like ducks to water. She wasn't sure that was true. Teenagers, in her experience, chafed under any form of authority. But then, the men in charge were authorised to do whatever it took to keep the conscripts working. Anyone who put up a fight would spend the rest of his life on a penal colony.

She stopped in at a lunch hall and purchased a sandwich and a mug of coffee. The sandwich tasted bland, as if it had been put together from algae-based ration bars; the coffee was foul enough to make her want to spit. The music was so loud the security monitors probably couldn't make out a word, something she was *sure* was intentional. She could see people—workers all—talking so quietly she couldn't hear a word either. They didn't seem inclined to invite her to join them. She was ruefully aware she stood out like a sore thumb. She was just too clean and tidy for the district.

Unfriendly eyes followed her as she put the remains of her lunch aside and walked back onto the streets. There was no open dissidence, as far as she could see, but...workers didn't seem to be *working* with any real enthusiasm. They didn't seem to believe the algorithms that monitored their working patterns would matter for much longer, if indeed at all. Her eyes drifted over a food store and noted how few items remained on the shelves, despite the paperwork claiming the city had plenty of food. Panic-buying was supposed to be impossible. The system monitored purchases closely. And yet...

There are plenty of ways to circumvent the system, she thought. She'd learnt, back on the battlecruiser, that people needed to have a *little* rebellion. They needed to think they were fighting the system and winning, even if they were claiming very petty victories that made no difference in the long run. *The shopkeepers are probably trading something other than money.*

She kept walking, unable to shake the feeling that the entire city was on a knife edge. There was nothing overt, nothing she could put her finger on, but...it was there. She was *sure* it was there. A hint of resentment, a hint of fear...and, perhaps, the hope of a better future once the corporation's power was broken. She felt her heart sink as she finally turned and started to walk back towards the centre of the city. She could *still* feel unfriendly eyes following her.

We need to win quickly, she thought. She couldn't allow herself any illusions. The comforting lies on the viewscreens were nothing more than... comforting lies. *We have to win quickly, or we won't win at all.*

CHAPTER TWENTY-FOUR

This point is never grasped by feudal lords or communist commissioners. They believe that setting impossible targets, and then threatening the proles with harsh punishments for failing to meet such targets, is the only way to convince them to generate a larger output. This is, of course, wrong. In the short term, it leads to either revolution or bitter resentment. In the long term, the effective brain drain leads to a complete lack of innovation and social collapse, stasis, or outside invasion.
—**Professor Leo Caesius**
The Rise and Fall of Interstellar Capitalism

"SIR," MAYBERRY SAID. "I'VE GOT MOVEMENT."

Haydn nodded as he peered into the distance. The marines had kept advancing, locating and isolating enemy positions before outflanking the enemy and shelling them into submission. It wasn't particularly fair, but he didn't care. The enemy might be in retreat, yet they weren't panicking and running for their lives. Instead, they were firing missiles or sniping at the marines, holding their positions long enough to land a blow and then retreating before the marines could return fire. Haydn's company hadn't lost many marines—two men had been killed, four more had been injured and handed over to the medics—but they were tired, cranky and sick of death of the endless sniping.

He frowned as he saw the enemy position. The landscape was a curious mix of farmland, forests and artificial dams and lakes. The enemy hadn't helped by flooding some of the terrain, reminding Haydn of the horror stories he'd heard from the final battles on Hameau even though they hadn't managed to drown any of the marines. It just made life harder for them as they pushed forward. Haydn understood the importance of keeping the pressure on—he'd spent half his career chasing terrorists until they could run no more—but he couldn't help feeling they were going to outrun their logistics at any moment. The logistics staff had pressed captured vehicles and enemy volunteers into service, yet it just wasn't enough. His men needed a break long enough to prepare themselves for the coming engagement.

Mortars cracked in the distance. He ducked as shells fell around them, then barked a command at the platoon. The machine gunners provided cover as the marines ran up the incline, forcing the enemy to duck. They'd dug a trench on the top, hiding their people from orbital or drone surveillance. Haydn would have been more impressed if they hadn't been shooting at him. The marines didn't give them a chance to react...

He froze, just for a second, as a handful of enemy troops threw down their weapons and raised their hands. Were they surrendering? Or was it a trick? Haydn was all too aware that terrorists and insurgents were fond of pretending to surrender, then picking up their weapons and opening fire when the marines got into range. Or their commanders would open fire on their own positions, mowing down their own men to get at the marines. It was never easy to tell if the surrendering men were *really* surrendering. Haydn had heard suggestions that some men were surrendering, only to find themselves used as bait by their fellows. The poor bastards hadn't stood a chance.

"Keep your hands in the air," he barked, as his eyes swept the surrounding countryside for enemy positions. The position they'd just stormed appeared to be completely isolated, as if the enemy hadn't really cared enough to provide any actual support. "If you touch anything, you will be shot!"

He eyed the men thoughtfully as the marines came closer. They looked young, too young. Haydn had joined the marines at eighteen and yet…the men they'd captured looked younger than the men who'd gone through Boot Camp and the Slaughterhouse with him. They looked younger than the lads he'd fought on Hameau, young enough to bother him. He'd seen children carrying grenades—and older kids carrying rifles—but he'd never expected to see it on Onge. The corprats had fought a surprisingly civilised war.

The marines searched the men roughly, confiscated their supplies and then ordered them to sit by the side of the trench to wait for the follow-up units. Haydn kept a wary eye on them, even as his platoon prepared to continue the advance. They really *did* look young. The oldest struck him as being around sixteen, perhaps younger. Teenagers? Haydn had wanted to join the marines from childhood, but he hadn't heard of anyone younger than seventeen getting into Boot Camp.

He peered down at the enemy troops. "What are you doing here?"

The oldest trooper peered at him, defiantly. "I can only give you my name, my rank and my serial number."

And anyone who went through the Conduct After Capture course would know better than to debate with the enemy, Haydn thought. He looked at the young men, suddenly realising they had very little training. *Are they throwing raw recruits into the fire?*

"True," he said. The spooks would get more out of them. They'd figure out how the lads had wound up in uniforms and ordered onto the front lines. "Behave yourselves and you'll get out of this alive."

He studied them for a long moment, then stood back as the MPs arrived and escorted the prisoners into captivity. The question of just what they were doing there didn't matter, not now. If they'd surrendered so quickly, perhaps it was a good sign. The corprats had lost a *lot* of troops on Hameau. They might be short of deployable manpower to throw at the marines… or they might be planning something big. Haydn had studied all the great battles of old, from infantry charges across no-man's land to fast-moving tank engagements as armoured monsters strove to break into the enemy rear. A calculating enemy CO might starve his front-line units of trained manpower, all the time preparing his masterstroke.

When it comes, we'll deal with it, he thought. It wouldn't be *long* before they reached the next megacity. *And then, hopefully, the war will be over.*

• • •

"It's confirmed, sir," Lieutenant Yu said. "The latest bunch of prisoners came from a labour battalion that was hastily thrown into the breach."

Gerald frowned as he studied the map. "They didn't have time to withdraw?"

"From what they said, when the spooks got to them, they were given weapons and told to hold the position as long as possible," Yu said. "They didn't really know what they were doing."

"Odd." Gerald looked up at him. "No training at all?"

"Only a little," Yu said. "They were in their final year of school when they were yanked out of the classroom and told to dig trenches. They weren't ready for a fight. They didn't even have more than an hour or two of weapons training."

"Odd," Gerald repeated.

He stroked his chin. The days when a new conscript could be given a rifle, an hour's training and then pointed at the front were long gone. Really, they had never existed outside the fevered dreams of politicians and armchair generals. It took months to turn a civilian into a soldier, let alone a marine. The enemy might have found it necessary to put schoolchildren to work digging trenches, but…he frowned. The poor kids were going to get killed, if they weren't careful. There was a good chance they'd be caught in the open by a prowling aircraft and strafed before they could run or hide.

His eyes wandered the map. It wasn't easy to estimate just how much trained manpower the enemy actually had. Their home-grown units were stiffened by ex-imperial officers and men who'd been scooped up and transported to Onge well before Earthfall had shattered galactic society beyond repair. Given time, the enemy certainly had the manpower and equipment to give the marines a real fight. It was part of the reason he was pushing the advance so hard. They couldn't afford to give the enemy a chance to get back on their feet and start punching back.

"They're up to something," he said. He was no stranger to military incompetence, or the simple fact that things often went wrong on the battlefield through no fault of the people in charge, but putting so many untrained men on the front lines was worrying. Either the advance had overwhelmed the defenders or...he had to assume the worst. "What are they doing?"

He frowned. What would *he* do? His lips quirked, humourlessly. He'd do what the *enemy* was doing. Bleed the marines, while buying time for the defence lines to stiffen and the fleet to return. And yet, the enemy didn't have much time. They could evacuate trained personnel from the factories, but they couldn't dismantle them before it was too late. The enemy needed to stop him in his tracks, then go on the offensive. He had to prepare his men for the worst.

"Push out more flankers," he ordered, grimly. "And see if we can speed up the logistics deployments."

"Yes, sir," Yu said.

Gerald rubbed his forehead. The advance would continue—it had to continue—until it ran into something that forced it to stop. He was all too aware his logistics were starting to break down. The shuttles were working night and day to bring down more ammunition as well as equipment and supplies, but they were running up against some very hard limits. He was starting to fear he'd made a mistake in pushing the advance so hard. The enemy was luring him onwards. He knew they might be preparing a trap.

He felt a pang of guilt. He was tired, so tired. And yet, what had he done? He'd spent the day sitting on his ass in a mansion, while younger men did all the *real* work. It had been a long time since he'd led troops in combat, a long time since he'd felt as if he was pulling his weight. He'd been in danger on Hameau, sure, but he hadn't been on the front lines. He understood why old-time generals had fought beside their men...they'd commanded their respect, even if they'd risked losing everything when they died. His training told him the generals had been selfish bastards. His emotions told him something different.

"Keep me informed," he said. Night was falling, but the war raged on. His men would snatch a few hours of sleep under the stars, then resume the march into enemy territory. "And alert me if anything changes."

His heart clenched as he walked along the corridor—the eerily-empty corridor—and out onto the lawn. Hundreds of vehicles had torn the lawn to pieces, churning up the grass and grinding the flowers into the mud. Now, the remnants of the charming gardens were dotted with mobile sensor platforms, air defence units and a single command vehicle. High overhead, lights flickered and flared before flashing out of existence, a grim reminder that the battle in space was far from over. He wished, not for the first time, that he was commanding from a hole in the ground. There was something about the mansion that promoted indolence.

You just need a kick in the backside, he thought. His old Drill Instructor would have laughed in his face. *And, when this is all over, perhaps you can ask for a demotion and go back to the front lines.*

He snorted. He knew that wasn't going to happen.

• • •

Lieutenant Simone Prescott shivered, despite herself, as she led the remnants of her unit back towards the front lines…the new front lines. The old front lines had been torn to pieces by the marines, just like the remainder of the defence lines that had been put together in a hurry before the marines reached them. Darkness was steadily falling, making it harder to keep going despite her enhanced eyesight. They didn't dare risk a light. They'd been warned the marines would fire on anything, even something as tiny as a cigarette.

She felt cold, even though it was a warm evening. Her men were falling apart. She'd never been trained to take command of a platoon, certainly not one that had been moved from garrison duty and thrown into combat.

Her original company—and her commanding officers—had effectively been smashed. The men under her command were largely strangers, survivors of previous encounters that had been swept up and put under her command. She was uneasily aware their morale was in the crapper. They'd been through hell in the last few days. Some of them had even been muttering about deserting.

Gunshots echoed through the air. She looked back, spotting a handful of fires where towns and hamlets had once been. She'd heard the marines were destroying everything, setting fire to empty homes and burning farms to the ground. She thought she could feel them behind her, driving her on. She hadn't slept in hours, perhaps days. She wasn't even sure they were going the right way. The jokes about lieutenants who'd been issued maps—and led their men into enemy positions—no longer seemed funny. For all she knew, they'd gotten turned around in the darkness.

"We shouldn't go back," someone muttered behind her. She didn't dare look to see who was talking. "There's nothing for us up there."

She gritted her teeth as she heard a mutter of agreement. The men had been through hell. None of them had been prepared for a high-intensity war. They'd expected time to prepare, not to shift from garrison duties to all-out war in the blink of an eye. She felt a sudden stab of fear. How many men were behind her? She knew several men had slipped away, into the darkness. And what would they do? They could desert, but what would happen after the war? They'd be hunted down and executed for desertion.

"They'll just send us back into the fire," someone else muttered. The voice was deeper, darker. "Why bother?"

Simone hesitated, unsure what to do. She was in command, technically. Half the men under her didn't know her and the other half saw her as a stupid greenie lieutenant. She'd heard the sly suggestions she'd slept her way into her rank, even though she'd gone through OCS with the rest of the officers in training. And…she felt her heart start to pound. Captain Dagon would have known what to say, if a bullet hadn't taken his head off a day or so ago. No one would have dared ignore him…

"If you desert, you'll be hunted down," she said, finally. It was the only argument that came to mind. She couldn't promise them anything when they reached safety. The new CO would turn them around, giving the marines yet another chance to kill them. "You can't leave now."

She realised, too late, that she'd made a mistake. A fist cracked into her back, knocking her to the ground. Simone grunted and tried to roll over, too late. Someone landed on her back, hands grabbing hold of her belt and yanking down her trousers. She heard someone chuckle as his hands slapped her butt, then caught hold of her hands and pinned them against the ground. Panic ran through her as she struggled, helplessly. They were going to rape her. They were going to gang-rape her and then…they'd cut her throat. They couldn't leave her alive afterwards, not when they'd be hunted down and killed. Better to kill her and hope, if anyone discovered the body, that they assumed the marines had raped her. She heard someone opening his zipper, felt fingers stabbing between her legs and forcing her to spread wide for them…

Something hit the ground, hard. Simone couldn't see anything, but… the weight on her back fell to one side and vanished. Someone cried out, swiftly silenced. The sound of running footsteps echoed in the air, then came to an abrupt halt. She wondered, suddenly, if she was dreaming. Perhaps they'd slit her throat and she was seeing things as her life slowly slipped away. They'd been completely alone. Who'd come to her rescue? And why?

"It's over," a voice said. Gruff, male…but somehow reassuring. "How are you?"

Simone rolled over, cursing the bastard who'd pulled down her trousers. The ground felt cold and wet against her bare ass. She hoped she wasn't sitting in a puddle of blood. It wasn't easy to pull them back up, then stumble to her feet. The newcomer was a shadowy form, barely visible within the darkness. She couldn't so much as make out his face.

"Fine," she managed. She'd never realised she could be raped by her own men. She'd been warned, in gruesome detail, what might happen if she fell into enemy hands, but…her own men shouldn't have been able to threaten her. "I … thank you."

"You're welcome," the newcomer said. He gave her space, something that surprised her. "I have to report back to my superiors in the city. Coming?"

"Yeah," Simone managed. She forced herself to calm down. "Who are you?"

"Commissioner Phelps," the newcomer said. "And I think we're going to be good friends."

Simone nodded. She'd never seen the commissioners as anything other than interfering assholes who made normal assholes look bland by comparison. The rumours suggested they had no qualms about taking advantage of their positions, although the commissioner attached to her old unit hadn't shown any interest in anything beyond his job. She eyed the shadowy form with a new respect. She'd certainly never expected a commissioner to be able to kill four men without batting an eyelid. He wasn't even breathing heavily.

And if he's going all the way back to the city, she thought, *and he takes me with him…*

She smiled. In truth, she'd had enough of war.

CHAPTER TWENTY-FIVE

The larger aspect of the problem, of course, is that corruption starts to rear its ugly head at once. Once you start setting targets, and threatening harsh punishments for failing to meet them, you can bet good money—as long as you have it—that your subordinates will start rewriting the records to 'prove' they succeeded. Your targets will rapidly become worthless.
—**Professor Leo Caesius**
The Rise and Fall of Interstellar Capitalism

"And what did you think you were doing?"

Rachel winced inwardly, feeling a stab of sympathy as Commander Archer berated an unfortunate staff officer for a tiny mistake. It wasn't even her fault, unless one counted following orders as a *mistake*. Rachel tried to keep her face blank as the asshole went on and on, reducing the poor girl to tears. It was easy to tell Commander Archer was enjoying himself. He wasn't just an asshole, but a sadist. Rachel dreaded to think what he might be like in bed.

She did her best to ignore the racket as she returned her attention to her console. The messages she'd sent had clearly attracted attention, although the enemy counterintelligence officers hadn't—yet—worked out where they'd come from. Rachel was fairly sure they couldn't, not without taking measures that would alert her long before they found even a hint of proof she was involved. They'd been forced to resort to doubling and even tripling the security officers on duty, ensuring they were practically tripping over each other as they tried to monitor the staff for signs of disloyalty. Rachel was almost tempted to stop making mistakes of her own. The enemy system was so screwed up she didn't need to bother.

"And you can report directly to HR for reassignment," Commander Archer snarled. "Don't think you're getting back here!"

Rachel kept her face impassive as Commander Archer resumed his pacing. She didn't know what would happen to the poor girl, when she reached HR, but Rachel was fairly sure it wouldn't be anything good. She'd probably wind up being given a rifle and told to join the front lines. Rachel had monitored the enemy mobilisation and noted it wasn't that efficient. She'd done her bit to make it a lot *more* inefficient.

The shift ended without further incident, much to her relief. Commander Archer dismissed them, then stamped off to make someone else's life miserable. Rachel didn't really care, as long as he stayed out of her way. She tossed a handful of ideas around to make sure he got the blame, if—when—she had to go active and do as much damage as she could before she fought her way out, but none of them were particularly *good* ideas. She shook her head at the thought as she walked into the barracks. The other staffers were heading down to the mess hall. She'd have at least half an hour to herself before the others came to get some sleep.

Not that it really matters, she thought. She could link into the datanet without doing anything that might alert the casual observer. *But it's well to be careful.*

She lay on the bed, in full view of the security monitors, and closed her eyes as she opened the datalink. The enemy hadn't set up more monitors, as far as she could tell, but she still felt nervous as she widened the link. They knew *someone* had hacked the datanet…she was sure, despite everything she'd written in the messages, that a few people would have reported them to higher authority. They'd be too afraid to do anything else. Rachel shivered as she remembered meeting a pair of missionaries, back when she'd been on leave. They'd felt that God Himself would punish them for *not* spreading the good word. Here…it was worse. The locals had no doubt they were being watched.

It didn't *look* as though the enemy had traced her, but she took extreme care as she poked and prodded her way towards the isolated data cache. Her instructors had taught her that it was relatively easy, if one knew what one was doing, to peer into and around the cache without setting off any red flags. The enemy couldn't take down their datanet without crippling themselves, but they could set traps to alert them if anyone opened the wrong file. Rachel allowed herself a moment of relief as she surveyed the cache, making sure it hadn't been uncovered. She'd gone to a lot of trouble to hide it, and ensure that any replies went on a grand tour of the network before finally reaching their destination, but it had been impossible to be *sure*. Someone could have caught on to what she was doing. The average staffer might know little about how the datanet worked, and someone who intended to play both sides might not know how to watch the message as it darted around the system, but the enemy had plenty of WebHeads in their service. Rachel doubted she could fool a WebHead for very long.

She smiled, inwardly, as she noted just how many officers and civilians had plucked up the nerve to reply. She'd sent hundreds of thousands of emails and received a few thousand replies. More than she'd expected, but less than she'd feared. She worked her way through them, silently wondering how many people intended to play both sides of the field. The military officers would certainly know the battle was far from decided, not yet. She composed a set of replies and sent them out, hoping their targets would respond properly. It was easier to convince people to join a movement if the hard work of starting the movement looked to have already been done.

Strength in numbers, she thought. *They can't put the entire planet in chains.*

The thought chilled her. She'd been on planets where slavery was legal, where men and women could be sold for a handful of coins, but…this planet *was* in chains. There was no way to get a protest movement started without everyone involved being noted, logged and arrested when the demonstration finally broke up. As long as the population monitoring system remained intact, there was little hope of a real uprising. Something would have to be done about it.

She led her mind roam through the system, searching for intelligence. The marines had studied the captured enemy personnel, they knew how the system worked. The implants were little more than transmitters, too low-powered to be detected from orbit. She suspected it was a security measure, but...it came with its weaknesses. Her mind jumped from datacore to datacore. The system had to be centralised, which meant there had to be a station somewhere within the megacity itself. Where? Her lips quirked as she traced the links and finally located the base. It wasn't too far from the military HQ.

Getting inside might pose a challenge, she mused. Commander Archer didn't have permission to enter the monitoring complex. General Gilbert probably didn't have permission, either. The chances were good that anyone who *did* have permission would be known to the guards. They probably had orders to call their superiors and check anyone who turned up, even if they were on the approved list. *If they start asking questions, I'm dead.*

She kept her eyes closed as she considered the possibilities. There had to be a way inside, but what? She couldn't pose as a guard. She couldn't pose as someone with permission to enter the complex. She couldn't...or could she? An idea ran through her head. It would be difficult, and risky, but it might be doable. If nothing else, it would give the enemy a fright.

And I have to put into action quickly, before something else changes, she thought. *It won't be easy.*

She started to fire orders into the system, silently thanking General Gilbert for keeping her nose to the grindstone. The system was easy to manipulate. The trick was to ensure that no one had a chance to put together the whole picture, then sound the alarm. She smiled as she watched the orders gliding through the system, then put the matter out of her mind long enough to get some proper sleep. Even if someone realised what she was doing, it was unlikely they could follow the path back to her. And...

Her heart sank. She knew what she'd have to do.

Her implants woke her, five hours later. Her shift wasn't scheduled to start for another four hours, long enough to go to work. She checked the security systems, making sure Commander Archer was in his suite. Alone. She raised an eyebrow, then decided not to worry about it as she slipped out of bed and donned her uniform. The commander wasn't a very nice man. Perhaps he'd simply failed to lure someone into his bed.

Or perhaps he's up to something himself, she mused, as she made her way through the corridors. It was early morning, the time when the human mind was least aware of its surroundings. Her old unit had always stood to at dawn, just in case the enemy was on the prowl. It had happened enough to convince her younger self that it was more than just paranoia. *If there was anyone who'd switch sides, it's him.*

She tapped on the commander's door, trying to look nonchalant. The officer quarters felt deserted. Rachel was fairly sure anyone who wasn't on duty was trying to sleep before they had to go back to work. Good. A half-asleep commander was unlikely to be thinking too clearly. The door opened with a hiss. Commander Archer stared at her, his eyes blinking in confusion.

He found his voice. "What do you want?"

"I need a favour," Rachel said. She fought down a twinge of disgust. Silk work had never been her forte. She lacked the aptitude as well as the body. "Can we discuss it inside?"

Commander Archer put his hand on her arm and pulled her inside. Rachel could have broken the grip easily, but restrained herself. The eagerness in his eyes bothered her at a very primal level. She wanted to break his neck. Instead, she allowed him to close and lock the door behind her. The sound of the lock was surprisingly loud. She wondered if he'd rigged it that way on purpose or if her enhanced senses were merely overreacting. It was certainly no coincidence he'd deliberately arranged his furniture to block the monitors. She was surprised no one had told him off for it.

He's probably got friends in high places, she thought. Commander Archer's behaviour represented a massive security risk. *There has to be a reason he hasn't been removed from office by now.*

"Well," Commander Archer said. "What do you want?"

"I need to send a message to my sister," Rachel said. Lieutenant Hannah Gresham's sister would be very surprised to receive a message from someone who was missing, presumed dead, but it hardly mattered. "I can't do it myself."

"Of course not." Commander Archer's eyes wandered over Rachel's chest. "All non-essential communications have been blocked."

"Yes, sir." Rachel tried to look endearing. "Please let me send the message. I'd be very grateful."

She licked her lips, meaningfully. Commander Archer smirked and keyed his terminal. "One message," he said. "And then you get down and suck."

"Yes, sir," Rachel said. It was hard not to shudder as his fingers slipped down to her rear and caressed her bottom. "Just let me send the message first."

She checked the terminal, making sure he'd unlocked it properly, then turned and kissed him as hard as she could. Commander Archer kissed her back, unaware she'd secreted a drug within her mouth. She'd never liked the idea of using it, but it worked. The commander fell forward as the drug took effect. His eyes went dull. Rachel smirked as she muttered a handful of erotic suggestions into his ears. He'd believe she'd given him a blowjob—and perhaps more—no matter the evidence against it. Her instructors had been very clear. People would believe anything, if they wanted to believe.

The terminal glowed as she pressed her fingers against the system. Commander Archer had more clearance than Lieutenant Gresham, particularly now. Rachel cut herself a handful of orders, then forwarded them to the right departments. In theory, the system would let her do as she wished without opposition. In practice…she shook her head. She'd have to find out later, when everything was in place. If she'd screwed up—or if someone noticed—she wondered, suddenly, if Commander Archer would get the blame. He didn't have the clearance to send messages into the datanet, nor the training to do it without clearance, but...it might take the enemy some time to realise it. And who knew? He might just be willing to join the fake coup himself.

Rachel finished her work, then stepped back from the console. Commander Archer would never ask about her sister. He simply wasn't interested in anyone but himself. She glanced into his bedroom—the monitors were covered there, too—and then helped him to his feet. He came willingly, too entranced to notice that she was leading him to bed. She rolled her eyes as she spotted the bottles of cheap alcohol beside the bed. She'd never seen him drunk on duty. She hated to give him any credit, but...

General Gilbert would probably kill him out of hand, she thought. Gilbert was an impressive figure. *Or have him shipped away to some hellhole on the other side of the galaxy.*

A thought struck her. She picked up the nearest bottle, sniffed it dubiously and then held it out to him. Commander Archer took it and drank, heavily. Rachel watched him finish the bottle, then gave him another and another. He nearly dropped the third one as the combination of bad alcohol and drugs overwhelmed him, sending him falling over backwards in a stupor. Rachel helped him into his bed. He was going to be in a very bad way when he woke up. She smiled coldly—she would have felt sorry for him if he hadn't been such an asshole—then slipped back into the office and started to search it from top to bottom. She'd heard stories about officers who filled their desks with booze, but she'd never actually seen it until now. She couldn't help wondering where Archer was *getting* the alcohol. There was normally a still somewhere within a giant starship, or a military base, but she doubted anyone running a still would trust *Archer* with the secret. Perhaps he was blackmailing them. It was quite likely.

And nothing of importance within the drawers at all, she thought. Commander Archer *had* worked on the anchor station, before the shit had hit the fan. She supposed his new office was a bit of a step down. *He isn't really doing anything here, is he?*

THE HALLS OF MONTEZUMA

She removed her top, then clambered into bed beside him. He groaned, loudly. She almost smiled as she closed her eyes, allowing herself to drift off to sleep. *That* wasn't the sort of reaction she normally got, when she climbed into bed with someone. She felt a flicker of guilt, hastily banished. Commander Archer deserved every moment of the hangover he was going to have, when the alarm sounded...

A hand struck her. The alarm rang, loudly. The lights came on. She jerked awake as Commander Archer spasmed against her, his hands covering his eyes. Rachel hid her amusement as she rolled out of bed, making a show of falling badly. Let him think he'd actually thrown her out of his bed, if he wished. It was important he didn't see her as a threat. She was tempted to let him suffer, but instead she walked into the bathroom and poured him a glass of water. The medical cabinet included strong painkillers, including a couple she'd thought were only available on prescription. She hesitated, then took them with her. Combined with the hangover, and the hypnotic drug, his memories of the previous night would be very blurred indeed.

His eyes rested on her bare breasts as he swallowed the painkillers and washed them down with the water. "What happened?"

"We had a good night," Rachel assured him. She forced herself to talk like a porn starlet. "You were fantastic."

Commander Archer nodded, as if she'd given him his due. She hoped it wouldn't occur to him to ask too many questions. If he started looking for the message she'd told him about...she doubted he knew how to search the system, but...she knew she could be wrong. Better he believed they'd spent the night in bed together than anything else...she smiled, inwardly. He would really *want* to believe they'd shared a bed together.

"I have to go get something to eat, sir," she said. She was fairly sure he wouldn't offer to share his breakfast. "I'll see you in the staff room."

"And you'll come back here afterwards," Commander Archer said. His eyes lingered on her muscled arms, then drifted to her chest. "Understand?"

Rachel stood and reached for her top, pulling it over her breasts. "Yes, sir."

She smiled, again, as she turned and left the suite. She'd done everything she needed to do to lay the groundwork, now...Commander Archer didn't know it, but he'd helped a great deal. And he was still helping her...

In a few hours, we will see just how well my plan actually works, she thought. *The plan was good, but no plan ever survived contact with the enemy. And if I'm really lucky, Commander Archer will get the blame.*

CHAPTER TWENTY-SIX

The smaller aspect of the problem is that resentment will also start to fester. The concept of "from each according to his ability, to each according to his needs" appears to make sense, in theory. In practice, who decides? The farmer who works his ass off, pardon the term, to support people he regards as idle layabouts is not going to be happy. Why should he? Is he not a needy person himself? It is simply impossible to keep people from exploiting the system, eventually bringing it down in ruins.
—**Professor Leo Caesius**
The Rise and Fall of Interstellar Capitalism

RACHEL HAD NEVER BEFORE been an object of pity. Not in her entire life.

She felt oddly exposed, as staffers—male and female alike—looked at her as one might look at someone who'd suffered a bereavement. Their eyes held nothing of spite or hatred, merely pity. She didn't need her enhanced hearing to know that Commander Archer had bragged of his sexual conquest to anyone who'd listen, that his imagination—and the drugs—had filled in the gaps spectacularly. She'd heard more than her fair share of crude crap and innuendo during Boot Camp and the Slaughterhouse, but this…she hid her amusement behind a carefully blank face as she worked her way through the daily tasks. Commander Archer would be amused, she was sure, to know he was cruder than the average recruit. She might tell him, right before she put a knife in his gut.

Commander Archer called her, the moment her shift ended. "Gresham, come with me."

Rachel tried to look eager as the other staffers tried not to make their sympathy too overt. Commander Archer would not be too amused if he knew what they were thinking. He'd probably send them to the front lines or worse...Rachel allowed herself a faint smile as she followed Commander Archer back to his rooms. Everything was in place. There was a good chance Commander Archer would be blamed for her actions. And if that happened, he'd probably be sent to the front lines himself.

Perhaps not, she thought. *They want to win the war.*

She showed no reaction as he opened the door and half-pulled her inside. The local security divisions had been going crazy, deploying troops and commissioners everywhere. Rachel had spotted two newcomers who were clearly more interested in keeping their eyes on their fellows, rather than their data screens. She was surprised they hadn't scattered more security monitors around, although she *was* in their HQ. They were probably more interested in keeping the civilians under control. She'd overheard a couple of people whispering about receiving messages from the underground. It was enough to make her wonder if there really *was* an underground.

Commander Archer pulled her to him and kissed her, hard. Rachel slipped her tongue into his mouth and drugged him, catching his body before he hit the floor. The temptation to let him fall was almost overpowering, but she didn't want to give him unexplained bruises that might jog his memory. Her instructors had warned her that the human mind was a funny thing. It was impossible to know what might bring a buried memory into the light, no matter what techniques were used to hide it. Commander Archer had to remain unaware of his role in the greater scheme of things until the time came for him to get the blame.

Rachel carried him to bed, muttered a handful of suggestions into his ears and then started to fiddle with the security monitors. The system would see her as sharing his bed...she hoped. It was hard to tell if the enemy had improved the system in the last week or so. They knew they had problems, even if they didn't know *precisely* what had happened. She'd heard a handful of other ex-imperial officers had been arrested and taken away. The poor bastards had made the mistake of reporting the messages they'd received to higher authority.

Which is never a good thing when higher authority is feeling paranoid, she mused, with a flicker of grim amusement. It wouldn't be the first time a system's paranoia about conspiracy had birthed a *real* conspiracy. *They merely earmarked themselves for arrest.*

She put the thought out of her mind as she checked the commander and stole one of his uniforms, then left the compartment and hurried down to the lower levels. The genius of the logistics system was that it allowed commanders to order what they needed and have it shipped to them; the curse that made life harder for them was that logistics officers rarely—if ever—questioned their orders. It was an improvement over the Imperial Army and Navy system, she conceded, but it was easy to misuse. She felt her heart start to beat as she walked into the garage. If someone had the sense to ask a few questions...

Rachel smiled as she saw the hovertruck, waiting right where she'd ordered it. She clambered into the rear, feeling her smile grow wider as she saw the collection of antitank rockets and plasma grenades. The corprats had improved upon the latter—the military had always regarded the standard design as dangerously unstable—but the antitank rockets were identical to the ones she'd used in her early career. They were designed to punch holes through hullmetal. Anything less wouldn't have any hope of slowing the rocket down for a moment.

She rigged the launchers quickly, moving with desperate speed, then climbed into the front seat and started the engine. The truck immediately came to life. Rachel smiled as she programmed a course into the ATC system, relying on the automated controllers to take the vehicle to its destination. The codes were all in place, insisting to anyone who cared to look that the hovertruck had military priority. She changed into the stolen uniform as the truck hummed down the ramp and onto the main road. It was packed with military convoys rushing half-trained troops to the front. Rachel smirked as the vehicles crawled along. She'd done her level best to ensure the locals called up the *wrong* classes of people. It was astonishing what you could do on a world where no one dared question orders.

Rachel kept a wary eye on her surroundings as the truck glided past a handful of patrols. The soldiers looked bored, rather than alert. Rachel supposed that they thought they were wasting their time. They were probably right. The patrols were in precisely the *wrong* area of town. They should have been in the poorer districts, making a show of force that might deter riots, rebellions and outright uprisings. Her lips tightened as the vehicle turned the corner and advanced towards the security headquarters. She was mildly surprised it didn't look like a fortress. Imperial Intelligence's headquarters on Earth had looked impregnable.

It'll be gone now, she thought, with a twinge of nostalgia. The old universe was gone. It would never return. *Between the riots and the falling asteroids, they'll be hardly anything left.*

The vehicle slowed to a halt automatically as it approached the checkpoint. Rachel felt a flicker of contempt. There were tanglefields and neural jammers, neither of which would stop a determined assault. She was fairly sure there'd be a QRA team somewhere within the building, but an ounce of prevention was worth a pound of cure. The contempt deepened as she spotted the security troopers manning the flimsy barricade. They looked too good to be true. The green tabs on their shoulders might be hellishly intimidating to the locals, but *Rachel* could tell they'd never seen a real fight. She wondered, idly, why their commanders hadn't insisted on rotating the troops in and out of active duty. They'd be a great deal sharper if they spent half their time on escort duty, even if they weren't put on the battlefield itself.

She checked the remote-control frequency as the guards ambled towards her, then opened the door and jumped to the ground. They were watching her hands—the first sign of actual competence she'd seen—but it wouldn't make any difference. She could use her implants to set off the rockets. She smiled at the guard, his eyes going wide as he realised she was female. The uniform was so baggy on her that it was hard to be sure. She wondered if he'd try to write her up for it, as if he wasn't about to have worse problems.

"Papers, please," the guard said. "I want..."

Rachel hit him, hard. She felt his neck snap. His body crumpled. Someone shouted, too late, as she triggered the rockets. A spread of anti-tank missiles launched from the truck and lanced towards the building, slamming into the facade. Rachel worried, just for a second, she might have done her work *too* well. If the rockets went right *through* the building without detonating...she grinned as the warheads detonated, a chain of explosions tearing the building apart. She sent the second signal and then turned and ran, boosting her legs to run at breakneck speed. Someone started shooting, bullets zipping through the air. The guards *had* to be stunned. None of the bullets came anywhere near her.

She hit the ground as her implants flashed up an alert, an instant before the plasma grenades detonated. A wave of heat washed over her. Rachel rolled over, in time to see the remains of the building catch fire. The flames would consume everything, at least until they ran out of fuel. If there was anyone still alive inside the building, they were probably doomed. The EMP thumper that had detonated before the plasma grenades probably hadn't helped matters any. The population monitoring system had been effectively disabled.

There was no time to waste. She picked herself up and continued to run, darting into an alley long enough to remove the uniform and tuck it up inside her shirt. The nearby buildings were emptying as the flames threatened to spread, men and women running in all directions as if the devil himself was after them. Rachel understood. Plasma fire was *dangerous*. A person who got burnt would be lucky if he *only* lost a limb. She forced herself to join the mob as it fled onwards, breaking free as she reached the military HQ. The guards were in a panic. Rachel had no trouble slipping past them and up the corridors to Commander Archer's room. There were no alarms. She was almost disappointed.

Commander Archer was moaning in his drugged sleep. Rachel undressed at speed, dumped the stolen uniform into the cleaning basket and jumped into bed with him. He couldn't be allowed to question his memories, not now. Her enhanced hearing picked out men running up and down the corridor, jackboots thudding against the floors as they swept the chambers...she tensed, wondering if she'd have to fight her way out after all. She'd covered her tracks, she thought, and she'd disabled the monitors, but...what if there was a back-up? The records insisted there wasn't one, yet...it was hardly the sort of thing she'd put in a datacore that *might* be accessed by enemy spies. She would want to keep it to herself.

If nothing else, it'll take them a long time to rebuild, she thought. The enemy would have to figure out what had happened first, not an easy task given that all the witnesses had died when the plasma grenades had detonated. The thumper would have damaged every exposed piece of technology within range. *They may even think I died in the blast, too.*

She lay back and accessed the datanet, tracking the distress signals and orders as they flowed through the system. No one seemed to know *quite* what to do, something that didn't really surprise her. The locals had never prepared for an attack in the middle of their city. They'd put most of their trained troops on the front lines. It had taken longer than it should for someone to take command of the scene, let alone deal with the fires and start picking through the rubble. She sardonically wished whoever was in charge good luck. There was no hope of rebuilding the system in time to make a difference.

Rachel smiled, then started to compose another mass email. The enemy government would try to deny what had happened, but who could miss a giant explosion in the centre of the city? They'd make themselves looked like fools if they tried. There was nothing more guaranteed to destroy their credibility than telling obvious lies. And they'd offend their people by treating them as idiots. They'd be better off trying to blame everything on the marines. Perhaps they could claim the explosion was a long-range missile strike.

She finished writing the email, checked to make sure the population monitoring system was definitely down for the count, then uploaded the message to the server. It would pass through a dozen datanodes, wiping all trace of its passage, before finally being sent out to everyone on the planet. The chances were good it would also cross the front lines…she'd written a handful of specific phrases into the message to inform her superiors she was still alive. She had no idea what had happened to the other three, but she was in place. They might even be able to get a message back to her.

The alarms rang. Rachel made a show of jerking awake as Commander Archer sat up, confused. Rachel knew the drug should have worked its way out of his bloodstream by now, but it was impossible to be sure. He looked like a dragon with a headache, too sore to pay attention to her naked body. She smiled shyly at him—he really *had* to be in a terrible state—and hastily grabbed for her clothes. He slapped her ass as she got out of bed. Rachel silently promised him, once again, a painful death.

"Attention," a voice thundered. "All off-duty personnel report to Hall A. I say again, all off-duty personnel report to Hall A."

Rachel scrambled into her clothes, then hurried for the door. She didn't want to be seen walking into the hall with Commander Archer, not when there was a reasonable chance the commander would be blamed for the bombing. She'd done everything in her power to cover her tracks, short of actually destroying the datacores themselves, but she knew a careful investigation would turn up all kinds of hints that would lead the investigators to Commander Archer. She wondered, idly, what he'd say when they arrested him. Would he realise what had happened? Or would he try to blame everything on his political enemies?

She made a show of adjusting her clothing as she walked into the hall. It was heaving with people, from staffers she knew to complete strangers who'd probably been recalled for duty after the shit hit the fan. She told herself to be grateful for the confusion. The more strangers running about, the harder it would be for the enemy counterintelligence personnel to locate an infiltrator. She made a mental note to check on her cover ID, just to make sure it was still solid. If someone did some vetting, they might spot gaps that would lead them to the truth. The *real* Hannah Gresham might already be dead.

An officer she didn't recognise took the stand. "There has been a terrorist attack within the city," he said. "Until further notice, all staff are required to remain inside the building and…"

Rachel listened as the officer outlined a series of precautions. None of them would be particularly hard to evade, for the moment. She knew there would come a time when she'd have to cut and run, doing as much damage as she could before the end came, but…so far, her cover was intact. She hoped that wouldn't change in a hurry. There were just too many things she needed to do before she left.

"Do not attempt to leave without permission," the officer finished. "Dismissed."

The hall slowly emptied. Rachel joined the crowds of tired-looking people as they headed back to the barracks. The alarms had gone off in the middle of their sleep cycle, ensuring they wouldn't be properly rested before they resumed their duties. Rachel hoped that meant they'd make a lot of mistakes, mistakes that would help to cover her genuine malice. She doubted Commander Archer would cover for her if she was accused of making mistakes, even if he thought she was his lover. There were plenty of other vulnerable young women where she came from.

The thought made her smile as she returned to the barracks, checking on the progress of her email as she walked. It was still spreading through the network, staying one step ahead of the censors as it flowed out to literally millions of terminals. The enemy would be going mad with rage. They couldn't hope to put the entire planet in jail…

A message popped up in front of her. She blinked. Who would be emailing Gresham's personnel account? Her family? If her family tried to contact her, Rachel knew she would have to run before she was exposed. If...

She smiled as she saw the name. Andrew Vanderveken would mean nothing to the censors, but it meant something to her. Phelps. It was the name Phelps had used, on their first undercover deployment. Phelps was alive! Rachel felt her smile grow wider. She hadn't let herself worry—too much—about the rest of the team, but she'd feared the worst. If they'd died in orbit...she wondered, briefly, if it could be a trick...no, it was impossible. No one outside the team knew about the Vanderveken ID.

He's alive, she thought. She hastily started sketching out a reply. *I'm not alone any more.*

CHAPTER TWENTY-SEVEN

But this is often not understood by political leaders. Promising bread and circuses has been a sure vote-getter for years. It is easy to promise free food, drink, education and everything else. Putting it into practice is much harder.
—**Professor Leo Caesius**
The Rise and Fall of Interstellar Capitalism

Julia had thought herself inured to horror.

She stood at the edge of the smouldering crater and watched, grimly, as the rescue and recovery crews dragged what they could from the wreckage. The entire city block had been burnt, the buildings on the outskirts badly scorched by plasma fires. It was sheer luck, from what she'd heard, that the flames hadn't spread much further. The emergency crews had been planning to knock down a dozen buildings in hopes of keeping the fires under control before the flames had finally abated. Julia shuddered as a twisted shape—it didn't *look* like a body, not really—was carried out of the wreckage. Male? Female? Human? Animal? She had no idea.

The wind shifted, blowing the stench of human flesh into her face. Her stomach twisted painfully. The director had sent her out to get her impressions of the disaster, but...she stared towards the crater, wondering if she'd made the wrong decision when she'd decided to return home. It was difficult to believe the marines had been able to carry out a bombing inside the city, the heavily-guarded city. It was far more likely some faction within the government had chosen to blow the population monitoring system to hell.

Julia turned away and stumbled towards her aircar. The early reports had stated the system had been smashed beyond all hope of repair. She saw no reason to doubt it. The entire building was gone. The senior staff, the people who made the system work, were dead. She shuddered as she realised the prisoners in the cells under the building were also dead. Perhaps *that* was why the bombing had been carried out, despite the risk. Someone had wanted to kill the prisoners to keep them from talking. It made sense, she thought as the aircar lifted up and carried her back to the government HQ. The prisoners had been earmarked for intensive interrogations. No one could keep their mouths shut forever.

She frowned as she peered down at the streets, empty save for patrolling soldiers and their vehicles. The civilian population had been told to stay home, out of the way...she dreaded to think how many work-hours would be lost even if the state of emergency was lifted in the next few hours. And if the civilians realised the government's prying eyes had been blinded...who knew what would happen? She had the nasty feeling *she* knew what would happen when word got out. Too many people hated and feared the government for the outcome to be *peaceful*. If Admiral Agate hadn't deserted when he'd been offered the chance...

The aircar landed on the pad on top of the building. Julia raised her arms and allowed the guards to search her, wincing as their fingers poked and prodded everywhere before they escorted her down to the director's suite. It felt as if they'd moved into a strange world, where nothing was entirely what it had been. She shivered helplessly, even though it was a warm sunny day. Someone had carried out a terrorist attack in the heart of the city, someone who might well hope to ride the chaos into power... how could they be so selfish? She glanced at the far walls. The marines were steadily advancing on the city. It was no time for civil war.

"Julia," the director said. "What have you learnt?"

Julia composed herself and gave her report. There was little *new* in it and she could tell the director was losing interest, even before she reached the final section. She might as well have been wasting her time. She scowled as he turned his back, his eyes tracking towards the latest reports from the front. He'd sent her out and he didn't want to hear the report? And yet, she knew he'd already heard it. His people hadn't been lying to him.

"We don't know who carried out the bombing," she said, finally. The preliminary reports had been unclear. Reading between the lines, it was fairly clear the forensic teams didn't know how the attack had been carried out. "It may have been an internal faction."

"That is quite likely," the director said. "They would have needed to manipulate the system to get a bomb within striking range of the complex."

Julia nodded. There weren't many people who could have put the attack together without setting off alarms. Whoever it was would need a high level of clearance *and* a demonstrated need for the bomb-making equipment. It wouldn't be some lowly clerk in the accounting office, but a high-ranking official. She doubted too many people would be in on the conspiracy. The more people involved, the greater the chance of a leak. And yet…she frowned. Something about the bombing didn't make sense. If the bombing had been carried out by someone inside the government, they'd destroyed a system they'd need to secure their positions after they launched a coup.

She put her thoughts into words. "Why would they destroy a system they desperately need?"

"They may assume they can rebuild the system." Director Onge smiled, coldly. "And if they left the system in place, they might find their plans impossible."

He stood. "Join me," he said. It was an order and there was no point in pretending otherwise. "I'll want your thoughts afterwards."

Julia schooled her expression as she followed him through the door into a conference room. The director's inner council were already gathering… she wondered, idly, if one of *them* had carried out the bombing. There was no one keener to climb the ladder than someone who was already so high they could *see* the top. It was quite possible... she allowed her eyes to wander the table, trying to decide which one of them it would be. They owed their positions to the director, but that didn't mean they wouldn't betray him. No doubt they'd already been approached by the director's rivals. It was what Julia would have done, if she'd been planning to unseat her patron.

Not that I am, she thought, wryly. Right now, she was in no place to risk moving against the director. She just didn't have a power base of her own. *It'll be years before that changes.*

"Twenty minutes ago, an email popped up almost everywhere," McManus said, once the table had been called to order. "As far as we can tell, *everyone* got the message. It may already have crossed the front lines and rushed into enemy territory. The message informed the entire world that the monitoring system has been destroyed."

The director said nothing for a long moment. "Who sent the message?"

"Again, we don't know," McManus said. "All we really know is that *everyone* got the message. Copies were dumped into every online email address on the planet, as well as corporate, military and personal terminals. It was coded urgent, so everyone who was online at the time will have seen it. We're working to scrub it from the system now, sir, but it's already too late."

Julia felt her heart sink. She'd been online for most of her adult life. She'd carried a terminal with her, just to make sure she was permanently in contact with her superiors. She'd even had to leave it on when she'd been in bed with her lovers. And... she cursed under her breath as the implications sank into her head. The vast majority of the population carried terminals wherever they went. If the message had been coded urgent, they'd have looked the moment it appeared in their inboxes. There was no hope of keeping word from spreading, even if they successfully wiped the message from the datanet. And that meant...

Trouble, she thought. She'd seen people looting on Hameau. The moment the police and security forces vanished, the streets had turned to chaos. The marines hadn't been able to restore order in a hurry. *How many people will seize the chance to run wild?*

The director spoke quietly, but with cold determination. "We have to nip this in the bud," he said, grimly. "And that means tracking down whoever inserted the messages into the datanet."

"We're looking at ways to trace them now," McManus said. He sounded as if he expected to be fired on the spot. "Sir, right now, we cannot afford to take the datanet offline. Even tightening the security measures will cause problems. We can and we will limit mass mailings in the future, making life harder for them, but...that might impede our ability to send orders to the entire population. Whatever we do, sir, they can manipulate to their own advantage."

"And we have the marines bearing down on us," Maryanne said. "When the wind is coming from the east, people can hear the shooting. It's only a matter of time until the truth gets out."

"It has already gotten out," McManus snapped. "We lied to the population. We told them that nothing happened on Hameau. But the underground has told them that we lost the battle and countless lives and...everyone who had a relative on the fleet is now wondering why they didn't so much as send a message home. There's no way we can keep them ignorant for much longer."

If we can keep them ignorant now, Julia thought. She was painfully aware the lower classes weren't stupid. They might be deliberately kept ignorant, but...they had eyes. They could tell when the government was lying. *They know we've lied to them. Why should they believe us if we start telling the truth?*

The director tapped the table, calling everyone's attention back to him. "Can an uprising unseat us?"

"Not on the face of it," McManus said. "The general population remains unarmed, for the moment. We must assume that'll change as dissent seeps through the city. Soldiers will desert, for example, taking their weapons with them. The underground's mystery backers will need to supply more weapons, if they want the dissidents to do more than annoy us. In the long term, however, there will be a whole string of problems. It is no longer possible to catch someone goofing off when they're meant to be working and kick him in the backside."

"And the marines will move to take advantage of the chaos," Julia said. She saw a handful of faces twist as they remembered the elephant in the room. They could beat the underground and coup-proof the government, only to be beaten by the invaders. "They provoked an insurgency in Haverford. They can do it again here."

"They had time to set up weapons dumps in Haverford," McManus said. "They didn't have time to do it here."

"They can ship weapons around the lines," Julia said. The marines were cunning. They'd have no trouble flying troops and supplies around the city, if they thought they had an opening. The last reports from Haverford had suggested the marines had done just that before the insurgents retook the streets. "We have to win quickly."

"Correct." The director looked at General Gilbert. "I understand you have a plan?"

"Yes, sir." Gilbert tapped a switch, displaying a holographic map. The marines were advancing across a broad front, but it was easy to see that the front was getting narrower as the marines moved further away from Roxon. "My intelligence staff has spent the last few days re-establishing contact with human agents within the megacity, as well as scattering observers on the far side of the front lines. The marines simply have not had the time or the resources to pull back and sweep the territory properly, to the point that they *really* only control the land under their guns."

"Which is quite a swathe of territory," Maryanne said, dryly. "Just by occupying it, they have driven thousands of refugees into our territory and forced us to evacuate and destroy installations we desperately need. They are costing us dearly."

"Yes," Gilbert agreed. "There is no point in trying to deny that they've done us a great deal of harm. They've advanced at breakneck speed, forcing us to throw untrained units into the lines. However, their success brings with it serious weaknesses."

He indicated the enemy icons. "We believe the marines are actually outrunning their logistics," he said. "They cannot drive forward, let alone shoot, if they don't have fuel and ammunition. We don't know how much they managed to capture when they took the megacity, yet even if we assume *everything* fell into their hands, they still wouldn't have anything like enough to maintain their offensive indefinitely. They're trained to operate on a shoestring, sir, but that shoestring is about to break."

The director frowned. "You are sure of this?"

"Yes." Gilbert sounded confident. "There are hard limits on how much the marines can bring down to the surface or steal from us. Even if we assume the absolute worst, their forward units have to be running short of all sorts of things. Their men probably aren't in the best of shapes either. I believe we will have a window of opportunity, shortly, to give them a bloody nose."

"We don't want to give them a bloody nose," McManus said. The cold determination in his voice echoed in the air. "We want to smash them flat."

Gilbert smiled. "We've been ruthlessly concentrating forces here and here," he said, tapping the map. "The marines are advancing into what looks and feels, to those on the front lines, a crumbling defence. They'll keep moving, in hopes of completing their mission before their supply lines snap. At that point, we'll hit them from both sides at once and either encircle or crush them. Even if they manage to break out, they'll be short on supplies. We'll have a chance to chase them back to Roxon and beat them for good."

Julia frowned. The plan looked good, but she knew from bitter experience that things always looked good on paper. Gilbert knew precisely how to present his concept—more likely, a concept dreamed up by one of his subordinates—to ensure his superiors didn't ask too many awkward questions before authorising the plan. Implementing the plan was often a great deal harder. The real world rarely deigned to cooperate with the humans as they struggled for supremacy. And, somehow, she had to remind them of it.

She cleared her throat. "How do you know they won't see you coming?"

"We've established a solid line of air defence units along the front,"

Gilbert said. "The PDCs have fired on everything in orbit that pokes its head out of the gap they carved in our defences. They shouldn't be able to see our units, which are heavily camouflaged anyway…just in case. Even if they do, and pull back before we can put them in the bag, they'll be giving up all hope of taking the city and destroying our industries before the fleet is re-concentrated. It may take longer, but we will still win."

"Good, good," the director said. "And what if it fails?"

"The worst that can happen, director, is that they get out of the trap before it snaps shut," Gilbert said. "And that will still give us the chance to run them down as they retreat."

"Then put the plan into operation," the director ordered. "And *don't* let them see what's coming before it's too late."

"Yes, sir," Gilbert said.

"Then we'd better all get back to work," the director said. "Good luck to us all."

He stood. Julia stood and followed him back to his office, considering the possibilities. If the plan worked, the marines would be broken. There would be no hope of them recovering before they were kicked off the planet. But if it didn't work…

The director called for coffee as he sat and looked at her. "What do you think?"

Julia clasped her hands behind her back. "I think the plan is workable," she said. She was mildly surprised he hadn't chewed her out for speaking out of turn. "But what if someone inside the government betrays us?"

"We're monitoring all communications that might be picked up by the invaders," the director said. "And we'd notice if someone used an unauthorised radio transmitter."

Julia had her doubts. "There were people in Haverford who were quite prepared to sell out," she said. The marines had taken the turncoats with them, when they'd abandoned the capital city and fallen back on their defence lines. "There will be people here who might be prepared to do the same."

"They'd still have to get in touch with the marines," the director pointed out. "Do you think they can without being detected?"

"I don't know, sir," Julia said. "The real question is...do *they* think they can do it without being detected?"

She remembered the map and scowled as the maid brought a tray of coffee and biscuits, then retreated without saying a word. There was just too *much* land in the disputed zone. Someone could walk east until they ran into the marines and surrender...she could imagine some of her fellows, men and women desperate for patronage, being willing to put their lives on the line for potential patrons. Or...someone might have a private radio set. Or...they might be planning a coup, intending to take power and *then* negotiate with the marines. She wondered, suddenly, if she should start thinking about options herself. The director wouldn't remain in power forever. If he fell before she clawed back enough power to protect herself...

"We'll have to wait and see," the director said. "We can't arrest everyone who received the messages."

"No, sir," Julia agreed. "We can't."

CHAPTER TWENTY-EIGHT

This happens even if the government avoids a collapse into outright tyranny. The system will be caught between two poles of injustice. On one hand, entitled scroungers who put their hands out for whatever they can get; on the other, people who literally cannot work—who genuinely cannot work—but are forced to do so by government beancounters. There is no way to avoid this. It is an injustice to support people who are perfectly capable of working, but it is also an injustice to refuse to support those who cannot work.
—Professor Leo Caesius
The Rise and Fall of Interstellar Capitalism

Percy kicked at a can as he walked home, uncomfortably anticipating an unpleasant chat with his uncle. The teacher had told him off at school, first for skiving and then for making rude gestures at the teacher's back. It wasn't *Percy's* fault he was bored stiff, learning facts and figures that were utterly meaningless. The man was an ignorant incompetent who should have been marched off to the front lines, like the older boys in the upper classes. Percy envied them. He'd have liked to wear a uniform and shoot people. He wanted to put a bullet through the teacher's head and…

He groaned, inwardly. His uncle was not going to be pleased. The man had threatened him with all sorts of punishments the last time Percy had been sent home from school. This time, perhaps, he might even go through with them. Perhaps he'd send Percy to a work farm on the other side of the world, as he'd threatened, or maybe he'd just apply his hand and his belt to Percy's backside. His uncle was a kind man, but he had his limits. And no one, absolutely no one, wanted to attract attention from the security services.

Bastards, Percy thought. There was no privacy. No freedom. Nothing...not even the prospect of a better life. He wanted something new, something different...he knew he wasn't going to get it. *My life is over and it won't ever end.*

He heard a hissing sound ahead of him as he turned into the alleyway. A man stood by the wall, painting on the stone. Percy blinked in surprise. A handful of kids had sketched out graffiti in the school bathrooms, only to be caught and punished by the police. They'd seen it as a joke, but...he stopped dead as the man started to write out a sentence. It was open defiance, the kind of thing everyone *knew* would end with the perpetrator in jail and...

"Hey." The man grinned at him. "What do you think?"

Percy hesitated, torn between awe and fear. He wanted to be like the man, showing his defiance to the police, yet...he didn't want to go to jail. He forced himself to read the sentence, word by word. BIG BROTHER IS NOT WATCHING YOU. He didn't know what it meant, or why the man had splashed bursts of paint around the alley. He swallowed, hard, as the man took a can of paint from his bag and held it out to him. It felt as if his entire life was hanging on a knife edge.

"I don't understand," he stammered. "What are you doing?"

"The security monitors are no longer on line," the man said. "I can do whatever I like and no one can see me. So can you."

He waved a hand at the splashes of paint. "You know where the monitors are? Cover them with paint now and they'll *never* be able to bring them back online."

Percy found himself gaping as he tried to wrap his head around the new reality. He'd seen the message on his terminal—it had vanished as he'd tried to read it—but he found it impossible to believe. One just couldn't get away with anything, not in the city. Things were supposed to be easier in the countryside, but…he'd heard too many horror stories of strange beasts praying on human farmers to want to go there. He knew he shouldn't talk to strangers. He knew he shouldn't even *think* about taking the can and using it…

He took the can. It was light, but it felt heavy in his hand.

"Give them hell," the man said. "And don't even think about letting them see you."

Percy nodded, staring down at the can. He could go home and disable all the monitors. He knew where they were. Everyone knew…they weren't even very well hidden. He swallowed, hard, at the thought of blinding them. If he did it alone, he'd be caught…but if everyone did it…he tightened his grip. He'd spread the word as far as he could. They couldn't put *everyone* in jail.

He turned and hurried down the alleyway. His uncle wouldn't be pleased, but…Percy knew the old man resented the constant surveillance as much as everyone else. He'd get over it in time. And the fact he'd have to thank Percy for giving the family back its privacy was just the icing on the cake.

• • •

Edna cursed under her breath as she waited in line for the storekeeper to finally attend to her. The person in front was taking her sweet time, even though she had only a handful of items. There was something wrong with her payment implant and she wasn't taking no for an answer…Edna felt a flash of frustration as she realised the silly woman had taken more than she needed. Bitch. It was people like her who made life difficult for everyone else. Edna knew the score. The rationing system was a headache, but it was the only way to make sure everyone got what they needed. Normally, they didn't make such a fuss.

She rubbed her pounding forehead as she heard angry muttering from behind her. The line was growing longer, yet the shopkeepers weren't opening more tills. The empty booths for the cashiers mocked her. Maybe half the staff had been called up and sent to the front, but that was no excuse. Edna didn't have *time* to wait much longer. She had to collect her daughter from daycare before time ran out or the meddling child protection agencies would start moaning at her again. Assholes. She had a job that didn't let her out until five in the afternoon, barely giving her an hour to shop before she had to pick up her daughter. It had been a lot easier before her husband had sailed off on *Hammerblow*. And...

Edna felt her heart sink. She'd known it might be months before her husband returned, but...rumour had it that the battlecruiser had been destroyed. Her husband might be dead. She was entitled to collect a widow's pension, if her husband had died on active service, but she'd been stonewalled when she'd called the navy personnel office to see if there was any truth to the story. She scowled as she tapped her fingers against the trolley, trying not to look at her watch. She could feel time ticking away, second by second. She would have to abandon her trolley and run if the line didn't start moving soon. She simply didn't have time to argue with the child protection officers. Meddling bitches, the lot of them. It was painfully obvious they didn't give a damn about the children. They just wanted to revel in their power to make parents squirm.

The manager appeared, scurrying towards the cashier. He was a dapper man who might have been handsome, if he clearly hadn't been sweating buckets. The entire line glared at him, wondering—she was sure—why he couldn't take a cashier's seat and start handling customers himself. Edna knew why. Managers thought they were too important to do menial work. And the few who didn't were almost worse. Her manager had tried to do some of her work for her, just to be nice, and he'd nearly driven her mad trying to fix it. She looked at her watch again, tears prickling at the corner of her eyes. She just didn't have *time* to go shopping again, after she picked up her kid. The frustration boiled up within her as the manager glanced at the crowd. The look of faint superiority in his face drove her over the edge.

She scooped up a tin of peaches and hurled it at him. A roar of anger echoed through the crowd as others started to hurl their own shopping, knocking the handful of cashiers to the floor. Edna picked up another tin, then stopped as an idea occurred to her. There was nothing stopping her from just pushing the trolley out of the store, loading everything into her bag and taking it home. The monitors would see her, but…the monitors were gone. She pushed forward, shoving the manager to one side as she moved. He was bleeding from a nasty gash on his temple…she told herself he deserved it as she kept moving, shoving her way onto the streets. Behind her, she heard shelves toppling and people screaming as they threw caution to the winds and started to grab whatever they wanted. The rationing system kept everyone alive, at the price of making sure no one had more than a couple of days' worth of food on hand. Now…

Edna wondered at herself as she packed her bag, abandoned the trolley and ran. The riot was spreading, more and more shops being looted as people—ordinary, decent people—started snatching everything that came to hand. Food stories were emptied rapidly, followed in turn by luxury shops that sold goods imported from Earth. Prices had gone up recently, although Edna wasn't sure why. Rumour insisted that Earth was gone, but she didn't believe it. What sort of crisis could destroy a whole planet?

She slipped into the shadows as she saw a line of policemen hurrying towards her. Fear washed down her spine. She'd heard terrifying rumours about what happened to women in prison, even though she didn't know *anyone* who'd gone to prison. The policemen ignored her as they ran towards the riot, clearly desperate to stop it before the chaos spread any further. Edna was sure it was too late. The crowd was no longer going to put up with their control. And anyone who escaped, now the monitoring systems were gone, was probably going to get away with it.

Her watch bleeped. It was time to pick up her daughter.

Edna squared her shoulders and kept walking, trying to look as innocent and uninvolved as possible. There was no reason for the police to catch her, right? There was no reason for them to search her. And…she wished, suddenly, that she'd taken the chance to grab *more* canned food. Her daughter was a growing girl, yet her records didn't reflect that. Her rations were more suited for a young girl than a preteen…

Behind her, she heard someone scream. She did her best to ignore it.

• • •

Constable Jimmy Parker felt his heart starting to race as he led the small force of policemen towards the riot. Fear congealed in his chest, almost choking him. He'd never really been afraid on the streets, not when everyone had known the entire city was monitored and anyone who committed a crime would be lucky if they stayed out of jail for more than a few hours. And yet…the last few days had been hellish. The bombing, the lost security monitors…someone had started teaching young boys and teenagers to block or destroy the monitors before the system could be brought back online. Jimmy had enjoyed the perks of being a police officer—it was astonishing what someone would do to stay out of jail—but now he was having second thoughts. There were so many rioters on the streets that the police were badly outnumbered.

He clutched his stunner in one hand, unsure if it would be any use. The captain had put out a call for a riot control unit, or even a company of armed soldiers, but it would take time for them to respond. The stunners weren't *bad* weapons, yet…even a wisp of clothing could provide enough protection to keep someone from collapsing into a stupor. An angry crowd couldn't be stunned before it was too late…he felt his heart skip a beat as the rioters turned to stare at him. There were more people on the streets than he'd ever believed to be possible. The worst thing he'd ever faced—a mugger who'd been bright enough to figure out the blind spots in the system—had been nothing compared to the sheer anger he saw on the streets. He felt hot liquid trickle down his legs as the crowd stared at him, their eyes hard an accusing. It took him longer than it should have done to realise what was *missing*. They weren't afraid any longer…

The crowd surged forward. Jimmy panicked and raised his stunner, sweeping it across the crowd. A handful fell to the ground, but the remainder kept coming, trampling on their former comrades before they reached the policemen. Jimmy turned to run, yet it was far too late. Something crashed into his back and he fell forward, a heavy weight slamming down on top of him. He tried to recall his training, to remember what he had to do, but...

Darkness.

...

General Gilbert was up to something.

Rachel knew it, even though she had no idea *what*. The last couple of days had been difficult, to say the least. She'd hoped to meet Phelps, to help him to slip into the building so she'd have an ally on the inside, but it had proven impossible. Phelps was now causing trouble on the streets, while she was building a conspiracy. The destruction of the monitoring system had unleashed a *lot* of pent-up resentment. It was surprisingly easy to start putting together a network of military officers and industrial managers who'd never see promotion, convincing them that they'd have a better future when the underground took over. They'd be surprised to discover who they'd been supporting, but...she shrugged. By then, it wouldn't matter.

And yet, General Gilbert *was* up to something.

She frowned, wondering if she'd done her work a little *too* well. General Gilbert didn't seem to trust anyone, save perhaps for a handful of people who'd been with him for years. He'd sent out hundreds of orders, often countermanding them hours later...if he was trying to confuse people, Rachel thought, he'd succeeded. It had crossed her mind to wonder if he was plotting a coup. Why not? She was doing the same thing, using the mobilisation and general chaos as a cover for her growing conspiracy. And yet, she wasn't so sure. A lot of his decisions wouldn't be useful if he intended to take power.

A hand dropped on her shoulder. "Hannah," Commander Archer said. He'd started to address her by her first name in public, something that had won her even more sympathy. "Come with me."

Rachel stood as her relief arrived, bracing herself. Commander Archer wasn't fool enough to insist on a quickie in the middle of his shift, was he? She frowned as she realised he might have that—or more—in mind. The senior officers were busy with their plans, leaving Archer unsupervised. Perhaps he thought he could get away with it. The hell of it was that he might well be right. General Gilbert had more important things to worry about.

And we probably made him look good, she thought. She knew she'd been a good little staff officer. She really didn't want to be sent away, not when she was precisely where she needed to be. *Damn it.*

She followed him into the office, looking around with interest. It was weirdly impersonal, although she supposed that shouldn't have surprised her. It was being used by a dozen different officers, half of whom probably believed the other half were plotting against them. Rachel had done what she could to heighten the paranoia, sending nagging messages to officers she knew to be loyal. They were screwed if they reported the messages and screwed if they didn't…

Archer locked the door, then turned to face her. "I know who you are."

Rachel froze, her implants snapping to full alert. If Archer knew who she was…her mind caught up before she could take his head off. He wouldn't have summoned her into an office, alone, if he *really* knew who and what she was. Archer was a coward. If he knew how close he'd come to death…

"You're going to be my escort to the ball, in two weeks," Archer said. "Make sure you wear something nice."

"I…I don't know how to dance," Rachel managed. She *had* had dancing lessons, but they'd been a very long time ago. "I…I thank you, but…"

Archer leaned forward until she could smell his breath. "You'll come with me or you'll go to the front."

Bastard, Rachel thought. He'd not only given her a fright, a fright that had nearly gotten him killed, he'd decided to blackmail her too. She was tempted to laugh in his face and see what happened, but…*I need to be here.*

"As you command, My Lord," she said. She tried to look alluring. "Perhaps you could teach me how to dance."

"It would be my pleasure," Archer said. He kissed her, hard enough to smear her make-up. "Now, get back to work."

"Yes, sir," Rachel said. Archer was going to pay. She'd make sure of it. "I'll get back to work at once."

CHAPTER TWENTY-NINE

Whatever the government does, it will be caught between those two poles. If it cancels benefits, however described, it will be accused of committing a grave injustice. If it gives benefits to people who manifestly do not deserve them, it is also committing a grave injustice.
—**Professor Leo Caesius**
The Rise and Fall of Interstellar Capitalism

THADDEUS SAT IN SOLITUDE.

It was impossible to know who to trust, now. The riots that had swept through the city—and over the entire planet—were a grim reminder the government's rule rested on force. The chaos had been shocking, all the more so for it being completely unprecedented. The security forces had been outmatched, unable to respond to more than a slight percentage of the incidents. Thaddeus knew it wouldn't be long before there was another cycle of riots. The people knew, now, that they were no longer being monitored. The omnipresent—and omnipotent—state had been broken. The people could say or do whatever they liked with little fear of punishment.

And we need to put dozens of men on the streets for each and every little arrest, he thought, darkly. The population no longer bent the knee to men in uniform. Entire districts had turned into no-go zones overnight. *We just don't have the manpower to keep the cities under control.*

His expression darkened as he looked at the latest set of reports without seeing a word. A wave of incidents, from stabbings and shootings to outright bombings. Men throwing rocks at policemen or swarming them by sheer weight of numbers; women seducing the policemen long enough to bury knives in their guts; kids destroying or blinding security monitors that would have to be replaced before the security systems could be brought back online. It was starting to look as though the marines—or someone—had decided to mount a terrorist campaign within the city, wearing down his forces and making them look weak. Each successful attack inspired two or three more.

His terminal bleeped. "Director," General Gilbert said. "Everything is in place. We're ready to mount the operation."

Thaddeus nodded, sourly. He'd hoped to play a waiting game, buying enough time for the fleet to return, take control of the high orbitals and smash the marines from orbit. The idea of risking everything on one throw of the dice was anathema to him. And yet, they had no choice. They wanted—they *needed*—a clear victory before the cities collapsed completely, before his enemies made a bid to take control of the system. The marines had to be crushed, then the troops redeployed before it was too late. His hands shook as he keyed the terminal. He'd thought himself prepared for the post-Earthfall universe, but he was wrong. The old rules were gone. They were never coming back.

"Do it," he ordered. There was nothing to be gained from making a fanciful speech. The historians would put words in his mouth, once the fighting was over. "And don't screw up."

"Yes, sir," Gilbert said.

Thaddeus closed the connection and scowled at the blank screen. Could Gilbert be trusted? Could anyone be trusted? The system was steadily breaking down. His closest allies would be looking for ways to jump ship, if someone else managed to gain control. Thaddeus didn't blame them—one didn't blame rats for doing what rats did—but that wouldn't stop him from punishing them if he kept his post. They'd know it, too. The old rules were definitely dead and gone. He wouldn't be sent into exile, if he lost power. He'd be killed by his own side.

He stood. It was time to go to the war room. He'd monitor the operation and, if it failed...

It isn't going to fail, he told himself. There was no point in drawing up contingency plans for defeat. Failure would lead, rapidly and mercilessly, to his execution. *We're going to win.*

...

Haydn frowned as the marines punched through a defence line and paused to gather themselves before pushing on. It had been a hard few days, an endless succession of enemy strongpoints, IEDs and brief ambushes designed to make the marines waste time clearing the trenches rather than stop them completely. He rubbed his eyes as he peered into the distance, wishing—again—that the company could rotate to the rear for a couple of days. They'd been fighting almost constantly for the last few days and it was taking a bitter toll.

A pair of tanks rumbled forward, advancing down the motorway. Haydn could hear gunfire in the distance, followed by an explosion. The enemy had been learning, for all that half the men they'd killed or captured had been untrained recruits. They'd sniped at the marines from a distance, they'd rigged houses to blow...they'd even managed, somehow, to put an IED under the motorway and flip a giant tank onto its back. Haydn would have been impressed, if they hadn't forced the marines to slow long enough to repair the road. The logistics chain was on the verge of breaking completely.

He felt his heart sink as he surveyed the town ahead of them. It was larger than the earlier hamlets, dozens of homes and bigger buildings scattered around a set of roads and parks that had clearly been dug up and turned into strongpoints. The enemy probably had hundreds of mortars hidden within the town, just waiting to rain shells on the advancing troops. Haydn's company was backed up by self-propelled guns—they'd lost their reluctance to fire into populated areas long ago—but the enemy had point-defence systems in place too. He was sure of it. They wouldn't let the marines silence their gunners *that* easily.

And they probably have orders to fire a couple of shells and shift positions, he thought, as he turned to look at his men. *It's what we'd do.*

Haydn gritted his teeth. The company had been hit hard in the last couple of days, then merged with two more companies into a single oversized unit. Marines were trained to swap companies at short notice, but there were limits. Too many of his men didn't know their new fellows. He would have sold his soul for the chance to run a training exercise, where the only real danger was being castigated for gross incompetence, but it wasn't going to happen. They had to keep the pressure on, rather than risk giving the enemy a chance to rally. He had no doubt the bastards were prepping the megacity for a long, drawn-out resistance. It was what he would have done, if he didn't have a trained army under his command. An urban environment would maximise the enemy's advantages, while minimising their weaknesses. And countless civilians would be killed in the fighting.

Mayberry came up behind him and held out a packet of cigarettes. "Smoke?"

"No, thank you," Haydn said. He'd never liked the habit. "You heard anything through the grapevine?"

"Nothing, beyond the insistence we should keep the pressure on," Mayberry said. "You think we can outflank the town?"

Haydn scowled. Leaving an enemy position in his rear struck him as a bad idea. The enemy could sneak out, cut the supply lines and then block his line of retreat. And yet...reducing the town was going to take time and effort. He wondered, idly, if he could convince the spacers to smash the town from orbit. They'd been deploying KEWs over the last few days, he'd heard. Picking through the rubble would be easier than taking the town building by building.

We knew we'd start hitting really built-up areas sooner or later, he told himself. *And now, we have.*

"I think we need reinforcements," he said, finally. "And probably a great deal more cover."

He sighed. The enemy had set up a *very* effective antiaircraft system. The drones he normally relied upon to watch their movements were effectively useless. The flyboys were making attempt to crack the system, but a couple had already been lost. Haydn knew he was advancing blind into terrain the enemy knew very well. Perhaps. He doubted they'd *planned* for a full-scale invasion. They'd assumed the orbital defences would be enough to keep any prospective opponent from landing troops.

His hand dropped to his belt and unhooked the canteen. The water tasted oddly flat, but he drank it anyway. They really *were* on the edge. He made a mental note to suggest the advance be slowed, if not halted, long enough to let his men catch their breath. None of their gains could be considered really secure, not yet. On paper, the marines had occupied a vast swathe of enemy territory. In practice, their control was so thin it might as well not exist.

As long as we keep the pressure on, we can keep them from striking back, he thought. He heard another series of explosions in the distance and frowned. *But if we don't get more men on the ground quickly...*

• • •

Lieutenant Ginny Patel gritted her teeth as she flew as low as she dared, passive sensors watching warily for signs of enemy contact. She, of everyone in the unit, knew the danger of letting the enemy have a clear shot at her. She'd been shot down once before, on Hameau, and she'd been very lucky to survive. Her former co-pilot hadn't been so lucky. She still had nightmares, sometimes, about a burning airframe and the time she'd spent in captivity. It was surprising she'd been allowed to return to active duty immediately, even though the corps was short on manpower. Normally, they'd be months of psych tests to make sure the enemy hadn't conditioned her before she was recovered by friendly forces.

She peered into the semi-darkness as the Raptor darted over an enemy town. It looked deserted, but the IR sensors picked up heat sources in the buildings. Ginny logged the details, adding them to the treasure trove of data being prepared for transmission. She didn't dare open a channel, not yet. Microbursts were supposed to be impossible to detect, but the enemy sensors were alarmingly good. They'd blown a dozen drones out of the air when they'd crossed the front lines, almost certainly because they'd been transmitting at the time. Ginny knew better. She'd only open the channel when she *knew* she was on the verge of being fired upon.

Her eyes narrowed as she picked up more and more hints of enemy activity. They were operating under a strict blackout—standard procedure, when the enemy knew what to watch for—but there were enough emissions to worry her. The sensors pinged an alarm as she flew over a troop of tanks, a troop that really shouldn't have been there. She yanked the Raptor to one side as a missile shot past her...the shot had come completely out of nowhere. She barked a command to the automated systems, ordering it to start transmitting as quickly as possible. The enemy had to have been tracking her on passive sensors, then...

She swore as she saw the sheer mass of enemy vehicles and soldiers for the first time. They were advancing along a broad front themselves, trying to take the marines in the side...her blood ran cold as she realised they'd managed to gain a certain degree of surprise. Her warning was already going out, but...she flipped a switch, arming her antitank rockets as she swooped down. The enemy guns were traversing rapidly, not quickly enough. She smiled as she saw a handful of vehicles exploding, then darted to one side as a hail of bullets shot though where she'd been. The enemy advance had been slowed, but...

Alerts flashed in front of her as the enemy self-propelled guns opened fire. Mobile missile launchers opened fire a second later, their missiles either climbing high to seek out targets or flying low to avoid point defence fire. Ginny winced in sympathy. The marines were going to take one hell of a pasting. She allowed the automated systems to fire on the enemy troops, expending what remained of her ammunition. She had no illusions. It wouldn't slow the enemy down for long, but...

Keep dodging, she told herself. There was no longer any point in trying to hide. Her active sensors noted and logged the enemy push in great detail, then forwarded it to higher authority. *Don't let them get a clear shot...*

She cursed as another wave of enemy shells flashed through the air. It was already too late. The enemy troops were on the move...and there was nothing she could do, any longer, to so much as slow them down.

...

Haydn's terminal bleeped an alert, an instant before the first wave of enemy shells crashed down on their position. He hit the ground as explosions filled the sky, the point defence lasers picking off hundreds of shells before they could reach their targets. But there were so many shells and missiles...the ground heaved, violently, as dozens of shells slammed down on their heads. Missiles followed, crashing down amongst the point defence units. Haydn swallowed a curse as he looked up, just in time to see a missile strike one of the tanks. An armoured vehicle that had shrugged off IEDs and gunfire exploded into a fireball so hot Haydn knew there was no point in searching for survivors.

He rolled over, snatching up his rifle as more and more shells cascaded down behind him. The enemy had played it smart, he acknowledged sourly. The point defence units needed to cover the marines at the sharp end, but in doing so they were exposing themselves to enemy attack. A missile rushed over his head and crashed down, somewhere in the distance. He saw a flash of light, followed by another fireball. A crack of thunder reached his ears a second or two later. There'd been a point defence unit there, if he recalled correctly. It wasn't there any longer. He dreaded to think how much damage the enemy had done in the opening bombardment.

And we're spread too thin, he thought. He heard the sound of vehicles in the distance and turned, just in time to see a line of aircars and hovertrucks emerge from the town. They had no place on a battlefield...his blood ran cold as he realised they might be makeshift VBIEDs, each one packed to the gunwales with explosives. The enemy wouldn't have any problems churning out enough explosives to fill their entire fleet...*They'd going to give us one hell of a kick in the ass.*

"Don't let them get any closer," he shouted. Normally, they'd hesitate to fire on civilian vehicles. Now...they had no choice. "Take them down..."

An aircar exploded, setting off a chain reaction. Haydn found himself sitting on the ground, unsure of quite what had happened. There was a smouldering crater where the aircars had been...the nearest buildings looked as if they'd been struck by an angry giant. In the distance, he could see enemy tanks advancing out of what remained of the town. The entire front line had been battered beyond repair. His terminal bleeped an alert, too late. Enemy forces were advancing from the north as well as the south... he realised, numbly, they were on the verge of being trapped in a vise. They were royally fucked.

He snapped orders, directing the antitank gunners to hit the tanks while the rest of the company prepared to run. They wouldn't slow the enemy for long, but every second counted. They *had* to get out of the trap before the jaws slammed shut. Haydn knew they didn't have the supplies to hold out, once they were trapped. There were heroic stories of men who'd been trapped in cauldrons and fighting to delay or escape the enemy, but those men had been armed to the teeth. And they'd often had longer to make their preparations. He had little more than a few seconds, at best. A handful of enemy tanks exploded into fireballs, but there were more right behind them. Bullets zipped through the air as they hosed the marine positions. Their shooting wasn't very accurate, but it didn't have to be.

Haydn keyed his throatmike and snapped out an update. The first moments of an enemy offensive were always chaotic, but Major-General Anderson and his staff would be working frantically to establish what was going on and take control. They needed to know the front line was breaking...no, that it had broken. Haydn swore inwardly as he barked more orders, men hurrying towards the rear as fast as they could while keeping their heads low. There wasn't any hope of stopping the enemy, not short of Roxon. They hadn't given any thought to preparing a proper defence line.

And we tore up the landscape pretty good during the march up, he thought, grimly. *We don't have a hope of preparing strongpoints because we smashed all the potential strongpoints ourselves.*

He glanced up as a flight of aircraft roared overhead, dropping bombs on a marine tanker unit. A pair of missiles rose up, blowing their targets out of the sky, but the remainder banked and escaped before they could be fired upon. The bastards had husbanded forces ruthlessly, he noted. It sounded as if they were advancing all along the front, as well as trying to trap the marines. He would have been more impressed if he wasn't on the verge of being trapped.

"Pass the word," he ordered, as the company kept moving. He could hear enemy troops behind him, *feel* shells passing through the air as they sought out targets in the distance. "No one is to stop until we get out of the trap."

But he knew, all too well, that it might already be too late.

CHAPTER THIRTY

The blunt truth is that ordered societies simply do not work. People act in their own self-interest—or, at least, what they think is their self-interest. They do not have a dedication to the vast majority of society, particularly when that dedication comes at the expense of their lives. They will not put the interests of society ahead of themselves. Indeed, a wise society will always bear in mind the interests of those who produce.
—**Professor Leo Caesius**
The Rise and Fall of Interstellar Capitalism

"We just received word from Captain Jalil," Lieutenant Yu reported. "His company is overwhelmed. He's requesting permission to surrender."

Major-General Anderson said nothing as he studied the display. The fog of war had enveloped the battlefield, to the point that far too many icons in front of him represented nothing more than educated guesswork, but the overall picture was all too clear. The enemy were advancing rapidly, their spearheads aimed at the weakest parts of the marine line. It was cunning, he admitted sourly. They'd timed it well. He had no choice but to order an immediate retreat if he wanted to preserve his men.

Unless they screwed up the timing instead, he thought. He shook his head.

I cannot afford to allow myself to believe it.

He cursed himself under his breath. He should have been out there, commanding from a battlesuit or a command vehicle somewhere along the front lines. He'd lost touch with the facts on the ground. He was no better than a snooty army officer who'd gotten his post through connections, rather than competence. He'd allowed his surroundings to lull him into a false sense of security. And…he told himself to stop woolgathering. The Commandant would deal with him, if the post-battle analysis decided the blame was his. He didn't have time to worry about it. Right now, he had to get his men out of the trap.

His eyes found Captain Jalil's position on the display. Jalil's men had been guarding the flanks, watching for insurgents or infiltrators rather than a full-scale enemy offensive. They'd been lucky to survive the opening blows…Gerald suspected they'd only survived because the enemy hadn't realised the company was there. Or maybe they'd been more intent on crushing the antiaircraft defences rather than dealing with a lightly-armed body of men. They'd claimed air superiority over the battlefield, if not air supremacy. Gerald knew it was just a matter of time until that changed.

"Order Captain Jalil to hold out as long as possible, then order his unit to break up and sneak through enemy lines," he said. He knew he was sending good men to their deaths, but there was no choice. They *had* to slow the enemy. "Tell him everything relies on him."

He knew, as he continued snapping orders, that it might already be too late. The enemy was pouring on the pressure. He'd never seen anything like it, even on Hameau. But then, he supposed the enemy had never been given a real chance to do something that hadn't happened for hundreds of years. Take on a marine division in open battle and give it one hell of a thrashing, perhaps even destroy it completely. He shuddered to think of how many men—and how much equipment—was going to go into the fire. They'd have to abandon anything that couldn't be moved quickly…thankfully, there wouldn't be much ammunition for the enemy to capture.

"We need to set up defence lines here, outside Roxon," he said. The megacity had never been fully in his grip. Now…he made a mental bet with himself the enemy had already slipped troops into the city. "And we need to stop them dead…"

A thought crossed his mind. The enemy had done everything right, so far, but…that might be about to change. If he was careful—and lucky—he might just have a chance to turn the battle around. It would be chancy—he disliked the idea of relying on the enemy making a mistake—but he couldn't think of anything else. He couldn't afford a long, drawn-out campaign. The enemy, hopefully, felt the same way too.

"Get me Captain Stumbaugh," he ordered. His staff could handle the retreat, although there was little they could do. Events had already moved out of their hands and there was no point in pretending otherwise. "I need to talk to her."

"Yes, sir."

...

Alan Beresford-Briggs lay on the ridge and peered towards the road below. He'd never expected to snipe at real humans, instead of wild animals in the forests, but his shooting was first-rate. Even his stepmother, bitch that she was, admitted he was a good shot even as she moaned about him spending all of his time hunting instead of climbing the corporate ladder. He felt a flicker of hatred for the wretched woman, even though he had no idea if she was alive or dead. The corporate ladder was driving his father into an early grave. Why would Alan waste his time trying to get onto the first rung when he could spend his days enjoying himself instead?

He lay very still as the first enemy troops came into view. They looked to be in retreat, running for their lives…he thought he spotted a handful of treacherous civilians accompanying them. He was tempted to shoot them first, but he had very clear orders to take out as many of the marines as possible instead. His eyes narrowed as a pair of vehicles drove into view, a truck and an armoured car…a tank? He'd never been particularly interested in the military. He loved shooting, and he enjoyed eating his kills, but the thought of marching around on a parade ground horrified him. It would be dreadfully dull...

Alan allowed himself a tight smile as he took aim, pointing his rifle directly at one of the enemy soldiers. He'd made harder shots. He'd picked off animals that could run at the speed of light...or close enough to it to make no difference, not to him. He squeezed the trigger, feeling the rifle jerk as the bullet left the barrel. The bullets were designed to take down wild animals. The target's head exploded. Alan blinked—he'd never shot a human before, not with a hunting rifle—and then moved to the next target. The tank moved forward, its guns rapidly turning toward him...

There was no time to run.

...

General Jim Gilbert studied the first set of reports with a flicker of pronounced satisfaction. It was clear to him, even if his superiors were in denial, that the datanet had been compromised. The messages that had been sent to everyone in the system, including military officers like himself, were proof that something was very wrong. He'd worked overtime to conceal his plans as much as possible, to the point of briefing trusted officers in sealed—and unmonitored—rooms and sending sealed orders to the men on the front lines. He hadn't really hoped for complete surprise, no matter what he'd told the director, but...

He nodded to himself. The marine lines were crumbling. They were putting up a stiff fight, but it was clear they'd been caught in the open. Some of his officers were already chattering about a rout, about the marines throwing down their guns and running for their lives. Jim knew better. The marines had realised the trap and done the only thing they could. He was almost relieved. Trapping thousands of marines in a cauldron might well have been akin to catching a tiger by the tail.

"Continue the offensive," he ordered, as he turned away from the displays. The first stage of the operation had proceeded smoothly, better than he'd expected. It was time to move to stage two. "Don't give them a moment to catch their breath."

"Yes, sir."

. . .

Haydn took a moment to rig an IED in hopes of slowing the enemy troops a little—a trick he'd learnt at the Slaughterhouse, back when the universe had made sense—and then resumed the march east. The lines had been thoroughly broken. Dozens of tanks, self-propelled guns and antiaircraft vehicles had been turned into burned-out ruins. He forced himself to keep moving, trying to decide if he had a front-row seat to the greatest disaster in the history of the Terran Marine Corps. There'd been other defeats—other disasters—but nothing quite as bad. And most of *them* had been nothing more than tactical defeats.

He motioned for his men to keep moving. The enemy shelling hadn't abated, although he wasn't sure what they were shooting at. They were tearing up the landscape, but little else. Perhaps they were monitoring the retreat, trying to harass the marines and keep them on the move…it was impossible to know. The command datanet had become strikingly patchy over the last few hours. He'd thought that was impossible.

They're probably tracking the communications nodes and taking them out, he mused, as they trudged onwards. The enemy forces were trying to trap them. He had no idea if they'd escaped the trap or not. *They keep us from talking to each other, they keep us from plotting a counterattack.*

His legs ached. Sweat poured down his back. The marines barely spoke as they kept moving, trudging through ground that had been torn up by the offensive and then churned up again by enemy shellfire. He felt dreadfully exposed. There was no sign of the enemy, but he was sure they were all around him. He hoped Major-General Anderson and his men had started setting up defence lines, somewhere close to the city. They'd need an anvil to stop the enemy hammer before their tanks got into the rear areas. If that happened, they were thoroughly screwed. The corps would be looking at the greatest disaster in its long history.

He turned as he heard an explosion behind him. A small enemy force was coming into view, driving up the road as if they didn't have a care in the world. He swore under his breath, ordering his men to take cover. The enemy was chasing them with light units...he was sure their tanks and other support vehicles were being held in reserve. His lips curved into a cold smile as he plotted an ambush. They could give the enemy a surprise before turning and resuming the retreat.

Mayberry tapped his shoulder. "There's a drone up there..."

Haydn glanced up. Nothing was visible in the blue sky, but he knew that was meaningless. The latest drones—and he was certain the corprats would have the very latest—flew high enough to be unseen by the naked eye, yet low enough to pick out the hairs on his head. Mayberry wouldn't have seen the drone without his optical sensors...Haydn put the thought aside as he thought, quickly. The drone had to be taken down. They couldn't hope to pull off the ambush while it's unblinking eyes watched the battlefield before.

"Hit it," Haydn ordered. "And then run."

Mayberry nodded and unslung the HVM launcher from his back, then crawled away. Haydn watched him go, trying not to wonder if he'd sent the sergeant to his death. The HVMs were single-shot weapons, and the enemy would gain little by trying to shell the sergeant's position, but there was no way to know if the enemy actually knew it. They might fire a salvo just to be assholes. Hell, the drone—or its controller—might spot the sergeant as he took aim and shot first. Drones weren't supposed to engage targets automatically—Haydn had yet to see a battlefield IFF system that worked perfectly—but the enemy might have disengaged the safety systems. They needed to keep their eyes in the sky.

Even at the cost of firing on their own people, Haydn thought. *That won't do wonders for morale...*

The sergeant fired. Haydn watched a streak of light shoot from the launcher and stab into the blue sky. The HVMs were fast. He'd been assured that any aircraft targeted by a launcher would be dead before the pilot realised it was under attack, although he knew better than to take it for granted. The drone was *very* high. He thought he saw a puff of smoke in the sky, then dismissed the thought as he raised his rifle. The enemy knew they were approaching the marines. His lips quirked. If they'd doubted it before the HVM had been fired, they didn't doubt it any longer.

"Fire," he snapped.

He squeezed the trigger. The lead vehicle skidded to a halt, two men jumping out and diving for cover. The driver slumped forward, dead. The two following vehicles evacuated themselves with commendable speed, too late. Haydn felt a flicker of cold delight as the enemy soldiers died, only a couple surviving long enough to return fire. They must have expected the marines to keep moving, rather than turning long enough to give them a bloody nose. The drone should have warned them. Perhaps someone hadn't kept his eye on the terminal.

Or perhaps their superiors didn't pass on the alert, he thought. *They don't believe in letting their junior officers have direct access to intelligence reports...*

"Keep walking," he ordered Mayberry. "I'm going to check out the enemy position."

He drew his pistol, then hurried forward. He knew he shouldn't go alone, but he wanted to get his men out of the trap as quickly as possible. A pair of enemy soldiers were moaning...he checked their wounds, then left them. Their reinforcements would arrive shortly, when their superiors realised the patrol hadn't reported back. Or something...he checked the vehicles quickly, unsurprised to find a complete lack of useful information. The vehicle's datanode had been smashed beyond repair. He scooped up a handful of grenades, then turned and hurried back to his men. They were waiting for him further down the road.

"We have to keep moving," he said. In the distance, he could hear aircraft. Friendly? It wasn't likely. "The jaws are slamming closed."

"That's all we can give you," the load officer said. "We're bugging out in half an hour."

Lieutenant Patel nodded, curtly, as she powered up the Raptor. She'd returned to the makeshift base, just in time to discover that Major-General Anderson had ordered a general retreat. Her records had been taken and analysed by the spooks, who'd told her she hadn't so much as slowed the enemy down. She was surprised she hadn't been ordered to fly vital personnel out of the trap. Instead, she'd been resupplied and ordered to attack targets of opportunity.

She glanced at the datanet terminal and frowned. The enemy had done well. She'd expected them to kill the drones, but they'd also managed to kill ninety percent of the active and passive sensors the marines had emplaced during the march up. There was hardly any coverage left…she shook her head as she steered the Raptor into the air and set course for the enemy lines. She'd just have to take potluck. It helped she had a rough idea of where the enemy were…and where friendly forces *weren't*.

Slow the bastards down, she thought. She stayed low, all too aware she was flying into the teeth of enemy air defences. It wouldn't take more than a single HVM to *really* ruin her day. Again. She tried not to think of the possibility of a blue-on-blue. To be shot down by the enemy again would be bad, but to be shot down by friendly forces…*Slow the bastards down, and then get out alive.*

Her passive sensors hummed as they picked up more and more radio and datanet chatter. It was difficult to localise the microbursts, but she had a rough idea of their location. She could get close enough to spot the troops visually, then hit them hard before running for her life. If she hit them hard enough, they might not even have time to aim a missile at her before she showed them her heels and rocketed out of range. Ginny checked the pistol at her belt, just in case. The last time she'd been captured had been quite bad enough. This time…she intended to make the enemy *hurt*.

Suddenly, far sooner than she'd expected, she saw a line of enemy tanks heading west. They crashed through the terrain, chewing up the remains of the farmland as they tried to trap the marines. She activated her missile launchers, firing a volley of antitank rockets into the enemy armour. A couple of tanks exploded, the remainder bringing their weapons to bear as quickly as they could. She evaded a handful of misaimed shots, then rocketed away. The threat receiver screamed a warning, a second later. A HVM shot past, so close she thought she could read the serial number on the wing. Thankfully, the missile was moving too fast for its own good. The explosion was too far away to do more than shake her craft.

Time to run, she thought, as she ducked low and fled back to friendly territory. She knew where the next airbase was supposed to be, but…was it there? The Raptor *could* fly all the way to Roxon, yet…there was a very good chance the air defences would see her as a threat and open fire. She didn't want to turn on her IFF. She'd be telling the enemy *precisely* where to shoot. *Go low, go fast.*

She glanced at the smoke rising behind her and shuddered. She'd hurt the enemy, but had she slowed them down? It was hard to tell. And even if she had…

We lost this one, she thought, tiredly. *All we can do is get out of the trap and regroup.*

CHAPTER THIRTY-ONE

Capitalism, in its purest form, is about rewarding people for producing. First, through hard work. This speaks to human nature. A person who works hard and is rewarded for it is incentivised to keep working hard. Furthermore, he sets a good example for everyone else. If Bob the Builder can work hard and earn enough to eventually start his own business, William the Wannabe can try too. He may even succeed.
—**Professor Leo Caesius**
The Rise and Fall of Interstellar Capitalism

RACHEL HAD NEVER FELT quite so helpless before.

She knew, now, what General Gilbert had been planning. She knew, now, just what he'd done to ensure the secret remained so, even from his staff officers. She had to admit he'd done a very good job of hiding the truth until it was too late for her to do anything, using the chaos Rachel and Phelps had caused to conceal his plans. The more she looked at the stream of reports flowing in from the battlefield, the more she wished she'd taken the opportunity to kill General Gilbert when she'd been on the anchor station. She might have died shortly afterwards, gunned down by his guards, but…the enemy CO wouldn't have lived long enough to plan and execute a counteroffensive.

Her thoughts raced as she tried to devise a way to slow or stop the offensive. She was prepared to sacrifice her cover, to throw away everything she'd done, but nothing came to mind. She thought she could get into the general's office, perhaps even into the director's headquarters, yet... it wouldn't be enough. General Gilbert's death wouldn't save the marines from the trap steadily tightening around them. All she could do was lose some orders and delay others, hoping there'd be enough gaps in the enemy lines to give her comrades a chance to escape. She had the uneasy feeling she might have lost everything. Her planned conspiracy wouldn't work so well if the conspirators thought they were joining the *losing* side.

And there are limits to how much damage the civilians can do, she thought. *They just don't have the weapons or supplies to pose a long-term threat.*

She cursed under her breath. She'd rerouted more trucks of weapons to the underground, but the enemy was starting to catch on. They'd started to insist on orders being checked and rechecked before they were actually followed, making it impossible for her to forge the correct paperwork and expect people to follow orders without question. There was a silver lining—checking orders took time—but it wasn't enough to make a real difference. She considered, again, simply walking into the general's office and opening fire. With a little preparation, she might even get out alive.

The shift ended. Rachel joined the throng as the staff officers hurried down to the canteen. It was better to remain in a group, if only to make a show of hiding from Commander Archer's roving eye. Her comrades had been sympathetic...she might have preferred it, almost, if they'd hated her for attracting his attention. Sympathy was often harder to duck. The giant viewscreen was displaying enemy propaganda, informing anyone who cared to watch that millions of marines had been killed. Rachel doubted anyone in the room believed the nonsense. They knew how hard it was to land even a thousand marines on a hostile world. There weren't millions of marines in the landing force. The offensive couldn't have killed anything like so many.

Idiots, she thought, coldly. *Do they really think people believe them?*

The thought bothered her. She knew she'd have to send out another email and soon, even though she had a feeling the searchers were getting closer. Perhaps that was why Commander Archer hadn't called her to his rooms…or perhaps he'd just decided she was no longer a challenge and moved on to someone else. Or…she smiled. Perhaps he'd just had an attack of competence. General Gilbert wouldn't hesitate to remove him if he fucked around—literally—during the grand offensive.

She ran her hand through her hair as she collected her tray and settled down to eat. The food had grown steadily worse, something that alternatively amused and annoyed her. The growing underground had managed to impede food supplies, for better or worse. The local government had made a mistake when it set up a rationing system. Keeping the population one or two missed meals from starvation had alienated nearly everyone.

And now they're looting the stores openly, she mused. *What'll they do next?*

Her lips quirked. The handful of reports she'd seen—or read, through the datanet—had suggested over a hundred marines were loose in the megacity. She knew there was only one, two if she counted herself. Phelps had moved quickly from place to place, regularly changing his appearance to ensure that no two people saw the same person. There was little hope of turning the dissidents into a proper army, but…it didn't matter. They had to do nothing more than upset the enemy and keep them off balance. If they knew how few marines were *really* within the city…

She finished her meal and stood. She had to move fast, before the enemy realised where she was and what she was doing. If she could get everything in place, she could mount a coup and win overnight. And if she failed…

At least I'll take their self-confidence down with me, she told herself. The enemy was starting to question the datanet, but they hadn't realised—yet—just how easily it could be manipulated. She was steadily collecting a small army's worth of fake IDs. *It'll be enough to give the troops on the ground a chance to rally and resume the offensive.*

"Shit!"

Haydn swore as the enemy shells crashed down around them. He hit the ground, then started crawling rapidly towards a ruined farmhouse. He'd broken up the platoon, when they'd reached the crossroads, but he still had thirty men with him. He glanced up, into the darkening sky. Was there a drone up there? Were the enemy tracking them? He knew it was unlikely to matter. They didn't have any HVMs left. The drone could direct the hunters towards them from a safe distance.

Mayberry joined him as they took cover. "They're closing in..."

"Looks like it," Haydn agreed. The company had shot its way through a handful of ambushes, exhausting their ammunition in the process. It felt as if they'd been singled out for special attention, although he was fairly sure it was unlikely. The enemy troops didn't know him from Adam. They couldn't know it had been his unit that had boarded *Hammerblow* and forced the battlecruiser to surrender. "I think we're in trouble."

He snorted, grimly, as they counted their remaining supplies. They were right down to the dregs, without a hope of surviving long enough to break contact and get back to friendly territory. The terminal had flashed up warnings of everything from snipers and insurgents to enemy aircraft roving on the wrong side of the lines. Haydn was grimly sure they were trapped. He could practically *feel* the enemy soldiers closing in.

His heart twisted. His men had been pushed right to the limit. It felt as if someone was going to snap. Haydn knew his marines were better trained than regular soldiers or guardsmen—the latter had a reputation for breaking and running whenever they ran into real danger—but even marines had their limits. He didn't need to hear grumbling from behind him to know morale was in the pits. He was pretty short on morale himself.

He surveyed their surroundings. The farmhouse wouldn't provide more than a few moments of cover...less, perhaps, if the enemy called in air support or simply dropped a handful of shells on the damaged roof. The fields around them had been burnt and then flattened, ensuring there was almost no cover. They might be able to escape after dark…no, he shook his head at the sheer absurdity of the thought. The enemy troops would have night-vision gear, if they didn't have enhanced eyesight. There was little hope of getting out alive.

And that left…what? Surrender?

He scowled. He'd grown up in a universe where insurgents, rebels and terrorists offered no mercy to surrendered soldiers. There were more than enough horror stories of prisoners being raped, tortured, mutilated or simply killed out of hand for him to have second and even third thoughts about surrendering. Better to be killed in battle than die in a POW camp. And yet…the Corprats hadn't been *complete* assholes to their prisoners. He knew a handful of men had been taken prisoner during the last campaign, only to be treated well and released after the fighting. Did he dare surrender?

If I don't, we die for nothing, he thought. A final desperate stand would be pointless. Worse than pointless. The enemy would simply drop a bomb on their position and move on. *If we surrender, we'll live to fight again.*

He looked at his men. He couldn't help feeling as though he was betraying them. If it had just been him…he would have fought, he would have tried to take a handful of men down with him before the end came. But he was responsible to the men under his command. He couldn't get them out, he couldn't hide them, he couldn't even sell their lives dearly. He…

"Stack arms," he ordered, harshly. The first moments of surrender were always the most dangerous. It only took one idiot to start a slaughter. The enemy troops would be jumpy as hell. He hoped they had orders to accept surrender. They should have orders, if only to encourage more surrenders, but…there was no way to be sure. "And wait."

He keyed his terminal to send the final message and self-destruct, before he stood, holding his hands up as he walked into clear view. There was no time to remove his armour, let alone strip naked. He'd been in places where forcing the locals to strip before they were allowed to leave had been the safest course of action, even though it humiliated the poor buggers and provoked resentment and hatred. The safety of his unit came first. He knew the enemy commander would feel the same way too.

"Keep your hands where I can see them," a voice barked. "And don't move!"

Haydn remained still as two men rushed towards him, moving with the squeamish determination of trained but untried troops. He winced inwardly—inexperienced men were not likely to prove good captors—and then kept his mouth firmly closed as they searched him roughly. They didn't really know what they were doing—he could have snapped their necks with ease—but it didn't matter. He was sure there were enough guns covering him to blow him to bits if he offered the slightest resistance. Strong hands gripped him, yanked his hands behind his back and bound them in place with a plastic tie. He winced, inwardly, as he was pushed back towards the enemy lines, forced to march into captivity.

The war isn't over, he told himself, sternly. *We aren't dead yet.*

But he knew, as they were pushed into walking faster, that he might well be wrong.

...

"Their troops have linked up, sir," Lieutenant Yu said. "The jaws have slammed shut."

Gerald nodded as he studied the map. The enemy lines had closed, sealing the trap shut. Anyone caught within the cordon would have a very hard time getting out before it was too late. The last—and probably the final—set of reports had made it clear the enemy were sweeping the cauldron, trying to make sure the marines didn't have a chance to dig in and fight to the death. Gerald made a face as he cursed his own mistake. Pushing the advance so hard had given the bastards a clear shot at his supply lines. And they'd taken full advantage of it.

He turned his attention to the datanet. The forward defence line was taking shape, but it just wasn't anything like strong enough to stop the enemy from punching through. They'd know it too. Probably. He was uncomfortably aware there were too many enemy spies within the occupied zone, poking and prying into everything between the two cities. It wasn't a bad thing, but he knew he was gambling. It would be a bad moment for the enemy to play it cool.

"Keep moving our men back to the defence line," he ordered. Too many of his people were exhausted. That, and the simple fact they'd been defeated, would gut them. They were trained to keep going, whatever happened, but…he had no idea if they *would*. Even the best men had their limits. "And get the relief forces into place before it's too late."

He sat back in his chair, forcing himself to think. The enemy had taken a page from *his* book, damn it. They knew what had happened during the last campaign and set out to duplicate it. There was no lake for them to turn into a weapon, no dam for them to destroy, but…it didn't matter. They'd taken advantage of their resources and used them masterfully.

And they'll want to keep the pressure on, he thought. *If they do…*

He checked the last set of logistics reports and scowled. The flow of troops and men to the surface was continuing, but…he shook his head. They'd need to use the dumpsters again and again, if they wanted to launch another planetary invasion. It was just impossible to get enough men down to the ground, if the enemy controlled the PDCs. It was…he shook his head, curtly. There was no point in worrying about it now. They'd learnt enough lessons, over the last few months, to fill a book. Three books. They'd spend the next year or so learning from them, adapting to the new universe. He'd worry about it when—if—they brought the campaign to a successful conclusion.

"The enemy tanks appear to be halting, for the moment," Lieutenant Yu said. New images flickered on the display. "Our drones report they're rearming."

"Night is falling," Gerald said. The enemy was presumably trained in night-fighting. They wouldn't want to give the marines a break. "They'll rearm and then resume the offensive. They have no choice."

And we'll be waiting, he thought, grimly. *Let them make one tiny mistake. Just one.*

Haydn relaxed, slightly, as the prisoners were marched to a mobile command unit and forced to wait as row upon row of enemy troops drove past, heading in the other direction. They laughed and jeered at the prisoners, but did nothing else. Haydn had no trouble recognising them as men who hadn't seen combat, yet thought they knew what was coming. He would have smiled, if he hadn't been so tired. The tie binding his wrists was starting to hurt.

He kept his face under tight control as a trio of trucks arrived, driven by men in unmarked uniforms. The green tabs on their shoulders meant trouble, if he recalled correctly; security troops, rather than *real* soldiers. Some things were universal. They had the finest uniforms, the finest equipment...he couldn't help noticing their boots were new, rather than worn out through constant use. He'd never understood why headquarters troops got the best equipment, even though they were rarely expected to do more than stand guard and look good. The few times they were sent into action, they never did well.

The security officers hauled him and his men to their feet, searched them again, then pushed them into the trucks. Haydn offered no resistance. There was no point. If the enemy was using trucks, without an escort, they presumably considered it safe. He groaned, inwardly, as the truck rattled to life. It was possible they were being watched from a distance, but unlikely. The front lines had been shattered. It was hard to believe his superiors were putting together a recovery operation. Did they even know Haydn and his men had been captured? He'd sent a message, but he had no way to know if it had been received.

We have a duty to escape, he reminded himself. They might have surrendered, but they hadn't given up. *We just need a chance.*

He studied their surroundings as they drove towards the megacity, burned-out towns slowly giving way to enemy strongpoints and deserted buildings. There were no civilians on the streets, just men in uniforms and armoured vehicles. Someone had been clearing lanes through the defences, allowing more and more men to join the offensive. Beyond the township... there was another road, leading up to the megacity itself. It looked like a giant old-time fortress, intimidating buildings towering over the people like gods looking down on men. Haydn knew it was deliberate, a trick to overawe civilians, but it still nagged at his mind. It was hard to force himself not to feel intimidated.

The poor bastards who grow up here are probably used to it, he thought. He'd been in uncomfortable places. He'd gotten used to them. *And it's clear some of the locals have had enough.*

Haydn turned his attention to the security troopers, silently gauging their worth. They were good at pushing unarmed civilians around, he decided, but would probably be hopelessly out of their depth on a real battlefield. It wasn't *them* who'd taken the marines captive.

But they'll probably take the credit, he thought. The troops looked alert, but not as alert as they should be. *If they give us an opening, we'll give them a nasty surprise.*

CHAPTER THIRTY-TWO

Second, through rewarding innovation. An experienced man may find a newer and better way to do something. If he is rewarded for his insight, he will be—as above—encouraged to innovate more as well as setting a good example for his peers.
—**Professor Leo Caesius**
The Rise and Fall of Interstellar Capitalism

"THE OFFENSIVE WAS A TOTAL SUCCESS," General Gilbert said. There was a hint of boasting in his voice, and who could blame him? "The invaders are in full retreat."

Julia frowned, uncomfortably. The map looked impressive—the occupied zone had shrunk rapidly—but she knew from grim experience that the marines were very good at recovering from their defeats and striking back. She'd watched a panorama of marines retreating, of prisoners being taken, of an endless procession of burnt-out vehicles and destroyed enemy strong points, yet...she found it hard to feel reassured. The enemy was tough. Sure, they'd been hurt...but they'd been hurt before, on Hameau. It hadn't been enough to keep them from striking back.

"Good," the director said.

"Our forces are poised to continue the offensive," General Gilbert said.

"We can drive them all the way back to Roxon and beyond…"

"No," Julia said, without thinking.

The director looked at her. Julia cursed herself, silently, as she realised her mistake. She was very junior…she would still be very junior even if she wasn't in disgrace. It wasn't her place to speak first, not unless she was called upon by her superiors. She'd been lucky to get away with it last time. And yet…the grim certainty they were on the verge of making a terrible mistake welled up within her. She knew she had to speak.

"Explain," the director ordered. "Now."

Julia took a moment to compose her argument. She needed to convince them. She needed…she felt her heart sink, the realisation dawning on her that they'd probably refuse to listen simply because she'd spoken out of turn. Again. They were amongst the most powerful men and women on the planet. She'd failed to wait.

"During the last war, the landing force drove the marines away from Haverford and chased them back towards their original landing sites," she said, carefully. "They kept falling back until our forces walked right into a trap, then drowned them. They blew a hole in a mountainside just to cause a flood and…"

"There are no dams between here and Roxon," General Gilbert said, tartly. "They have not had *time* to set up any kind of traps. If the reports are accurate, they are in full retreat. We cannot afford to give them time to regroup and establish new defensive lines. We have to push them back now."

"The longer they remain on the surface, the greater the chance of losing control of a city or two," McManus added. "We need those troops on the streets."

"And if we lose the next battle," Julia asked, "what will it do to us?"

"Poppycock." McManus looked at her as if she was something nasty he'd scraped off his shoe. "Once bitten, twice shy?"

"I learnt from my mistakes, sir," Julia said. "I should never have authorised the last offensive. We are on the verge of repeating the same mistake."

McManus shook his head. "We cannot give them time to recover, nor can we keep our troops on the front lines when we need them back here."

"We should be able to drive them all the way back," General Gilbert said. "If our figures are accurate, and we worked a considerable margin for error into the calculations, the marines are operating on a shoestring. They simply haven't had *time* to land enough supplies to set up a defence line and eventually resume the offensive, but that will change. We cannot afford, from a purely military point of view, to give them the chance. We have to act now."

"Quite." McManus sounded irked, as if he disliked the idea of agreeing with the general. "If we don't move now..."

Julia sat back in her chair, wondering what sort of hammer would fall. Exile? Death? Or...or what? Resentment burned in her gut. She'd given them her advice and they'd chosen to ignore it because *she* was the one who'd given it. She cursed her own mistake as the board moved to discuss other matters, wishing she'd had the sense to raise the matter with the director privately. He'd be much more reasonable, she was sure, if no one was watching. He certainly wouldn't be afraid of looking weak, just for listening to plainspoken advice.

"You will continue the offensive as quickly as possible," the director said. He smiled, humourlessly. "My family has been nagging me to recover the mansions."

It'll take months to repair the damage even if the marines surrendered without a fight, Julia thought, savagely. *And what will you do then? Remain there, alone?*

"Now that's settled," McManus said, "we have a more important matter to address."

He leaned forward. "My department wishes to take custody of the enemy prisoners."

"Out of the question," General Gilbert said. "The marine prisoners surrendered in accordance with the laws of war..."

"The laws of war no longer exist," McManus snapped. "The Empire is gone. We are not obliged to honour treaties and agreements we never signed, let alone rules handed down by the Grand Senate and enforced by the Imperial Navy. The marines are invaders who landed on our world, little better than terrorists and traitors. They can be legally put against the wall and shot! Now!"

His eyes roamed the table. "They know things. We have to know those things. My people are experts in…convincing…prisoners to talk. We need to *make* them talk."

The director looked at the general. "General?"

"There are two points that need to be raised," General Gilbert said. "The first is that the prisoners are unlikely to know very much, even if we *could* convince them to talk. Troops on the front line are rarely told anything important, simply because they might fall into enemy hands. I think trying to get information out of them will be, at best, pointless. At worst, they might be conditioned to the point that a suitably…*rigorous*…interrogation will kill them before they can say a word."

"My people are experts," McManus insisted.

"There are plenty of ways to keep one's people from talking," General Gilbert said. "And the marines are reputed to use all of them."

He indicated the map. "The second point, sir, is that they've taken a hell of a lot of *our* people prisoner. They've swept up tens of thousands, perhaps hundreds of thousands, of our people. They even hold an entire megacity, complete with millions of our civilians. If we start mistreating their people, they will start mistreating ours."

McManus snorted. "So what?"

"The laws of war do not rest on…treaties and agreements," General Gilbert said. "They rest on the ability and *willingness* to retaliate in kind for any breaches. The marines will be well aware of it, sir, if only because they were often charged with doing the retaliation. They will not want to risk setting any precedents, precedents that will make it harder to convince later captors not to mistreat their men. If we mistreat their men, they will mistreat ours."

"I ask again," McManus said. "So what?"

"So our people will know we don't give a shit about them," General Gilbert snapped. "And we, should we be taken prisoner, will be mistreated too. The marines have a long history of risking their lives so they can take people who break the rules prisoner, just so they can be properly tried and hung. Do not think for a moment, sir, that you can escape. If they win the war, they will demand an accounting and punish those who commit atrocities."

"If they win the war," McManus repeated. "If."

Julia took a breath, then spoke. "They can be held prisoner now, without being mistreated," she said. She could hardly do any more damage to her career at this point. "Afterwards…things will be different."

"We need to know what they know," McManus said.

"It is unlikely, as I said, that they know anything useful." General Gilbert spoke with icy patience. "Whatever plans they had presumably didn't include a headlong retreat from a major counterattack. It's clear they didn't expect us to regroup and push back."

"At the very least, we need them somewhere secure," McManus insisted. "Can we move them to the Security HQ?"

The director raised a hand. "They are to be held within the HQ, but not interrogated or mistreated in any way," he said. "If we have to come to terms with the marines, we can return them…perhaps in trade for our people. If not, if the war ends victorious, we can decide what to do with them then."

"My people will wish to speak to them," General Gilbert said. "I think…"

"The Security HQ is my territory," McManus insisted. "My people can handle them and…"

"Share, children." The director's voice was wryly amused. "If you can't play nicely together, you'll have to give up your toys."

He stood. "Julia, come with me," he said. "The rest of you…you know what to do."

Julia sighed inwardly as she stood and followed the director through the door. She was probably in trouble. Real trouble. She was only here on the director's sufferance and she knew, all too well, that she'd embarrassed him in front of the board. Perhaps she'd have a chance to convince him, if they spoke privately…she shook her head, knowing it was far too late. Too many people knew she'd spoken out of turn. They'd wonder what she'd said to him, when they were alone, if he changed his mind. They'd wonder even if she hadn't said a word to him. Bastards.

She gritted her teeth. The marines had treated her well, when she'd been their prisoner. She hated to admit it, but things could have been a great deal worse. She'd heard the horror stories…she'd heard the rumours, same as everyone else, about Security HQ. People went in and didn't come out again. She wanted to believe the rumours were exaggerated, but…

"That was unwise," the director said. "You shouldn't have spoken so openly."

"Yes, sir," Julia said. She braced herself for a lecture—or worse. "I understand."

...

Rachel found it hard to believe a marine division had been defeated in open battle. It had never happened before, not for hundreds—perhaps thousands—of years. Small units could be destroyed, sure, but an entire division? It was unthinkable. And yet…the figures were exaggerated, to the point the entire corps would have been wiped out several times over, but the reports definitely suggested the marines had taken a beating. She tried to pull them together, risking everything as she accessed files and reports from the secure sections of the datanet. It looked as though the marines really had lost a battle.

Her blood ran cold as she realised the enemy had taken prisoners. A couple were so badly wounded they'd been rushed to a military hospital—she supposed the corprats were at least *trying* to honour their obligations, under the laws of war—but the remainder were being shipped into the city. She swore inwardly as she accessed the transfer orders. They were being moved to the Security HQ, a grim-faced building in the middle of the government district. She'd heard the rumours, spoken in whispers, of what happened to people who were taken inside. They were never seen again.

Their soldiers may try to honour the laws of war, she thought, numbly. *But their security officers may feel differently.*

She stared at the terminal without really seeing it. The security officers *would* feel differently. She'd met enough security officers, on a dozen worlds, to know they felt themselves totally above any threat of retaliation. The handful who were smart enough to fear retaliation for committing atrocities were *also* smart enough to know their superiors would kill them for *refusing* to commit atrocities. Even at the Empire's height, it was difficult to guarantee that there *would* be punishment. She was all too aware there was little stopping the corprats from breaking out the rack and thumbscrews. Or simply executing the captives before anyone on the outside realised they'd been taken prisoner.

And that means we have to get them out, quickly, she thought. She readied a datapacket for Phelps. He'd have to do the heavy lifting. There were so many guards surrounding the building now that she couldn't hope to leave and then return. Not now. *I may need to get some better codes...*

She grimaced as her shift came to an end. General Gilbert was sending orders to his staffers...orders to check on the prisoners. It crossed her mind to wonder if the orders were a trap—the general had deduced that elements of the datanet had been compromised—but she didn't have time to worry about it. She stood and glanced towards Commander Archer, who was eying another young staffer. The poor girl was barely out of Basic. She wasn't remotely secure enough to handle a predator. Rachel smirked as she winked at the commander, drawing his attention. If Phelps did his part of the operation, there was a better than even chance Commander Archer would get the blame. It couldn't happen to a nicer person.

Commander Archer caught her arm and half-pulled her into the corridor, pressing her into the wall. "What do you want?"

"I need to send another message," Rachel said. She'd do whatever she had to do to get into his office. "I'll pay..."

She licked her lips, suggestively. Commander Archer eyed her for a moment, then stepped back and led her down the corridor. Rachel studied his back. The asshole probably fancied himself a predator, probably the apex predator. She knew the type. He no longer saw her as a challenge before he'd *had* her, as far as he knew. Rachel concealed her amusement and annoyance with an effort. She'd done her work a little too well.

"Drop your trousers," Commander Archer ordered. "Bend over the desk."

Rachel caught his arm and kissed him hard. He let out a gasp of surprise, which turned into a groan as the drug took effect. She didn't really *want* to let him fuck her if she had a choice...and besides, there'd been hints in his tone he hadn't intended to keep his side of the bargain. She carried him to his bed, muttered a handful of suggestions into his ear and pulled down his trousers. His imagination would, again, fill in the rest. She didn't want to know.

The other staffers wouldn't be feeling sorry for me if he was into something vanilla, Rachel thought. She'd met too many staff officers to care for the breed. They had no qualms about putting out for their superiors. Hell, they'd be jealous of a young officer who won her commander's favour. She dreaded to think what might make them feel *sorry* for her. *I suppose ropes and chains would be a little too light for him.*

She sat at his terminal and began to work. General Gilbert seemed to have assigned a handful of officers to monitor the prisoners in the Security HQ. He hadn't assigned Archer, even though it would be an excellent way to get rid of the bastard. Rachel wondered, idly, if Archer had hidden talents, then dismissed the thought. He was probably only kept on active service because there was a shortage of other staff officers. Here, at least, he couldn't do much damage. She smirked at the thought as she hacked the system, added Archer's name to the list and fiddled with his biometrics. The enemy would notice, eventually, but by the time the hammer fell it would be far too late. And, if she was lucky, it would fall on Archer first.

Rachel forwarded the second datapacket to Phelps, then stood. She disliked the thought of relying on something outside her control, even though she had total confidence in her commanding officer. There was no way to know how long it would be before Phelps saw the message, let alone did something about it. He was on the streets, causing so much trouble the enemy honestly believed there were over a thousand infiltrators within the city. Who knew if he'd be able to react before the enemy realised they'd been tricked?

She walked into the bedroom, undressed and clambered into bed. Archer shifted against her, a trickle of drool running from his mouth. She could feel his heart pounding in his chest. It would be easy, so easy, to snap his neck like a twig. Her lips quirked as she closed her eyes, opening the link to the local datanode processors. Killing Archer would be of inestimable help to the enemy. Her superiors probably wouldn't bother with a court-martial before they shot her for treason.

I can't stay here much longer, she thought. She'd laid the plans for a soft coup, but…she didn't know how many of her allies would jump when she hit the button. It was easy to talk, harder to put one's life on the line. *And if the enemy really is close to winning the war…*

She scowled. People didn't switch sides if they thought they were leaving the *winning* side. It was absurd. Why would anyone commit suicide? She sighed as she devised the next set of messages, including a stern warning about backsliding. Too many people had pledged themselves to her. They'd have no place to hide if the corprats won the war. She'd make sure of it. The purges would keep the corprats from threatening the rest of the galaxy for a few years or so…

Shitty way to win, she told herself. *But what other choice is there?*

CHAPTER THIRTY-THREE

Indeed, smart capitalists treat their workers very well. They invest in them. They find ways to put them in places their talents can be used. A poor engineer might make a good manager or vice versa. And good workers respond to this. Good treatment leads to loyalty. Loyalty leads to a worker who will go the extra mile for his boss.
—**Professor Leo Caesius**
The Rise and Fall of Interstellar Capitalism

GERALD HAD EXPECTED TO SEE the enemy troops go on the offensive, after they swept the pocket, and regrouped, but it was still unpleasant to watch a giant army advancing steadily towards his flimsy defence lines. His men had regrouped and rearmed, as best as they could, yet he was all too aware they simply didn't have time to set up a solid defence line before the enemy overwhelmed them. The reports of unrest within the city were merely the icing on the cake. Gerald knew, for better or worse, that the city simply didn't matter. There was no point in fighting for it when the war would be decided elsewhere.

He watched the microburst reports from the stealthed drones as the enemy continually outraced their antiaircraft defences. They were moving with commendable speed, he acknowledged, clearly determined to pour on the pressure until the marines broke or the enemy hit something so solid they had to stop. Gerald knew it would be the former, unless the marines changed the rules. The defence lines were simply too weak to do more than slow the enemy down. It was sheer luck they were so determined to win quickly they were overlooking their flanks.

"Sir," Lieutenant Yu said. "The latest shuttle flights report taking fire from the ground as they dropped to the landing zone."

Gerald nodded, curtly. He'd expected that, too. The enemy was throwing everything at the marines, up to and including the kitchen sink. He was mildly surprised they hadn't used nukes. His forces were in no position to duck and cover, even if they realised what was coming before it was too late. The enemy knew the marines couldn't retaliate in kind, not as long as the PDCs remained intact. They probably didn't want to turn the aristocratic estates into radioactive nightmares...the thought galled him. He told himself he should be grateful. The marines had quite enough problems without adding nukes to the mix.

"Understood," he said. It was a shame they hadn't had time to rig up more dumpsters. "Tell the shuttles to halt resupply, at least for the moment. We should have enough in place on the ground."

He concealed his irritation as Yu turned back to his terminals. There was a second reason to cancel the shuttle flights, one the younger man probably hadn't realised. The division was standing on the cusp of victory or total defeat. If the plan failed, if the lines broke, the entire division would be shattered beyond repair. Gerald had no doubt his men would fight to the last, exhausting their ammunition before finally surrendering, but it wouldn't matter. The war would be lost and...they'd have to save what little they could. Gerald had already rewritten his logs, accepting complete responsibility for the disaster. It was the least he could do.

"Order the marines to keep falling back, as planned," he added. "We'll let them keep moving into the trap."

"Yes, sir," Yu said.

Gerald nodded, thinking of the pistol at his belt. He knew too much to fall into enemy hands...he knew too much and there was no guarantee he couldn't be forced to talk. If the lines broke, he'd have no choice but to destroy as much of the command network as possible before putting the pistol to his head and pulling the trigger. Suicide was rare amongst the corps—it had only happened once in his career, to an officer who'd been relieved of duty for being insufficiently aggressive—but he might not have a choice. His rank came with responsibilities.

You knew the job was dangerous when you took it, he told himself, calmly. *And that your life might be on the line if you fucked up.*

He turned his attention to the display and forced himself to wait. He'd issued all the orders he could. His men knew what to do. There was no point in trying to micromanage them, not when he didn't know *precisely* what was going on. All he could do was wait and hope.

And pray, he thought. *There's nothing else to do.*

...

Captain Dylan Hiller had heard stories of fast-moving tank battles, but he'd never actually taken part in one. The training ground—and endless exercises—had made it clear the modern tank had nothing more than a very restricted role on the battlefield. An infantryman could take a tank out with a rocket, if the armoured behemoth wasn't lured onto an IED or simply bogged down. The bold strokes, driving hard into the enemy's flanks, had seemed a thing of the past. And yet...

He felt a thrill of excitement as his tank roared onwards. The Defender had a maximum speed of fifty kilometres per hour, but it felt as if they were moving faster as they crashed through the remains of towns and crushed the fields under their treads. A handful of bullets cracked into the hull and bounced off harmlessly, barely noticed by the crew. The machine guns traversed automatically, unleashing hell towards the snipers before they could run. The marines didn't seem so tough, now they were in retreat. Dylan laughed in delight as the driver managed to put on even *more* speed. The marines had taken several days to fight their way from Roxon to the cauldron. He was going to be in Roxon by the end of the day.

His terminal bleeped, flashing up a string of alerts. The tanks had roared right past a handful of marines, their guns snapping at them in passing. The follow-up units—the mounted and unmounted infantry—would deal with the bastards, if they didn't have the sense to surrender. And if the infantry could be bothered to take prisoners. Dylan had orders to accept surrender, but he intended to be the first to get to the megacity. There were few chances for promotion in the armoured divisions. He was damn sure he wasn't going to waste time when he had a chance to put his name in lights. He'd be rewarded and promoted and…he'd finally reach the level he deserved.

He smiled, again, as he studied the terminal. They were advancing so rapidly the marines simply didn't have time to prepare any traps. A couple of tanks had been disabled by rockets and a third by plasma grenades, but the remainder were untouched. Dylan would mourn the dead later. Someone would complain, later, that he'd thrown away lives for nothing, but he knew better. He'd had the word directly from a cousin who worked under General Gilbert himself. The marines had to be crushed, even if it meant pushing the offensive forward at breakneck speed. Dylan promised himself he'd ignore all complaints. The idea of war was to win…

An alert flashed up in front of him. The marines were trying to shell the tanks, but the tankers were charging forward too quickly for dumb shells to find their targets. They were probably running short of guided shells, projectiles that could be counted upon to hit their targets. Dylan wasn't too surprised. Commanding a troop of tanks had given him an excellent understanding of logistics. The reports suggested the marines were running short of everything and it looked, from his point of view, that the reports were actually accurate. He snapped commands into the terminal, trying to call down shells of his own onto the enemy targets. The advance was more than a little chaotic—they'd been given warnings about outrunning their antiaircraft defences, giving the enemy pilots a chance to land a blow—but it hardly mattered. They were piling so many soldiers and firepower onto the enemy lines that they could easily trade ten for one and still come out ahead.

It'll be over soon, he thought, as another bullet cracked off the hull. *And then we'll all be promoted.*

• • •

General Jim Gilbert knew, without false modesty, that he was no fool. He also knew he was short on options. Too many staff officers had received seditious emails for him to feel entirely comfortable drawing the war out, even though a more sedate advance might preserve men and equipment for future campaigns. Julia Ganister-Onge hadn't been entirely wrong, he conceded, although the marines hadn't had any time to devise a trap. The problem was that they needed to win quickly or not at all.

He studied the reports as they flowed into his console. He'd prefer to wait for the fleet, but…there just wasn't time. He wasn't sure how many enemy agents were on the streets—the security forces had issued a series of estimates, each one more absurd than the last—yet it was clear they were causing too much damage. They had to get the troops on the streets too… he sighed, bitterly. Why couldn't people just accept their place? Why did they have to aim for the skies?

The advance was picking up speed, an endless row of men and machines racing into what had been enemy-held territory. The marine lines were breaking. The tactical staff were projecting that Roxon would be back in friendly hands by the end of the day, then…there'd be no reason to stop. A couple of days would see the end of the marines, unless they did something desperate. But what? They'd played their last cards and lost.

He keyed his terminal. "Continue the offence," he ordered. "And don't stop until you reach Roxon."

• • •

"Captain," Tomas said. "The enemy are entering the killzone."

Kerri let out a breath as she studied the live feed from the stealthed sensor platforms. The fighting in space had continued, friendly and enemy forces alike paying no attention to the struggles on the ground. Both sides had refrained from committing atrocities—slamming a missile into an asteroid habitat was an atrocity, no matter how one looked at it—but there was a steady stream of debris spinning out in all directions. It hadn't been *hard* to deploy stealthed weapons platforms as well, knowing they wouldn't be detected until they brought their targeting systems online. Hell, they barely even needed *those*. The ships—and the sensor platforms—would do all the targeting the weapons needed.

"Check with Major-General Anderson," she ordered. "Is he ready for us to deploy the first salvo?"

She gritted her teeth as she waited. She'd known Imperial Navy officers who would have gloated if the Imperial Army had taken a bloody nose. *She* knew too many people on the ground to even *think* it might be a good thing...even if defeat hadn't ensured more work for her and her people. They'd have problems lifting even a tiny fraction of the survivors out of the wreckage before it was too late. She knew they might have to abandon the remainder to their fate.

Her eyes moved to the in-system display. It was blank—the enemy facilities had largely gone dark—but that was meaningless. Their ships were supposed to be returning piecemeal, yet...she shook her head. There was no point in worrying about it. Either Anderson's plan worked, or they'd suffer the greatest defeat in their long history. By the time the enemy concentrated its fleet, the engagement would be decided...

"Captain," Susan said. "Major-General Anderson has cleared us to engage."

Kerri nodded. "Begin firing sequence one," she ordered. She doubted the firing would be very accurate, but it shouldn't be an issue. All that mattered was that the projectiles would be falling in the right general area. "And move to firing sequence two the moment the enemy reacts."

"Aye, Captain," Tomas said.

Colonel Hank Feingold scowled as he sat in the command core and watched the display. The high orbitals were crammed with debris, enough to make life difficult for his crew as they struggled to monitor events in orbit. The PDC had enough firepower to give an enemy ship a very nasty surprise indeed, if her CO was foolish enough to come within range, but...there was little they could do about the fighting in space. Hank was entirely sure the enemy hoped he'd try to engage suited men with ship-killing plasma cannons. He'd blow away half the orbital industry if he tried.

"Colonel!" The display filled with red lights. "They're firing on us!"

Hank stood. The enemy had taken out one PDC with a shipkiller or something—the sensor records weren't entirely clear on just *what* had smashed an entire mountain—but so far, they'd refrained from targeting the remaining PDCs. They'd probably thought they could take the installations for themselves, when they won the war on the ground...a war they were currently losing. And yet...he swallowed as he saw the red icons gaining speed. The enemy were suddenly firing on all five PDCs within range.

"Deploy point defence," he ordered. If the enemy widened their control over the high orbitals, they might still win. They could start dropping KEWs into the cities, harrying the government until it conceded defeat. "Take them all down."

He sucked in his breath. The star system was *littered* with space junk that could be turned into simple kinetic projectiles. They wouldn't be *that* accurate, but the marines could just keep raining them on the PDCs until they overwhelmed the defences and pounded the installation into scrap. Hank's operators were already trying to prioritise the targets, shooting the projectiles that seemed most likely to strike the PDC. The remainder would have to be ignored. Bad news for anyone nearby, he thought, but the marines were unlikely to fire on civilian targets. They hadn't set out to slaughter people for fun...

"Sir! They're firing again!"

Hank saw it, too late. They'd been tricked…

…And the men on the ground were going to pay.

• • •

The terminal bleeped an alert, too late.

Something hit the ground, close enough to the tank for the shockwave to pick the vehicle up and throw it over and over until it slammed down again. Captain Hiller's body ached as the straps held him firmly in place, his head pounding as a series of crashing sounds echoed through the tank. He blacked out—he must have—for a second, only slowly realising that he was upside-down. The tank was upside-down! Ice ran through him as he fumbled with the straps, allowing himself to fall to the floor. No, the ceiling. Everything was topsy-turvy. The display was dead, the screen cracked…

He crawled towards the hatch and peered into the gunner's compartment. His body was a mangled wreck, his head crushed as if an angry giant had popped it like a grape. Dylan couldn't bring himself to touch the remains. He'd mourn later, if there was a later. Instead, he opened the emergency hatch and scrambled out of the vehicle, dropping neatly to the ground. The driver's hatch was firmly closed. Dylan knew that wasn't a good sign.

His head spun as he tried to process what he saw. The tank was upside-down, half-buried in a ditch. The remainder of the troop was a shattered ruin, from what little he could see. Half the tanks under his command appeared to be completely missing. As far as he could tell, he was the only survivor. He saw smoke rising along the battlefield and shuddered as he realised what had happened. They'd been clobbered from orbit. They'd been told the PDCs would cover them, but…they'd been wrong.

Dylan forced himself to scramble onto the tank. He could see flames licking up from a dozen places, each marking a destroyed vehicle. The ground itself was blackened and dimpled, what little left after two successive campaigns wiped from existence…he stumbled, nearly tumbling off the tank as he heard aircraft in the distance. He turned to peer towards

Roxon, towards the marine lines…it was just a matter of time, he knew, before they went back on the offensive. His troop had been destroyed… no, the entire army had been destroyed. He couldn't imagine the marines holding back, not now. It was easy to believe he was the sole survivor.

He felt numb. He'd known victory was within their grasp. He'd known they were going to crush the marines. He'd known…he'd been wrong. He felt weak as he tried to find something—anything—that would make him feel hopeful. But there was nothing. If the marines had taken out the PDCs, they could hammer the entire planet into submission. The war was coming to an end…

There's no point in going on, he told himself. The men under his command were dead. He'd failed them, as surely as he'd failed himself. *This is the end.*

He sagged, dropping to his knees. The tank felt hot under him. He knew he should start walking, he knew he should report back to his superiors, but…he felt liquid under his shirt and realised, dully, that he'd been wounded. It was hard to understand how. Had he been shot? Or…or had he been wounded when his tank had been hit and he simply hadn't noticed? He wanted to cover the wound, to try to stop it from bleeding, but it was hard to muster the will. The war was over…

Dylan closed his eyes. He didn't open them again.

CHAPTER THIRTY-FOUR

Capitalism, therefore, holds out the promise of eternally bettering one's self. A poor man might climb into the middle class, while his son climbs into the upper class. A wealthy man who inherited his money might discover, too late, that he simply isn't the man his father was and lose his business to cutthroat competition.
—**Professor Leo Caesius**
The Rise and Fall of Interstellar Capitalism

LIEUTENANT BORIS TIMBISHA felt a flicker of fear as he looked at the sky.

The entire city had seen the flashes; the entire city had heard the thunder. Boris didn't know what they meant, but he was certain they weren't good news. He glanced at his rifle, wondering if he'd have to use it soon. The days when a pair of green tabs on one's shoulders had been enough to compel instant obedience were long gone. Boris had lost friends and comrades who'd gone into the disputed parts of the city and never come out again. A couple of bodies had been recovered, hideously mutilated. He knew it was just a matter of time before he was ordered to re-join his unit and start patrolling the rougher parts of the city. He wouldn't be allowed to keep his cushy billet forever…

He tensed as an aircar came into view, landing neatly outside the security HQ. There was no reason to think he really *had* a cushy billet. The underground had bombed buildings inside the security zone, somehow; they'd even killed the population monitoring system. He watched the aircar hatch open, disgorging a man wearing a staff officer's uniform. Boris's lips thinned. The man wore a uniform that suggested he had powerful connections, perhaps powerful enough to punish Boris for doing his job. He certainly wouldn't show the proper respect.

"I'm here to check on the prisoners," the newcomer said. He shoved a datachip at Boris, seemingly unaware of the rifle in his hand. "Take me to them."

Boris kept his face impassive as he slotted the datachip into his terminal and scanned the orders quickly. Commander Archer, special aide to General Gilbert…a man who could make *real* trouble for a lowly security officer if Boris got in his way. Boris was fairly sure his superiors wouldn't protect him. General Gilbert had the ear of the director himself, if the rumours were true. Who knew?

He checked the biometrics quickly, then called for a replacement guard before leading Commander Archer into the building. The HQ was dangerously understaffed, the majority of the guards ordered away on short notice. Boris didn't know what was going on, but he'd heard enough hints to be glad his unit hadn't been ordered away as well. He led Commander Archer though the security scanners, half-hoping they'd sound the alert. The guards had standing orders to give anyone who triggered the alarm a full-body search, something that always knocked people down a peg or two. But there was nothing. Commander Archer wasn't even armed.

Idiot, Boris thought. A staff officer might be more dangerous to himself than anyone else, if he carried a pistol, but the streets were unsafe these days. *You should have drawn a gun from the armoury if you knew you were going out in the open.*

The air grew colder as they walked down a long flight of stairs. The prisoners were being held in the lower cells, being treated reasonably well.

Boris was mildly surprised they hadn't been sent further below ground. Very few people left the building, if they were arrested and marched to the cells. They'd be lucky if they were simply executed, their bodies thrown into the furnace and their ashes dumped somewhere nicely isolated. The marines were unusual prisoners, but...they'd invaded the planet. They deserved to die.

"You can see the prisoners through the viewscreens," he said, as he led Commander Archer into the monitoring room. There was no privacy in the cells beyond. The bored-looking operator glanced up at them, then returned his attention to the screens. "If you want to talk to them in person, you'll have to go through that door..."

"Good," Commander Archer said. "And now..."

He reached out in one smooth motion and yanked the operator away from the console, throwing him right across the room. Boris gaped, his hand dropping—too late—to his pistol. He was still trying to draw it when a hand gripped his throat and tightened. Boris had only a second to realise that he'd failed in his duty before he felt something snap...

• • •

Haydn stood in the cell and waited. The guards had clearly received at least three sets of orders while they'd been driving the prisoners around, practically giving them a tour of the city before finally arriving at the prison complex. The cell didn't feel like a POW camp. It was dark and dingy, clearly designed for only a handful of prisoners. The forty marines, including some who'd been captured separately, barely had room to move. He couldn't decide if it was a form of torture without quite breaking the rules or if the enemy hadn't been able to decide what to do with them. The cell boded ill for the future. He hadn't been able to think of a way to escape, not yet. Most of the ideas he'd come up with required being on the other side of the bars.

He studied the cell thoughtfully. It reminded him of the brig on a starship, complete with metal bars keeping the prisoners in place, except on a far larger scale. The chamber seemed completely airtight. The enemy interrogators could shoot into the cell, if they wanted, or simply dump knock-out gas into the vents. Or poison them...he was starting to fear their rights as POWs weren't going to be respected after all.

The hatch snapped open. A man hurried into the chamber. "Family Man," he said, as he started to fiddle with the lock on the bars. "I say again, Family Man."

Haydn blinked. He'd been told the code Pathfinders used to identify themselves, when they were behind enemy lines, but he'd never expected to use it here. He hadn't even known there *were* Pathfinders on the surface, until...he blinked as he recognised the man. "You're a Pathfinder who just wanted in through the door?"

"Yep." The door clicked open. The newcomer pushed a rifle into Haydn's hands, then motioned for the marines to hurry out of the cell. "We need to move. The streets are in chaos right now, but that'll change pretty damn quickly."

He cocked his head, clearly accessing the complex's security systems. Haydn didn't envy him, even though he'd wanted to be a Pathfinder. The neural links weren't always reliable. If they went wrong, when someone was attached to a computer net, the results could be utterly disastrous. Or...he followed the newcomer out into the next room, spotting a pair of bodies on the floor. They both looked as if they'd had their necks snapped.

"There's an armoury on the upper levels, but I want to try to sneak out if possible," the Pathfinder said. "You being here might come in handy."

"We should get back to the lines," Haydn said. "Quickly."

The Pathfinder glanced at him. "That might not be possible. From what I picked up before I arrived, the enemy advance has just been smashed from orbit. You'll have miles to go before you reach safety, if you made it through at all. And you could do something much more useful here."

He held up a hand as they reached the top of the stairs, then ran forward so fast he almost blurred. Haydn glanced forward, just in time to see the Pathfinder taking down two guards at incredible speed. The bodies didn't even have time to hit the ground before the enhanced soldier was pulling open the door, revealing the armoury. The marines hurried forward, scooping up enough weapons and ammunition to fight a small war. Haydn couldn't help wondering if that was what the Pathfinder had in mind.

"Son of a bitch," Rifleman Curry said. "Why aren't we all like you?"

The Pathfinder smiled. "The drugs within my system have a very short lifespan," he said. "You boost for a few minutes, at best, and then you have to cope with the side effects. I can use other drugs and enhancements to handle the effects, for a while, but it comes at a cost and they'll catch up with me sooner or later. There's a very good chance I won't survive long enough to take retirement."

"Thanks," Curry muttered.

Haydn cleared his throat. "What now?"

"This way," the Pathfinder said. "I'm currently telling the security systems a handful of comforting lies, but they won't last forever. We have to be out of here before the bastards realise what we're doing."

They hurried down a corridor and into an underground garage. A pair of trucks were sitting in the middle of the chamber, looking surprisingly new. Haydn guessed the security forces had grabbed the first models, rather than letting the troops have them. The marines scrambled inside, then started the engines. A moment later, they were gliding up the ramp and onto the streets.

He stared at the Pathfinder. "Isn't anyone going to stop us?"

The Pathfinder laughed. "Why should they? We have official authorisation to be on the streets. We're in more danger, right now, from insurgents than the security forces. That'll change, when they realise what we've done, but by then we should be well away."

Haydn had to smile. "They just let you walk in and rescue us?"

"They trusted what they read in the datanet," the Pathfinder said. "And that was their fatal mistake."

Haydn said nothing as they drove through the streets. He was no stranger to chaotic cities, but *this* city was a nightmare. People were glancing east as they walked, as if they feared a giant monster was about to come over the horizon. The giant viewscreens—so large they covered entire buildings—were dark and silent. Thousands of men in uniform rushed from place to place, waving weapons around so frantically it was clear it was only a matter of time until they had a friendly fire incident. Haydn understood, finally, what the Pathfinder had meant. The marines could go anywhere, as long as no one saw their uniforms.

He frowned as they reached a warehouse. "We're going to need to change our clothes."

"Already arranged," the Pathfinder assured him. "Will you have a problem wearing enemy uniforms?"

"No," Haydn said. The enemy would be perfectly within their legal rights to shoot them, but…they'd also be within their rights to shoot escaping prisoners. They were within the enemy's city, in the middle of a state of emergency…"I don't think we have a choice."

"No," the Pathfinder agreed. "You don't."

...

Colonel Nancy Braithwaite had never liked visiting the Security HQ. The guards were leering monsters and the prisoners, most of them, were worse. One didn't wind up a permanent guest in the cells unless one had crossed practically all of the lines. The prisoners had nothing to lose, save perhaps for the marines. She gritted her teeth as she strode out of the aircar and advanced on the gate, cursing her superior under her breath. The last time she'd visited, the guards had found an excuse to strip-search her. And they'd laughed when she'd complained.

Her eyes narrowed as she approached the checkpoint. The guards looked as if they wanted to run around like headless chickens. A pair of senior officers stood just behind the barrier, arguing in low voices; a handful of others were visible by the doors, looking as if they wanted to be somewhere—anywhere—else. Nancy wasn't sure *quite* what had happened outside the city—the datanet hadn't told her anything useful—but she doubted the guards gave much of a damn. It was far more likely that something had gone terribly wrong inside the HQ.

She held up her ID. "Colonel Braithwaite, here to see the prisoners."

She'd expected some kind of reaction, from mockery to sarcasm and bitter indifference. She hadn't expected fear. The guards stared at her, as if she'd suddenly grown two heads. Or if there was someone higher-ranking behind her. She kept her face as impassive as possible, pushing her sudden advantage as far as it would go. She owed the security troopers a little payback for how they'd treated her.

"I have authorisation from the Board of Directors to see the prisoners," she said, calmly. "Take me to them at once."

The guards glanced at their commanders, who looked as if they were on the verge of calling someone higher up the food chain. Nancy hid her amusement, and her growing concern. She had all the permissions she needed, right from the very highest levels. The guards should have taken her into the building at once, without hesitation. Instead…

"Do I have to call your superiors?" She allowed a trace of irritation to slip into her voice. "I have strict orders…"

An officer—she didn't recognise him—stepped forward. "The prisoners are gone."

"What?" Nancy was sure she'd misheard. "Gone?"

Her mind raced. General Gilbert had told her, in confidence, that the security forces might just make the POWs disappear. They were practically a law unto themselves. They might try to get intelligence out of the prisoners, then kill them and burn the bodies to make sure no evidence survived. Nancy believed him. If the guards were willing to sexually harass, if not assault, an army officer…there were probably no limits to their depravity. She shuddered in bitter memory. They might just have killed the prisoners themselves…

She met his eyes. "This is no time for games," she said, curtly. "I need to see the prisoners."

"They're gone!" It was the hint of naked fear in his voice that convinced her he was telling the truth. "They just walked out!"

"Impossible," Nancy said. She tried hard not to sneer. "I suppose you left them with their weapons? Perhaps you forgot to shackle them? Perhaps…"

Another officer—his nametag read NILES- came over to her. "If you'll come with me, please?"

Nancy nodded and followed him into the building. The lobby was in utter chaos. Officers were shouting at each other, while the enlisted men kept their heads down. No one moved to insist she went through the scanners as she walked through the chamber and into a small office. An open bottle of alcohol sat on the desk. A pistol rested beside it. Niles had been drowning his sorrows, she recognised dully, when she'd arrived. She wondered if he'd been considering suicide. The security forces would be looking for a scapegoat soon, if they weren't already.

She tried to keep her voice under tight control, speaking as gently to him as she could. "What happened?"

"We don't know!" Niles sat behind the desk and poured himself a glass. He didn't offer Nancy any. "The local datanodes have been scrambled. We just don't know."

Nancy frowned. General Gilbert had kept her busy hand-carrying orders all over the city, warning her in no uncertain terms not to use the datanet any more than strictly necessary. He didn't *trust* the system any longer. If the enemy had gained access…her mind raced. She'd deleted the handful of messages that had arrived in her inbox, unwilling to risk answering or reporting them. Messages were one thing, but this…? She didn't want to think about it.

"They escaped," she said. How the hell had the trick been done? Someone on the inside? General Gilbert had hinted as much. "Where did they go?"

"We don't know," Niles said, again. "We just don't know."

"I see." Nancy thought, fast. "I have to report to my superiors."

She stood, brushing down her trousers. General Gilbert was unlikely to believe the truth. He'd want to believe the security forces had killed the marines, rather than let them escape. She found it hard to believe herself.

If she hadn't been sure Niles was telling the truth...

"Put out more patrols and track them down," she advised. If they were lucky, the marines would be caught before they could do any real damage. She dreaded to think what they could do, if they were given time. "Quickly."

There was a sharp knock on the door. Niles's hand reached for his pistol, then fell into his lap. "Come!"

The door opened, revealing a grim-faced woman. "Sir, we found two bodies, shoved into makeshift hiding places," she said. "One of them was Lieutenant Boris Timbisha. He...he was showing Commander Archer to the prisoners."

"What?" Nancy stared. She knew Commander Archer. It was quite possible there was more than one, but...somehow, she doubted it was a coincidence. "Commander Archer?

"Yes," the woman said. She wore no rank tabs, suggesting she was high enough up the ladder for everyone to know who she was. "According to the guards, he had authorisation to visit the prisoners. He had all the paperwork and everything."

"That can't be right," Nancy said. Archer was loyal to his superior, she thought, but a complete idiot otherwise. He would have been replaced if there hadn't been a constant shortage of trained personnel. "Commander Archer wouldn't have any such permission."

"Then it's time we had a few words with Commander Archer." Niles stood, picking up his gun and returning it to his belt. "And you can accompany us."

Nancy nodded. She'd have to alert her superior, as quickly as possible. He wouldn't thank her for letting him be surprised. If Commander Archer really was a spy, working for the internal or external enemy, it would reflect badly on his superior officer. She couldn't let that happen. He'd take it out on her.

She took a breath. "It will be my pleasure."

CHAPTER THIRTY-FIVE

So why did it go so wrong?
—**Professor Leo Caesius**
The Rise and Fall of Interstellar Capitalism

Julia felt cold as she walked into the conference room.

She'd been right. She knew, now, she'd been right. And yet, being right was no protection when her superiors had been so badly embarrassed. No, they hadn't been *embarrassed*. They'd been defeated. The advancing army had been hammered so badly there'd only been a handful of survivors, if the reports were accurate. The entire city had seen the flashes of light as the kinetic projectiles smashed the army flat.

They lured us on, again, she thought. *And we walked straight into their trap.*

She kept her face under tight control as she took her seat and waited. The director had scolded her as one would scold a child, something she'd found maddening. How *dare* he not take her seriously? She supposed, politically, he'd had little choice—her branch of the family had practically disowned her, despite her heroism in saving the director's life, but it was *still* maddening. And she'd been right. She was tempted to be genuinely childish and hold her breath until she got an apology, but she knew it wasn't going to work. If there hadn't been tight controls on people moving in and out of the city, she would have retired to the country estate and tried to make her peace with whatever government arose from the ruins.

"There's no time for the formalities," the director said. His voice was so flat it was easy to tell he was shocked. "General, what happened?"

"We overextended ourselves," General Gilbert said, tonelessly. "They deployed stealthed KEW platforms into the high orbitals, then divided their fire between the PDC and our advancing forces. The PDCs largely protected themselves. The advancing forces got hammered."

"*Crushed* would be a better word," McManus said. He'd been pushing for more power for weeks. The crisis spelled opportunity for him, if they survived long enough for him to make *use* of his new power. "Were there *any* survivors inside the blast radius?"

"Only a handful," General Gilbert said. "We lost."

Julia felt her heart sink at his blunt words. She was tempted, very tempted, to remind the board that she'd *warned* them. The urge to say 'I told you so' was overwhelming. But she knew better. The board would start looking for a scapegoat shortly, if it wasn't already. She couldn't logically be blamed for anything—it wasn't as if she'd been anything more than an advisor—but what did logic and reason have to do with anything? The board would sooner avoid the blame itself, rather than face up to the sheer scale of the disaster.

"We lost," Maryanne repeated. "How *badly* did we lose?"

"The forces we carefully husbanded over the past two weeks are gone," General Gilbert said, flatly. "We lost thousands of trained men and almost all of their equipment. The marines are plunking away at a handful of surviving tanks, as they ready their own forces to resume the offensive. In short, we have effectively *nothing* between the marines and the city walls."

"And so the only hope of a realistic defence rests in the hands of *my* men," McManus said, coldly. He looked at the director. "I request full control over all deployable military forces within the city."

"Your troops are good for beating up unarmed civilians," General

Gilbert said. He spoke with the air of a man so far gone he no longer cared about anything. "The marines will make hash out of them."

"We'll be holding the walls," McManus said. "They'll break the walls, of course, but that will lead them into a maze of defences that will wear them down. They'll be wiped out before they get anywhere near this place."

He waved a hand at the walls. "We can stop them, sir," he said. "We just need the authority to do it."

Julia leaned forward. "Do you think they don't *know* it?"

McManus snorted. "Whatever do you mean?"

"The marines know the dangers of being lured into a city fight," Julia said. She was aware she was making an enemy out of the most dangerous man on the planet, and someone known to be vindictive, but she owed it to her family to try. "They'll do everything in their power to avoid it."

Like wheeling around and seizing the industrial nodes instead, she thought. *They'll win without ever fighting their way through the city.*

"They have no choice, if they want to win quickly," McManus said. He looked at the director. "Sir, there's still time for the fleet to regroup and retake the high orbitals. We can still win."

Julia tasted desperation in the air and knew McManus was going to win the argument. The board couldn't imagine a situation in which they could lose, despite everything that had happened over the last six months. They certainly couldn't imagine contacting the marines and trying to seek terms...not, she supposed, that the marines had any reason to offer terms the board might accept. They were standing on the cusp of total victory or crushing defeat. If the fleet returned and regrouped in time, they might still come out ahead...

If, she thought. The fleet wasn't concentrated. The ships would return, one by one, and fly straight into a trap. *They don't have anything left to bargain with.*

It wasn't entirely true, she knew. They still controlled the industrial nodes. But their control was starting to slip. Parts of the giant megacity were already rising up against the central government. The workers were already looking beyond, to the days when they would have to deal with a *new* government. She knew, better than most, just how much resentment lurked behind their bland expressions. They had a chance to take power for themselves. It was foolish to expect them to waste it.

"Yes," the director said. "Can we stall?"

He looked at Julia. "Can we?"

"I don't know, sir," Julia said. "The marines might listen, if we tried to offer them terms, but they have…"

She broke off. They wouldn't thank her for giving them *more* bad news. And besides…she looked from face to face, accepting—deep inside—that it was over. The corporation's days were numbered. Even if they won the war—somehow—the population control system had been shattered beyond repair. The entire planet was on the verge of rising against them. It was only a matter of time before a spark ignited an explosion. The forces they'd need to keep the chaos under control were gone.

"I think we should at least try to stall," she said, carefully. She doubted it would work, but it would keep them focused on an attainable goal. "If they agree to talk, we can keep them busy dickering over the size and shape of the table…"

The director's wristcom bleeped. "Excuse me."

Julia felt cold. No one, absolutely no one, would interrupt the meeting unless it was truly urgent. The board was supposed to debate in absolute privacy…

"I see," the director said. "Come."

The door opened. A mid-ranking military officer—a staff officer, judging by her uniform—stepped into the chamber. She was pretty, her uniform neatly tailored to show off her curves, but she looked as if she were sweating bullets. Julia had no difficulty spotting a social climber, one who'd just come face to face with the simple fact her climb up might have been derailed by circumstances beyond her control. She tasted bile in her mouth. The newcomer and Julia had a great deal in common.

She doesn't have so far to fall, Julia thought. *Does she?*

"Nancy?" General Gilbert sounded astonished. "What are you doing here?"

"Sir, there's been a development," Nancy said. "Ah"—she saluted the table—"Colonel Nancy Braithwaite, reporting."

"Report," the director said.

"The marine prisoners have escaped," Nancy said. She sounded as if she expected to be shot on the spot. Her eyes flickered to General Gilbert, then looked back at the table. "They were aided by Commander Archer or…or someone using his ID."

"Commander Archer?" McManus smirked, eying General Gilbert with a predatory stare. "One of your staff officers?"

"A man on my staff, yes," General Gilbert said. He sounded completely astonished. "Nancy, report. What happened?"

"The intruder used the ID to get into the security complex," Nancy said. "He made his way down to the prison cells, freed and armed the marines, then drove them out in a truck and headed into the city. So far, we have not been able to locate the truck, let alone the former prisoners. The traffic control system has been badly compromised."

"Shit," General Gilbert said.

"Quite," McManus said. "A traitor in your ranks. How did *that* happen, I wonder?"

There's no guarantee Commander Archer is actually *the traitor*, Julia thought. *He might simply have been the victim of identity theft.*

"I have no reason to think he's a traitor," General Gilbert said. "It is true his competence is limited, but…"

"Or he could be pretending to be incompetent," McManus said. "He might have been a long-term undercover agent, burrowing his way into your confidence until he was in a position to strike. Your entire staff could have been compromised."

"That is unlikely," General Gilbert said. He sounded as if he didn't quite believe himself. "I think we have to approach the situation carefully and…"

"No." McManus stared at him. "There's no time. We have to arrest your staff now..."

General Gilbert spoke over him. "And if we do that, we'll be unable to regroup our forces before it's too late."

"And can we do that"—McManus sneered—"if your staff is compromised?"

He looked from face to face. "I request, again, complete control of military forces within the city. I will arrest the staff, preventing the compromised officers from doing any further damage, then prepare a defence that will bleed the marines white if they ignore our attempts at negotiation and resume the offensive."

"This is not the time for a sudden change in command," General Gilbert insisted. "The war is not yet decided..."

"And if we allow an enemy operative to remain in position within your ranks," McManus snapped, "the war *will* be decided."

The director silently assessed the mood of the table. "General Gilbert, transfer command authority to Director McManus. We'll have to find and capture the spy before things get any worse."

"Yes, sir," General Gilbert said, coldly.

Julia felt a flicker of sympathy. General Gilbert was no traitor—he could have launched a coup in all the confusion, if he'd wished—but his career had been destroyed in less than a minute. The board would never forgive him for harbouring a spy...if, of course, there was a spy. Not, she supposed, that it would matter that much. General Gilbert had enemies who hated him personally and enemies who had nothing against him, but wanted his position filled by one of their clients. And McManus would hardly leave a potential threat at his back, not now that the daggers were drawn. General Gilbert would be thrown in one of the cells soon enough.

"Regroup our forces, then hold the line as long as possible," the Director ordered McManus. "Julia, prepare a diplomatic message for the marines. Let us see if they're willing to talk."

"Yes, sir," Julia said. She'd already made up her mind. She'd play nice, right up until the moment it was time to play nasty. "I'll get right on it."

"General, stay behind," the director ordered. "Everyone else, return to your duties."

Julia stood and followed McManus out the door. The security director seemed to have a new spring in his step. She watched him greet a pair of armed guards, then hurry down the stairs to his office. He was already barking orders for command and control to be shifted to his men, even as his troops fanned out to capture General Gilbert's staff officers. Julia wondered, as she turned to head back to her own office, how many of the poor bastards would survive the experience. Many of them personally owed their positions to General Gilbert. McManus was hardly likely to leave them alive.

She opened the door and stepped into the office, then sagged against the door. Her heart was pounding. The population monitoring system might be down—the last report had insisted it would take months, at least, to repair the system and replace the destroyed monitors—but it was quite possible someone had concealed bugs in her chambers. The director's security staff had no reason to think she was harmless. They might fear she'd been conditioned, even though she'd passed all the tests. How could they catch her lying when she didn't *know* she was lying?

Great, her thoughts muttered. *You can go to jail in the knowledge you're perfectly innocent.*

She pushed herself off the door and headed for the desk. It looked a mess, but she'd placed everything with a certain degree of malice aforethought. If someone—anyone—had been in her chambers and searched her desk, it wouldn't be easy for them to put *everything* back when they'd found it. Not, she supposed, that she'd been stupid enough to leave something incriminating lying around where a searcher might find it. It hadn't taken her long, as she'd grown into adulthood and started her career, to learn random searches were a fact of life. The academy staff had been fond of them…and woe betide anyone who got caught.

The terminal—and the junk she'd put on top of it—looked unmoved.

She sat down, wondering if she was about to make the greatest mistake of her career. Second greatest, perhaps. In hindsight, returning to Onge had been a mistake. She should have known better. She should have known... she put the thought out of her mind as she opened the terminal, wondering if she was going to spend the rest of a short and miserable life in McManus's cells. If someone was watching her...

They think I'm harmless, she thought, sourly. She supposed it was true. She was unarmed, effectively powerless. *What can I do, without the director's permission?*

Her heart thudded as she opened her inbox. The message was where she'd left it, a call to rebellion and war. She hadn't dared so much as delete it, for fear of acknowledging its existence. She supposed she should be glad that so *many* officers and men had received the message. No one, not even McManus, could purge *everyone*. He might as well surrender to the invaders and save time. And yet...

Bracing herself, she opened the message and started to compose a reply.

• • •

Thaddeus felt...old.

He was in his second century. Few humans lived so long, even with the advantages of modern medicine. And...he wondered, suddenly, if his parents had made a mistake when they'd raised him. He'd been subject to his father, at least until the old man had died, but he hadn't had to climb the ladder himself. Nothing short of a truly disastrous screw-up would have kept him from sitting on the board, even if he didn't become CEO. He wasn't sure how to handle a crisis when all the tools at his disposal broke, one by one. The systems his ancestors had spent years building were starting to come apart at the seams.

General Gilbert cleared his throat. "Sir, I..."

Thaddeus looked at him. "How long have you known Commander Archer?"

"He was assigned to the anchor station," General Gilbert said. "And he attached himself to me as we fled to the surface."

"I see." Thaddeus felt his heart sink. An ambitious officer would attach himself to a superior, but so would a spy. There'd been so much confusion during the invasion, and afterwards, that it was hard to properly vet one's officers before putting them to work. It was easy to see how the mistake had happened...easy, too, to see how Gilbert would never be allowed to recover from it. "It wasn't your fault."

"Thank you, sir," General Gilbert said, stiffly. He'd stood with the others and remained standing. "Do you want anything else from me?"

Thaddeus read the younger man's future in his eyes and shivered. General Gilbert had *no* future. He would go back to his quarters, put a gun to his head and pull the trigger. And why not? What did he have to live for? Gilbert couldn't retire to the family estate and spend his declining years writing largely fictitious memoirs. McManus or one of the others would want him dead. Hell, the board would want a scapegoat for everything...

"No," he said, quietly. He wanted to say something reassuring, but what could he say? Nothing came to mind. "I'll see you later."

He closed his eyes. There were few cards left to play now. The marines might let themselves be stalled...it wasn't much, he told himself, but it was all he had. The only other option was surrender and that was unthinkable. He knew he couldn't give up. Centuries of work would be lost if he ran up the white flag. And who knew what sort of universe the marines would create?

I won't live long enough to see it, he thought. He was tempted to call Julia and demand an update, even though it had only been a few minutes since he'd dismissed her. In hindsight, he should have *listened* to her. She'd been right and he'd been wrong and it was too late to make amends. *Whatever they build...*

He shook his head. There were still cards to play. The game wasn't over yet.

CHAPTER THIRTY-SIX

There were several separate problems. The empire saw itself, incorrectly, as a paternalistic state. It tried to compensate for what it saw as injustices, only to make matters worse. Wage laws drove profits down, for example; regulations that made little sense, even from a bureaucratic point of view, made further expansion difficult.
—**Professor Leo Caesius**
The Rise and Fall of Interstellar Capitalism

RACHEL WAS HALF-ASLEEP, despite everything, when she heard someone knock. It sounded as though they were on the verge of breaking down the door, even though it was made of solid metal. Commander Archer shifted against her, still trapped in a drugged stupor. She was mildly surprised he hadn't woken up. The dreams she'd given him must have been more appealing than the real world. Given the alerts she'd seen flashing through the datanet, the real world was steadily turning into a nightmare.

She rolled out of bed as the knocking grew louder. She didn't bother to get dressed as she padded to the door. Her enhanced ears could pick up at least four people on the other side, speaking in gruff, cold tones. A quick check revealed that Commander Archer's access permissions had been unceremoniously cancelled. She smiled, despite everything, as she keyed the door. Commander Archer was about to wake up to find himself in very deep shit.

The security officers pushed in as soon as the door opened. They were well-trained, Rachel had to admit; the leader didn't so much as look at her naked body as he pushed her against the wall and secured her hands behind her back with a plastic tie. Rachel concentrated on looking harmless as the others flowed into the bedroom, Commander Archer letting out a shout as he was unceremoniously yanked out of bed and thrown to the floor. She could hear him alternatively cursing and begging, then yelping in pain. Rachel guessed the security officers had orders not to put up with any nonsense. It was hard not to feel a flicker of satisfaction. Commander Archer hadn't been a traitor, not in any real sense of the word, but he *had* been a complete asshole. He deserved pretty much everything that was going to happen to him.

They already know his codes were used to hack the system, she mused. *They won't believe he's innocent until it's far too late.*

She widened her senses as the security troops searched the office roughly. The entire building datanet had been locked down, to the point where only high-level officers were permitted access. It was hard to be sure, but it sounded as though the entire building was being searched. She heard someone crying in the distance, perhaps one of the junior staffers. The poor girl would be lucky if she left the security complex alive. Rachel wished, suddenly, that Phelps had blown it to hell when he'd liberated the prisoners...

A hand grabbed her arm and yanked her around. "What are you doing here?"

"He told me I had to suck him or get sent to the front," Rachel said, doing her best to sound like a victim. "He told me..."

"Get her out of here, down to the trucks," the officer snapped. He shoved Rachel towards another security officer. "And then report back here."

"Yes, sir," the officer said.

THE HALLS OF MONTEZUMA

Rachel eyed him as he took her arm and steered her through the door and down the corridor. Professional enough, she admitted sourly. He kept his eyes on her, but there was no hint he might take advantage of her nakedness. *That* was annoying. She'd sooner deal with a lusty idiot than a professional. She forced herself to hang back as they walked past a row of bound staffers, sitting on the floor contemplating the remainder of their short and miserable lives. A handful of people she knew, from her formal duties, looked at her and then looked away. She felt a twinge of guilt. They didn't deserve to be arrested and marched straight to hell.

The security officer kept pushing her as they walked down the stairs. Rachel listened carefully, trying to determine if they were alone. The lower levels seemed to have already been cleared, but it was hard to be sure. There were just too many sounds running through the air. She was tempted to hack the datanet, but if they had WebHeads watching the net…she braced herself, then shrank back. The guard turned to grab her and she headbutted him in the nose with enhanced strength. He crumpled and started to fall. Rachel boosted her strength, snapped the tie and caught her former captor. He stared at her in shock, then opened his mouth. She crushed his throat before he could make a sound.

Idiot, she thought, as she dragged him into the next room and stripped him bare. *Just because someone's naked it doesn't mean they're harmless.*

Rachel changed into his uniform, hid her hair under his cap and checked his equipment. His gun was fairly standard, as was his neural whip; the terminal was a design she didn't recognise. She tried to hack it and drew a blank. The system was locked down. She put it to one side, hid the body in the closet and headed for the door. The corridor outside was empty, but she could hear voices in the distance. It sounded as though a small army of security troops had arrived. Good. No one would notice one more.

She walked down the corridor and into the garage. Row upon row of prisoners sat on the concrete floor, being watched by armed guards. Others were being searched or marched into trucks. Rachel was tempted to assign herself to one of the guard platoons and make life difficult for the security troops, but she didn't have time. Instead, she walked to the garage door and out into the light. The troops outside paid no attention to her. Rachel smirked as she continued her walk. They were paranoid, but they weren't paranoid enough.

There were no civilians on the streets, she noted; there weren't many soldiers. The vast majority of people on the ground were security troopers, holding their weapons at the ready as they stood guard in front of the government complexes. They looked jittery, as if they expected to be attacked at any moment. It wasn't an unjustified fear. The reports she'd read had been optimistic to the point of mindlessness, but it was clear security officers were under constant attack. She allowed herself another smile as she walked past a pair of antiaircraft vehicles, their sensors scanning the skies for incoming aircraft. There were so many security officers and military units on the streets that they'd be getting in each other's way when the shit hit the fan.

She kept walking until she was out of the secure zone, then briefly linked into the datanet and sent a message. Phelps and the others would be hiding inside the city, but she had no idea where. She couldn't tell what she didn't know, if she got captured. She could feel unfriendly eyes following her as she walked into an alleyway, sense a pair of men following her. They felt like thugs, rather than insurgents or rebels. Somehow, she wasn't surprised. There was always a criminal element, even in the best-behaved societies. The security officers probably didn't care as long as no one important got harassed.

A voice came from behind her. "Hey! You come here, you pay the toll."

Rachel turned, slowly. Two men, barely out of their teens. They carried a pair of rifles in a manner that suggested they didn't know how to use them. She guessed they'd been taken off dead policemen or security officers. There was an outside chance the weapons didn't even work, although she could hardly risk her life on it. She was fast, but dodging a bullet was beyond her.

"That's right," the second man said. "Give us everything…"

Rachel boosted and lunged at them. She was past their rifles before they could even start to pull the trigger. She slapped one in the head with enhanced strength, his skull cracking under the blow; she punched the other in the stomach, the force of the impact crushing his heart. She felt nothing as their bodies hit the ground. They were little more than parasites, draining the lifeblood of their communities. She stripped the first man, donning his shirt and trousers herself. Hopefully, people wouldn't pay close attention to her now she was no longer dressed as a security officer. She took the rifles, checked them—she was amused to note the thugs only had one clip each—and then wrapped them in a stolen jacket. It would hide them from prying eyes.

Smiling, she turned and resumed her walk. She didn't think anyone else was watching her, but she made sure to run an evasive course before linking to another datanet node. Phelps had sent a reply, ordering her to a particular location. Rachel grinned and started to walk, passing through cramped alleyways rather than walking onto the empty streets. There were few other in view, save for a security convoy that looked as if it was driving through the streets of Han. Rachel shivered in remembrance. The security officers had no idea how bad it could become.

Phelps was waiting for her at the RV point, wearing a hat and coat long enough to conceal a small arsenal. He'd taken his talents in a different direction, doing his best to look like an overweight slob rather than a helpless young woman; Rachel had to admit she wouldn't have recognised him if she hadn't known him so well. There was no sign of the other two. She'd hoped—prayed—they'd been sent into the city as well, even if no one had told her. They would have had good reasons for leaving her in the dark.

"It's good to see you again," Phelps said. He'd recognised her as easily as she'd recognised him. "Did you get out without leaving a trail?"

"I think so." Rachel had no way to be sure, but it would take some time before the searchers discovered the body. By the time they started looking for her, it would be too late. "They have good reason to suspect my former commanding officer. It'll take them some time to realise he's innocent."

"Good." Phelps led her through a maze of alleyways. "And your planned soft coup?"

"I have a number of people who replied to my emails," Rachel said. Soft coups were never easy. The temptation to just sit on one's hand and wait for a clear winner to emerge could be overwhelming. "There's no way to know how many of them will actually commit, when the time comes."

"True." Phelps glanced at her. "We need to move quickly."

"Agreed," Rachel said. She'd already prepared the messages, storing them within her implants. "Are the former prisoners ready?"

"Ready, and eager for some payback," Phelps said. "All we need is to finalise the plan."

"That should be easy enough," Rachel said. "Right now, the streets are in chaos. We'll never have a better chance."

She braced herself as he led the way into a mid-sized warehouse and up a flight of rickety stairs. The lower floor felt deserted, but the upper floor offices were crammed. Rachel glanced, automatically, towards the window, breathing a sigh of relief when she saw there were none. The warehouse had probably been deserted before Phelps had turned it into a makeshift base, and the surrounding area was hardly populated with people who'd call the cops, but it only took one flicker of light to draw attention. She wondered, idly, who owned the warehouse. If they decided to come visit...

"Welcome home," Phelps said. "Can I offer you a cup of coffee?"

"Yes, please," Rachel said, a deadpan look on her face. She shook hands with Captain Steel, who appeared to be the senior man amongst the former prisoners. "When do we move?"

"As soon as things are ready," Phelps said. He waved a hand at a terminal. "Get started."

"Sir," Rachel said. "Where are the others?"

"I don't know," Phelps said. His voice was flat, suggesting he was concerned too. "They didn't report in."

Rachel nodded as she hurried over to the terminal. There would be time to worry about the rest of the unit later. The datanet was still in place, allowing her to access her secret inboxes, but...it was clearly being monitored a great deal more carefully. She was mildly surprised it hadn't been shut down completely. The reports from the KEW bombardment suggested there was literally *nothing* between the two megacities. The locals didn't *need* their datanet so much now. Her lips quirked as she skimmed through a handful if replies. The security officers taking power had certainly concentrated a number of minds.

She frowned as she read one message in particular. She *knew* Julia Ganister-Onge. The former Political Commissioner was hardly the sort of person she'd expected to reply positively, if she replied at all. And yet... Rachel stroked her chin, sipping her coffee as she considered the issue. Julia had already given her a pearl beyond price by confirming the negotiations were little more than a stalling tactic. Given that Rachel hadn't even known there *were* negotiations...

"The government is concentrated in Government House," she said, slowly. It was impossible to trust Julia completely, but her emails matched what Rachel had learnt from other sources. She'd spent hours trying to locate the enemy centre of gravity when she'd been working under Commander Archer. "We could go there. If she helps us, we could get inside without a problem."

Phelps cleared his throat. "Can we trust her?"

"I don't know," Rachel said. The woman she'd met had been willing to return to her homeworld, despite the possibility of being put against the nearest wall and shot. Or simply sent into internal exile. "If the security officers are launching a coup...it's possible Julia and the others are hoping to get their own coup underway."

She rubbed her forehead. "I think we have to move fast," she said. "If they realise Commander Archer isn't a traitor, no matter what else he might have done, they'll start wondering what happened. And it's only a matter of time before they find the body I left behind."

"Understood," Phelps said. He glanced at the rest of the marines. "You and I will sneak into the building. The remainder of the force will attack on the ground. Prepare your allies."

And see how many of them live up to their commitments, Rachel thought. It was easy to be a keyboard warrior. She'd met hundreds of armchair generals and admirals who'd thought they could do better than the men on the spot. The fact they had the advantage of hindsight had never really dawned on them. *This could go horribly wrong.*

She smiled. "And send a message to Major-General Anderson," she said. "We're going to need reinforcements in a hurry."

"I'll see to it," Phelps said.

"Tell him to play along with the diplomatic stalling," she added. "We're going to need some cover to get through their defences."

"Of course," Phelps assured her.

Rachel let him handle the debate with Captain Steel as she plunged her mind back into the datanet. Everything would have to be put in place ahead of time, to ensure that her contacts found themselves forced to rush into making a commitment. It was a simple rule of thumb that anyone who tried to bully someone into making a hasty decision was not a friend, but...there was no *time* to sound out people properly. She didn't dare try. There'd be no room for manoeuvre if someone had an attack of conscience and reported the affair to their superiors. If the enemy took precautions the coup might never get off the ground.

She composed a message for Julia, then uploaded it. If she said no...

We can handle it, she assured herself. *There's more than one way to skin a cat.*

...

Julia had never felt so naked in her life, even when it had dawned on her—finally—just how closely her life was monitored. She was fully dressed and yet she felt naked, unable to shake the feeling no matter how many times she looked down at herself. Her heart was pounding so loudly, as she made her way past the pair of security officers on duty outside the director's office, that she was surprised they couldn't hear it. She suspected they had other problems. From what little she'd heard, McManus was moving rapidly to consolidate his power.

The director didn't look up as she entered. "What is it?"

"I signalled the marines," Julia said. She wouldn't have dared to lie about *that*. "They have agreed to discuss a truce."

"Good," the director said. He never took his eyes off the terminal. "You may proceed."

Julia took a breath. "I need diplomatic advice," she said. "There are two people in the city with diplomatic experience...such as it is. I'd like to call them both to the complex."

The director said nothing for a long, chilling moment, long enough to make her fear she'd made a dreadful mistake. Her request was reasonable—there weren't *many* people with diplomatic experience—but...what if he expected her to handle it alone? Or...or was McManus already in complete charge? Julia found it hard to believe, but...

"If you feel it necessary," the director said, finally. He still didn't look at her. "General Gilbert killed himself, two hours ago."

Julia swallowed, hard. "He did?"

"Yes."

"I..." Julia swallowed, again. Had it really been a suicide? McManus could easily have killed the general and made it *look* like a suicide. "I'm sorry."

"Just end the war, quickly," the director said. "Give us time to recall the fleet and win."

"Yes, sir," Julia said. She felt sorry for him—the director and his general had been friends—but she knew it was already too late. "I'll make the call now."

CHAPTER THIRTY-SEVEN

The corporations responded by buying their way into the corridors of power, demanding laws that made life harder for workers as well as competitors.
—**Professor Leo Caesius**
The Rise and Fall of Interstellar Capitalism

"THEY DIDN'T FIND THE TRUCKS," Mayberry said, surprised.

Haydn grinned at him as they slipped into the abandoned warehouse. The Pathfinders had been fairly sure the trucks would remain undiscovered for some time, as the population and traffic monitoring systems had been crippled, but he hadn't been so sure. He was used to serving on a battlefield where everything moving could be located and blown away from orbit, not sneaking around a city big enough to house over a million people. There were so many refugees on the streets, outside the government complex, that the marines had no trouble hiding as long as they didn't attract attention. It helped, he supposed, that the enemy security officers were too busy mounting a coup.

Which is the problem with security forces, he thought. *You just can't trust them.*

They checked the trucks quickly, altered their IFF beacons and then readied themselves for the task ahead. It would hardly be the first building

Haydn had stormed, but…he felt oddly uneasy as he addressed his men. They were using dishonourable tactics, even if they were using them against dishonourable men. He'd seriously considered insisting that they should sneak out of the city instead, making their way back to join the remainder of the division. Only the blunt truth that they had a chance to end the war overnight had kept him in place.

"Maybe I wouldn't make such a good Pathfinder after all," he muttered.

Mayberry looked at him. "Sir?"

"Never mind." Haydn looked at his men. The drivers, who'd be sitting in the cabs, wore enemy uniforms. The remainder wore their regular BDUs, although it probably wouldn't keep them from being shot if they were recaptured. "Is it time?"

"Just about," Mayberry said. He indicated the first truck. "Shall we go?"

"Yes," Haydn said. He raised his voice. "Mount up!"

A moment later, they were on their way.

• • •

McManus had no qualms about doing whatever he needed to do to extract confessions, up to and including making them up. He had no intention of becoming CEO himself—there were too many risks—but he wanted, needed, to be the power behind the throne. It was the only way to keep himself safe in a dog-eat-dog world. He was perfectly aware that the vast majority of the people who knew him hated him, as the vast majority of the population hated the security officers under his command. He didn't care. Let them hate, as long as they feared. But they were starting *not* to fear.

He felt nothing as he surveyed the live feed from the interrogation cell. Commander Archer looked as if he'd been beaten to within an inch of his life, by men who knew precisely how to cause the maximum of pain with the minimum of permanent damage. It didn't matter, to McManus, if Commander Archer was guilty or innocent. The point was to justify the security lockdown beyond all doubt. Commander Archer would be confessing to being responsible for Earthfall shortly, McManus was certain, as well as a number of other crimes he couldn't possibly have committed. The trick was to ensure the confession that reached his nominal superiors was one that was reasonably plausible...

And yet ... he frowned as he watched the interrogators resume the beating. Commander Archer was an asshole. His staff had been quite happy to detail Commander Archer's proclivities, pretty much involving each and every one of his subordinates, but...they'd never suggested he was particularly strong. He certainly couldn't have killed the security officer whose body had been found in a closet. And...the naked staffer was missing. It couldn't be a coincidence. The file on her was curiously vague. It was starting to look as though *she* had been the traitor.

Not a traitor, he corrected himself. *An enemy infiltrator.*

Commander Archer groaned and started to babble. McManus watched, unmoved, as the interrogators moved in to hear his confession. He had a nasty feeling it didn't matter as much as the broken commander might have hoped. If he'd been guilty of little more than being a horny idiot at the worst possible time...McManus scowled as he turned his attention to the reports from his staffers. General Gilbert's death had robbed Commander Archer of any real purpose. After his confession, he'd be shot and his body dumped in the incinerator.

His wristcom bleeped. "Sir," his staffer said. "Long-range sensors are reporting enemy aircraft launching from Roxon."

"Do whatever you have to do," McManus ordered. There was no point in fighting in the muddy sea between the two cities. The marines had the edge in the open, certainly against untrained men. "Just don't let them fly over the city."

"Yes, sir," his staffer said.

McManus nodded. It was time to make himself the kingmaker. By the time the fleet returned, by the time the marines were beaten, his position would be impregnable. He already had a small army on the streets, as well as the commissioners reporting directly to him. The soldiers would follow orders or they'd be executed. General Gilbert had been the only military officer with some degree of independence—and a power base of his own—and *he* was dead by his own hand. McManus found that delightful. The fool might have lost most of his army, but he hadn't been powerless. And yet, he'd killed himself. Idiot. He could have recovered his power base or launched a coup himself.

It's time, he thought. *And I will finally know true power.*

...

"It's time," Phelps said, quietly.

Rachel nodded as the groundcar glided towards the security checkpoint. They'd taken Julia's permissions and checked them carefully, but there was no way to be *sure* she wasn't trying to pull a double-cross. The woman she'd met back on the MEU had been smart, yet…she'd been dumb enough to want to return home. Rachel supposed she would have done the same, if she'd been captured by the enemy, but still…*her* people didn't have a habit of searching for scapegoats. She put the thought aside as she started to upload the first set of messages onto the datanet. If nothing else, the enemy would be ripped apart by civil war. The marines would win by default.

She let Phelps handle the talking as she hunched down in her chair, allowing the wig to cover her eyes. She looked different to the person who'd fled the staff offices, but…she had no idea who'd seen her, who might *recognise* her. There was so much activity moving around the secure zone, from the antiaircraft vehicles she'd noted earlier to heavy AFVs and troop transports, that it was easy to believe she might cross paths with someone who'd seen her. It was a relief when the groundcar started to move again, leaving the checkpoint behind. They passed through two more before they reached Government House.

"Impressive," Phelps breathed.

Rachel shrugged. Government House looked like any other government house—the design had been standardised centuries ago—but it had been built to a far greater scale. There were at least twenty floors, each one covering four times as much space as the standard design. She looked up, spotting troops patrolling the roof with handheld antiaircraft weapons and sniper rifles. Someone was feeling paranoid, she decided, as they parked in the parking lot and climbed out. A pair of grim-faced security officers checked their permissions before searching them quickly, thoroughly and professionally. The enemy had brought their A-Team to the party.

"This way," she said. She'd memorised the building's floor plans, although she wasn't sure how close they were to reality. The prefabricated design was intended to allow the beancounters to reconfigure their surroundings, at least before the original government complex was replaced by something new. "We don't want to be late."

Her implants pinged an alert as they passed through the doors and into the building. The enemy datanet was locked down tight, the local nodes reprogrammed to prevent remote access. She suspected the enemy feared remote terminals, rather than enhanced soldiers, but it hardly mattered. She'd assumed they'd have to get the messages out before they entered the building and met their contact. She braced herself, readying herself to run—again—if they'd been betrayed. She was all too aware Julia could win herself whatever reward she wanted if she lured the marines into a trap.

Her eyes wandered across the lobby. It was huge, so large she had the impression it had been built for giants. Her lips quirked, humourlessly. Had the designers just scaled up the plans with no regard for the implications? Or were they just trying to impress visitors? The security officers scattered around the room looked like midgets as they watched the doors and visitors with wary eyes. She put the thought out of her head as Julia emerged from a side door and hurried towards them. The older woman looked frightened, as if she expected the hammer to land on their heads at any moment. Rachel tensed, despite herself. Julia could betray them quite by accident, if the guards noticed she was jumpy.

"This way, please," Julia said. If she recognised Rachel, she said nothing. "We have a lot of work to do."

Rachel nodded as Julia led them into the elevator. The security officers weren't even *trying* to hide the pickups in the cramped compartment. Rachel noted their positions absently, then swept her eyes around the rest of the elevator, trying to determine if there were any more. People weren't lazy, she'd been told once, but they did have a habit of slowing once they thought they'd reached the goal. A person who thought he'd found and disabled all the bugs would stop looking for *more*. She kept her mouth tightly closed as she noted three more, all concealed within the decor. There might even be more.

The upper levels felt strange as they slipped out of the elevator and made their way down to one of the guest suites. Rachel guessed it was Julia's office. She slipped inside, hastily scanning the room for surveillance devices. There were only four, all surprisingly easy to find. She checked the rest of the suite, her eyes narrowing in disapproval as she found one concealed within the shower head. Bastards. She knew that one would be almost impossible to find, let alone remove, without the proper equipment.

"The room appears clean," Phelps said, after he ran his own sweep. "Julia, can you unlock your terminal?"

"Yes, but I don't have total access," Julia said. "The entire system is operating on restricted mode."

"It doesn't matter," Rachel said. "Where is the command suite?"

"One floor up," Julia said. She bit her lip. "The…the security troops are in control."

"No worries," Rachel said. "Let us deal with it."

• • •

Colonel Parker Haworth was entirely sure the reports of General Gilbert's suicide were total bullshit. He didn't need to spent most of his career in the military, first for the empire and then for the corprats, to know that ninety percent of everything the media put out was utter crap. General Gilbert was an experienced officer. Sure, he'd taken a beating—Parker knew it was sheer luck his unit had been outside the blast zone when the KEWs started to fall—but the war wasn't over. No, he'd been killed by the wretched brownshirts. The security officers had killed the general, just to cement their control over the military.

Parker smiled to himself as he glanced at his wristcom, silently counting down the seconds to zero. He'd hesitated—he'd thought long and hard—before joining the coup plotters, although he'd kept the fact they'd contacted him a secret. Everyone knew what had happened to the dumb fool who'd reported the contact. The idiot had been interrogated so intensively he'd died in the chair. Parker knew he wasn't going to die like that, not while he had a gun in his hand. In truth, he acknowledged silently, he'd committed himself the moment he'd heard about the general's death.

His eyes swept the FOB, noting the positions of the commissioner—a wretched rodent of a man—and his two escorts, armed security troopers. It was sheer luck everything was in total chaos. The remaining military units had been pulled back to the city and slotted into position along the walls, as if someone with only the barest understanding of military reality had been issuing orders. Parker had never seen the marines, but anyone who could advance so far in a handful of days…he shook his head. The sooner they took power, the better.

He unbuttoned his holster as he turned away, drawing his gun before turning and opening fire. The security troopers died first, shot through the head. The commissioner gaped at him, his gaze moving from Parker to the dead bodies as if he couldn't wrap his head around what had happened. Parker keyed his wristcom, snapping out a command to his men on the outside. He hadn't been able to prime them as much as he might like, but…they should obey orders. The corprats had no one but themselves to blame. They'd been the ones who insisted that strict obedience to orders, no matter how insane, was the priority.

"The security forces are mounting a coup," he said, as he kept the gun trained on the commissioner. He thought he could trust his men, all of whom were unarmed, but it was impossible to be sure. Rumour had it that there were undercover spies within the ranks. "We are moving to stop them."

"This is insane," the commissioner spluttered. "This is…"

Parker shot him, then keyed his wristcom again. The rest of the plotters should be moving now, trying to seize control of the military before it was too late. Unless…he shook his head as the first set of replies came rattling in. He'd feared it might be a demented test of his loyalty, when he'd seen the first message, but no one in their right mind would stage a test in the middle of a war.

He gritted his teeth as he heard the sound of gunfire in the distance. He had his orders—hold his position, purge the commissioners and the security troops, prepare for further offensive operations—but he knew it wasn't going to be easy. Some units wouldn't be taken over so quickly, others would start shooting in all directions or sit on their hands as their commanders, who didn't have the slightest idea what was going on, did nothing. And there would be the problem of dealing with the marines afterwards…

Parker shook his head. The coup had to succeed quickly, or not at all. They could worry about everything else later.

• • •

Julia felt oddly free as the two marines checked the room, then started to fiddle with the terminal. She wasn't clear on precisely what they were doing, but…she felt as if she had finally committed herself. The decision had been made. She found herself looking at the marines—there was something familiar about the woman—and waiting for them to tell her what to do. Maybe they'd want her to sit and wait for the fighting to end. It wasn't as if she was any good with a gun.

She frowned as the female marine looked up. "The coup is underway," she said. "Haydn and the others should be *en route*."

Julia frowned. "How many of the plotters know who's *really* behind the coup?"

"Just you," the female marine said. "Although I imagine a few of them have guessed, given that we played on loyalty to the empire in some of the messages."

She glanced back at the terminal. "We need to move," she said. "We have to snatch the director before it's too late."

Julia nodded. "I'll take you there," she said. "Do you have any weapons?"

The marines exchanged glances. "We couldn't carry weapons through the security cordon," the female marine said. "But we have a plan."

"I'll take your word for it," Julia said, biting down on a far sharper response. "Let's go."

She led them through the door and up the stairs to the next level. There were no alarms, but she thought she could feel *something* shift in the air as they approached the director's suite. The three men standing in front of the door looked more like prison guards than protectors, their weapons constantly sweeping the air as if they expected to be attacked at any moment. Julia almost took a step back when they looked at her, despite the marines moving up behind her.

"Well," the guard said. "What do we have…?"

The marines moved so quickly they blurred. Julia threw herself to the floor as they crashed into the guards, knocking them down. Julia felt the floor shake under the impact and looked up. All three guards were dead, blood leaking from wounds that…she swallowed hard, unable to comprehend what had happened. The marines had said they were unarmed. They'd said…no wonder they were unarmed. They didn't *need* weapons to be lethally effective.

"Fuck," she managed.

"Get up," the male marine ordered. "Hurry!"

His voice compelled obedience. Julia scrambled to her feet and stumbled forwards, pressing her hand against the buzzer as the marines searched the dead bodies and removed the weapons. The door hissed open, revealing the director sitting on a sofa. He looked to have aged fifty years overnight. It dawned on Julia, as she was pushed into the room, that the marines weren't the only ones mounting a coup.

McManus, she thought. *He didn't waste any time.*

And then the alarms started to ring.

CHAPTER THIRTY-EIGHT

Indeed, by Earthfall, the line between the corprats—as they came to be called—and the senators was effectively non-existent. The corprats had become part of the aristocracy. They were no longer so concerned with innovation. All they really cared about was preserving their power.
—**Professor Leo Caesius**
The Rise and Fall of Interstellar Capitalism

THE CHECKPOINT DIDN'T LOOK VERY TOUGH, not to Haydn's experienced eye. It had clearly been thrown up on very short notice, by troops more used to policing than soldiering. The handful of air defence vehicles behind the lines, their sensors swinging from side to side, were far too close to the barricades for comfort. If *he'd* been setting up the defence lines, he would have placed them much further away. But then, it looked as if their coup was taking place in the middle of another coup.

"They're checking everyone who goes in and out," Mayberry muttered, as they drove towards the checkpoint. "Our paperwork probably won't hold up."

Haydn nodded, then glanced back at the marines hiding in the rear of the truck. "Jump when the first grenade explodes."

He braced himself as they drove up to the checkpoint. The guards looked alert—and deeply worried. One of them was constantly glancing into the distance, not in the direction Haydn would have expected. Did he think the marines were going to circle around the city and strike from the rear? Or... he heard an explosion towards the edge of the city and winced, inwardly. The Pathfinders had promised that some of the ex-imperial officers would jump towards the marines, but nothing had been guaranteed. The enemy chain of command was about to collapse. It didn't sit well with him.

The guard poked his rifle through the opened window. "Papers, please."

Haydn pushed the rifle up, then unhooked a stolen grenade from his belt and hurled it into the checkpoint. The HE grenade detonated a second later, taking out the guards inside the guardpost before they could react. The guard who'd accosted him pulled the trigger, the bullet going through the vehicle's roof and heading onwards. Haydn's ears rang as he yanked the rifle away, then punched the guard out. He snapped orders, directing the marines to seize the guardpost and the escorting vehicles. They had to be captured before some bright spark organised a counterattack.

Mayberry followed him as he led the charge towards the antiaircraft vehicles. They were standard designs, meant to provide cover for military bases rather than advance with the remainder of the mobile units. Their hatches weren't even buttoned up! He pulled them open, ordered the crews out at gunpoint and then directed a handful of his men to shut the vehicles down. The enemy would be—hopefully—reluctant to bomb their centre of government. He snapped more orders as the forward squad raced towards the main entrance, pushing through before the shutters could come down. He was fairly sure the enemy commanders would already be on their way to the bunkers.

And they really should have bugged out long ago, he thought. He could understand a reluctance to abandon one's capital city—it could not fail to have a demoralising effect on the defenders—but common sense should have sent the enemy leadership to a PDC or somewhere else safely away from the fighting. *They must have thought they'd thrashed us.*

He shot down a pair of guards as they swept through the lower levels, keeping a wary eye out for rooms and elevators that weren't on the plans.

The enemy would have plenty of ways to get to their boltholes, unless they'd really been caught by surprise. His men hauled open elevator tubes and jammed them, ensuring the tubes and cars themselves were useless. There was no point in keeping them operational, not now. Elevator cars could turn into death traps at a moment's notice.

"Sir," Mayberry shouted. "The enemy are massing outside the lines!"

Haydn cursed under his breath. They'd caught the enemy by surprise, but...they'd regrouped with impressive speed. There must have been a bunch of patrols outside the lines, under an officer with the authority and initiative to take action. It probably shouldn't have surprised him. The enemy knew they were losing control of their city. They'd probably been drawing up plans for countering an insurgent uprising well before the population monitoring systems had been destroyed.

"Hold the line," he snapped back. The prisoners were being marched into the lobby, where they'd be guarded by his men, but there was no time to secure them. They didn't have any ties. They hadn't even thought to bring duct tape! If the prisoners decided to cause trouble, they'd have to be stamped on fast before things got out of hand. "Don't let them get back inside."

He cursed, again, as the shooting started. He'd thought the enemy had thrown their defence lines together too quickly to do a good job of it. Now...he found himself wondering if they'd been one step ahead of him all along. Had they intended to counterattack right from the start? Or was he overthinking it? The enemy might just have had a stroke of good luck to match the bad.

We have to hold the line long enough for the Pathfinders to do their job, and for the reinforcements to arrive, he told himself. *We can assess what worked, and what didn't, later.*

• • •

"Sir, we just lost contact with two more garrisons," the operator said. "The..."

The building shook. McManus scowled, eying the rapidly-darkening display with a jaundiced eye. He'd never trusted the ex-imperials—turning one's coat tended to be habit-forming—but he'd never expected an outright uprising. Too many fighting units had dropped out of the command network, along with the commissioners who were supposed to be keeping an eye on them. McManus would have liked to believe they were trying to regain control, but he knew better. The commissioners were deeply disliked and completely outnumbered. And their charges no longer had reason to think they would be caught and shot if they raised a hand to the watchdogs.

He rubbed his forehead as he tried to think. The command network was starting to break down completely. It was no longer possible to trust what he was seeing on the display. It was clear *someone* had attacked the building below, but...who? The marines? A rebel unit? He didn't know. The last report from outside the lines suggested that one of his most trusted officers was mounting a counteroffensive, forcing the original attackers to defend themselves rather than sweep the building for the corporate leadership...

McManus swore. It wasn't fair. It just wasn't fair! He'd finally reached a position of power and it was already falling apart. He couldn't just run... he wasn't sure he could so much as get down to the bunker. In theory, the drop shaft was impregnable; in practice, the attackers might already have cut it from behind. He could drop down and straight into their waiting arms. He forced himself to think. It wasn't over yet. If he could get to the aircraft and slip out of the city before the hammer came down...

"Team One, you're with me," he ordered, as he slotted a command earpiece into place. He'd need to fetch the director before leaving the city. The old man would give McManus the legitimacy he needed to secure his position, once he reached safety and organised a counterattack. "Team Two, concentrate on keeping the routes open as long as possible."

He took one last look at the display, silently noting how many military units had gone dark, then drew his pistol and headed for the door. There'd be time for revenge later. He'd use nukes and shipkillers on the marine position, turning the mansions to radioactive ash rather than waste time and men trying to recapture them. The sentiment that had saved the marines, during the first offensive, meant nothing to *him*. Oh, he was going to *enjoy* watching them burn. And then he'd hunt down their base and kill the rest of them.

The hatch hissed open. He checked his terminal—the internal security net was coming apart too—and then nodded for his close-protection team to lead the way. He'd reward them later for their loyalty. They'd stayed with him when it would be easy to run the other way and escape. And...

Get to the director, then to the aircraft, he thought. *And then get to safety.*

• • •

Rachel's eyes adapted instantly to the darkness as she stepped into the director's suite. It was smaller than she'd expected, smaller and less fancy than the rooms she'd seen when she'd been working under General Gilbert. The director himself sat in a chair, staring down at his hands. He didn't look up as she entered, as if nothing mattered to him. Rachel guessed he'd lost everything in the last few days, including his power. The security officers were in charge now.

She keyed the lights. The room brightened. Behind her, she heard Julia gasp. The woman might have thrown her lot in with the marines—finally—but she still had to worry if she was doing something wrong. The howling alarms—and the shooting, clearly audible even though the thick walls—were a clear sign the marines were not in full control. Not yet. Rachel could hear enough shooting to be fairly sure there was a pitched battle going on downstairs.

The director looked up, his eyes old and hard. "What do you want?"

Rachel chose her words carefully. "I represent the Terran Marine Corps," she said. "I have authority to guarantee your safety—and the safety of your families—if you surrender the planet without delay."

"I doubt it," the director said. His voice was flat, his face unchanging, but she could still *hear* the sneer. "There are too many people who'll want revenge."

It was a good point, Rachel conceded silently. There would be people on the planet—and elsewhere—who'd be horrified at the corprats being allowed to get away with everything. And yet...she understood the logic. The enemy wouldn't surrender if they thought they'd be put in front of a kangaroo court and executed, or shot without the formalities of a trial. An endless cycle of revenge, and revenge for the revenge, wouldn't help anyone. She'd seen it before, on too many planets to name. Sometimes, you just had to draw a line under the past and refuse to allow it to overshadow the future.

"We can take you off-world," she said. "*All* of you. All you have to do is surrender and assist us in transferring power to a provisional government."

The director said nothing for a long moment. "How do I know I can trust you?"

Julia stepped forward. "Sir...they did keep their word on Hameau," she said. "They protected the former government, often to the point of risking their own men..."

"This isn't Hameau," the director reminded her. "This is Onge."

Rachel met his eyes. "The war is effectively over," she said. "Half your military is in revolt. The security forces are launching a coup. Your population, simmering with anger, is out on the streets. There's no way you, and your people, can regain control. The only question is just how much blood is going to be shed, between now and the end of the war. You can concede defeat and help us minimise the bloodshed. Or you can refuse and watch as the entire planet burns to the ground. You've already lost. You can only decide if you're willing to die, for your entire family to die, just to spite us."

Phelps tapped her shoulder. "We have incoming!"

"Shit," Rachel muttered back. She checked the internal datanet. It looked as if there was a full-scale war going on below them. Haydn and his men were armed, but they couldn't stand up to tanks and AFVs. "We need to finish this quickly."

• • •

Thaddeus had always prided himself on being ruthlessly pragmatic, although—in hindsight—it was clear he hadn't been ruthless enough. He'd been losing his grip from the moment the marines landed on his estate, well before McManus effectively took power for himself. Thaddeus wasn't blind to the younger man's manipulations. He'd hoped there would be time for McManus to overreach himself—the man didn't realise it, but taking power and using it were two very different things—yet...he was running out of time. They were *all* running out of time.

He looked at Julia, wondering when she'd made the choice to betray him. Had she been a traitor all along? Or had she turned on him after he'd refused to listen to her? Or...did it matter? He was old enough to put his anger aside, to consider his legacy logically. His family would be wiped out, if civil war raged across the planet. They had too many enemies. They'd die unless they came out on top and he was pragmatic enough to realise they might not. The offer was a good one, as frustrating as it was. They might lose their power, but at least they'd keep their lives. And they might be able to claw back their power.

"You safeguard our people," he said, softly. "And we will place the world into your hands."

"They're coming," the other marine said. "We have to hurry."

• • •

Haydn kept low and fired carefully, conserving his ammunition. It wasn't easy to tell how many enemy soldiers were out there, but it felt as if a small army was bearing down on them. They seemed reluctant to use heavy weapons, for which he was grateful, but it was just a matter of time before that changed. He snapped orders at the marines manning the antiaircraft vehicles, directing them to turn the missiles into makeshift field artillery. They didn't have much ammunition—it was starting to look as though the defenders had never planned for a long siege—but it would give the attackers a fright.

"They're bringing up riot-control vehicles," Mayberry said.

Haydn cursed. The police vehicles weren't designed for the battlefield, but...his lips quirked. It wasn't as if his men had antitank rockets or plasma cannons or even heavy machine guns that would punch through the advancing armour like a knife through butter and leave the vehicles flaming wrecks. No...

He turned to the antiaircraft crews. "Don't let them get any closer," he snapped. The guns on the vehicles were hardly designed for a siege, but the defences were too weak to stand up for long. "Hit them!"

Moments later, the first riot vehicle exploded into a massive fireball.

• • •

McManus staggered as the building shook, violently. His earpiece seemed to fall silent, before filling—again—with excited chatter. The people below him had stopped the riot control vehicles in their tracks. They had antitank rockets! Where had they found antitank rockets? McManus knew there were none in the building. After a batch had been stolen, he'd made sure to keep the remainder of the stockpile under tight control...

"Keep moving," he snapped, as they reached the top of the stairs. "I..."

His voice trailed off. There were *bodies* outside the director's room. The door itself gaped open. He could hear voices inside. McManus swore, his arm shaking as he levelled his pistol. Someone had gotten there first. Someone had beaten him. Someone...

"Grenade," he snapped. If someone had control of the director...he felt a surge of naked hatred as his dreams threatened to crash into nightmares. No one would have the director, he vowed; he'd turn the man's death into a rallying cry after he'd escaped the building and reached a PDC. "Now!"

He took the grenade and hurled it through the door.

• • •

Rachel blinked as she saw the grenade. She'd assumed the newcomers, whoever they were, would hesitate to kill the director. Killing the only person who could order a surrender was never a good idea, yet...there was no time to kick the grenade back out of the room. Phelps hurled himself forward, landing on top of the grenade. It exploded a second later...Rachel knew, without looking, that he was dead. No one, not even an enhanced marine, could take such a blast and survive. Her head spun. She almost wished it had been Julia or the director who'd taken the blast...

Mourn later, she told herself, savagely.

She hurled herself forward, running down the corridor. The newcomers raised their guns, too late. Only one of them managed a shot, missing her by inches. She ploughed into them, blinking away tears as she ripped them apart with enhanced strength. She'd pay for it later, she knew, but she didn't care. Her best friend was dead and...

Rachel caught herself and stumbled back to the room. The director was staring at the body, looking stunned. Rachel felt a hot flash of anger. The director had ruled a dog-eat-dog world. Was he surprised his subordinates had decided to remove him? A dead figurehead might be more useful than a living man. Whoever took power would be able to use his death to justify all kinds of things.

"Order the surrender," she said. The datanet was flickering and fading. She scowled as she heard another explosion outside, shaking the building once again. "Quickly."

The director nodded stiffly and walked to his desk. "Keep your word," he said, as he keyed the console. "Too many lives are at stake."

"I know," Rachel said. Phelps was dead. The rest of her comrades—her brothers—were missing. She shuddered to think how many others had died in the last few weeks. If the fighting continued, hundreds of thousands more were going to die as well. "End it, now. Please."

Five minutes later, the guns outside fell silent.

It was over.

CHAPTER THIRTY-NINE

This might not have been so bad, if they hadn't realised—as we had—that the empire was doomed. Like us, they had no idea when the crunch would finally come; like us, they started to prepare themselves. They assumed they would be the masters of the new universal order.
—**Professor Leo Caesius**
The Rise and Fall of Interstellar Capitalism

GERALD WATCHED, COOLLY, as the Raptor flew over the burning city and headed directly for Government House. The military and police forces had largely surrendered—and had been ordered to hold position and wait for relief—but the local population wasn't interested in going back to their homes. Too much hatred and fear had built up over the last few decades for the people to take their freedom calmly. The marines had already established camps to take the corprats—and an astonishing number of managers, directors and HR specialists—into protective custody. God alone knew how many had been killed before the marines had started trying to re-establish order.

The only thing worse than a battle lost is a battle won, he thought. The Duke of Wellington had said it, after a battle that most people had forgotten long ago. *And he wasn't quite right.*

He smiled, but there was little real humour in the expression. Hundreds of marines were dead or wounded. Millions of credits worth of equipment had been lost. The corps had its own industrial base, established long enough to stop corrupt or penny-pinching beancounters from cutting the safety margins to the limits, but replacing everything that had been destroyed or damaged beyond repair would take years. The tanks, in particular...he made a mental note to look into the captured stockpiles. He disliked the idea of using vehicles designed for the corprats, but not using them would be considerably worse.

These are the problems of victory, he told himself. *The other side is in an even worse mess.*

The thought didn't cheer him. There were just too many things that needed to be done. The enemy industrial nodes had been occupied, their cloudscoops had been secured...he had a feeling their design for newer and better cloudscoops would unlock an economic resurgence, when the chaos of Earthfall finally came to an end. The enemy fleet was still out there, but he was fairly sure the ships would be secured as they returned, one by one. If some of them became pirates or independent...he shrugged. They wouldn't have much of a support base, at least at first. They would be hunted down before they became a real threat.

He felt a twinge of...*something*...as the Raptor circled the building, giving him time to see the burned-out vehicles on the ground before the aircraft landed neatly on the roof. The final battle had been chancy as hell, the sort of plan that would probably be rejected out of hand by any *sane* military. It was hard not to think of all the things that could have gone wrong...that nearly had gone wrong. The thought bothered him as he unstrapped and headed for the opening hatch. Major-General Foxtrot would take command shortly, allowing Gerald to head back to Safehouse to face the music. If the Commandant and the other Major-Generals decided they'd done the wrong thing...

I did what I had to do, he thought, as he stepped onto the roof. The air tasted of smoke and burnt human flesh. *And we did come out ahead. In the end.*

"Major-General," Julia Ganister-Onge said. "Welcome."

Gerald nodded. Julia Ganister-Onge had apparently become a liaison officer between the provisional government, such as it was, and the marines. He doubted it would last. The bemused coup plotters and their allies might have hung together, throughout the chaos of the last few days and the shock of discovering who'd *really* led the coup, but…they'd start bickering over power very soon. The provisional government had no legitimacy worthy of the name. He wondered, idly, how long it would be until the various post-corprat factions started setting up political parties and fighting for dominance. Probably not very long at all.

"The director chose to head straight into protective custody," Julia informed him. She sounded older than he remembered, as if she'd learnt more than a few hard lessons in the last few weeks. "He hopes you'll keep your word."

"We will," Gerald said. He had no trouble spotting the signs of someone wanting to have a private chat. "What do you want to say?"

"We're getting organised," Julia said. "A lot of the industrial nodes survived intact. The personnel who ran them have…more or less…claimed ownership. It'll be a long time before things straighten themselves out, but…they will."

"That's good to hear," Gerald said. It was true. A decently-run planet would have an uplifting effect on the entire sector. "Is that what you wanted to tell me?"

"No." Julia stopped and turned to face him. "We assume you have a plan for the future, for the post-Earthfall universe. What *is* it?"

Good question, Gerald conceded. The planners had advanced a number of options, but none of them were truly viable. The sheer scale of the collapse, and just how many Core Worlds had been turned into radioactive ruins, had stunned everyone. *We're not sure what we want to do.*

He met her eyes. "We're working on it," he said. "If there's one thing we've learnt, over the last few centuries, it is that plans often need to be adapted as circumstances change."

"You need a plan," Julia said. She turned away from him. "The plan here...it wasn't very good, in hindsight, but it was the best they could come up with at the time. You need a plan, too."

Gerald nodded, curtly. "I know," he said. He could hardly deny it. "But, right now, we have to handle the present before we look to the future."

...

Rachel felt oddly at a loose end, even though she'd been working with Captain Steel and his men ever since the director had ordered the surrender and the fighting had—finally—come to an end. She'd contacted the staff officers she'd known when she'd been undercover and invited them to join the new government, once they'd been released from the prison cells. They hadn't been mistreated, which was more than could be said for Commander Archer. He'd been beaten to death, after confessing to a long list of crimes he couldn't possibly have committed. Rachel wasn't sure if the security forces had given much of a damn. The commander hadn't been any use to them whatsoever.

She let out a breath as she stood on the rooftop and stared over the city. It was slowly quietening down as the marines patrolled the streets, making it clear they would tolerate no nonsense. Groups of looters and vandals had been placed in shackles and put to work clearing up the mess. It was more useful than throwing them in a camp and, hopefully, it would discourage others from burning and looting if they thought they might have to clean up after themselves. She smiled, then sobered as she looked towards the distant countryside. She was alone...

Her heart sank. Phelps had died to save the mission...she couldn't help feeling it hadn't been worth it. And the other two had vanished. She wanted to believe they'd remained underground, after the anchor station had been taken, but it was inconceivable they'd have stayed underground all this time. The war was over. They'd had ample opportunity to come forward and make contact, even if they weren't pulled out. They must be dead and she was alone. She was almost tempted to take a step forward and allow gravity to pull her down, ending her life.

Bad idea, she told herself. *Really bad idea.*

She turned as she heard someone open the door behind her. She turned to see Major-General Anderson stepping onto the rooftop, looking remarkably tired for someone who'd done nothing more strenuous than sit at a conference table for the last few hours. She silently told herself off for being mean-spirited. The locals meant well, she supposed, but they were trying to put together a government out of spit and baling wire. There just wasn't enough of the old government *left* for the task to be simple, even though the lower managing class had largely remained on duty. And they now thought *they* should be running things.

"General," she said. "What can I do for you?"

Anderson stood beside her and looked at the city. "It's a very strange design, isn't it?"

Rachel nodded. "It looks like a giant chessboard," she agreed. "Everything is laid out…soullessly. Whoever designed this was an academic who knew nothing of the real world."

She smiled at the thought, although it wasn't funny. What sort of lunatic would place the residential areas on one side of the city and the shopping complexes on the other? And then expect the residents to get to the shops when they wanted something as small as a pint of milk? Not to mention how easy it was to turn electronic currency into a means of social control, denying people access to their funds…the system was always going to explode, she was sure. The marines might have saved the corprats from a far worse fate.

"I'm sorry about the rest of your team," Anderson said. "They deserved better."

"They died doing what they loved," Rachel said. She knew she'd never know what happened to the other two. The medals she'd been promised were no compensation for the loss of her friends. "I'll miss them, but…"

"You'll be going home with me," Anderson said. "You'll spend some time on Safehouse before they assign you to a new team."

You mean, I'll spend some time being mercilessly poked and prodded by the headshrinkers, Rachel translated silently. She understood the logic, but...she shook her head. The marine corps employed better psychologists than the rest of the military, men and women who'd seen the elephant themselves, yet it was never easy to unburden herself in front of them. She'd heard all the stories, all the warnings whispered during basic training. Say too much to a headshrinker, they'd warned, and you'd never see active duty again. *I suppose I don't have a choice.*

She sighed, inwardly. She didn't want to think about a new team right now. She wasn't even sure there *was* a team waiting for her. Empty slots were rapidly filled...she winced at the thought of being the FNG again. It wasn't going to be easy, even though she had a stellar record since she'd earned her wings. Too many teams would ride her hard until they were sure she still had it.

"Yes, sir," she said. There was no point in trying to fight it. "When do we leave?"

"Two weeks, I think," Anderson said. "We'll see."

You're probably not too keen to hand command to Major-General Foxtrot, Rachel thought, silently. She understood the impulse. Very few marines had ever commanded multiple divisions in combat. *And when you go home...*

She winced, again. She had a *lot* of reports to write. She'd have to go through everything she'd done, everything the rest of the team had done that she'd known about, everything the *division* had done...she dreaded the thought of assessing the division's overall effectiveness when she honestly hadn't seen much of it. She'd been undercover for the majority of the campaign. The thought made her smile, reluctantly. Her report was going to be required reading if—when, she told herself firmly—the Slaughterhouse was reopened.

A thought struck her. "They didn't destroy the Slaughterhouse."

Anderson looked irked. "If they did, we haven't been able to find any record of it," he agreed. "They had means, motive and opportunity, but they didn't actually *do* it. And we don't know who did."

Rachel nodded. The corps was not short of enemies. There were plenty of factions who had a vested interest in crippling the corps, ranging from corprats to warlords...she scowled as she realised the attackers might *never* be identified. She'd heard a rumour that the Commandant had assigned a team of Pathfinders to finding the attackers, but nothing concrete. Maybe she could get herself assigned to the team. It would give her something to do.

"We'll find them," she said.

"Yes," Anderson agreed. He turned to head back downstairs, then stopped and looked at her. "Until then...there'll always be something for us to do."

"Yes, sir," Rachel said. "I look forward to it."

...

"We must get captured more often," Rifleman Young said, as the remains of the company settled into the berth. The makeshift unit had been left intact, although that would change if—when—the division was rebuilt from scratch. "If it means going home earlier..."

"That's enough of that," Command Sergeant Mayberry said, sharply. "We haven't been ordered home as a *reward*."

Haydn agreed, silently. They'd been relieved by airborne forces, then assigned to guard duty until enough reinforcements had arrived to take the POWs—and the city—in hand. It was clear his makeshift unit was being treated with kid gloves, although he hadn't figured out why until they'd been given orders to report to the shuttles. They'd been in enemy hands long enough for the bastards to have tampered with their minds. Haydn knew no one had done anything to his mind, but his superiors wouldn't take his word for it. His programmers would have programmed him to say they hadn't programmed him to say anything...

He rubbed his forehead. He had to be tired. That was almost funny.

"Get some rest, sir," Mayberry advised. "I'll handle things here."

Haydn nodded and left the compartment. *Havoc* and the remains of her original squadron had been earmarked to go home first, along with a pair of MEUs. It certainly *felt* as though the men were going to get some downtime, before they were thrown back into the fire. Safehouse didn't have much in the way of facilities, but…he shook his head. He'd settle for a few days of lolling in bed, without duty yanking him out of his pit and demanding he went back to work. He was too high-ranking for a sergeant to drag him out of bed any longer…

He smiled, then scowled. He'd met too many Imperial Army officers who'd got their posts through connections, rather than training. They'd often been unfit for duty. The corps, by contrast, put its prospective officers through hell before allowing them to take command. It helped that they'd spent time in the field first. Every marine was a rifleman first and that went double for officers…

The observation blister lay open in front of him. He stepped inside and looked down at the planet below. There was no hint of scarring on the blue-green orb, no suggestion a pair of armies had been locked in titanic conflict for the last few weeks. It seemed obscene, somehow, to think that the world was unmarked. But then, the stars and planets were practically eternal compared to the human gnats who swarmed and multiplied around them. It was easy to understand, now, why so many people *worshipped* the life-giving stars.

He heard someone behind him and turned. Kerri stood there, looking tired. "Hi."

Kerri smiled. "Hi to you, too," she said. She might not be classically pretty, but his heart leapt anyway. "Welcome back."

Haydn hesitated, suddenly unsure of what to say. They'd been lovers, but…had it been nothing more than a quick affair that had ended when he'd been redeployed? Or…or what? He felt a flicker of doubt, followed by concern. Did she want more? Did he? It was going to be uncomfortable sharing the same ship if they had different ideas…

"Thanks," he said. "How was it for you?"

"We dropped a hammer on them," Kerri said. "And since then, we've been securing the remains of the orbital defences before we go home."

Haydn had to smile. "You probably saved us all, you know."

"We'll be gloating about it for the entire trip," Kerri agreed. "You were lucky they overstepped themselves."

"I suppose." Haydn looked back at the planet. "Are you…are you busy right now?"

Kerri had to laugh. "Smooth."

Haydn snorted. "I downloaded five books of romantic poetry and decided they were written by clueless virgins who wanted to sabotage their rivals," he said, a deadpan look on his face. "I think anyone daft enough to try those lines will be lucky if the poor girl doesn't throw up in disgust."

"Everyone goes through a stage when they want a handsome prince," Kerri said. "And if they're lucky, they grow out of it before they find one."

"That's very insightful," Haydn said.

"I spent a chunk of my time as XO comforting young officers and crew who were having relationship problems," Kerri said. "Half the time, I had to reassure them that there was more than one fish in the sea. Too many of them had problems believing it."

"I don't believe it," Haydn said.

"You're in your thirties," Kerri said. "Can you remember being a teenager?"

Haydn shrugged. He'd been a rowdy teenager who hadn't really knuckled down and worked at anything until he'd joined the marines, where he'd learnt that Drill Instructors were rarely impressed with teenage smartasses. It was humbling, in hindsight, to realise that most of his daringly original teenage rebellions had been nothing of the sort. The DIs had seen it all before, time and time again. Of *course* they hadn't been impressed.

He winced at the memory. "I try not to."

"I don't blame you," Kerri said. She made a show of consulting her wristcom. "I have to be back on the bridge in five hours, but until then…"

She held out a hand. "Coming?"

CHAPTER FORTY

And, alas, far too many people had to die to convince them they were wrong.
—**Professor Leo Caesius**
The Rise and Fall of Interstellar Capitalism

IT WAS ALWAYS SNOWING ON SAFEHOUSE.

Major-General Jeremy Damiani, Commandant of the Terran Marine Corps, stood by the conference room window and peered out over a scene from hell. Safehouse's atmosphere was poison for an unprotected human, the pools of liquid and ice on the ground deadly…the flickers of weird lightning in the cloudy purple sky a grim warning the world was very far from safe. It was the last place anyone would look for a marine base, he thought, which was why the Major-Generals had chosen it. But it couldn't be the *only* major base any longer…

He turned to face Major-General Anderson. "We made mistakes."

"Yes, sir," Anderson said. His report had been both complete and conclusive. It hadn't made for comforting reading. "We made a lot of mistakes."

Jeremy nodded. The marines had underestimated their enemy and overestimated their own potency on the battlefield. It was an understandable mistake, he conceded, but not an excusable one. They should have realised what would happen when they faced an enemy that matched them in equipment and technical skill. Air and space supremacy could no longer be taken for granted. They'd still come out ahead, but it had been costly. Seven hundred marines had died in the fighting. Many of the bodies had never been recovered.

"We didn't realise what we were facing," Anderson added. "If we'd known we were picking a fight with a multi-system power before we committed ourselves..."

"We might not have had a choice," Jeremy said. It was comforting to *believe* the corprat system would have collapsed into bloody chaos, with or without the marines, but he knew he couldn't put his faith in it. There'd been hundreds of governments and systems that had tottered for decades before finally expiring. The people who'd predicted their demise had often been wrong. "We couldn't let them reshape the galaxy to suit themselves."

"Yes, sir," Anderson said. "We can no longer remain in the shadows. We have to start forging a new order."

"I know." Jeremy let out a breath. He'd never considered himself a politician, for all that he'd spent most of his career rebuilding societies that had torn themselves apart. "We can't take the risk of letting someone else do it."

His eyes wandered to the starchart. There were a disturbing amount of unknowns in what had once been *very* well explored regions of space. How many *other* corporations had set up their own boltholes? How many warlords would survive long enough to become a significant threat? And how many defenceless colony worlds would be forcibly integrated into the growing empires, broken and crushed before they had a chance to grow into something interesting. Jeremy knew he had the most complete picture of what was going on in the known universe, yet he also knew it was dangerously out of date. A whole new threat could be growing, even now, on the other side of the Core Worlds. And they'd have to be ready to deal with it.

"We need to establish a new form of interstellar government," he said. Military rule was rarely effective in the short term and *never* in the long term. "And we need a figurehead."

Anderson nodded. "Prince Roland?"

"It's possible." Jeremy grimaced. "He's making his way through Boot Camp. It's possible he might be suitable, but…"

He shook his head. It had been common, before Earthfall, to blame the Empire's problems on the Head of State, but the blunt truth had been that the real cause of the problems had been the overconcentration of power in too few hands. The Grand Senators had been the worst, followed rapidly by the interstellar corporations and the massive ever-growing government bureaucracy. There was no way anyone who'd survived Earthfall would go along with putting so much power right back in the hands of a central government, particularly as the former government had done more damage through ineptitude than malice. They'd need to sort out a balancing act, quickly. They couldn't lurk in the shadows any longer.

"I've asked for a report on the prince's progress," he said. "If he's suitable…we'll see if we can use him. If not, we'll have to think of something else."

He took his chair. "Right now, that's a matter for the future," he said. "We have other matters to discuss."

Anderson tensed. "Yes, sir."

"I think you made the right call," Jeremy said. "There will be people, years from now, who will question your decision, but I think you made the right one. The corprats could not be allowed a chance to get back on their feet and come looking for us. And the liberated planets have been quite grateful to us."

"Hameau offered to host a new Slaughterhouse," Anderson said. "I said we'd consider it."

"We might be better off finding an uninhabited world," Jeremy said. "They literally killed *everything* on *the* Slaughterhouse. Whoever did that… they didn't give a shit about civilian casualties."

His eyes hardened. He was used to atrocity, but he'd never seen a whole *world* effectively destroyed before. The attackers had drenched the planet in radioactive particles…he felt sick at the thought. There wouldn't have been any survivors, if the planet hadn't been evacuated before the hammer fell. People in bunkers might have survived, but getting out and off-world would have been tricky. Jeremy was relieved they wouldn't have to try.

Anderson made a face. "We still don't know who did it, then?"

"No." Jeremy had hoped it had been the corprats. It would have given him some closure and allowed them to start work on a new training world. Instead…they were still guessing. He found it hard to imagine anyone, even religious fanatics, being willing to obliterate an entire world. "We don't know."

He stood. "We'll find them," he said. "And then we'll make them regret they ever heard of us."

"Yes, sir," Anderson said.

"We'll hold a formal debrief tomorrow," Jeremy said. "Dismissed."

Anderson stood, saluted and headed for the hatch. Jeremy turned aside to stare out of the window again. The reports really *hadn't* made comforting reading, although they would have been a great deal worse if the marines had actually *lost*. As it was…it had been a close-run thing. Their mistakes had nearly taken them down completely. He let out a breath as he studied the poisonous snowfall. There was no way they could return to the shadows now.

He frowned, his reflection frowning back. The Empire had been *too* large, *too* concentrated. And yet, there'd been no choice. The fractured states before the Unification Wars had been *too* scattered for effective governance. The Empire had brought order, at a price. But it had failed to balance government with freedom, and the bill had finally come due.

The problem was all too clear. Too many worlds would refuse to submit themselves, once again, to a central authority. They'd demand some very stringent safeguards to protect themselves before they'd even consider it. Others would expect handouts, to be assisted by their wealthier neighbours…something that would make the neighbours reluctant to offer their assistance to anyone. And still others had nursed grudges they had no intention of putting down…it still shocked him, even now, just how many people had died in the last few months. The precise number would never be known, but…it was impossible to grasp—to truly grasp—how many people had died. It was nothing more than a statistic.

Every one of those figures represents a living breathing human wiped from existence, he thought, sharply. *And if we don't find a way to put the brakes on, the number will just keep getting higher.*

And yet, as he stared over the poisonous landscape, he knew there might be no way to stop the chaos before it was too late.

We won the battle, he thought. *But can we win the war?*

. . .

THE END

The Empire's Corps **will return in:**
The Prince's Way
COMING SOON

AFTERWORD

Fools that we were! We thought that all this wealth and prosperity were sent us by Providence, and could not stop coming. In our blindness we did not see that we were merely a big workshop, making up the things which came from all parts of the world; and that if other nations stopped sending us raw goods to work up, we could not produce them ourselves. True, we had in those days an advantage in our cheap coal and iron; and had we taken care not to waste the fuel, it might have lasted us longer. And yet, if ever a nation had a plain warning, we had.
—The Battle of Dorking, George Chesney

IT'S GETTING HARDER TO FIND THINGS to write about for these afterwords...

(Of course, some people aren't going to consider it a bad thing.)

I went through several different ideas, when I was thinking about it. The last three years have been crazy, with the world feeling as if the elites are determined to play 'dog in the manger' until their universe finally crashes down around them and the rest of the population quite willing to throw the baby out with the bathwater...a problem that, in places as diverse as Cambodia, China and France, led to utter disaster. Sane people would have taken a breath, calmed down and concentrated on learning from their experiences. We don't seem to be led by sane people. And, really, by the time this book is published a lot of what I want to say will be out of date.

So…I'm going to focus on something else.

Imagine…a pair of battleships steaming through the waves, heading towards the enemy landing sites. Kings of the seas, their crews quietly confident of victory as they approach their targets. And then the sun is blotted out by wave after wave of dive bombers falling towards the ships. The guns rise and open fire, but the bombers keep coming. The ships take hit after hit, until they are ablaze and sinking. There are only a handful of survivors, all stunned by the sheer scale of the disaster. Two battleships have been lost…and so has an empire.

This happened in 1942. The British Government made a series of catastrophic misjudgements as it became increasingly aware there was going to be war with Japan. They sent two battleships, the *Prince of Wales* and *Repulse*, in the hopes their mere presence would deter the Japanese. This was folly, all the more so as the Royal Navy itself had used aircraft to cripple or sink German and Italian battleships. If relatively primitive aircraft could do so much, what could the more modern Japanese aircraft do? And even if one chose to assume the Japanese aircraft would not be much more effective than their British counterparts, the Japanese Navy would be deploying ten battleships to the British two. The Royal Navy might outnumber the Japanese—leaving the issue of quality out for the moment—but the British couldn't concentrate their fleet in eastern waters. There was no way to avoid the simple fact that the British Government made a terrible mistake.

Prince of Wales and *Repulse* were hardly the first battleships lost by the Royal Navy. HMS *Hood* had been sunk only a year ago. But their sinking represented far more than just a major tactical defeat. The British Empire rested its supremacy on the Royal Navy and the Royal Navy was dependent on battleships. Losing two battleships under such circumstances, circumstances that were predictable even without the advantage of hindsight, discredited the underpinnings of the British Empire itself. It wasn't the first time the British had lost a battle—the British Imperialists were fond of saying they lost all battles save for the last—but it was the first insurmountable defeat. And so the British Empire, for better or worse, was consigned to the dustbin of history.

This is not an uncommon pattern, throughout the history of empires. The battlefield defeat of Imperial Germany, in 1917-8, spelt the end of the Second *Reich*. The defeat of China, in the Opium and Arrow Wars, undermined Imperial China beyond repair. The defeat of the Romans at Adrianople undermined the Roman Empire, ensuring the Goths would remain a powerful—and separate—force that would eventually sack Rome and destroy the Roman Empire. It is perhaps unsurprising that so many people who really should have known better tried to deny it, to pretend—with horrific consequences, in Hitler's case—that nothing had really changed. The shock of the defeat was just too much to handle.

Why did these defeats happen?

It is often said that generals always try to fight the *last* war. There is some truth in this. Military planners need to know what can happen and they study previous wars in hopes of predicting future wars. This is often misleading. Much of the Royal Navy's tactics, in the years between Napoleon and the First World War, became impractical as technology advanced. The idea of landing a small army, in the days of motorised infantry, tanks and aircraft, is dangerous, to say the least. The Royal Navy's battle to land troops on the Falklands meant running risks that would have been alien to Nelson and Drake.

It is also true that militaries, particularly victorious militaries, are dangerously conservative. The British Army of 1918 was the most advanced military in the world. It had mastered the art of using tanks and aircraft, burying the Germans under a tidal wave of men and machines they simply couldn't match. (The myth the German soldiers were stabbed in the back was never anything more than a myth.) And yet, many of those lessons were simply forgotten as the First World War receded into the past. The British and French chose to ignore the warning signs, chose to pretend that war hadn't changed. The Germans, who couldn't ignore the truth, took those lessons and ran with them. The German Army of 1939-40 had its weaknesses, many of them. It was also the most capable force on the planet at the time, to the point it beat the British and French in open battle.

And yet, there are risks in being *too* innovative. The Germans wasted a considerable amount of their limited resources in trying to develop wonder weapons (and even naval units they couldn't really use, like battleships and carriers.) The history of military development is littered with boondoggles that absorbed money and returned little. One doesn't need to look further than Arthur C. Clarke's *Superiority* to realise that a technologically-advanced military could be defeated by a primitive, but more numerous force (as happened to Custer at Little Big Horn). The trick, as always, is to remain on the cutting edge without sacrificing the keystones of survival and eventual victory.

...

In 2000, the Bush Administration believed the only major threat to the United States—and the global order it had created—was China, a rising power. The reforms to the American military proposed by Donald Rumsfeld, amongst others, were designed to fight and win a war that was assumed to be something akin to the Falklands War, although on a much larger scale. The war would be limited. The Americans would either safeguard Taiwan and put the Chinese back in their box or lose control over the waters surrounding China, in which case China would dominate Taiwan and the surrounding nations. There was no concept the war would turn general, with engagements being fought all over the world, or nuclear.

This was not an unreasonable assumption, at the time. However, it didn't account for terrorists who could—and did—turn airliners into makeshift cruise missiles. (Not unlike submarines and aircraft, the threat was first discussed in fiction and largely ignored by the militaries.) The United States and its allies found themselves grappling with a new kind of war, facing challenges they were not mentally prepared to handle. They had to deploy forces to Afghanistan and later Iraq, becoming embroiled in complex issues that were either unprecedented or, in the past, had been handled in ways that were now politically unacceptable. Worse, the terrorists and insurgents who survived their first encounters with American and allied firepower learnt from their experiences. They found ways to minimise American advantages, they found ways to circumvent or outsmart American technology and they found ways to create legal and ethical problems for their American opponents. Worst of all, the terrorists were ever-present. When the allied forces pulled out, the terrorists moved back and undid all their good works.

The problem exists on a much bigger scale. China, Russia and Iran—and other enemy states—have a very good motive to find ways to circumvent American advantages and bring the United States to heel. The Chinese investment in antiship missiles, for example, can only be explained as a bid to deter American carriers from approaching the South China Sea or preparation to sink one if she *did*. The Russians have been working on building up their deployable technology, claiming that it can match American technology (and, just incidentally, selling it without strings attached). The assumption the United States—and the West in general—will retain its technological edge for the foreseeable future is nothing more than wishful thinking.

Technology is not the only issue. Saudi Arabia, for example, has spent vast sums of money on buying everything from modern tanks to aircraft. It has one of the largest defence budgets in the world. And yet, the Saudis are quite unable to protect themselves against a peer power. The Saudis have spent so much time coup-proofing their military and setting up rival units that their actual fighting power is quite low. Even basic maintenance is a non-issue. It is true the Saudis did better than their critics expected, during the Gulf War, but the bar was not set very high. Modern militaries require more than giving a man a rifle and pointing him at the front. They need training in how to handle and maintain their weapons, then training that draws directly from real-life experiences. It is all too easy, when there is no sense of urgency, to allow standards to fall by the wayside.

THE HALLS OF MONTEZUMA

The belief that the West will maintain its superiority tends to breed complacency. The planners of Operation Iraqi Freedom overlooked a number of factors that made the invasion and occupation a great deal harder than it could have been. Their mindset refused to allow them to grasp the nettle and admit that they would *have* to make hard decisions and yes, there would be casualties. In a sense, the complacency continues to pervade American and Western military thinking. Our governments are often more interested in looking good than actually making hard decisions and sticking to them, because they believe—deep inside—that total defeat is simply not a possibility. This is, unfortunately, untrue.

There are three basic possibilities that must be acknowledged, considered and prepared for:

First, we may face another paradigm shift in wartime. Instead of a major invasion, we may see insurgencies and uprisings within major cities, particularly in districts dominated by ethnic and religious groups hostile to the government. This would present us with a legal and ethical quandary, as we would start by treating the matter as a police issue rather than calling on the military. The insurgents, in such a scenario, would try to play on this as much as possible, alternatively claiming to be a rival government or demanding the protection of the law depending on the exact situation. This would rapidly lead to hardening attitudes, particularly if the government refused to commit itself to defending the country until it was too late. If this happened, our values as a society would be effectively dead.

Second, we might face an enemy force that outnumbers us so badly the tech advantage is effectively meaningless. China, for example, might throw hundreds of primitive cruise missiles at a carrier battle group and count it a victory; Russia might launch a massive invasion of Europe, accepting the loss of ten Russian tanks for every European tank and coming out ahead. If this happened, the world order would be completely reshaped.

Third, we might face a different paradigm shift. The Russians or the Chinese might manage to gain effective control of space, allowing them to bombard the United States from orbit until the United States surrendered.

This would not require (much) additional technological development, merely the will to invest money and resources and the determination to overlook early failures. If this happened, the world order would be shattered beyond repair.

...

In these books, the Terran Marine Corps met—for the first time in centuries—an opponent that matched them in technology and came close to them, although not completely, in training. The marines had problems handling the challenge because they assumed, even though they should have known better, that they were the best. They were too used to enemies who were unable or unwilling to match them in a straight fight.

In the real world, the results might not be so kind. The world is not a safe place. The current global order has its problems, some of which are easy to see, but it is far better than the alternative. There is no reason to believe—and quite a few reasons to *disbelieve*—that a world dominated by Russia, China, Iran or Islamic State's successors would be any better. We must ready ourselves for battle, for being ready to fight is the only way to prevent a war.

And now you've read the book, I have a favour to ask.

It's getting harder to earn a living through indie writing these days, for a number of reasons (my health is one of them, unfortunately). If you liked this book, please post a review wherever you bought it; the more reviews a book gets, the more promotion.

Christopher G. Nuttall
Edinburgh, 2020

If You Liked This, You Might Like...*Hell's Horizon*
BY RICHARD FOX AND JONATHAN BRAZEE

A war with no end. A vendetta that will destroy two commanders.

The war between the Alliance and the Hegemony has spanned countless stars, and shed untold blood on a hundred worlds. For two commanders, Alliance Captain Alcazar and Major Richter of the Hegemony, the war has spiraled into a personal feud.

Both lead fierce Marines and mechanized soldiers into battle against the other on the green hell planet, Ayutthaya, and each new fallen warrior only deepens the bitterness and hatred between the two.

But as the conflict rages, the two warriors discover they have more in common than they dare to admit, and their own codes of honor may be what can bring the bloodshed to an end...if they don't kill each other first.

Military veterans and authors Fox and Brazee bring their war-time experiences and years as officers in the United States military to the page in this grueling, head-to-head action driven story.

PROLOGUE

This war's getting to me. Shouldn't, right? I fought on Hansen's World and managed to get out of that one. Lost a bit of myself there, but I made it. Plenty of boys went home feet first. Why didn't I join them? Just enough luck to make it to the next battlefield. My luck's still holding out.

Fighting on Ayutthaya's nothing like the tundra of Keppler-22 from my last deployment. The jungle…we don't have this back home. We'll patrol into the deep canopy, and it'll get dark as night. Yeah, we have optics, but they're made by the lowest bidder and maybe they work, maybe they don't. We'll be in that dark, the smell of rot and mud all around us. Every step and sound we make gives us away to the enemy.

Then there's the big cats. Imagine a tiger and a bear had a bad-tempered cub. Locals call them chayseux, and hunting them used to be big business on the planet before the war. They'll hide up in the branches, drop down, and take a man in full gear. At least, that's what we tell the new recruits. That way they keep an eye to the sky for traps that've been left behind. Couple years of the front line's changing and the smart mines don't act so smart. The attack drones' targeting gets real wonky.

At least there's no orbital bombardment. The navies are up there above this godforsaken planet, but so far, it's just us ground pounders.

But the enemy's bad enough, and he's out there. Always. Most fights are blind shots at wherever we think they are. Sometimes we'll rip the jungle up and find not a damn trace of them. Sometimes we'll find them lying there, waiting for us as they bleed.

I've seen the dead before. I worked the mass graves after the Battle of Bellis when some officer deep in a bunker decided to send a battalion's worth of green recruits against an armor advance. You'd think he wanted those boys to throw themselves into the tracks to slow them down.

But those few times we see proof that we're fighting someone real, that the brass don't have us chasing ghosts in the jungle…it's almost worse than when we have to bag up our own.

When a man dies of violence, he don't lay right. Arms and legs at bad angles. Uncomfortable just to look at. It's how the wrist bends that gets me. Like they were reaching to touch God's face at the end, but they lost strength a moment too soon. No one would choose to die like that, but they wouldn't have chosen to go anyway.

We'll find them. Half in, half out of a bush. Maybe on a path with a mess of first aid stuff around them. Guess everyone quit when the kid gave up the ghost or they heard us coming and thought we'd finish them all off in one go.

We don't do that. And don't you believe what the vids tell you either. The war here's bad, but we still got our dignity. Other side will kill us just as quick as we'll kill them, but they don't fight like godless barbarians. Don't let their looks fool you.

After so long in the shit, you'd think my boys and I would start to slip. Nah. We'll go home with our heads high.

When we find them…they look just like us. Same nothing in their eyes as our dead. The dead kid at my feet's no different than the new guy just assigned to my squad. Just dressed different. The officers keep telling us they're the enemy, and I guess they are, but when they're dead, I don't see much difference. Just another body whose mother or wife is going to cry over.

That's what it comes down to out here. Kill the other. But every time I find them bled out, or I hear their wounded crying out there in the jungle… there's no other. It's me that's dying. Only person I kill in this war is myself.

Like I said. This war's getting to me. Got to prep for the next patrol. Be—

—*Partial document recovered during routine intercept. Belligerent party unknown.*

Supreme Union Humanitarian Mission. Ayutthaya Civil War. Day 1,733

CHAPTER 1

MARINES

"Don't get bunched up, Trace. I want to see dispersion."

Captain Mateo Alcazar, Alliance of Democratic Peoples' Marines and Kilo Company commander, ran down the beaten path as he followed the movements of Third Platoon on his CCD, his Command Combat Display. He knew he should hold back, but he was an enlisted grunt before his battlefield commission, and that hands-on approach to combat was too deeply ingrained into his very DNA to lead from the rear. He'd probably get his ass chewed by the battalion CO, but so be it. He wasn't going to stand back and let Third get bunched up where a single Hegemony mortar round could wreak havoc upon them.

He watched as First Lieutenant Trace Okanjo took charge and spread his platoon out. The lieutenant was an Academy grad and a rising star, destined to go far in the Corps, but that didn't mean he didn't need supervision.

At least, that was what Teo told himself as an excuse to get closer to the fight.

Up ahead, he could hear the sounds of combat as First Platoon opened up their base of fire on tiny, abandoned Rawai, hoping to fix the Hegemony infantry in place. Up until a day ago, the destroyed village no longer had any tactical or strategic value, but with the crabs nosing around, Teo couldn't let them get a foothold so close to his company's lines. He had to slap them hard to remind them that even with the peace talks on Phoenix, the war wasn't over yet.

"*Skipper, where're you heading?*" First Sergeant Oak Lippmaa asked over the Person-to-Person.

Teo winced. The first sergeant was his minder—part nanny, part teacher—tasked by the battalion commanding officer and sergeant major to keep the junior officer acting as a commander, not as a sergeant. Teo out-ranked his first sergeant, but he understood the dynamics involved.

"*Just had to get better positioning,*" he said as he ran forward.

"*And Rios? Why isn't he with you?*"

Because I didn't want him in the line of fire. Or to keep me out of the action.

Big, goofy Rios, married just before the deployment and someone with whom Teo had formed a deep connection in the short time he'd been company commander. Just because Teo was being stupid didn't mean he wanted to put Rios needlessly at risk.

"*He's securing my six,*" Teo said of the sergeant assigned as the one-man security force to keep him safe.

The first sergeant didn't respond, but Teo could picture him reporting up to the CO. He'd been angry when he first realized the first sergeant's real job, but that had long faded. The first sergeant was a good man, and he was just following orders. To Teo he was simply part of the landscape now.

He turned his attention back to his CCD and the battle forming just 200 meters ahead of him. This should be a cakewalk—"should" being the operative word. Marine drones, in a moment of clarity, had spotted a four-man crab team setting up in what was left of the Sawadi Friend Hotel. The drones were lost soon thereafter, but Teo had already sprung into action, using one of his hip-pocket contingency plans in sending First and Third forward, leaving Second and Weapons back at camp. Only this time, there was a difference. The CO had been pushing him to engage the tank section that had just been assigned to Kilo Company. The three MT-49 Badger tanks were waiting just down Provincial Route 3 a klick out, ready to move in as soon as First secured the village.

Staff Sergeant Horatio, the tank section leader, had protested that wasn't the best use of his tanks, and maybe he was right, but Teo didn't think Krabi, with its heavy jungle vegetation and limited roads, was good armor country. He'd decided to keep a tight lid on the armor boys, using them just enough to get the CO off his back.

The lead squad of Third Platoon was approaching their Final Coordination Line, the FCL. It was almost go-time. Out of habit from too many battles, he went through his almost superstitious routine for the third time today. First, he checked the charge on his VP-51, then visually sighted down the barrel and the mag rings. A bent mag ring could render the dart-thrower ineffective. Next, he seated his VW-9 Jonas in its holster. Not many of his Marines carried the crossbow handgun, only those who'd served on anti-pirate patrol. Then, he patted the ornate Eagle Warrior handle of his tecpatl, the modern version of the Aztec knife that his ancient ancestors used to cut the hearts out of their enemies. Next, a quick glance at his Command Combat Display gave him all greens for both his Individual Fighting Uniform and internal nanos. Finally, he punched himself hard in the chest, feeling his IFU's Protective Outer Layer stiffen up, the shear-thickening armor in action.

The five steps weren't just superstition. He was checking his equipment—but he realized there was that superstitious element to it. No matter. Everything was green. He was ready for bear.

Teo pulled up Sergeant Gauta's Individual Combat Display feed and switched to meshed view. It took a moment for Teo's AI to coordinate the sergeant's feed with that of the Marines around him, but after a brief flicker, Teo was looking ahead as if he were there. He could turn his head, and the viewpoint would shift, the view synched by his AI. As long as someone in the squad had visuals, Teo could see what he wanted.

Teo adjusted the feed to 75% opacity, leaving 25% for the real world in front of him. Alone, without Sergeant Rios watching his back, that was bordering on dangerous, but Teo had lots of experience with overlaid displays. He slowed to a walk, putting his personal tactical view on mental autopilot as he focused on what was facing his Marines.

Maybe not enough experience. He grimaced as his shin slammed into a chunk of cerrocrete—his POL's armor needed a stronger, quicker impact to thicken. For a moment, he contemplated adjusting the feed to 66% opacity, but he left it there. He could take bruised shins.

The shell of what had once been a restaurant, pock-marked by battles past, stood just to his left, the jungle already taking it over. This was the visual reference for the FCL and for First Platoon to shift its base of fire. Third Squad, led by Sergeant Gauta, would clear the mostly destroyed buildings on the west side of the main drag while First Squad, led by Sergeant Adoud, would clear the east side. Then both squads would provide security around the objective for Sergeant Win's Second Squad to clear the hotel itself.

Speed was of the essence. Teo had considered an envelopment, but with only four crabs, they probably had orders to withdraw in the face of a Marine reaction, and he didn't want to give them time to escape. Using one squad from First Platoon as a blocking force on the other side of the village was his security blanket to ensure they killed or captured the crabs. Most likely killed. The crabs weren't in the habit of surrendering, much like his own Marines.

The lead team reached the restaurant and crossed the FCL, and Teo had to bite his tongue as First Platoon kept up the base. He was just about to break in when Trace ordered the shift fire.

Almost immediately, the two lead squads rushed forward. It made Teo's heart sing as he watched the choreographed ballet that was MOUT, Military Operations in an Urban Terrain. To call Rawai "urban" might be a stretch, but the techniques were the same had this been an archology holding tens of millions on Lancaster or Nouveau Niue.

The Alliance Marines might lack all the newest military equipment, but no one could deny their training and discipline. This could have been a training demonstration back at The Infantry Warrior School at Camp Woramo, not actual combat, and Teo was filled with pride as two teams from the squad rushed into the first husk of a building, clearing it in seconds before crossing the alley to the rubble of the next.

With the squad breaking into teams, Teo's feed became somewhat more disjointed. He hungered for the thrill of the fight, but duty took over. He couldn't indulge himself. He backed out of the meshed feed, then relegated it to the upper left corner of his CCD. Real life snapped in front of him. He'd been advancing on autopilot and hadn't realized he'd moved as far as he had. Right in front of him was Lieutenant Okanjo and Second Squad. Sergeant Win, the squad leader, swiveled and nodded at Teo before turning back to the front.

Teo held up. He needed to let Okanjo fight this battle.

That didn't mean he wasn't going to listen in, however. His Combat AI was monitoring all comms, ready to alert him based on any of a thousand messages being sent.

That also didn't mean he was going to hang back and out of the fight. If he wanted to do that, he'd have stuck with Rios. So, as Okanjo led his platoon across the FCL, Teo followed in trace.

Teo almost chuckled as he realized what he was doing: following *Trace* in *trace*.

Come on, Mateo! No time for stupid jokes.

Razor Fuentes reported taking fire from the crabs at the objective, which was the plan. Hopefully, that would give Lieutenant Okanjo and his platoon time to get close before the crabs knew he was there.

Probably not. The crabs weren't stupid. But hopefully, there wouldn't be much they could do.

Most of the buildings were shells or rubble, so as Teo watched though the feed, Third Platoon was quickly able to clear them, reaching the objective within six minutes. First and Third Squads surrounded the old hotel's main building while Second moved in for the assault.

Teo stopped short of the objective despite an almost overwhelming desire to be in on the assault. With his back against a chunk of rubble, he switched back to meshed view on his CCD as Second Squad was given the order to kick off the final assault. He couldn't help it. He needed the rush of combat. His display flickered, and he was *inside* the hotel lobby. A blood trail led across the floor to the far wall where a crab sat, his head lolled slackly onto his chest. His weapon at the ready, one of the Marines kicked the crab hard in the chest, knocking him over, but this crab was gone.

Teo's heart pounded as if he were a sergeant again, back in combat instead of merely hitching a ride. He didn't even realize when he drew his tecpatl, so deeply was he immersed in the fight.

Sergeant Win led his Marines across the lobby and to the stairwell. A string of fire reached down, peppering the stairs and sending splinters flying. PFC Ramirez yelped and jumped back out of the line of fire, holding his chest. His avatar didn't pop up light blue on Teo's CCD, so, if he'd been hit, his armor had held.

"Use a Gryphon, Win!" Staff Sergeant Weiss yelled from somewhere behind the squad.

The Gryphon was a small, fire-and-forget anti-armor missile. Made on the independent planet Waterson, they weren't part of the Marine standard issue, but they were available through a parallel supply chain if the Marines paid for the missiles themselves.

Teo started to protest, then held his tongue. He didn't want to waste a Gryphon on clearing a hotel, but then again, he wasn't the one taking fire.

Sergeant Win motioned to Lance Corporal White Horse, who pulled the small tube out of his assault pack and extended it, arming the impeller.

"Impact plus two," Win told White Horse.

Teo nodded. The impact on the ceiling above would start the fuze, and the missile's warhead would detonate two meters after that. The Gryphon wasn't designed as an anti-personnel weapon, but it could sure mess up someone's day.

Sergeant Win pointed to a spot on the ceiling, some ten meters above the deck. White Horse nodded and got ready while the rest of the squad moved closer to the stairwell. The Gryphon was powered by ram-impellers, so there wasn't a backblast to worry about, but there would probably be debris raining down.

"On three," Sergeant Win said. "One...two...three!"

With a whuff, the little missile shot out of the tube, its fins snapping into place, followed a micro-instant later by a boom as it detonated.

The Marines were already moving, bounding up the wide stairs, peppering the area with fire. Teo's mind was with them, leading the charge, just like in the old days before he was yanked out and commissioned. His body, sitting in the rubble 60 meters away from the hotel, subconsciously swung his 51 around with one hand as if he had a target, his other gripping the handle of his tecpatl.

The lead Marines charged over the top of the stairs. One stumbled and fell, cut down by a crab flanker ten meters away in what looked to have once been a ballroom or conference room, now filled with smoke. The crab was on his knees, looking stunned, but not stunned enough to keep him from fighting.

"*Get him!*" Teo instinctively shouted over the platoon battle net.

His Marines didn't need him for that. Four Marines converged their fire on the crab. A dart hit his hand, making him drop his weapon, and he tried to get up, screaming in defiance before he fell under the Marine's combined onslaught.

Teo shifted his view. The smoke was clearing. Chairs were flung around, and a curtain was flickering with fire as the breeze from outside fed the flame. Another crab body lay still on the deck, one hand pointed up to nothing as if beseeching Valhalla.

A grey avatar blinked on Teo's CCD. He didn't want to look, as if he didn't acknowledge it, it wouldn't be true. But he couldn't ignore facts. Lance Corporal Carl Mooney was dead. He'd just gotten married before the deployment, and Teo had attended the wedding. One more Marine killed under Teo's command, one of the ghosts he'd have to answer to for the rest of his life.

"*All clear,*" Sergeant Win passed. "*Three crabs down. One friendly KIA.*"

"*Roger that,*" Lieutenant Okanjo passed. "*Hold fast, Second. Third, go in and clear the rest of the hotel.*"

Not quite what Teo would have ordered, but it was Okanjo's platoon. Now all that was left was to clear the rest of the village. He wasn't going to attempt to hold it, but maybe this would be a message to the crab commander that he shouldn't try and make inroads like this again.

Sergeant Win walked over to the smoldering curtain and yanked it off the rod. He stomped out the flames, then took a moment to look out what must have once been a huge picture window.

Teo lowered his 51, just now sheepishly aware that he'd been ready to blast away at the bad guys. He was about to switch back to general command mode when Sergeant Win's head and upper chest exploded into a pink mist. Before the rest of the sergeant's body had time to fall, the sound of heavy fire reverberated down the main street.

"*Horatio! Bring your Badgers forward now,*" he ordered even before he'd consciously realized what was happening.

Teo recognized the reports. He switched off of mesh mode and stood, poking his head out from around the chunk of cerrocrete behind which he'd taken cover. From beyond the edge of the village, crabs in their jacks were moving forward and had engaged the blocking force.

"*Staff Sergeant Horatio, respond,*" he ordered again before the flashing yellow triangle on the edge of his CCD caught his attention. Comms were down, jammed. His AI would be frequency hopping to try and break through, but when and if it would be successful was anyone's guess. He had the Quantum Communicators, so he could communicate with the XO, the battalion S-3, and the four platoon commanders, but he didn't have a repeater for the tank section commander. All he could do was hope his initial message got through, or if not, that Staff Sergeant Horatio would realize that the situation had just gone to shit.

Teo ducked his head and ran forward, taking cover behind the burnt-out husk of a car, poking his head up to try and spot the crabs. Bits of a wall

150 meters up the road exploded as it was hit by one of the crabs' cyclers, their 8mm heavy machine gun. The unique *tot-tot-tot* of the nasty weapon was something once heard, never forgotten.

"*Razor, what do you have there?*" Teo asked First Lieutenant Razor Fuentes, his First Platoon commander, over the QC company net.

Costing more than any other piece of company equipment, the quantum-matched sets were essentially jam-proof…when they worked. They were notoriously finicky.

"*I've lost comms with Sergeant Roy, but we're moving to support him now,*" the lieutenant passed. "*Are we getting the Badgers?*"

Teo turned around to look down the road. Nothing. He swore under his breath. As a grunt, he didn't completely trust armor, but he wanted them now. One shot from a Badger's 90mm smoothbore, much less the 70mm anti-armor round, and the crabs' vaunted jacks were just so much mangled metal.

He was just about to order Trace to send a runner back when the first Badger coalesced from out of the light rain as it bolted into the village, followed by the next two.

"We've got the Badgers," Teo passed. "*Keep your heads up.*"

The fighting from up ahead intensified as Teo crouched behind the wreck. He waited until the first tank almost reached him before he jumped up, waving at it to stop…and then had to dive out of the way before the beast ran him over. He ate a faceful of muddy water and came up sputtering.

"Stop!"

But the Badger kept going, firing its first round.

"Son-of-a-bitch!"

The Badger was an adequate chunk of armor, but it was hardly invincible. Made in Waterson as the MT-23, it was a medium tank, light and maneuverable, with the ADP Marines' model being amphibious for up to twenty minutes. The cost of being light was that it could be knocked out, and with their muscles augmented by their jacks, the crabs could carry heavy-enough weapons to do the job.

The second two tanks rushed past, surprisingly quiet with their fuel-cell powerplants, but still making the ground tremble.

Teo stared at them for a moment, then passed, "*Razor, the Badgers are going cowboy. Get Sergeant Roy and his squad out of the Badgers' line of fire.*"

"Roger that."

Up ahead, barely visible in the rain, a crab appeared as he awkwardly ran between two ruined buildings. Almost immediately, the lead tank opened fire, and Teo almost shouted out in excitement. The round hit with a flash, but when the debris settled, Teo couldn't see if the crab had been taken out or not.

Flashes sparkled off of the second tank—it was taking fire. Teo half-expected to see that followed with something more powerful, but the three tanks split up in a smooth move, getting off the road.

"At least they're well-trained," he mumbled to himself.

His CCD flashed for a moment as a free frequency was found, and the frozen forces display jumped ahead before freezing again. Two Marines from Sergeant Roy's squad were the light blue of WIA, but their vitals weren't in the critical range.

Roy had started a bounding overwatch to rejoin the rest of First Platoon, engaging at least a squad of crabs to the north of them.

At least. Maybe more.

Without working drones, Teo didn't have a full picture of what faced him. All he could see was a compilation of what any of his Marines could detect. Unis to doughnuts, if he had eleven of them on his CCD, then there were more out there.

How many more? Do I engage or withdraw?

As a private, and up through sergeant, Teo didn't have to make decisions like this. His job had been to close with and kill the enemy. Period.

He needed to know what he faced, and he couldn't get that sitting on his ass. It was time to move forward. But he hesitated. His VP-51 was in dart mode—which was fine for the crab flankers, but not the best weapon for a jacked crab. There weren't many places where one of the 2mm hypervelocity darts could penetrate. He had the grenade module in his assault pack, which packed a bigger punch, but it had a minimum arming distance, and in among the buildings, he probably would be too close.

No, darts it is.

Teo looked down the road then sprinted across and inside a half-standing shop of some sort—whatever had been in it had either been long destroyed or long looted.

His CCD flashed again as the system momentarily defeated the jamming.

Shit!

From his display, he could see that crabs had bypassed Sergeant Roy and his squad and were now intermixed within his Marines, two of whom were down hard. Lieutenant Fuentes was consolidating the rest of his platoon. The three tanks were separated on the ground, and Teo didn't have a clue if they were coordinated with each other or they were fighting independently.

Okanjo and Third were moving forward, but another twenty-three crabs had now appeared on his CCD.

This wasn't a mere squad.

Teo had to act. His ancient Aztec ancestors didn't have modern comms, yet they conquered Mesoamerica. He didn't need comms to fight, either. It took him a second to create an image of the battle area in his mind, and he knew what he wanted to do.

"Trace, set up a hasty defense across PL Juniper. Deploy the Switchblades across your frontage, but leave First a way back in. Hold that line. Razor, I'm going to get you some covering fire. Use it to get Roy, then move back and consolidate on Third's left flank. Make the crabs come to you, then take them down.

"Harris, fire mission. I want three anti-armor rounds each on…targets Robin, Osprey, and Vulture," he passed to his Weapons Platoon commander, who he knew had been anxiously waiting for a mission. Rawai no longer had any civilians, so it was weapons free, no need to go up the chain for permission to use their supporting arms.

"Roger that. Three rounds each on Robin, Osprey, and Vulture. Time of impact…forty-three seconds."

Teo hoped the nine rockets would be enough to slow down the crabs. The seeker heads on the anti-armor rockets gave them limited smart capability, and a direct hit would take down a jacked trooper. Even near misses, however, should catch their attention, and the rounds would convince the enemy to back off First Platoon's flank, giving them room to maneuver or find better cover.

The rockets swooped in, hitting in rapid succession, and lighting up the village and surrounding jungle. Teo wished he could tie into Roy and his squad, but for the moment, he had to trust his Marines' training.

Hoping to be able to spot the tanks, he moved forward another twenty meters before he realized that with his orders to the two rifle platoons, he was now isolated on the wrong side of the main road. As if listening to his thoughts, one of the Badgers crossed the road fifty meters ahead and disappeared into the buildings. He considered crossing back, but with the tank up ahead, he thought he was secure, at least for the moment. And he was going to take advantage of that.

He bounded forward, dashing from one bit of cover to another, straining to make out what was happening. The intense, continual firing had died out, changing to sporadic bursts of fire from both sides. His CCD flickered again, giving him a new snapshot. First Platoon had retrieved their blocking force and was falling back to link with Third. Two more Marines were WIA. The defense was coming together...except for the damned tanks. Two were pushing forward and were well beyond PL Juniper and were approaching PL Pine, which had been their limit of advance. With them back in the fold, Teo was confident that he could withstand anything the crab commander would be willing to throw at them.

The tank on his side of the road, *Blue Ice* stenciled on the bore extractor, a metal hump halfway down the barrel, kept firing. Sergeant Bean, as the tank commander, was hanging back, sending measured round after measured round downrange. If Teo could reach him, maybe Bean could get a hold of Staff Sergeant Horatio.

Teo knew he was exposed, and as the commander, he needed to be with the Marines he was commanding. He had to rejoin them instead of cowboying it like a fool. The CO would be able to track what he did, and the man would be livid. But the *Blue Ice* was just ahead of him, and the colonel was going to go off on him no matter what now. He might as well make the ass-chewing worth it.

He crouched and ran along the back alley. At one time, it might have given him cover, but with most of the buildings destroyed, he felt like the turkey in a turkey shoot. With enough time, he'd low-crawl, making full use of every bit of cover. But, as was often the case, he had no time.

He turned in when he reached the tank…but it wasn't there. His CCD disposition of troops display was still frozen, not showing the here and now.

Teo hesitated. He couldn't afford to go wandering around in bad-guy territory, looking for a Badger. He needed to get back to his Marines and lead the defense.

But the Badgers would sure help. If I could only get eyes on…

He had to go forward and see if Sergeant Bean could contact Horatio. That hadn't changed.

He pulled up the map of the village, trying to envision where a tanker might move his Badger. There weren't many choices, but right at the village's main intersection might be a good choice. He could move forward another 70 meters or so. If Bean was gone, then he'd abandon the effort and rejoin the rest of the company.

Teo kept low, running around the back of the building, jumping what was a surprisingly intact pig pen, the former resident now a bloated mass of putrefying flesh rising out of the mud. Luckily, his IFU, his Individual Fighting Unit, filtered the air, and he didn't experience the stench that thing must be putting out.

Back against the next wall, he gave the carcass one more look before he started around the next corner…and jerked back. A crab was slowly edging toward the main street, using what was left of what the sign said was the best Indian food in Krabi for cover. Even jacked, Teo had read the body language of a soldier moving forward to engage.

He had to act.

Teo didn't trust his 51 against the crab. Killing a jacked crab with the darts was more chance than skill, and at maybe ten meters away, he was too close to switch to grenade mode. For a moment he considered his blade. Within the Marines, there were kills, and then there were *kills*. Long-range kills didn't count as much within Marine culture as those with personal weapons, and those didn't count as much as killing hand-to-hand. Teo had sent many an enemy to his grave, but never with his tecpatl, and the temptation was strong.

He fingered the ornate handle for a brief moment. It might be patterned after the ceremonial knife made of flint, the blade itself was high-tech, made by Okinawan bladesmiths back on Earth itself. He didn't doubt that it could pierce the crab's Cataphract armor.

Stop chasing glory, Mateo! Just kill the son-of-a-bitch.

He knew he had to use his Jonas anti-pirate gun. Normally carried by spaceborne Marines, it was essentially a crossbow without the cross, firing two different bolts: one with an expanding head that would keep it from puncturing the skin of a spacecraft, and another that would pierce through almost anything, to include body armor. The range was short in an atmosphere, but at ten meters, it was deadly.

He gave the indicator a quick check—using the expanding head would only piss the crab off—but he had the armor-piercing bolt in the slot.

His CCD flickered again, and his battleview updated before freezing in place once more.

Hell!

The crab was now on his display, but so was another just around the corner of the restaurant. That made things a little more dicey. He had to take out the crab without alerting the next one. The Jonas was silent, but dying soldiers rarely went quietly into the night. He had to get a quick kill.

He never considered withdrawing. His mental targeting was locked on, and the only acceptable outcome was a dead crab.

The sound of a shod foot knocking rubble away was the trigger. He had to move now before the two crabs hooked up and engaged his Marines with enfilade fire. With one smooth movement, Teo swung around the corner, bringing his anti-pirate gun to bear. His target was the back of the crab's helmet, and at this range, it was impossible to miss. With a click, the bolt flew forward, hitting the back of the helmet, almost tearing it off, and sending the crab to his knees. Teo was already rushing forward as his Jonas cycled the next bolt and the retention spring returned to the ready position, something that took a long second-and-a-half.

The bolt had destroyed the crab's helmet, and blood splattered from his head, but he wasn't dead. The helmet must have been able to deflect the bolt, a miraculous escape from the crab's point of view.

But a short-lived miracle.

The crab started to raise one hand to his head when Teo kicked him in the ass and knocked him down, brought the muzzle of his Jonas up to the back of the crab's head, and fired. The bolt passed through his skull as the crab collapsed.

Teo didn't stop to admire his kill. There was still the other crab indicated on his frozen display. Back against the restaurant wall, he edged forward until he reached the corner, then spun around, Jonas at the ready... but there was no one there, and now he was exposed. Teo jumped back.

His CCD might have picked up a ghost, but more likely, there was another crab nearby, and he was pretty vulnerable on his own. Across the main road and just behind was the rest of the company, where he should be.

But he still needed the tanks. That hadn't changed. And that last update showed that Sergeant Bean was just two alleys over.

He might still be there, he might not, but Teo had to find out. If he could only get a better picture of what was happening around him. Looking at his display, he had an idea...if it was still standing. With one last look at the dead soldier, his kill, he sidled to the back of the restaurant, then peeked around the corner.

Just ahead, visible over the next ruined shop, the sat tower still stood, canted, but surprisingly upright. If he could climb that, he might be able to get a better picture of the Area of Operations, where the crabs were, and what they were doing. And what his wayward tanks were doing.

That excuse wasn't going to hold up with the CO, but Teo let it be enough for him. The tower was wide enough to protect a single person from fire from the front, and it would only take a few moments of time.

He holstered his Jonas, brought up his 51, and poked his head around the edge of the building before darting across the small alley to the next one. He hit it with his back and froze for a second, waiting to see if he'd been spotted. The sounds of battle filled the village, but nothing seemed directed at him. He gave a quick glance around the next corner. It was clear. Teo took a moment to check his 51, wondering if he should switch to grenade mode, but nothing had changed about minimum arming range, and he was more likely to run into a flanker than a jacked crab.

Time to go, Mateo!

He bolted around the corner…and a crab was right in front of him, 15 meters away. Teo fired on instinct, darts blasting around the crab as the enemy jumped forward and out of the line of fire. Teo jerked back out of sight, behind the building.

Shit!

If the crab had been looking in his direction, he'd have been a dead man.
What now?

Teo could hear the creak of road wheels. The *Blue Ice* was near, but so was the crab. He could withdraw and rejoin the rest of the company, and that was the text-book answer. But Marine infantry were embedded with the need to protect armor.

He knew what he was going to do and a smile spread across his face. He drew his knife and moved into the attack.

CHAPTER 2

PALADINS

Major Richter of the Hegemony Army flinched as a bullet burst through the wall right next to his head. Cerrocrete fragments spattered his face shield, and dust caked against the rain-wet lenses. He ducked and spun into the wall as the Alliance Marine kept firing, punching more holes in the wall, each another stab at Richter.

He ran in a crouch toward a metal door on the alley side of a small building, his optics sputtering as they vibrated to dislodge the dust coating. A round cracked past his head as he lowered the armored pauldron on one shoulder and bashed through the door, losing his footing. He fell forward, twisting to land on his armor and spare the cycler rifle held by the augmented frame in his other hand.

A puddle exploded as he landed and slid forward. He rolled to his back and fired a burst through the broken doorway. The jack frames down his back around the outside of his legs stiffened up, programmed to brace his body every time he used the heavy-caliber weapon—vital for accurate fire when he was on his feet. On his back, he felt like a turtle with broken legs.

"Briem? Kontos? Report, damn you," Richter sent over the infrared broadcasting system built into his helmet. He rolled hard to his left and used the frame down his gun arm to push off against the floor to shift the forward weight of his armor up and over. The ballistic plates bolted to his frame gave him the look of a medieval knight, but the protection cost him maneuverability.

The company net holo on the inside of his optics blinked several times; the IR had no connection through the rain and humidity.

Richter grabbed a moldy reception desk and shoved it at the doorway. Putting a boot to the edge, he used his frame to augment his strength and kicked it into the opening, where it buckled. Not much of an obstacle, but it would slow down any Marine trying to charge in after him.

His IR crackled and he tapped the receiver built into the side of his helmet, just as a squeal rose in the air, the squeak of treads over wet asphalt roads. He looked through a broken window and saw an Alliance Badger come around a corner, the double-barreled turret scanning from side to side.

"Ah … shit." Richter gripped the ammo belt connected to his cycler, a band around his wrist pulsed, and the breach released the feed. Slotting the lead round into a port on his forearm, he reached back to a drum on his left hip and slapped a magazine loaded with armor-piercing rounds into the weapon. A tremor went up his arm as a round locked into the breach.

The Badger's turret froze then traversed to point straight at him.

Richter dove forward as a main gun shell blew through the building. The blast wave slapped him into the wall as it collapsed, and he exploded through in a shower of mortar and dust. He landed hard, the armor plating knocking the air out of his lungs before his frame could compensate for the landing.

He kept rolling with the momentum and thrust out a foot to dig into a wet, overgrown yard, stopping him. The Badger was a dozen yards ahead of him, the turret still trained on the building from which he'd been ejected. Richter laid his aiming reticle on the vision blocks on the driver's hatch and opened fire.

The antitank rounds were self-contained sabot shell, designed to impart a tungsten bolt with tremendous velocity. Even with his jack's frame to compensate, each shot kicked like a mule.

His rounds sparked off the Badger's hull, but two struck the vision blocks, sending spider-web cracks through the thick ballistics glass. He shifted his fire up and blew a small sensor dome mounted on top of the turret into fragments. He didn't have the firepower to destroy the tank, but at least he could make the crew's job harder.

If he had a Spike antitank grenade, this fight would already be over, but the expensive, rare hand-thrown weapons with their explosively formed tungsten lances were all with his flanker troops, none of whom were near enough to help him.

The tank's barrels slewed toward him and Richter lurched to one side, lowering his aim. Firing from the hip, he ran for a low, blown-out wall. He emptied the rest of the magazine into the forward tread, breaking the links between the flat sections. The tread dropped off the road wheel like a drawbridge.

A bullet struck the back of his pauldron and knocked him off-balance. Instead of bounding over the low wall like he planned, his shin struck hard, and he went head over heels forward. He got a brief glimpse of the deep shell hole on the other side before he went tumbling down the side. Mud smeared across his visor and filled his mouth as he splashed into water and sank.

Richter felt panic at the back of his mind as he thrashed around. The Hegemony's Cataphract armor was an advanced, lethal battlefield weapon system, but a jacked trooper could not swim. Grasping a rock with one hand, he pulled his head and shoulders out of the water.

A bloated corpse of a dead pig floated right in front of him, pus and maggots seeping through torn skin. Richter had to swallow the water in the back of his mouth, and he got to his feet, the dark, fetid pool coming up just over his knees. Shaking his cycler hard to dislodge mud and water, he felt a sticky warmth drain down the body glove within his jack.

The empty magazine fell out of his rifle with a chop from his hand, and he reloaded the weapon with the antipersonnel ammo belt feeding into another magazine on his back.

"Any Paladin element, this is Richter." He looked up the slope of the crater to the gray sky as the *chunk-chunk-chunk* sound of the enemy tank rolling off its broken tread sounded through the pouring rain. "Requesting backup."

The sound of the tank grew louder, and its forward edge poked over the lip, the soil buckling slightly beneath the weight, sending twin falls of mud and water down into the pool. Richter looked around the shell hole. The walls were steep and slick—no way he could get out quick or easy.

The dead pig bumped against his leg.

"Paladins, fall back to rally point alpha," he said as he cranked his IR up to maximum power, having no faith the signal could reach anyone. He switched to radio, knowing that any broadcast would be traced within seconds.

The Badger sank a bit deeper into the mud, almost aiming the turret level with him. He had to give credit to the crew's tenacity.

Richter repeated his message through radio frequencies and brought his cycler up to his shoulder, firing single shots at the auxiliary sensor nodes. Between rounds, he heard the tank load a shell into the breach.

This is how it ends, he thought. *What a grave.*

A rocket slammed into the back of the tank, and it tipped forward, smoke billowing out of the back as it slid down the crater straight toward Richter. He sloughed through the water as the twin turrets struck the bottom and bent like plastic straws. The ammo compartments on the back of the tank began cooking off, sending brief showers of sparks and dull thuds as warheads exploded.

Richter used the side of the tank to haul himself up and out of the crater as explosions grew faster. The top hatch clanged against the hull as the crew tried to escape, and Richter reached up and grabbed a hunk of concrete still firm in the foundation of nearby building. He pulled his chest up and over the edge as screaming began behind him.

The tank crew was burning alive.

The major swung his legs up and out as the last of the shells went off. Fire and metal fragments shotgunned out of the crater, and another blast wave slapped against his body, pushing him into a roll. He came to a stop against a wall, chest heaving as he tried to regain his bearings.

The turret slammed into the ground a few yards away, licks of flame dancing as they died in the rain.

Pressing his back to the wall, Richter used it as a brace to stand back up. He checked his cycler for damage and the comms overlay on his visor blinked. Another of his troopers had connected to his IR.

A shadow cast across the edge of a wall between him and the burning turret.

"Park," said Richter, giving his company's battlefield challenge. If the other man didn't respond with "dog" in the next heartbeat, he'd know it was an enemy.

He swung his cycler up as a Marine vaulted over the top of the wall. The Marine's active camo swirled with grays of the wall and green of the nearby jungle as he dropped onto Richter and knocked his weapon aside.

Richter bashed his shoulder into the Marine, and the other man thudded into the wall. The metal on the back of his close-fitting helmet whacked against the bricks, the padding absorbing most of the impact. The Marine came right back at Richter, slashing an almost ornate knife up and cutting through Richter's beard, nicking his jawline.

When the Marine reversed his grip on the knife, Richter saw an eagle warrior carved into the base of the hilt. That he was almost killed by a blade modeled off something so primitive almost struck him as absurd. A Hegemony officer in a full jack frame killed by some savage with an obsidian knife?

Ignoring the sharp pain, Richter opened fire, shooting into the ground and wall as he brought the muzzle up to his enemy with his jack's help. The Marine jumped forward and into the sweep of the cycler before it could hit him, stabbing his knife into Richter's breastplate. The armor turned the blade, and the Marine's arm shot around Richter's side.

Richter pinned the Marine's arm to his body and held him as he hauled them both backwards, twisting as they fell. He landed on top of the Marine with his entire weight—enough force to crack the bones of a normal man.

The Marine's body armor stiffened against the impact and Richter slid off.

Grasping the ammo belt, the Marine ripped the links apart as Richter struggled to get space between the two of them. Richter raised his cycler up and fired, but the Marine kicked the weapon to one side as the last two bullets shot out, missing him.

Richter grabbed the barrel with his other hand and shoved the cycler at the Marine's chest. The enemy took the hit on the outside of one arm, then stabbed at Richter's face with his knife. The blade hit above the vision slit, gouging the metal.

Richter grabbed the front of the Marine's uniform and jerked him close as he slammed his head forward. His helmet connected with the Marine's faceplate, making his knees give out.

Richter kicked forward and missed. The Marine swept one hand across the ground and flung a handful of mud up at Richter's head.

The trooper backpedaled, sputtering and cursing, as he brought a hand up and hit the emergency release. The helmet popped off and he saw the Marine draw from a thigh holster a long-barreled pistol, one of their specialist weapons, a bolt-thrower that packed enough of a punch to defeat his jack's plates.

Richter ducked his exposed head behind his armored pauldron as a bolt struck the plate and punched through, stopping inches from his face. Dropping his cycler, Richter drew his own pistol. He swung the pauldron up to one side, keeping half his face protected…but the Marine was gone.

Cycler fire sounded nearby, and a squad of Cataphracts raced toward him.

"Sir!" Lieutenant Briem called out, firing a burst past Richter and shuffling against the wall. "Got your radio signal."

"'Bout God damn time." Richter swiped a hand across his cut chin, noting a little blood, and slapped his helmet back on. The holo overlays within came alive with a map showing all his nearby troopers.

"Think that pattie got away." The lieutenant turned his head to one side and mumbled orders to his platoon. "Tank didn't. There's that."

"There's that." Richter glanced into the crater at the smoking hull. One

Alliance soldier had made it out, and his charred body bobbed up and down in the water. "Who got the hit?"

"Ozol," Briem said. "I don't think he'll ever shut up about it either."

"He's earned his spurs. Finally." Richter paused as a coded message hit his system. "Squadron commander's ordering us back to our lines. No air support available."

"Figures." Briem glanced at the sky. "Can't expect them to fly through anything but perfect weather, can we?"

"Tanks," Richter said. "The patties commit tanks to a fight and you'd think the pilots would be all over the chance to do some plinking. Paladins!" he said as he reached to his back and removed a mud-caked cylinder. "Active seeking, three minutes!"

He twisted the base of the cylinder and two lights lit up on the side. He pulled the base out until it clicked three times, then tossed it toward the direction the Marine had retreated. Cataphract troopers repeated the order up and down the line and threw out their own cylinders.

The Benedict-37 Smart Mines hit the ground and the shells broke apart and reformed into tiny legs for the weapons. They crawled like crabs over broken walls, each communicating with each other to identify likely dismounted avenues of approach and then burrow into rubble or dig into mud.

An icon pinged inside Richter's HUD. The minefield would lock on to and swarm any enemy that tried to follow them. The smart mines would stay active for hours, then self-destruct. At least, that was how they were designed. The 37s used across Ayutthaya had a reputation for being buggy.

"Emplaced, fall back." Richter slapped Briem on the shoulder and ran down a sidewalk, his jack's servos stiff with mud and grit, a dull pain rising along his jawline.

A red-cross holo hovered over a nearby building and he went inside. Flankers, Hegemony troopers who fought in lighter armor with no jack support and carried smaller carbines, guarded a perimeter around the roofless building with a mortar tube at the center. A robot stood against a wall where a medic knelt over a pair of downed Cataphracts.

Richter went to the medic, who had his helmet off and carbine slung over his back. His kit was open, but Richter noted that the contents were undisturbed.

Both Cataphracts' armor were facedown, but the troopers within had been flipped over. One—dead eyes staring at the sky, unmoved by the patter of rain—had a scruffy beard and small triangles tattooed over one brow. The other didn't have much face left.

"Parn. Cengic." The medic flopped the back of his hand against his knee. "Both flatlined before I could reach them. I pulled their chips. Winnie's got their gear."

"Unit at eighty-seven percent load capacity," the robot chimed.

"Fucking patties," the medic said, shaking his head. "You get some, sir?"

"Kill tally's still on our side, Shala." Richter put a hand to the man's shoulder. "Let's get them back for the deacon."

Shala stood and canted his head to one side, examining the cut on the major's chin.

"It's nothing." Richter crossed himself then beat a knuckle against his chest twice, the metal ringing, as the faint chime of other Cataphracts doing the same echoed through the space. He grabbed a carry handle on one of the dead trooper's armor as Briem grabbed the man's feet, and they lifted the body up.

"Flankers out," Richter said. "Armor close. Orders are to return to base. Heads on swivels. I don't want to carry anyone else."

He waited a moment as another pair of Cataphracts picked up their comrade, then began the trek back. His jack carried most of the weight, but his mind was heavy with nearly dying in that shell hole and the fight with the Marine.

Death had taken notice of him before, but today was not his day to die.

More time to kill Alliance, he thought. *That one with the eagle warrior knife is still out there. I'll find him again.*

HELL'S HORIZON

...

Pre-order *HELL'S HORIZON* right now
and read the rest on October 13th!

GET IT FROM:

iBooks: https://books.apple.com/us/book/hells-horizon/id1531196532
Amazon: https://www.amazon.com/dp/B08HR6VH6W
Barnes & Noble: https://www.barnesandnoble.com/w/hells-horizon-richard-fox/1137613212
Kobo: https://www.kobo.com/us/en/ebook/hell-s-horizon-2